The Tales of Abel and Mitra: Part I

Yisei Ishkhan

This novel's story and characters are fictitious. Certain places and historical figures and events are mentioned or based in reality, but this story is a product of the author's imagination.

Copyright © 2024 by Yisei Ishkhan

Cover design created with the assistance of OpenAI's DALL-E 3.

All rights reserved. This book or any portion thereof may not be reproduced or used in any manner without the written permission of the publisher, except for the use of brief quotations in a book review.

First edition: December 2024

The Tales of Abel and Mitra

Part I

It was Night.

Two young foragers, a boy and a girl, trekked silently through the towering treetops of the Forest of Shambhala. The sun had disappeared over the horizon nearly a hundred hours ago, which meant they were nearing the midpoint of Night–the darkest, most dangerous time to venture beyond the Village. Still, they were on patrol. As members of the *Kamkara Morung*, it was their duty to journey across the Lightside Quadrant of Shambhala between the ninetieth and hundredth hours of Night, keeping an eye out for any ratri rakshas that might have crossed over the Purvanchal Range.

"This way," the boy whispered as he leaped from one tree branch to the next, clearing a five-meter gap with ease.

"Abel! Slow down!" The girl cracked through the stillness of the trees as she lagged behind.

Abel glanced back at his sister as he waited for her to catch up. Sweat beaded his brow, and he unhooked his waterskin, taking a sip before offering it to her.

"You can't speak so loudly out here, Esta," Abel hissed once his sister had caught up. "We don't wanna draw unwanted attention to us. C'mon, let's hurry. Akavi has gone up ahead. We can't lose him."

Esta rolled her eyes, resting her back against the trunk of the tree as she let out an exaggerated sigh. "We know where he's going. Can't we just chill for a bit? I'm exhausted."

"Two minutes," Abel conceded. "That's it. I'm only letting this slide because it's your third Night out, but this can't become a habit. If you're gonna be part of the *Kamkara Morung*, you've gotta work on your stamina. Otherwise, they'll send you to the *Oyeba* or *Lukano Morung* with mum and dad. You can't be taking breaks every ten minutes. We've got work to do."

Yisei Ishkhan

"Yeah, yeah, I know…" Esta grumbled, breathing heavily between her words. She took a sip of water.

"I'm not trying to be strict," Abel whispered, scanning their vicinity. "There are a lot of dangers out here. You've gotta stay alert, prepared for the situation to change at any moment. You never know what you'll run into out here."

Esta snorted, wiping her mouth with the back of her hand. "We haven't run into any ratri rakshas tonight. Or last time we were out, or the first time for that matter."

"Oh, they were there," Abel assured. "You just didn't notice them. But you can be sure that at least some of them noticed *you*."

"When?" A chill ran up Esta's spine as her eyes darted around the shadowy forest. "I didn't see anything."

"The first time you stopped for a break," Abel said. "You were right above a lukano burrow. You didn't see it, but I spotted its eyes glowing in the dark right beneath your feet. That's why I told you to hop over to my branch."

Esta shivered, casting a nervous glance over her shoulder at the tree trunk she was leaning on, half-expecting something to pop out. "Why didn't you tell me?!"

"I didn't want you to panic. Lukano are called "lurkers" for a reason. They're ambush predators. They aren't a threat to humans unless we fall into one of their burrows. I was worried that if I told you, you'd freak out, lose your balance, and fall inside."

Esta rolled her eyes as she tried to mask her unease.

"Then there was that incident earlier tonight when you almost walked right into that web." Abel's tone was a mix of exasperation and amusement.

The Tales of Abel and Mitra

"That was a *web*?" Esta's face twisted with disgust. "I thought it was some kind of weird plant."

"It was an oyeba web," Abel explained. "Webspinners. Like lukano, they aren't too dangerous unless you get caught in their trap. But again, you have to stay alert. I know it's difficult to see when it's this dark—that's why it's important to stick close to Akavi. He has better vision than we do and can sense which branches are safe to tread on and which should be avoided."

"Well then," Esta crossed her arms, suddenly regretting her decision to let Akavi go on without them, "we should probably catch up with him before we come across something waiting to eat us."

They pressed on along the path Akavi had taken, making a gradual descent toward the forest floor. The further they dropped, the lighter it became, revealing a breathtaking world of bioluminescence blooming along the forest floor. Up in the canopy, hundreds of meters above the ground, only the dim cold light of distant stars pierced the blackness of Night. But down below, the forest came alive with colour. There were fungi that glowed neon blue and green, fluorescent rocks shimmering underfoot, and strange, luminous creatures flitting through the air and scurrying along the branches. Most were just blurs of light zipping past them—fleeting flashes and dazzling displays that fizzled in and out like a Night sky alight with miniature fireworks. But some lingered, moving along slowly enough to be seen in full.

Tiny ganaan, a decapod species no larger than a fingernail, scattered as Abel and Esta landed on a low branch twenty meters above the ground. Ganaan were one of the most common species inhabiting the Valley, regarded as pests in the Village that fed on roots and killed crops. Their eyestalks peeked out of their rounded shells that glowed with a faint blue light, eyeing the humans for a moment before skittering away into the shadows.

Nearby, a colony of four-legged gubara bugs puffed up the orange, bioluminescent membranes atop their heads like tiny balloons. They floated up from below, bobbing gently in the breeze and drifting with a strange elegance to the higher levels of the forest.

But no creature could surpass the spectacle of the silver phoenixes. These six-winged creatures, about the length of a human forearm, glided with a mesmerizing, fluid motion, giving off a shimmering silver glow that illuminated the darkness. Their translucent wings beat in a slow, graceful rhythm as if they were swimming through the air.

"Amazing!" Esta gasped, for once without a trace of sarcasm in her tone.

The glow of the silver phoenixes bathed the forest floor in a silver light. For the first time since they'd set out from the Village that Night, Esta glimpsed her brother's face. A mess of curly, black locks hung down over his dainty visage. In the pale luminescence, his fair appearance seemed almost ghostly. His black uniform clung tightly to his thin frame. His wide, almond-shaped eyes reflected the light with an eerie, faintly crimson glow. He bore an aloof look in those eyes, unfazed by the dazzling scene that surrounded them. His attention was fixed on the forest floor, scanning for threats rather than appreciating the scenery.

"We get to see this every Night when the silver phoenixes come up to feed on the starflowers," he muttered matter-of-factly.

The Tales of Abel and Mitra

"Yeah, but mum and dad never let me get this close to them!"

"I suppose it's strange to see them come this far onto Lightside..." Abel noted absently.

But where there were silver phoenixes, golden dragons were sure to follow. It wasn't long before Abel spotted the first of the predators. About half the size of the silver phoenixes, golden dragons shared the same streamlined body and six translucent wings as their prey. But they were much swifter. The predators struck, darting through the undergrowth and snatching their prey mid-flight. The silver phoenixes were drained of their life force before their bodies had even hit the ground.

Esta yelped as the desiccated remains of one of a silver phoenix tumbled down from above, landing at her feet as little more than a shriveled husk.

"Gross!" She recoiled.

"Let's keep going," Abel muttered nonchalantly. "We've almost caught up to Akavi."

Esta sighed, eyeing the fallen creature with sadness as she followed her brother. "The poor thing..."

"It's the circle of life," Abel said gently. "And if we don't want to fall prey to whatever other things are lurking out here, we should rendezvous with Akavi."

They continued, lower and lower into the depths of the forest. Fifteen meters...ten meters. They came to a halt five meters above the ground after leaping across a ten-meter gap and landing on the roots of a small tree.

"Are you sure it was around here?" Abel asked.

"I'm sure! Isn't this where the waterfall is?"

"It's just up ahead," Abel confirmed. "As for Akavi..."

Yisei Ishkhan

A flash of turquoise caught his eye. In the branches of a nearby tree, Akavi waved two of his furry legs. The tiny pku, a decapod about the size of a human fist, blinked his four bulbous eyes, clicking his mandibles, and flashing a bioluminescent turquoise display across his back to signal to them.

"There he is!" Esta beamed. "Told you this was the right spot."

"Let's find out if Avi and Noa were right about this place," Abel said, leaping up to the branch where Akavi was perched.

They followed his gaze downward. Around the bases of nearly every tree, a massive colony of hkaru shells clustered around the roots and trailed their way up the trunks, some reaching heights of twenty or thirty meters.

"Amazing..." Esta gasped. "I've never seen so many hkaru all in one place."

The hkaru had tough, almond-shaped shells, nearly indistinguishable from rocks at first glance, and just as difficult to crack open. Rare and difficult to cultivate, but a prized delicacy back at the Village, they were one of the most sought-after resources for foragers during Night Missions. It was debated whether the hkaru were plants or animals, but whatever they were, they served as a major part of the Village's diet. To conserve moisture, their shells only opened at Night, but when they did, they revealed a fleshy interior that could be harvested by simply plucking them out of the shells.

"Let's get to work," Abel said with determination, pulling out his gathering packs. "We'll have a big harvest to carry back at the end of our shift."

The Tales of Abel and Mitra

"You make it sound like we're saving the world," Esta quipped. "We're just gathering dinner."

They descended on the colony, plucking at as many hkaru as they could get their hands on. There were only three hours left until their ten-hour shift ended, and the Village was still more than an hour away. As Akavi kept watch for trouble, Abel and Esta filled seven packs. Hkaru bodies were soft and could easily be packed together by the hundreds within a single container. Said containers were compact and easy to transport, making them perfect for gathering resources during Night Missions.

"I think that's enough for tonight," Abel said, once their seventh pack had been filled.

"That's it?" Esta frowned. "I still have two more packs on me, and we've only been here for an hour. What's the rush?"

"The packs will slow us down on our return," Abel pointed out. "If they get snagged in the trees or attract unwanted scavengers, it won't be worth the risk. We'll let the next shift know of this spot, and they can come back to harvest more."

"Fine," Esta sighed. "You're the boss. I'm exhausted anyway."

They secured their packs with rope around their waists, inflating them and dragging them along like balloons as they prepared to make the journey back to the Village. Akavi guided them, weaving his way between the branches as he propelled himself forward with powerful jumps, occasionally shooting out a silky threat to bridge the gaps when the distance between one branch and another was too wide for him to cross. The higher they ascended, the less foliage surrounded them. The branches were sparse up in the canopy, and strong winds blew down into the Valley from the Purvanchal Range, allowing them to navigate back to the Village with ease, their packs trailing behind them. They neared the upper reaches of the forest, some three hundred meters above the forest floor. The shimmering stars of the Night sky flickered faintly in the distance. But one star stood out from the others, catching Esta's eye as she glanced overhead.

"Hey, Abel, do you see that?" She pointed toward Lightside, where a star hanging low on the horizon burned with an unusually bright intensity.

"*Hm?*" Abel muttered. He'd been so focused on scanning for threats that he hadn't yet looked up at the sky. "What is it?"

"That star over there. Which one is it? You're always staring up at the Night sky, aren't you? Do you recognize it?"

Abel made a final jump to the highest branch of their tree, joining Esta and Akavi as they stared up in bewilderment. He'd always found solace in watching the stars and could spend hours at Night staring at them. By now, the layout of the Night sky was etched into his mind. But that star on the Lightside horizon was unfamiliar to him. It didn't belong.

"No…" he admitted, his eyes reflecting its eerie, crimson glow. "I've never seen that one before…"

Akavi chirped nervously, his bioluminescent display flickering wildly in uneven pulses. Abel frowned. Something wasn't right.

"Do you think it could be a Falling Star?"

Abel was about to respond, but as the glowing red light grew brighter and larger, it seemed to answer the question for itself. Falling Stars weren't unusual on Lightside, especially at

The Tales of Abel and Mitra

Night. His friend Noa had explained once that it had to do with Blue Sky's gravity on Darkside pulling in space debris. But most of the time, they burned up long before reaching the ground. Something about this Falling Star seemed different…

The red glow flared, becoming a blinding flash of light even brighter than the skies of Lightside during the Day. Abel instinctively shielded his eyes, but the brilliance pierced through his fingers. Then came the trembling–a deep vibration that shook not just their tree, but the entire Valley. Abel staggered, losing his footing on the branch. He barely had the chance to stabilize himself, grabbing hold of a nearby vine as the violent shockwave rippled out from the force of the impact.

"Abel?! Abel, are you alright?!" Esta's shrill voice cried out. "Abel, where are you?!"

"I'm fine…" Abel managed, his voice distant as his gaze was drawn toward Lightside. Not far in the distance, the forest was alight with towering flames leaping high into the air, illuminating the forest with an intensity only eclipsed by the light of Day.

"Great!" Esta's tone was sharp with irritation. "Then do you mind giving me a hand?!"

Abel blinked as if surfacing from a trance. His gaze dropped to the branch below, where Esta dangled precariously upside down. The vine wrapped around her ankle was the only thing preventing her from tumbling three hundred meters down to the forest floor. The three packs she'd been dragging along had been torn loose, drifting through the canopy as they were carried off by the winds.

"Ah!" Abel cried. "Akavi, help her!"

Yisei Ishkhan

From his perch on Abel's shoulder, Akavi leaped down, scuttling over to Esta's position. The pku tilted his head, his four globular eyes blinking as he examined Esta's predicament. Without hesitation, he shot out a silken thread that firmly latched around the girl's hand.

"I–I don't know about this!" Esta squeaked, swinging slightly back and forth as she clutched the line.

"There's nothing to fear!" Abel called out. "Just trust Akavi! His silk has never failed before, has it?"

"There was that one time when Avi pushed me from the tree and–"

"That was *once*!" Abel said. "You'll be fine!"

"Ugh! Alright, alright. I trust him. But if this fails–"

"It *won't*. But you'll have to cut yourself free from that vine before we can pull you up!"

"I know! I *know*! Look, here's my knife. I'm gonna cut now. This better hold me, Akavi! Do you hear me? This better hold or I'm frying you up with the hkaru for dinner!"

She sliced through the vine with a clean swipe, and the tension snapped. A piercing scream escaped her throat as she plummeted several meters before Akavi's silk snapped taut, jerking her to a halt in mid-air.

"What did I tell you?" Abel breathed a sigh of relief. He pulled on the silk thread and helped his sister climb her way safely back to the top of the tree. "Well, how was that for our third Night Mission out together? Not so boring after all."

Esta glared at him. "I lost all the packs I filled. Mission. Failed."

The Tales of Abel and Mitra

"Yeah…" Abel muttered. His attention was once again fixed on Lightside, obliviously unaware that they'd lost half their harvest.

"Wow," Esta sucked in a breath as she followed his gaze. "That's…a *huge* fire. Did that Falling Star actually hit the ground?"

"It must've. We should check it out."

"You wanna go *into* those flames?!" Esta scoffed. "Really?! I think we've had enough for one Night!"

"If it landed, there could be valuable resources out there," Abel said. "Remember the last one a few dozen Cycles ago? They found all sorts of ore and precious metals—things we can't get anywhere else."

"Or we could let the next shift handle it. We have less than two hours to get back, and the flames would've died down a bit by then."

"Protocol says that *Kamkara Morung* teams who are already on duty are responsible for investigating anomalies immediately. We're probably the closest team to the impact site. They'll understand if we make it back a few hours late."

Esta let out a long, drawn-out sigh. "Ugh, fine, Mister *Protocol*. And here I thought I'd get to call it early tonight."

They decided to leave their remaining packs fastened to the upper branches of the canopy rather than carrying them to the impact site. The packs would only slow them down, and hkaru flesh would likely be dried out by the intense flames. They'd come back for their harvest after investigating.

Esta lagged considerably behind the others as they made their way toward the impact site. It wasn't that she was slow; Abel was moving far quicker through the trees than she'd ever seen before, his cautious footing replaced by a reckless drive, barely allowing his feet to settle on one branch before leaping to the next. Akavi darted ahead, nimble and precise, as he made a beeline for the impact site.

As they neared the flames, the environment shifted. Thick smoke obscured any light given off by the flames. The heat was oppressive, far exceeding any heat that Abel had experienced, forcing the nocturnal species to retreat into hibernation. Flowers and fungi dimmed, and the forest's bioluminescent glow flickered out as animals sought shelter in their burrows.

Abel came to a sudden stop at the crest of a hill, Akavi perched beside him. Esta took a while longer to catch up to the two of them, panting as she ascended to their position.

"That's strange…" she said. "I don't remember this hill being here before…"

As she joined the others, she soon realized they weren't on a hill at all, but the crest of a ridge that formed the edge of an impact crater. Inside the crater, nearly every tree had been uprooted, their charred forms aflame. But beyond the ridge, the forest was largely untouched. The towering trees acted as a natural barrier that shielded the forest from flaming debris, while the swampy terrain prevented fires from spreading far beyond the immediate vicinity. Already, the flames within the crater were starting to subside.

"What is that?" Esta gasped.

A massive triangular structure jutted out from the center of the crater, its metallic surface glinting through the haze. It stood nearly as tall as the trees, and with its base buried in the ground, it was likely even taller. The structure's edges were unnaturally sharp, its shape alien against the backdrop of the pristine forest.

The Tales of Abel and Mitra

"Is it the Falling Star?"

"It must be…" whispered Abel.

"The last one didn't look like this," Esta recalled. "It was just a lump of rock. This one is so…so…"

"Perfect," Abel said, his gaze unwavering.

Esta snorted. "I guess you could say that."

"Its edges are so straight," Abel murmured. "It doesn't look natural at all…"

Esta glanced at her brother. His eyes were wide, brimming with fascination. It was the same look he had whenever he spent hours staring up at the Night sky.

"Alright," he pushed forward, hopping onto the first fallen tree within the crater. "Let's go."

"What?" Esta exclaimed. "You wanna keep going? Isn't this close enough? Let's head back and, I dunno, get a *proper* exploration team to come out here to deal with this!"

But Abel was already out of earshot, intent on continuing their exploration. Esta sighed in frustration, glancing down at Akavi as he skittered by her feet.

"Is he *always* like this on Night Missions?"

Akavi's turquoise glow pulsed softly, and the pku raised two legs in what Esta could only interpret as a shrug.

"I guess we're doing this, then," Esta sighed.

She chased after Abel. By the time she'd caught up, he was standing at the base of the massive structure, his hand pressed up against its smooth, gleaming surface.

"What are you doing down there?" She called out. She cast a nervous gaze left and right, scanning the eerie landscape around them. There were no creatures in sight, not even the faintest buzz of a ganaan. "You're always the one lecturing me about how dangerous it is to be on the ground!"

Yisei Ishkhan

"Just look at this thing," Abel mused. "It's completely smooth. No seams, no cracks–nothing like any material I've ever seen."

"It's giving me the creeps," Esta grumbled. "Let's report back to the Village."

"Look!" Abel's voice rose with excitement as he pointed off to the right. "There's a tunnel!"

Esta followed his gaze to a perfectly round opening in the side of the structure a few meters up from the ground. It was just large enough for someone to crawl through.

"You're kidding, right? You want to *go in there*?!"

"There could be resources inside! I'm not going back to the Village before we figure out what this thing is–and if there's anything we can bring back."

"Or we could *not* crawl into a hole that leads to who knows where. How does that sound?"

"You don't have to come, but I'm going. C'mon Akavi. Let's leave Esta to stand guard."

"No way," Esta huffed. "You're always telling me never to split up on Night Missions. You think I'm gonna wait out here by myself?"

Abel smiled, the kind of earnest boyish smile that both annoyed her and softened her resolve. "Then quit complaining, and let's get going. We'll turn back once we figure out what's at the end of that tunnel."

"Famous last words," Esta muttered under her breath. "Is that a promise?"

Abel nodded slightly without giving a verbal response. Akavi had already scurried up the side of the structure, leaving behind a silk thread in his wake for the others to climb. They

The Tales of Abel and Mitra

pulled themselves through the tunnel opening, slipping into the dimly lit passage, with only the soft turquoise glow of the patterns along Akavi's back to guide their way. There wasn't much to see. The tunnel was unnervingly pristine. Perfectly round, with a cold, smooth interior, it lacked any other distinguishing features.

"Are you *sure* we'll find anything here?" Esta hissed, her voice breaking the claustrophobic silence as she trailed her brother from behind.

"Maybe. Maybe not. Let's just see where it takes us."

The tunnel stretched forward in a perfectly straight line for about a dozen meters before it opened into a small, domed chamber. The space was just large enough for them to comfortably stand in. Where the walls met the floor, a thin band of pale, glowing light pulsed in a hypotonic rhythm.

"What is that?" Esta whispered. "Some kind of glowing stone?"

"I have no idea," Abel said, crouching to inspect the ground more closely.

He reached down to touch the luminous band, but the moment his fingers brushed the surface, the ground beneath his feet gave way. Esta cried out in surprise. Akavi sprang into action, shooting a thread of silk that caught Abel mid-air. He dangled there for a moment, glancing up at them with a sheepish smile.

"Thanks, Akavi," he called out. "But don't worry–the drop isn't too far. I'm gonna hop down the rest of the way."

He severed himself from the thread, and a moment later, landed on the ground below with a gentle thud.

"C'mon!" He called out from the darkness.

Yisei Ishkhan

"Ugh," Esta groaned, shooting a glance at Akavi. "What are we getting ourselves into?"

They hopped down after him, landing on a smooth, flat metallic surface.

"You *promised* we'd turn back when we reached the end of the tunnel," Esta said. "Well, guess what? This isn't the tunnel anymore."

"Let's just have a quick look around."

"Fine."

With only Akavi's faint glow to offer them light, it was difficult to make out their surroundings. They moved cautiously, tiptoeing about the room.

"Over here," Abel hissed. His voice echoed off the walls. "I found something."

Esta followed the sound of his voice toward the center of the room, where an oval-shaped object protruded from the ground.

"What is it?"

"I don't know, but there are lines running along the side. Akavi, can you come a little closer and light this area up?"

The pku skittered forward, and Abel brushed his hand across some of the lines, clearing a thick layer of dust. Without warning, the object flared to life, emitting a piercing light.

"Ah!" Esta shielded her eyes. "Are you trying to blind us?!"

"It isn't that bright," Abel assured. "Just give it a few minutes. Our eyes need to adjust."

Abel's heart thumped loudly in his chest as he anticipated what they'd find once their vision returned. A couple minutes passed. Abel was right, the light wasn't as intense as it had first seemed, about as faint as the rays of Dawn.

The Tales of Abel and Mitra

"Can you see it now?" Esta asked, still blinking away the spots in her eyes.

"Yeah," Abel nodded, his voice brimming with wonder. "They look like symbols. I think they're letters from some kind of script. But I've never seen anything like it before."

"What? How is that possible? Why would there be letters written inside some Falling Star that came from the sky?"

"Take a look for yourself. Don't these look like letters to you?"

Esta leaned in, but just as she was about to inspect the markings, the oval-shaped object suddenly began to shift. Its surface split apart with a low hiss, unfurling like a metallic flower in bloom. A burst of steam erupted from inside, forcing them to shield their faces.

"What *now*?" Esta cried.

When the steam cleared, they saw the object had fully opened, revealing something inside. No, not something. *Someone.* A face.

The two siblings screamed, stumbling backward. Esta tripped over her own feet and landed sprawled out on the cold, hard ground.

"Who is *that*?!"

"How am I supposed to know?!" Abel stammered.

"Is he *dead*?!"

Regaining his bearings, Abel helped his sister back to her feet. They cautiously approached the figure that had appeared before them. He lay upright against an elevated platform, partially obscured by the unfolded petals of the metallic oval that he'd emerged from. His body, visible from the waist up, was unclothed, with unblemished bronze skin, and luscious white hair that spilled down to his waist. He had broad shoulders, a chiseled chest, and a defined abdomen, but it was his face that truly left them speechless. He had perfectly symmetrical features, with a straight nose, and full rose-tinted lips. His jawline was sharp and angular, ending in a smooth, pointed chin. His eyes remain shut, hidden behind thick, white lashes. The contrast between his masculine build and the delicate beauty of his face gave him an otherworldly appearance that was simultaneously handsome and beautiful. It was difficult to determine his age just by looking at him—he could've been anywhere from Abel's age to twice that.

"Is that even a real person?" Esta whispered, worried that her voice might rouse this man from his slumber.

"What do you mean?" Abel frowned. "What else would he be?"

"He just looks so…perfect." She glanced up and down at his figure. "I've never seen anyone who looks so surreal. What if it's just a really fancy statue?"

Abel scoffed. "Does he look like a statue to you?"

"I don't know. Why don't you give him a poke and find out?"

"I'm not touching him!"

"Fine. Then I will."

"Esta, wait–!"

Before Abel could stop the girl, she'd already reached out, her curiosity getting the better of her. The figure was significantly taller than either of them, and the easiest place for her to reach was his chest. She poked her finger against his left pectoral.

"It's soft…" she said in surprise. "I've never felt skin so soft before."

The Tales of Abel and Mitra

Abel's face turned red. "Esta, you can't just *touch* someone without asking them first!"

"Are you sure he's alive?" Esta asked, pressing her hand flat against his chest. "I don't feel a heartbeat or see him breathing—"

Before she could finish, the man's hand shot forward and grabbed Esta by the wrist. She shrieked and yanked her arm away. The man's eyes fluttered open, revealing irises that glowed with a mesmerizing, golden hue, even more vibrant than golden dragons.

"I was just checking to see if you were alive!" Esta blurted.

The man's gaze flicked curiously between the two young foragers, and down at Akavi. He opened his mouth, and a melodic sound came out that took Abel a moment to realize was speech, though he couldn't understand the tongue that was being spoken.

"I'm sorry, sir," Abel spoke up nervously. "We don't understand what you're saying. Do you speak our tongue?"

The man stared back blankly at them. Suddenly, a monotonous voice of a woman reverberated throughout the chamber, smooth and disembodied, and seeming to come from every direction at once. Esta glanced around, frantically searching the room as she tried to pin down the source of that voice.

"Who is that...?" She asked. "There's no one else here!"

"I have no idea..." Abel admitted.

"I *told* you we should've turned back earlier!"

The voice of the woman continued to speak, her alien cadence softening as some of her words caught Abel's attention.

"Did you hear that?" Abel asked.

Yisei Ishkhan

Esta threw her arms up. "Hear *what?*"

What, echoed the voice.

"That!" Abel exclaimed. "She's repeating some of the things we're saying. At first, it was just gibberish. But now, she's using some of our words! Do you hear it?"

I...you...we...is...that...what...no...have...

At first, she could only say simple, one-syllable words. But after a couple more seconds, she began repeating some of the longer words and even started to say things that neither Abel nor Esta had spoken since they'd entered the room.

Begin...beginning...translate...translation...beginning translation...

"Beginning translation!" Abel exclaimed, his face lighting up with excitement.

The mysterious man tilted his head, his golden eyes twinkling as a calm expression rested on his face.

Translation complete.

The woman's voice ceased. Then the man raised two of his fingers against the back of his ear, where a faint glow flashed briefly before disappearing.

"I have completed translating your language," he said in a smooth voice. "I should now be able to understand your speech and communicate with you."

Esta crossed her arms. "Took you long enough."

"Who are you?" Abel asked, staring in awe at the man.

"I have gone by many names."

"Then what should we call you?"

The man paused for a moment. "You may call me Mitra. That was the name I first went by."

The Tales of Abel and Mitra

"Mitra," Abel repeated. "And who was the voice we heard speaking just now? The woman?"

"That was not a woman. That was Aida."

"Aida?"

"She sounded like a woman to me," Esta scoffed.

Mitra chuckled. "She is an…" he uttered a couple of words that neither Abel nor Esta understood.

"And what does that mean?" Abel wondered.

"There is no word for it in your tongue. I suppose you could say that she is not a conscious being."

"S-she's dead?" Esta murmured with unease. "Like a ghost?"

"Not dead. She was never alive to begin with."

"Oh…I see…" Abel said, trying but failing to wrap his mind around that thought. "Then are you the only one here?"

"Yes, it is just me," said Mitra. "This place is my…"

Again, more words came from his mouth that neither of the siblings understood.

"What does *that* mean?" Abel pressed.

"This place is a vessel that carried me across the sky to reach this place. Now, may I ask where exactly I am? Is this EP-Tianyuan2.2?"

"EP-what?" Esta shook her head. "No. This is Shambhala."

"Shambhala," Mitra repeated, as if savouring the word on his lips.

"The Valley of Shambhala," Abel nodded with enthusiasm. "But where do *you* come from, Mitra? We saw your vessel crossing over from Lightside, from the other side of the Purvanchal Range."

"Purvanchal Range…" Mitra murmured, more to himself than to either of them.

"That's what we call the mountains that encircle the Valley."

"I see," nodded Mitra. "No, I do not hail from the other side of that range. I come from much farther away."

Abel's eyes lit up. "You mean the colony at the other Pole! The Elders say that Lightside is mostly desert–too hot for humans to live in during Day. I've always wanted to see it myself, but they won't let us venture near the mountains. But there are rumors of other colonies out there, at the other Pole. The Elders told us they were just stories, but I guess those stories are true!"

Mitra shook his head. "No. I do not hail from there either."

Abel fell silent.

"Then?" Esta crossed her arms. "Where *do* you come from?"

"Another world, beyond this one."

Silence descended upon the room. Abel stared at Mitra in confusion, trying to make sense of his words. Esta leaned in and tugged at his sleeve.

"This guy is sketchy," she hissed. "We should go back to the Village and inform the Elders."

Abel frowned. "We can't just leave him here."

"What? You want to bring him back with us? The Elders are gonna freak out."

"He doesn't know anything about our world," Abel said. "If he really does come from somewhere else, he'll be in

The Tales of Abel and Mitra

danger on his own. What if he comes across a kamkara—or worse, the makarasa?"

They glanced back at Mitra. Akavi had jumped up next to him on the platform, and he eyed the pku with curiosity.

"Hello there," Mitra said in a gentle tone, extending a single finger out to him. "And who might you be?"

Akavi reached up with one of his legs and pressed it against Mitra's finger, as if the two were shaking hands.

"That's Akavi," Abel said. "Oh, I never introduced myself, did I? My name is Abel Imsong, and this is my sister, Esta."

"It's a pleasure to meet you, Mister Abel and Miss Esta."

"Just 'Abel' and 'Esta' is fine," Abel assured with a smile. "Akavi never lets anyone touch him. He must really like you."

"Akavi..." Mitra repeated the name. "What kind of creature is he? Are they native to this world?"

"He's a pku," Abel explained. "And yes, the pku can be found throughout Shambhala."

"Fascinating," Mitra murmured, turning his gaze back up to them. "Are the two of you discussing what you should do with me?"

Esta flushed. "What? No! We're just...figuring out how to get out of this place."

"Esta wants to leave you here and return to the Village," Abel blurted out.

"*Tch*," Esta glared at her brother. "You weren't supposed to tell him that!"

"You are debating whether or not you can trust me," Mitra said calmly. "That is understandable. You are wise to exercise caution around a stranger."

"We just…we aren't sure what to make of you exactly," Abel admitted sheepishly.

Esta crossed her arms. "What is your purpose for coming here?"

"I am an archivist."

Abel cocked his head. "Archivist?"

"I collect and store information–specifically stories."

"Stories?" Esta eyed him skeptically. She glanced around the room. "Where? I don't see any books lying around here."

"Most of what I collect are not physical records," Mitra explained, tapping the side of his temple. "All of the information is stored here."

Esta scoffed. "So, Mister Falling Star has a perfect memory to go along with his perfect voice, perfect face, *and* perfect body. Why am I not surprised?"

"Esta!" Abel turned red. "Sorry about her. I think my sister is just jealous that your skin is so soft compared to hers. She's always complaining about how rough her hands get because of all the climbing we have to do."

"So what if I'm jealous!" Esta said. "Why does a *man* need to have such flawless skin? And just *look* at those muscles! You're worried he can't handle the ratri rakshas out here? Please. He can probably take them down without breaking a sweat."

"I apologize if my form displeases you," Mitra said in a steady tone, a hint of humor in his gaze. "This was the form given to me by my creator."

Esta stared at him blankly. "Creator? We call those 'parents' around here."

The Tales of Abel and Mitra

"Alright, alright," Abel sighed, stepping between the two of them. "Esta gets grumpy when she's tired. It's been a long Night for us, and we should really get back to the Village. So, let's quit arguing and get going."

"How far is this Village from here?" Mitra wondered.

"About a two-hour journey through the forest."

"Two hours by foot?"

"How else?"

"There are a couple of hovercycles in storage that could get us there faster," Mitra suggested.

"Hovercycles?"

"We're going on foot," Esta interrupted. "I'm already reluctant to let you return to the Village with us, Mister Falling Star. I doubt the Elders are gonna throw a party when they see you. Don't push your luck. We're not bringing anything from this place back with us."

Mitra nodded. "Very well."

He began pushing himself to his feet, rising from the metallic flower.

"W-wait!" Abel called out, his face suddenly flushing red.

Mitra paused. "What is it?"

"Ah…" Abel let out a nervous laugh. "Are you…unclothed down there…?"

Mitra glanced down at himself, unbothered. "I removed all my clothing before entering hibernation."

"I…I see…" Abel averted his gaze. He fumbled through his pack, pulling out a thin piece of black fabric and tossing it at the man. "You should wear this. They're the spare undergarments of my jumpsuit. Unfortunately, they're all I have on me."

Yisei Ishkhan

Mitra examined the fabric. "I suspect that these will be too small for me. I am much taller and have a larger build than you."

"It'll fit," Abel assured. "The material is flexible. It can stretch or shrink to fit different body types."

"I see. How practical. Thank you for this."

Akavi shot another string of silk up the way they came, and Esta climbed up first. Abel followed her, glancing back before he pulled himself through the hole.

"How does it look?" Mitra wondered.

Mitra stood below him, now clad in the bodysuit. It clung to his body in a way that revealed every detail of his lean, muscular build, leaving little to the imagination.

"A bit revealing..." Abel muttered. "But it'll do until we get to the Village."

Mitra nodded without a trace of embarrassment. "Lead the way."

Once they emerged from the opening, they crawled back through the narrow tunnel that led to the exterior. The cramped space was just wide enough for Mitra to squeeze his way through.

"This tunnel is a pretty inconvenient exit to the vessel," Esta's voice echoed from up ahead.

"It was not intended to be an exit," Mitra explained. "This is part of the ventilation system. It must have opened during the landing."

When they finally made it outside, the air was thick with the scent of charred wood. Smoke still hung in the sky, but most of the flames had subsided. Warm droplets of rain poured steadily from above, soaking their clothes and turning the scorched earth beneath them into mud. Mitra tilted his head back, closing his eyes as he let the rain trickle down his face.

"It is humid. Would you like to reconsider taking my vehicles? It may take more than two hours to reach your Village with all this mud on the ground."

Esta scoffed. "Why would we travel on the ground?" She leaped effortlessly into the lower branches of a nearby tree, landing three meters up. She looked down at them, a wide grin spreading across her face. "Rule number one of Night Missions–always travel through the trees."

Abel shook his head with a chuckle. "It's her third Night out, and she already thinks she's an expert."

He and Akavi leaped up, joining his sister on the branch. Mitra remained on the ground, staring up at them in fascination.

"C'mon!" Abel called out. "What's wrong?"

"That was quite the jump."

Esta rolled her eyes. "Maybe Mister Falling Star is too weighed down with all that muscle to make it up–"

Thud. Esta hadn't finished her words before she found herself staring up at Mitra as he balanced gracefully on a branch several meters above them.

Abel stared at him in awe. "Looks like you're a natural!"

"Show off," scoffed Esta.

As they began to make their way back, Abel and Esta quickly fell behind. Even Akavi struggled to keep pace with Mitra's strides as he leaped between the branches.

"Hey!" Esta called out. "Slow down! You don't even know where you're going!"

Yisei Ishkhan

"My apologies," Mitra came to a halt. "Are the two of you tired? I could carry you back the rest of the way."

"Excuse me?" Esta landed on a branch near him, doubling over to catch her breath. She glanced at Mitra up and down. He hadn't even broken a sweat! "I'm perfectly capable of traveling on my own, thank you very much."

"Suit yourself," Abel gasped for air as he reached them. "I'm all worn out. I'd love it if someone carried me back."

Mitra nodded with perfect seriousness. "Would you prefer I carry you in my arms or on my back?"

Abel stared at him in disbelief. "You're...you're being serious?"

"You said you were tired," Mitra noted. "A piggyback ride would be most practical, given the terrain. That way, I can have my hands free to stabilize us during a jump."

"Are...you sure...?" Abel stammered. He still couldn't tell whether the man was being serious. "You won't get tired having to carry me?"

"Not at all," said Mitra. "Your weight is negligible to me, given this world's gravity."

Before Abel could argue, Mitra crouched down. Abel glanced at Esta, and the girl shrugged. Abel awkwardly climbed up onto Mitra's back, barely able to wrap his limbs around the man's body. Akavi, ever resourceful, reinforced Abel's grip by wrapping him with strands of silk.

"I could carry you as well," Mitra offered, glancing at Esta.

"No way!" The girl snapped. "I'm fine on my own."

"Very well. Let me know if you change your mind."

The Tales of Abel and Mitra

They set off again, Mitra moving effortlessly through the trees while Abel clung tightly to him. Occasionally, he would glance back. Unsurprisingly, Esta had already fallen far behind.

"Would you mind slowing down for my sister?" Abel asked softly. "She isn't as familiar with this part of the woods as I am. It's dangerous out here at Night. I don't want her to get lost."

"Of course," Mitra immediately adjusted his pace. "Though I am curious–if it is dangerous, why are you out at this hour?"

"Night Missions," Abel explained. "We're part of the *Kamkara Morung*, so it's our duty to carry out a ten-hour shift each Night once we turn two hundred."

"Two hundred?" Mitra repeated. "You hardly appear to be that old."

"Two hundred Cycles," Abel clarified.

"I see. I assume that your world measures time differently than mine. You said you patrol for ten hours each night. How long does an hour last here?"

"Each hour is sixty minutes; each minute is sixty seconds. As for seconds: one…two…three…"

"I see," Mitra nodded. "Our units of measurement appear to be the same. But how long are these 'Cycles' you speak of?"

"It depends. Here in the Valley, we don't experience Day, only Night, Dawn, and Dusk. Night lasts for about two hundred hours. Dawn and Dusk combined are five hundred and fifty hours. One Cycle here consists of Night, Dawn, and Dusk–seven hundred and fifty hours in total. If you cross the Purvanchal Range onto Lightside you get Day, but if you journey to Darkside, it is always Night."

"Then your world must be tidally locked," Mitra noted.

"Is it different on your world?" Abel wondered.

"Very much so."

"I'd like to hear about your world. You said that you collect stories, right? Can you tell me a story about where you come from?"

"Very well," Mitra said. "Let me tell you a story–a story of two worlds colliding; of strangers who bridged the gap between their peoples…"

The Tales of Abel and Mitra
I. The Tale of Domingo and Nezahualatzin
August 14, 1521 AD
Tenochtitlan, Valley of Mexico, Ēxcān Tlahtōlōyān

Huēyi Teōcalli–the Templo Mayor, as the Spaniards called it. That was where Domingo de Granada was headed.

Sandoval. Juan Alonso Sandoval. I must find him. I must.

That thought burned in his mind as he navigated the blood-soaked streets of the once-great city. His dark eyes were locked on the towering temple in the distance, its silhouette sharp against the haze of smoke and ash as it glowed in the rays of the setting sun. That was where they had taken Sandoval. Domingo hadn't witnessed it himself but had heard what had happened from the accounts of Díaz and de Leon. The Mexica had dragged their Spanish captives up the steps of the Templo Mayor, cutting out their hearts on the altar, and devouring them.

That was over a week ago.

It can't be true, Domingo thought to himself. *Sandoval is alive. I know he is.*

Crossing into the Sacred Precinct, Domingo's focus faltered as the scene around him set in. Blood. So much blood. The air reeked of it. The ground was slick with it, drenched in pools around hundreds of bodies that lay scattered about– Mexica warriors, civilians, and nobles alike. Among them were dozens of Tlaxcalan corpses, and other native allies of the Spaniards. There were even a couple of Spaniards themselves, their metal armour caked in dirt and gore. Domingo's gaze flicked past a Spaniard with dark curls, and another with sun-bleached golden hair. He averted his eyes, refusing to linger. He didn't get close enough to see who they were, but he knew he would recognize them. He didn't want to see their faces–their gray, lifeless eyes staring up at him. He'd seen enough death in these past months to last a lifetime.

His boots squelched in the crimson-soaked earth. The fringes of his pants were damp with blood that wasn't his own. How many bodies had he stepped over to get here? Hundreds? Thousands? He'd lost count.

The acrid stench made his stomach churn. He stumbled to a halt, retching up his last meal onto the grounds of the Sacred Precinct. Soggy bits of corn tortilla splattered into the pools of blood. The taste burned his throat. He coughed, closing his eyes and steadying himself with a sharp breath.

"Oi! Spaniard! Where are you going?"

The voice echoed across the square in the Mayan tongue.

Domingo glanced up to where a group of Tlaxcalan soldiers lingered nearby, their faces streaked with blood and sweat. He recognized one of them–a wiry man with a crude grin on his face. *Tizoc? Or was it Atonal?* Domingo was unsure, but he knew it was one of the Tlaxcalan translators.

Domingo straightened his posture, wiping the vomit from his mouth. "Soldier," he addressed the man in Mayan, the only tongue the two of them shared.

Tizoc–or Atonal–gestured to his comrades. Each man held a bundle of ceremonial artifacts: a feathered headdress adorned with jewels, sacred statues carved of gold, obsidian blades, incense burners, and other relics stripped from one of the nearby temples.

"Hoping to find your own prize?" Tizoc grinned with amusement. "Better hurry, Spaniard. Most of the good stuff's already gone."

The Tales of Abel and Mitra

"I'm looking for a man," Domingo said, the words falling hollow in his raw throat. "A young Spaniard, about my age. Pale skin, wavy brown hair, no beard. Have you seen him?"

"Alive or dead?"

Domingo flinched at how casual his tone was. "I...I don't know. He was taken hostage by the Mexica during the siege. I heard they took him to the *Huēyi Teōcalli* to be...to be..."

"Sacrificed."

Domingo managed a weak nod.

The Tlaxcalan sighed impatiently. "Any Spaniards taken to the temple have already been killed. The most you'll find might be a severed head." He drew his finger across his neck, mimicking the motion.

Domingo grew tense, a cold shiver creeping up his spine. "And where...where would they keep the remains?"

The Tlaxcalan gestured up the massive steps of the Templo Mayor. "Go see for yourself."

Domingo swallowed hard as he began his slow ascent up the steps. The Templo Mayor was almost the height of the tallest church buildings he'd seen back in Europe, a steep incline where bodies were cast down after they were sacrificed at the top. With each step, his heart grew tighter in his chest.

I must find Sandoval. I must.

But as he drew near the top, the undeniable truth he'd been suppressing for the past week settled in. Sandoval was dead.

No. He can't be dead. He can't be.

Sandoval was the one person that mattered to him in this strange land. Even in Spain, there was no one he truly cared for. After his parents died, the Sandovals had taken him in as their servant. Despite his Morisco heritage, they treated Domingo well. But deep down, he felt that their kindness was simply pity for an orphaned child.

It was their son, Juan Alonso Sandoval, that made Domingo feel like he was part of the family. He was the reason Domingo had decided to leave behind the Old World on this grand adventure. It all started three years ago, when the young nobleman approached Domingo with a grin. He announced with excitement that he'd manage to secure passage to Hispaniola, and asked Domingo to accompany him there.

"You want *me* to come with you?" Domingo had asked in disbelief.

"Of course I do!" Sandoval laughed, slapping him on the back. "You're my best friend! Why wouldn't I want you at my side when I strike it rich in the New World?"

Domingo's heart skipped a beat. *Best friend?* That was the first time Sandoval had called him that. He had never thought of Sandoval that way before. Domingo was his servant. Always had been. He'd never once considered that he might be seen as anything more than that. The Sandovals weren't wealthy by any stretch, despite their noble lineage. Still, they'd welcomed him into their home and given him everything he had. But it had never occurred to him that they genuinely cared for him–he had never allowed himself to believe that.

"So, what do you say?" Sandoval grinned, extending his hand to Domingo. "Shall we head off on an adventure?"

Domingo's mind snapped back to the present. He paused at the top of the Templo Mayor, struggling to catch his breath. The area had been cleared of bodies, yet the metallic scent of blood still hung thick in the air. Broken candles, smashed

The Tales of Abel and Mitra

idols, and shattered images were strewn across the ground. The temple had already been stripped of its valuables, just as the Tlaxcalan soldier had said.

He waded cautiously through the debris. The darkness was oppressive, swallowing up the faint streams of evening light. Domingo touched the stone wall with one hand, guiding himself along as he navigated deeper into the chamber. After tripping over a couple of scattered relics, he realized he'd come to a dead end. He cursed under his breath. Turning back, he retraced his steps but quickly became disoriented by the darkness. In his despair, he sank to the cold floor, drawing his knees to his chest. The toll of the past few months was getting to him. He didn't realize he'd dozed off until he was roused from his slumber by a voice echoing across the temple walls.

"Hey! Domingo! Hey! Are you alive?"

Domingo's eyes fluttered open, squinting as the burning light of a torch filled the chamber.

"Vincente?" Domingo croaked in a raspy voice.

Vincente stepped closer, his torchlight illuminating the grime on Domingo's face. "What in God's name are you doing on the ground here? I nearly tripped over you! Thought you were a corpse!"

Domingo pushed himself to his feet, his limbs stiff. "I came looking for the hostages…"

"Sandoval and the others," Vincente's face darkened. "Cortés sent us here for them too. Said they deserve a proper Christian burial after what those heathen savages did to them. Come," Vincente offered his torch. "Help us look. There's a lot of ground to cover."

Domingo reluctantly accepted the torch. He followed Vincente toward a group of other Spanish soldiers that had gathered along the rear wall of the chamber. The flickering light illuminated a massive carving that spanned the stone from floor to ceiling. One of the Spaniards raised his torch to the middle of the carving, revealing a grotesque face with bulging eyes, encircled by what looked to be feathers, or perhaps rays of light.

The Spaniard recoiled in disgust. "What the devil is this?"

"Huītzilōpōchtli," Domingo whispered.

Vincente turned to him with a frown. "What was that?"

"Huītzilōpōchtli," Domingo repeated. "The name of the deity represented by that image. God of the sun. And of war."

"Some god of war," one of the Spaniards sneered. "He couldn't even save his own city." He spat at the carving's base.

"Let's keep moving," Domingo said. "I've already checked this area. There's nothing here."

They pressed onward, the torches casting erratic shadows along the walls that made Domingo feel uneasy. Narrow corridors branched out ahead of them, some leading further into the temple and others winding down steep stairwells.

"We should split up," suggested Vincente. "Cover more ground."

Domingo crouched as he entered the narrow path on the left, the low ceiling forcing him to stoop. The air was suffocating, thick with the scent of decay. He trod carefully, his free hand trailing along the wall. The corridor ended abruptly ahead of him. He sighed in frustration, turning back as he planned to regroup with the others. As he did so, the stone under his hand shifted loose, falling into an empty darkness behind the wall. More stones crumbled, revealing a

The Tales of Abel and Mitra

hidden chamber. Domingo froze, raising his torch to get a better look inside.

That's when he felt a blade against his throat.

Instinct kicked in. Domingo jerked back, but a hand clamped over his mouth, stifling his cry. His torch dropped, sputtering as it hit the ground. In the dimming light, an elderly native man emerged from the darkness, dragging him into the hidden chamber and in the process knocking down what remained of the makeshift wall. Before the torchlight could die out, a tiny pair of hands grabbed hold and lifted it back up. The old man wasn't alone here. Women, children, and a few elderly faces huddled in the cramped space, pale with fear.

The old man muttered in Nahuatl, his knife still pressed against Domingo's throat.

"I don't understand," Domingo stammered in Spanish. Desperate, he switched to Mayan. "I don't understand your tongue!"

A figure stepped forward, tall and imposing, his calculating gaze fixed on Domingo. He looked to be only a couple of years older than Domingo and was the only young man in the room. He spoke in a commanding tone. "You speak Mayan?"

The dialect was different from what Domingo had learned in the Yucatán, but it was similar enough for him to understand.

"Yes," Domingo said quickly.

"Good," the man replied. "Now shut up. If you alert your comrades, this knife will silence you before they arrive. Understood?"

Yisei Ishkhan

Domingo nodded frantically. The man narrowed his gaze at him, mimicking his head movements.

"What is that? Do you understand or not?"

"I understand…" Domingo quivered.

The old man spoke again in Nahuatl, and the young man responded with quiet authority. After the brief exchange, the young man turned back to Domingo.

"You're going to help us escape."

"Escape?" Domingo gasped. "How?"

"You're a Spaniard," the man huffed. "If you lead us through the streets, no one will stop us."

"But I'm not a soldier. I'm just a translator."

The young man frowned. "Translator or not, you're still a Spaniard. Now, tell us how many soldiers there are in the temple."

Domingo hesitated. "I saw five. There might be more outside."

"We can worry about that later. Just get us out of the temple first."

The group filed out one by one into the narrow corridor, Domingo leading the way. The old man was close behind him, his blade pressed against Domingo's back. The others followed in silence. They moved through the temple's winding passageways, veering left and right down a gradual slope as they snaked their way through the pyramid's interior.

One of the women called out softly behind them.

"They've found rope," the young man explained to Domingo.

The Tales of Abel and Mitra

"Rope?" Domingo glanced back in confusion to find that the woman had begun tying the children's hands together before doing the same to themselves. "What are they doing?"

"We need to look convincing," the young man said, taking the knife from the old man who'd begun wrapping his own hands in binds. "We'll lead them out together, you as a Spaniard, and me as a Tlaxcalan soldier."

He leaned down, scooping a feathered headdress up from the ground and taking up a spear to complete the look.

It was only then that Domingo noticed that there were bodies scattered across the ground. In the dim light, it was difficult to make out the fallen figures, but from their armour, he could tell that they were some of his Tlaxcalan allies. His heartbeat raced. It wasn't just Tlaxcalans that littered the floor. There were also Spaniards. Domingo froze as he spotted a pale, naked corpse, its chest torn open.

"Shine the torch here," he said with a trembling voice.

The young man stared at him. "What?"

"Just do it," Domingo snapped.

The man obliged, lowering the torch to the ground. Domingo knelt to the body, his shaking hand reaching for its wrist. *It can't be him...it can't be...*

The man had been decapitated, but as Domingo's fingers brushed against the wooden bead bracelet on his hand, he knew at once who it was. He had a matching bracelet on his own wrist. He and Sandoval had gotten them during their pilgrimage to Santiago before setting sail for the New World.

Domingo cried out, his vision becoming blurry with tears.

"What are you doing?" Hissed the young native, pressing his blade harder against his back. "We don't have time for this. Get up."

Yisei Ishkhan

Voices echoed from the way they'd come from. Vincente and the others were drawing near.

"We need to move," the young man yanked Domingo to his feet.

Domingo's hand shot forth, grabbing Sandoval's bracelet as the young native pulled him back. *I'm sorry, Sandoval.* The bracelet slipped free from the corpse. *I'm sorry…*

The bracelet was caked in dried blood, and several of its beads were chipped or missing. It wasn't much, but it was the only keepsake he had of his friend, the only piece of him he'd be able to bring back to his family.

As he was nudged down the corridor, Domingo didn't even get the chance to glance back at his friend one last time.

***

Under the cover of night, they navigated the Sacred Precinct without garnering much attention. Chaos enveloped the city, with fires devouring whole neighbourhoods and looters running rampant like packs of wolves. Any civilians caught by themselves were easy pickings, with men slaughtered and women and children dragged into the shadows.

A sharp cry pierced the darkness behind them. One of the women in their group had fallen behind, cornered by several men. In the flickering firelight, it was impossible to tell if they were Spaniards, Tlaxcalans, or native inhabitants of the city taking advantage of the anarchy.

The young man holding Domingo shouted a command at them in Nahuatl. They ignored him.

"Hey!" Domingo barked, first in Spanish, then in Mayan. "Leave them alone!"

"Spaniard?" One of the men harassing them asked in broken Mayan. "What are you doing with these prisoners?"

The Tales of Abel and Mitra

"Taking them to Cortés," Domingo snapped. "What does it look like?"

"Cortés, huh?" The man sneered. "Why don't we take them off your hands, hm? We'll treat them well, I promise."

The group of men chuckled. Domingo drew out the arquebus slinging across his shoulder, firing once into the air. A sharp *crack* echoed down the wide street. Both soldiers and prisoners alike cried out and ducked for cover, cowering as they covered their ears.

"I said *I* would deal with them," Domingo repeated in a low voice. "If I catch you harassing civilians again, you'll wish I'd shot you first. Understood?"

The men grumbled, but backed off, disappearing into the night.

"Let's keep moving," Domingo said. "Make sure no one strays from the group this time."

The young native raised an eyebrow as he studied Domingo's arquebus. "So, these are the infamous Spanish weapons that crack like thunder. I didn't realize you had one on you. I've never seen one for myself."

Domingo met his eyes. "Are you going to confiscate it?"

"Keep it. I'm sure you shoot better than I could."

They pressed on, reaching the house of the old man in their group before long. Though his home had been ransacked, the shed where he kept his boats remained untouched. They pushed two large canoes into the canal and piled aboard. As the group prepared to take off, one of the women muttered to the young man in Nahuatl, casting a sharp glance in Domingo's direction.

"You're coming with us," the young man said.

"I've already done what you asked!" Domingo gasped.

Yisei Ishkhan

"We can't risk you running to Cortés and having troops sent after us."

As the flames spread closer to them, lighting up the area, Domingo got a good look at the group for the first time since he'd encountered them. They were dressed in fine pelts and furs, many adorned with gold and precious stones. The realization struck Domingo–these were no ordinary refugees.

"You're–!"

"So, now you understand," the young man huffed, dragging Domingo onto the canoe.

Domingo didn't attempt to resist. He took up a paddle of his own, and together with the others, cruised along the canal and out onto Lake Tetzcoco. They weren't alone. All around, dozens of canoes had taken to the lake, fleeing the burning city as it fell to ruin. The distant roar of flames, agonizing screams of civilians, and sporadic crackle of gunfire echoed in the night. Domingo kept his eyes forward, trying to block out the horror unfolding behind them.

One of the women, a regal figure adorned in gold, spat a couple venomous words at him in Nahuatl. Her accusatory gaze was fixed on Domingo, but underneath the cold look in her eyes, Domingo could sense that she was struggling to hold back tears. Two small children sat by her side, burying their faces in her garments.

"Princess Atotozli says you should be killed," the young man said bluntly. "Her husband was murdered by your people. She says you should be sacrificed as an atonement."

Domingo flinched, his heart pounding in his chest as he imagined himself laid out across a sacrificial altar.

The Tales of Abel and Mitra

The young native turned to the princess, speaking softly in Nahuatl. Atotozli glared at him for a long moment before turning away, her expression bitter but resigned.

"What did you say?" Domingo trembled.

The young native sighed. "We've seen enough death to last a lifetime. You helped us to escape the city. That can be your atonement."

Domingo fell silent.

"So," the young man continued. "Have you killed anyone?"

"Of course not!" Domingo protested. "Didn't I tell you? I'm a translator, not a soldier!"

"One's profession does not dictate the depths they might descend to in war."

Domingo looked away.

They rowed on, the silence stretching between them as the echoes of burning flames and anguished cries began to fade.

"What do they call you?" Domingo finally asked. "Your name, I mean."

The young man glanced up at him. "Nezahualatzin."

"Neza...what?"

"Nezahualatzin."

"Nezahual...I think I'll just call you 'Neza.' Easier on the tongue"

"Don't."

"Well, it's the best I can do," Domingo shrugged. "My name is Domingo, by the way. Domingo Humeya de Granada."

Yisei Ishkhan

He turned his gaze eastward, toward the massive dike separating the salt water of Lake Tetzcoco from the freshwater.

"That dike," Domingo said thoughtfully as he recounted his tour of the city two years prior with Cortés, "doesn't it share the same name as you?"

"Nezahualcoyōtl," Nezahualatzin corrected. "It's named after a previous ruler."

"I see. Are you related to him?"

"No."

"But you are of noble descent?"

"I am. But I'm not originally from Tenochtitlan. I was born in Tlaxcala."

"A noble from Tlaxcala?" Domingo said in surprise. "Then what are you doing here?"

Nezahualatzin scoffed. "You think just because my people have sided with you Spaniards that I'm on the wrong side of this war? I was sent to Tenochtitlan as a child and have not returned since."

"Sent here? As a hostage?" Domingo wondered, recalling how the Mexica demanded annual sacrifices from their tributaries.

"Yes. But not for sacrifice. I became a priest."

"A priest?" Domingo blinked. "Is that why you were at the temple? Are you...are you the one who–?"

"I do not serve at the *Huēyi Teōcalli*," Nezahualatzin said, his face twisting with a look of disgust. "I am not a priest of Huītzilōpōchtli."

"Then which god do you serve?"

The Tales of Abel and Mitra

"Quetzalcōātl," Nezahualatzin's voice softened to reveal a hint of reverence. "His temple stands across the Sacred Precinct from the *Huēyi Teōcalli*."

"Quetzalcōātl," Domingo murmured. "The feathered serpent?"

"He is the God of Life, the God of Light, the God of Wisdom, Ruler of the West…"

Domingo hesitated. "Have you carried out sacrifices in his name?"

Nezahualatzin paused. "Not of humans."

"But you're a priest. I've seen the sacrifices your people carry out at the temples, including the Temple of Quetzalcōātl. I was here last year with Cortés—I saw it for myself!"

"So, you were here on the Night of Sorrows," Nezahualatzin said. "The night you Spaniards and Tlaxcalans slaughtered hundreds of our nobles and priests in the Sacred Precinct. Yes, I recall that night as well. I lost many friends that day…and many more tonight. For all I know, everyone I care about back in the city could already be dead."

Domingo fell silent. He averted his gaze from Nezahualatzin, glancing back toward the burning city. The crackle of flames and distant cries were muffled by the lapping of water against their canoe.

"No," Nezahualatzin continued, his tone softening. "I have never taken part in human sacrifices myself. I'm against it, as is my god. You found me at the *Huēyi Teōcalli* because I was there to free Princess Atotozli and the others. They were to be offered up as sacrifices in a last-ditch attempt to appease the gods."

Domingo scoffed. "How can you and your god be against sacrifices when they are offered at his temple?"

Yisei Ishkhan

"Is everything you Spaniards do in the name of your god condoned by him? There have always been those who perverted their devotion to Quetzalcōātl. I became a priest to reform the way he is worshiped."

"Reform? How can you reform such barbaric devotion?"

"And what would you have had me do instead?" Nezahualatzin asked.

"Tear it all down!"

"Like how you Spaniards have done? You've killed more people in this city these past weeks than human sacrifice has claimed in decades."

Domingo fell silent again. His fingers tightened around the bloodstained bracelet he'd taken from Sandoval's body.

Nezahualatzin's voice softened. "Was he someone important to you? A friend?"

"More than just a friend," Domingo's voice dropped to a whisper. "He was family to me."

"I am sorry for your loss."

Domingo nodded slowly. "I'm sorry too. For everything. I wish it hadn't come to this."

"If only there were more Spaniards who thought the same as you do," Nezahualatzin said, "perhaps it wouldn't have. But I can't be quick to judge. Most of the soldiers out there are my people. Tlaxcala and Tenochtitlan have been bitter rivals for generations. Tenochtitlan conquered and subdued many of her neighbours over the years— Āzcapōtzalco, Chālco, Xōchimīlco, Xoconochco. It was only a matter of time before one of her enemies rose against her to strike back."

The Tales of Abel and Mitra

Their canoe bumped against the northern shore of the lake. The nobles scrambled out in haste, joining dozens of other refugees who had fled the city.

Princess Atotozli lingered on the boat, clutching the hands of her two young children. She blocked Domingo's path as he tried to disembark, glaring at him with daggers in her eyes. Domingo shot a glance at Nezahualatzin. The priest uttered a couple of words to Atotozli. She scowled at him but backed down. With a huff, she gathered her children and hurried to join the others.

"She wants me to kill you," Nezahualatzin said matter-of-factly.

Domingo remained silent.

"You may go now," the priest continued. "Take the canoe back to the city or find your way to the causeway."

Domingo blinked in surprise. "I thought you were worried I'd have soldiers sent after you."

"We've made it across the lake," Nezahualatzin said. "Even if you were to inform Cortés, we'll be long gone by the time his men arrive. But I don't think you will say anything."

"Where will you go?" Domingo asked.

Nezahualatzin chuckled. "Do you think I'm foolish enough to tell you?"

"Let me come with you."

Nezahualatzin's gaze narrowed. "Come with us? Why? You saw how much Princess Atotozli wants your head. I won't be able to shield you from her for long."

"I don't want to go back to the city," Domingo said. "There's nothing for me there. I have no reason to stay with Cortés."

Yisei Ishkhan

Nezahualatzin folded his arms across his chest. "Then return to Yokatlān. Or the islands out at sea. Or Spain. You don't belong here."

"I don't belong anywhere," Domingo faltered. "There's nothing for me in Spain. I came to this world because Sandoval asked me to. We were going to build a better life for ourselves. But now…" he squeezed the bead bracelet tightly in his hand, "I have no reason to go back."

Nezahualatzin let forth a deep sigh. "Fine. Come, if you insist. But if you stir up trouble, I won't hesitate to abandon you to the coyotes in the valley."

Nezahualatzin strode off to join the others. Domingo lingered by the shore for a moment longer as the first light of dawn painted the sky. In the early light, Tenochtitlan's silhouette emerged–the towering peak of the Templo Mayor rising like a ghostly specter above the smaller pyramids and palaces. The canals, once bustling with life, were now clogged with boats carrying desperate refugees. Hundreds of bodies floated in the waters of the lake.

This must've been what it was like to witness the Fall of Constantinople, Domingo thought to himself. Sandoval's great-grandfather had been part of an Aragonese fleet that witnessed the fall of the great city. Domingo had never laid eyes on the Queen of Cities, but somehow, he felt that its majesty and splendor was surpassed by the glory of Tenochtitlan. He remembered the awe he felt two years prior when he'd ridden into the city with Cortés. He could hardly believe his eyes. It was unlike anything he'd ever imagined– floating gardens dotted Lake Tetzcoco, with the Nezahualcoyōtl dike separating saltwater from fresh; aqueducts only rivaled by those built by the Romans brought

The Tales of Abel and Mitra

crystal-clear water to the city's half a million inhabitants; the meticulous grid layout of the streets and canals, and towering temples surpassed the architectural feats of any city back in Europe.

He wasn't just witnessing the fall of a great city, but the death of a civilization. The end had come for the Empire of the Mexica. A new day was dawning in the New World.

***

They made their way from the shore of the lake, climbing one of the nearby hills where Nezahualatzin said there was a shrine that would offer them temporary refuge. The night had been long, and as the sun climbed higher, the heat quickly became stifling. Nezahualatzin suggested they rest at the shrine for a while before continuing their journey later in the evening. One of the nobles—the old man who had held his knife to Domingo's throat—had a residence a couple of days' travel from the city. He said he would offer sanctuary there, hoping its remote location would be overlooked by the Spaniards for a while.

When they arrived at the shrine hidden among the trees on Tepeyac Hill, they found hundreds of other refugees already gathered there. The few caretakers of the shrine, overwhelmed by the sheer number of people, struggled to maintain order. Fear clung to the faces of those who sought shelter, their desperate prayers rising to the local goddess for deliverance. Nearby, the sick and injured were being tended to under makeshift tents. Women and children wept openly, while the elderly stared vacantly into the distance. There were few men present among them—most had fallen in the siege.

Nezahualatzin had given Domingo his outer *tilmàtli* cloak to blend in. He kept his head low, careful not to draw attention to himself.

Yisei Ishkhan

"Princess Atotozli?!" A woman's voice cried out. One of the shrine's keepers hurried toward them. "Princess Atotozli!"

The princess barely acknowledged the call, continuing to stride forward without pause. But the mention of her name quickly drew the attention of others around them.

"Princess Atotozli?"

"It's her! She's really here!"

"I can't believe she made it out of the city!"

Domingo lingered behind Nezahualatzin as the crowd swarmed the princess and the other nobles. Their words were lost on him, but the growing sense of tension in the area was palpable.

"Princess Atotozli, what should we do?"

"You must save us! The gods have abandoned us!"

The princess gripped her children tightly as the people threw themselves at her feet and pleaded before her. Her gaze was distant and unfocused, looking past the crowd and somewhere beyond the trees.

"The gods have *not* abandoned us," she said firmly. "In fact, they've sent us a sacrifice today!"

With a swift motion, she turned and pointed directly at Domingo. His heart froze as all eyes rested on him. Domingo shrunk back. Before he knew it, several people lunged forward, grabbing at him and tearing at his cloak.

"A Spaniard!" Someone shrieked.

"Rip his heart out!"

"That's enough!" Nezahualatzin's voice rang out in Nahuatl. He pulled Domingo close to him and pushed the crowd back. "Step back at once! This man is not here as a sacrifice. He is under *my* protection! Is that understood?"

The Tales of Abel and Mitra

Atotozli flew into a rage. "Nezahualatzin, you're a Tlaxcalan by blood and still a Tlaxcalan at heart! No wonder you're defending a filthy Spaniard! We should've never let people like you into our priesthood! You wish to do away with our ritual sacrifices! No wonder the gods have decided to punish us!"

Nezahualatzin narrowed his gaze. "Need I remind you, Princess Atotozli, just *who* it was that the priests had planned to sacrifice last night?"

The princess shrank back, shielding her children.

"You are mistaken," the priest continued calmly. "It is not because we haven't offered enough sacrifices that our city has fallen. It's because we have sacrificed far, far too many."

"Blasphemy!" The princess spat.

"Is it? Think for yourself. Why have the Tlaxcalans, the Tetzcocoans, the Totonacapans, and so many others sided with the Spaniards against Tenochtitlan? It is because they've been oppressed and downtrodden by Tenochtitlan for decades! Tenochtitlan demands an annual tribute and fights endless Flower Wars to capture sacrifices for the gods. Of course, the people would rise up and throw in their lot with the Spaniards when the chance arose!"

"You're a traitor!" Atotozli fumed.

She was about to confront the priest, but just then, her young daughter spewed vomit across the ground. The onlookers froze, then recoiled in a panic away from the child. The girl's hood fell back, revealing a red rash that spread from her ear across her cheek and down to her chin.

"She's infected!" Someone cried.

"It's the pestilence that struck last year!"

"We're all going to die!"

Yisei Ishkhan

Despair rippled through the crowd. Several people collapsed to the ground and wept uncontrollably. Others turned toward the shrine, offering their most fervent prayers. A few stared vacantly at the sky, at the mountains in the distance, or in the direction of the ruined city.

"Smallpox," Domingo muttered in Spanish as he studied the girl's symptoms.

"What was that?" Nezahualatzin asked.

"The disease the girl has," Domingo switched back to Mayan. "We call it smallpox."

"I've never encountered this sickness before you Spaniards arrived in Tenochtitlan," Nezahualatzin said. "You brought it here on your ships–a plague from your world that has devastated our people. Half of Tenochtitlan's population was wiped out by it just a few months ago."

"Half?" Domingo paled. "It shouldn't be that deadly…"

"Tell me how it can be treated."

"I…I'm sorry," Domingo shook his head. "I'm afraid there isn't much that can be done."

Atotozli sank to her knees, clutching her daughter to her chest as tears streamed down her face. Her son stood beside her, staring at them with an empty look in his eyes.

Nezahualatzin grabbed Domingo by the arm and began pulling him through the crowd.

"Where are we going?" Domingo asked.

"When there is nothing else that can be done, we pray."

Once it was clear that Domingo was with Nezahualatzin, no one dared to lay a finger on him. They ducked through the low stone doorway of the shrine. A statue of a goddess stood at the altar, with a feather headdress and a skirt made of serpents. She was surrounded by offerings brought by the faithful–various kinds of feathers, fruits, and flowers. One of the flowers in particular caught Domingo's eye–a pink species of rose that he recognized.

Castile rose? What is that doing here? I didn't realize they grew in the New World…

Nezahualatzin knelt before the altar, pulling Domingo down beside him.

"Who is the goddess of this shrine?" Domingo whispered, nodding toward the statue.

"Cōātlīcue," said Nezahualatzin. "They call her Tonāntziné around here. 'The Mother Goddess.'"

"You want me to…pray to her…?" Domingo hesitated.

Nezahualatzin waved his question aside. "Pray to whomever you'd like–your own God, or your own Mother Goddess. You have one too, don't you? I've seen you Spaniards carry the banner of her–the Virgin Goddess."

"She's not a goddess," Domingo corrected. "She was merely a human. We only have one God."

"She must be someone quite important to revere in such a manner," Nezahualatzin noted.

The priest bowed his head, closing his eyes as he began reciting a prayer in Nahuatl. The others in the shrine, and even those gathered outside, joined along. Domingo watched from the corner in silence, absently tracing his fingers along the beads of Sandoval's bracelet.

Before he knew it, he was reciting a hymn in his head:

Salve, Regina, Mater misericordiæ, (Hail, holy Queen, Mother of Mercy;)
vita, dulcedo, et spes nostra, salve (Hail our life, our sweetness and our hope.)

Yisei Ishkhan

Ad te clamamus exsules filii Hevæ (To thee do we cry, poor banished children of Eve)
Ad te suspiramus, gementes et flentes (To thee do we send up our sighs, mourning and weeping)
in hac lacrimarum valle. (In this valley of tears.)

Eia, ergo, advocata nostra, illos tuos (Here, then, our advocate,)
misericordes oculos ad nos converte; (Turn then, most gracious advocate, thine eyes of mercy toward us;)
Et Iesum, benedictum fructum ventris tui, (And Jesus, blessed fruit of thy womb,
nobis post hoc exsilium ostende. (Show us after this exile.)
O clemens, O pia, O dulcis Virgo Maria. (O merciful, O pious, O sweet Virgin Mary.)

Nezahualatzin tapped Domingo lightly on the shoulder. His eyes fluttered open. He'd fallen into a trance, losing track of the time as the prayers echoed in his head. Dry remnants of tears stained his face. One of the beads on Sandoval's bracelet was the shape of a cross. When he had squeezed the bracelet during his prayers, the cross had dug into his palm, drawing blood that slowly dripped down his hand.

"It's time to go," Nezahualatzin whispered.

Domingo followed the young priest as they departed the shrine. More refugees had poured into Tepayac Hill from the city, but Nezahualatzin paid them no heed. They moved east, toward the trees, the ground sloping down toward the northern shore of Lake Tetzcoco.

"Where are we going?" Domingo asked.

The Tales of Abel and Mitra

"You may not wish to return to your homeland, but I do. Tlaxcala lies to the east, across the lake and over the mountains."

"What about Princess Atotozli and the others?" Domingo wondered. "I thought we were traveling to the old man's estate with them?"

"They don't need me to accompany them," Nezahualatzin said. "You heard what Princess Atotozli said– I'm a Tlaxcalan by blood and still a Tlaxcalan at heart. Because of my heritage, she never liked me. Do you know how many struggles I faced just to enter the Priesthood of Quetzalcōātl? How many times I was told the best way I could serve the gods was to be offered up as a sacrifice to appease them? But I persevered. I worked my way into the Priesthood with the hope that I could reform the system, with the hope that I could somehow bridge the gap between Tlaxcala and Tenochtitlan." He gazed distantly to the east, a bitter chuckle escaping his lips. "And for what? In the end, the Tlaxcalans destroyed Tenochtitlan. The Spaniards will tear down the temples of Quetzalcōātl. Do you know what the shrine keepers told me back there? Before the siege, they heard the goddess cry out *'My beloved children, your destruction is next.'* Last night, when the city fell, they heard her voice once again. She was weeping. Tonāntziné was weeping for her children. The prophecy has been fulfilled. This is the end."

Domingo said nothing. On the ground next to Nezahualatzin's feet, he noticed a couple of Castile roses in bloom. Had they always been there?

"Don't say that." Domingo stepped forward. "I thought your people didn't believe in absolute beginnings and ends. The end of one cycle is the beginning of another. Perhaps

Yisei Ishkhan

Tenochtitlan's time has come, but that doesn't mean the story is finished. Her people are still here. *You* are still here."

Nezahualatzin brushed away the tears forming in the corners of his eyes. "For now," he whispered. "Let's keep moving."

By evening, they reached the shores of the lake. An abandoned village sat before them, with a few dozen dilapidated houses and a creaky wooden dock. By chance, a canoe was tied to shore, bobbing gently in the waves. They decided to borrow it.

"You've been to Tlaxcala, haven't you?" Nezahualatzin said.

"Cortés had us stationed there before we launched the siege."

"Good. Then you'll know the way back."

"You don't?"

"I haven't been there since I was a child. As a priest, I rarely leave the city. I've studied the maps, but it's different when you're actually on the ground."

"Is that why you wanted me to come with you?"

"You're the one who chose to stay with me," Nezahualatzin reminded him.

They set out onto the lake as night fell, rowing in silence. The winds began to pick up as they drifted toward the middle of the lake.

"We're nearing Tetzcoco," Nezahualatzin said after a while, breaking the silence as they approached the eastern shore. "Do you know the way to Tlaxcala from there?"

Domingo nodded.

"What does that mean?"

The Tales of Abel and Mitra

"What?" Domingo glanced at him in confusion.

"When you do this," Nezahualatzin repeated the head movement. "What does it mean?"

"Oh. It's a way of answering in the affirmative."

Nezahualatzin made a face. "Then why don't you just say 'yes'?"

Domingo shrugged.

"I don't know what that means either."

"It means 'I don't know.'"

Nezahualatzin looked amused. "You Spaniards and your strange customs."

"Is it strange? I always assumed those gestures had a universal meaning."

"Why would they?" Nezahualatzin scoffed. "What is it about nodding your head that means 'yes,' or shrugging your shoulders that means 'I don't know'?"

"I suppose I never gave it much thought," Domingo admitted.

"Perhaps that's what's wrong with this world," Nezahualatzin sighed. "We make assumptions about what others are thinking without truly understanding our differences."

"Perhaps."

Nezahualatzin glanced back at Domingo, studying him intently with his gaze. "Tell me about your homeland–Spain."

Domingo glanced at him. "What is it to you?"

"I want to know about the land of your people. We'll be spending the next few days together as we journey to Tlaxcala, so I'd like to have a better understanding of who you are."

Yisei Ishkhan

"There isn't much to say. I'm from Granada, in the south of the country. The climate and terrain aren't too different from here in the valley, only we're closer to the sea than you are."

"And the people?"

Domingo scoffed. "You've met the people for yourself."

"I've met soldiers," Nezahualatzin said. "I'm sure they're hardly representative of all Spaniards."

Light rain began to fall. The distant lights of the city of Tetzcoco ahead grew dim as dark clouds rolled in overhead, shrouding the valley in darkness.

"People are the same anywhere you go in the world," Domingo said without looking up.

Nezahualatzin chuckled. "So, your people also fight petty wars of expansion against neighbours who worship the same God as you, form alliances only to break them, and conquer others before you are conquered in turn."

"We do. Spain fought a seven-hundred-year war to reclaim Iberia from the Moors. They only succeeded in driving the Moors off the peninsula the year that Columbus landed in the New World."

"So, there are other people who live in your world besides the Spaniards."

"There are plenty. Spain is only one small country at the edge of Europe, and Europe is only a small part of the Old World. There are much greater empires that stretch across the vast lands of Africa and Asia that even the Spaniards have yet to explore. Even within Spain, there are many different peoples. The kingdoms of Leon, Navarre, Aragon, and Castile came together under one crown, similar to how Tenochtitlan, Tlacopan, and Tetzcoco united to form the Triple Alliance.

The Tales of Abel and Mitra

Then there are the Conversos—Jews who converted to Catholicism and their descendants. Moriscos are the Muslim equivalent. My parents were Moriscos."

"I see," said Nezahualatzin. "Then you are no more a Spaniard than I am Mexica."

"I suppose you could say that."

"And what do you mean when you say they 'converted'? They went from being one thing to another?"

"They stopped worshiping their old god and became devoted to the Christian God instead. At least officially. Some continue to hold onto their old faith in secret."

"You said earlier that your god isn't the Virgin they wave on the banners," Nezahualatzin recalled.

"She's the one who gave birth to God's human incarnation but is not a deity herself."

"How can a human give birth to a god?"

"Because his incarnation wasn't just divine. He was also human. I know it's difficult to comprehend."

By this point, the rain had turned into a downpour; the wind picked up, and waves knocked violently against their boat.

"I think I understand," said Nezahualatzin. "We have a similar story in our legends—some believe that Quetzalcōātl came to Earth as a human king a few centuries ago. It is said that during his reign, he ended human sacrifices, before eventually giving up his own life, and promising to one day return." He smiled wryly. "When Cortés first landed, there were some who claimed that he was Quetzalcōātl's second coming. I wonder what they would say now."

They could no longer see the shore. With the storm growing stronger, a sudden gust of wind sent a large wave

Yisei Ishkhan

crashing upon them. They tried their best to steady themselves with their paddles, but the canoe capsized. Domingo plunged into the icy waters, struggling to find his way back to the surface. He managed to grab onto the side of the boat, but when he reemerged, he found that he was alone. Nezahualatzin was nowhere to be seen.

"Neza!" He called out for the priest, coughing out a mouthful of water as he struggled to catch his breath. "Nezahualatzin! Where are you?!"

Lightning split across the sky, zigzagging between the clouds like an enormous serpent swimming through the heavens. A shiver shot up Domingo's spine as the light dissipated. In that brief flash, he had spotted an island nearby, and the shadow of a large, winged creature hovering above the shore. It looked like a large bird, perhaps an eagle. But as another bolt of lightning struck, the eagle was gone, instead replaced by the silhouette of a man.

A deafening crack of thunder followed moments later, shaking Domingo to the core. He paddled furiously toward the island, struggling against the relentless assault of the waves. Every muscle in his body strained; every stroke was a battle against the forces of nature. But finally, he found himself ashore. The island, however, was desolate. There wasn't a single tree or even the slightest shrub jutting from the rocks.

I'm sure I saw someone here, Domingo thought to himself. He reached instinctively for Sandoval's bracelet, hoping to pray with it in hand. But the bracelet was gone.

***

Nezahualatzin didn't know how to swim. Each frantic movement sent him deeper into the chaos of the abyss. The storm roared above him, water pressing against his chest and

The Tales of Abel and Mitra

pulling him under. But the lower he sank, the calmer the lake became, until there was only stillness. He floated there in the murky depths, feeling neither warm nor cold. The sensation was strangely peaceful, and his struggle to make it to the surface seemed meaningless now. Perhaps it wasn't so bad if the lake pulled him deeper into its depths.

A flash of light arched across the sky, its brilliance refracting through the water like the shimmer of a thousand stars. Then he saw it–a hand extending toward him from above.

Domingo?

He couldn't see who the hand belonged to but assumed it must be his companion. But then, the voice of a man spoke out to him in perfect Nahuatl.

It is not the end for you. Come. Follow me.

Nezahualatzin froze. That voice–firm yet calm–didn't belong to Domingo. Not only was it speaking Nahuatl, but it spoke in the dialect of Tlaxcala that Nezahualatzin had first learned as a child.

Do not be afraid. Just trust me. That's all you need to do.

The words cut through the haze clouding Nezahualatzin's mind. Against every instinct screaming at him to let go, to give into the depths of the lake, Nezahualatzin thrust his hand forward, his fingers intertwined with those of the stranger. Water surged past him as he rose, higher and higher, until his head breached the surface of the waves.

***

Domingo could hardly believe his eyes as he squinted through the dissipating storm. A figure was walking across the surface of the waves, steady and unwavering, as though the water beneath his feet were solid ground. As the storm let up, and the figure drew near to the island, his features came into focus. Domingo's breath caught in his throat.

"Nezahualatzin?!" He gasped in disbelief. "I thought I saw you on the island, but when I got here it was empty! You...what happened to you?! How did you do that?!"

"I sank beneath the waves," Nezahualatzin said. "I thought it was over for me. I had given up. But then, a hand reached out to me. At first, I thought it was you, but the man spoke to me in perfect Nahuatl."

"A man? Where is he now? What did he look like?"

"I don't know. I only saw him for a moment when I resurfaced. His face was shrouded in light, too bright for me to make out the features."

Domingo laughed with excitement. "When I saw you walking toward me on the waters, I thought you must be Señor Jesucristo!"

"Your God?" Nezahualatzin wondered. "Does he often walk on water?"

"Occasionally," Domingo chuckled. He glanced down at Nezahualatzin's hands, suddenly noticing a familiar object around the man's wrist. "Wait...is that...?"

Nezahualatzin raised his hand, frowning in confusion as he noticed the bracelet for the first time. "Sandoval's bracelet?"

Domingo nodded, his mouth agape. "How did you get a hold of it? I thought I lost it in the storm!"

"I don't know," Nezahualatzin admitted. "That man who saved me must've put it on me."

They stood in silence as the remnants of the storm faded away. The night sky became clear, revealing the lights of

Tetzcoco on the eastern shore, and the distant stars in the heavens above.

Domingo exhaled, the tension leaving his body as he looked out across the waters. "The storm has calmed. It really is a miracle."

"I think you were right, Domingo," said Nezahualatzin.

Domingo cocked his head. "About what?"

"When that man saved me, he told me that this wasn't the end for me. You said something similar earlier. Maybe you were right–this isn't the end of the story. It's only the beginning."

Yisei Ishkhan

The Tale of Abel and Mitra

Abel frowned as Mitra's tale came to a close. "Why'd you pick such a sad story!"

Mitra cocked his head. "You asked for a story from my world. Most stories carry the weight of tragedy."

"You could've picked one that was slightly less depressing."

"The story had a happy ending," Mitra said. "Besides, I think we learn more from experiences of sorrow than joy."

"The ending was more bittersweet than happy," Abel argued. "And it wasn't *really* the end! As Nezahualatzin said, it was just the beginning! So, what happened next?"

"I'm afraid the remainder of the story is fragmented into different records."

"I'm sure you could fill in some of the blanks!"

Mitra paused as he considered the boy's words. "There is a 98% chance that Domingo and Nezahualatzin eventually reached Tlaxcala, where Domingo recorded his story. Eventually, it found its way to my archives. Beyond that, it would be reckless to speculate on the details. If I did, you might be disappointed in what happened next."

"I won't complain, I swear! I just wanna know what happened after. What happened to the other characters in the story? Princess Atotozli and her children? Did they escape to the old man's estate? Did her daughter recover from the illness?"

"I have no records of their whereabouts after Domingo's account. But I imagine they met a similar fate as most of their subjects."

The Tales of Abel and Mitra

"And what was that?"

"Up to ninety percent of the population perished from Old World diseases in the subsequent decades, not just across the lands of the Mexica's empire, but the entire continents of North and South America."

Abel fell silent for a while, his fingers fidgeting with the edges of his cloak. After a couple of minutes, he looked up, forcing a smile. "Tell me another story. A happy one this time."

Mitra chuckled. "We're nearly back at the Village. I think it'll have to wait until later."

Ahead, the warm glow of lanterns flickered through the dense trees. Abel detached himself from the silk that held him to Mitra, and they waited for Akavi and Esta to catch up before making their way into the Village.

The Village was the sole human settlement in the Valley of Shambhala, home to a couple thousand inhabitants. The trees that grew here were less densely packed than other parts of the forest, and it was even possible to glimpse through the canopy out at the sky from certain locations. The forest floor was a lush, swampy ecosystem, carved out by enormous roots rising from the ground in one place and sinking back into the soil a dozen meters away. This created shallow pools between the trees that were ideal for hosting a range of crops—rice, bamboo shoots, duskroots, and dawnberries. Barriers had been erected along the perimeter of the Village to prevent unwanted ratri rakshas from wandering through, thus the forest floor within the grounds of the Village was safe to traverse.

Despite this, there were no buildings on the ground, only storage facilities in the complex subterranean tunnel systems that ran beneath the forest floor. The lowest buildings perched atop branches thirty meters above the ground, though even these were few and far between. Most houses and shops were found at higher elevations, a hundred meters or more above the ground.

Branches and foliage in the Village were sparser than elsewhere in the forest, partly because the trees stood further apart and partly due to careful grooming and upkeep. This made jumping and climbing between the branches more difficult, so most trees in the Village were connected through a complex series of ladders, hanging bridges, zip lines, and pulley elevators that crisscrossed their way between the forest floor and the canopy.

Abel and the others landed on one of the docking platforms at the Village's edge, a hundred meters above the ground. Normally, only the team taking over their shift would be waiting for them there. But today, a dozen people had gathered. His friend Avi was leaning against the railing with his usual nervous energy, alongside Nineveh of the *Makarasa Morung*, who oversaw security for the Lightside Quadrant. A few old Village Elders were also present, including the priest Vishel with his graying beard and bald head, and Inali, the oldest and most respected of the Elders. But Abel's attention was fixed on his parents. Kitoli and Nyimang's faces lit up in relief as they spotted Abel and Esta emerge from the trees.

"Thank God you've returned!" Cried Kitoli, their mother, wrapping her children in an embrace. "We were so worried when you didn't return at the end of your shift!"

"We heard the explosion out there and saw that blinding flash of light," said Nyimang. "What happened?"

"We're fine," Esta said with an exaggerated sigh, casting a glance at her brother. "But I'm *exhausted*. *Someone* insisted on staying out to investigate the anomaly."

The Tales of Abel and Mitra

"That is protocol," Nineveh said, adjusting her spectacles with an air of quiet authority. She cast a glance at Mitra. "And who is this? You're not part of the *Kamkara* or *Makarasa Morung*."

"This is Mitra," Abel said. "He's...how should I put this...?"

A look of amusement crossed Mitra's face. "I suppose you could say *I* am the anomaly."

The group fell silent, staring at the man in confusion.

"The anomaly?" Avi piped up, his eyes sparkling with curiosity. "What do you mean?"

"My vessel fell from the sky and crashed in the forest. That was the flash of light you saw and the explosion you heard."

"A *vessel?*" Vishel repeated. The old priest stroked his beard, his face twisting in skepticism as he studied Mitra with a cautious gaze. "What do you mean by 'vessel'? Who are you, and where do you come from?"

Mitra glanced at Abel, as though seeking permission to explain further. Abel hesitated for a moment before nodding slightly.

"I come from another world."

Vishel snorted. "Another world? And what world would that be?"

"It is called by many names, but it is most commonly known as 'Earth.'"

"Earth..." Inali repeated. The old woman's gaze was distant.

Mitra nodded. "I am not sure if you have a different name for it in your tongue."

Yisei Ishkhan

"In *our* tongue?" Nineveh echoed. "Does that mean you originally speak another language? How did you come to acquire our tongue if you just arrived in Shambhala today?"

"He's a man of many talents," Esta huffed. "I'd be surprised if there was something he *couldn't* do!"

"I would like to take you in for questioning," said Nineveh.

"As would I," Vishel added. "I'll convene a meeting with the Elders at once. Nineveh, please take this man into custody."

"Of course."

"W-wait!" Abel protested. "Custody? He did nothing wrong!"

"This is all part of standard protocol," Nineveh assured. "Not that we've ever dealt with an outworlder before. Once we can determine that he poses no threat, he'll be released."

"No need to worry, Abel," Mitra said. "I'll be fine. Why don't you get some rest?"

"Yes," Kitoli put a hand on her son's shoulder. "You must be exhausted. Come, let's get you some dinner before you head off to bed."

Abel was reluctant to leave, but he couldn't deny that he wanted to sleep. Even during Mitra's story, he'd found it difficult to keep his eyes open until the end. He watched as Nineveh escorted Mitra away before following Esta and his parents home.

***

Most of the homes in the Village consisted of burrows within the tree trunks or round huts nestled along the branches. These homes were modest, with little more than a central

The Tales of Abel and Mitra

kitchen and two or three adjacent bedrooms. Abel's house was near the end of their branch, almost two hundred meters from the forest floor, with a hanging bridge nearby to connect them to the neighbouring trees.

Abel fell asleep before Kitoli finished cooking dinner. He awoke a short while later, just before the hundred and tenth hour of Night. By then, his parents and Esta were asleep, so he ate quietly on his own before heading out.

He hurried along the branch to the pulley elevator near the trunk of their tree. From there, he dropped down to the forest floor, ready to start his shift harvesting duskroots. As their name suggested, duskroot only bloomed during the hours of Dusk. Once Night fell, it was time for the harvest to begin.

"Avi!" Abel called out. He spotted his friend already at work, knee-deep in one of the shallow pools.

Avi waved him over, wiping the sweat from his brow. He wore a basket like a backpack, nearly filled to the rim with duskroots. "I'm almost done with this pool. We can move to the next one soon."

Abel nodded. "Have you seen Mitra around?"

"That guy you found out there? The Elders sent him on a Night Mission with Nineveh and some of the more experienced members of the *Makarasa Morung*."

"A Night Mission? What for?"

Avi shrugged. "Noa told me they were gonna recover some stuff from his vessel. Plus, Esta said you two forgot to pick up the hkaru you harvested on the way back. So, they went to grab those too."

Yisei Ishkhan

Abel slapped his palm to his forehead. He'd been so caught up in the excitement of Mitra's arrival that he'd completely forgotten to pick up their packs on the way back.

"So, I guess the Elders don't see him as a threat?" Abel said.

"Guess not. Vishel and some of the others are suspicious, but Inali vouched for him, so the Elders agreed to let him stay. Still, don't you think it's a little strange? That guy said he came from another world. Do you believe him? Sounds a little far-fetched, don't you think? My guess is that he came from the other Pole."

"He said he's an archivist," Abel noted. "He even told me about the world he came from. I think he was telling the truth."

"Anyone can tell a story," Avi smirked. "You remember all the tales I used to tell you when we were kids? About the colonies of monsters out in the woods? You actually believed them and got so scared you said you'd never go on a Night Mission!"

"H-hey!" Abel blushed. "Just because I was scared doesn't mean I *believed* them! Besides, there *are* monsters out there. Some of the ratri rakshas are scarier than any monsters you made up in your stories."

Avi chuckled. "And yet, here you are. You could have joined the *Oyeba* or *Lukano Morung* like your parents, but you still chose the *Kamkara Morung* and became a forager."

"Only because you did," Abel huffed. "*Someone* had to keep an eye on you. You have no sense of direction. I had to make sure you didn't get lost."

"Uh-huh," Avi brushed his comment aside. "Well, that doesn't matter now since we're no longer partners out there.

The Tales of Abel and Mitra

Noa's sense of direction is just as bad as mine, but we still make it back after every shift."

"I'm surprised that you do," Abel shook his head.

"How's Esta out there? Third Night, right?"

"She's fine. She needs to work on her stamina, but she'll get there."

"Oh, so *you're* no longer the slowest forager in our Quadrant. Congratulations!"

"Shut up," Abel flushed.

They soon finished harvesting the pool and moved on to the next one. Akavi and Avi's pku friend, Spinner, joined them. Prowling along the roots at the edge of the pool, the pku hunted down ganaan and other pests that damaged the crops.

It was almost the hundred and fifteenth hour of Night when Esta's voice echoed from above.

"Hey Abel! Get up here! Mister Falling Star is back!"

Abel dropped his basket as he rushed over to the elevator.

"Hey!" Avi shouted. "Where are you going?!"

"I wanna see what they brought back!"

"Your shift isn't over yet!"

"Don't worry, I'll be back soon!"

Abel ascended the elevator, crossing the bridges that led back to the docking platform.

Nineveh was there, alongside the other members of the *Makarasa Morung* as they changed out of their gear. Mitra stood by a stack of crates they'd brought back from the expedition. The man was no longer dressed in the thin undergarments Abel had lent him but instead donned the same uniform as the others.

Yisei Ishkhan

"How'd you bring this all back with you?" Abel asked as he glanced at the crates.

Mitra gestured to the strange vehicles the stacks of crates were resting on, and it was only then that Abel realized they were levitating slightly above the ground. Mitra ran his hand along the seated portion of the platform and up to a handle lined with buttons. "These are the hovercycles I mentioned earlier. Miss Nineveh insisted we bring them back. She said she'd send out another team later to retrieve more of the artifacts."

"Artifacts?" Abel wondered. "Is that what's in these boxes?"

"For the most part."

"I think the Elders will confiscate them from you."

"It is fine," Mitra assured. "They only asked to inspect what I brought with me. They believe it would be safer to bring the artifacts to the Village rather than keep them aboard the vessel. They mentioned that ratri rakshas were on the prowl."

"Are you planning to stay here a while?" Abel wondered. "Or do you have another destination in mind?"

"Aida ran diagnostics and found that the vessel sustained damage during the landing. It will take some time to repair. I will also require an adequate fuel source to get off-world. Otherwise, I will be forced to remain on your world." He chuckled when he noticed a look of concern on Abel's face. "I do not mind. Shambhala has proven to be more habitable than I initially expected."

Nineveh approached the two of them, gripping the handle of one of the levitating vehicles. After a couple of button clicks, the hovercycle sprung to life, rising slightly

The Tales of Abel and Mitra

higher above the ground. Despite the heavy load, she maneuvered the vehicle along with ease.

"Do you require my assistance with anything, Miss Nineveh?" Mitra wondered.

"We're fine," Nineveh assured. "We'll take these down to storage for investigation. Perhaps Abel can show you around the Village."

Mitra turned to the boy expectantly.

"Ah...yes...I could do that," Abel nodded.

Nineveh strode off alongside the others with the cargo.

"Nineveh is a quick learner," Mitra mused. "She learned how to steer the hovercycle without struggle. Her brother, on the other hand..."

Abel glimpsed Noa as the young man struggled to pull his hovercycle along. Nineveh reprimanded him, hurrying over to take hold of the vehicle before he lost control and accidentally drove it over the edge of the platform.

Mitra watched with amusement as the scene unfolded. "He nearly crashed on several occasions."

"That sounds like Noa," Abel sighed. "So, where would you like to head first? We've got the farms down on the forest floor, the houses up in the branches, and the Village Center with all the shops and gathering spaces."

"The Village Center sounds like a good place to begin."

As they made their way toward the Village Center, Abel couldn't help but notice the curious glances from the villagers they crossed paths with. Word about Mitra's arrival had spread quickly, and the stranger from the stars had been the talk of the town since his arrival. Despite the attention, few dared to approach him directly. Shambhala had no history of outworlders arriving, and Mitra's sudden appearance provoked unease in the community.

Mitra, though, didn't appear troubled by this.

"Is the Village the only settlement in the Valley of Shambhala?" He asked.

"There are some houses scattered here and there throughout the forest," said Abel. "Most of them are abandoned, but sometimes members of the *Kamkara* or *Makarasa Morung* will sleep under their roof if they're caught outside on a Night Mission. It's dangerous to stray too far from the Village, especially at Night."

"I asked the Elders, Miss Nineveh, and some of the others a few questions about your world," said Mitra. "But it seemed they often did not know the answer."

"What is it that you wanted to know?"

"Many things. For instance, how long have your people resided in Shambhala? What exists beyond the Purvanchal Range, on what you call Lightside and Darkside? And are you aware of other worlds that contain life?"

"I don't know the answers to those questions either," said Abel. "Before I met you, I didn't even know that there *were* other worlds out there, let alone that they were home to people like us. Your world sounds like an amazing place, with all kinds of different people."

"It was," Mitra mused.

"Was?"

"The story I told you was from a long time ago. The world has changed much since then."

They reached the Village Center, where layers of additional platforms stretched across the empty gaps between

The Tales of Abel and Mitra

the trees. Shops, homes, and other buildings sat along the edge of a central square, while a large, circular building sat atop a tree, cradled between its branches like an enormous bird's nest. The building had high walls, with a conical roof that had a cross perched atop it.

But none of the buildings seemed to catch Mitra's attention. A flash of blue and red feathers scurried between some of the food stalls in the square. One of the vendors cried out as the creature snagged some food from him before scampering off and soaring down to a branch in the distance that was just out of the man's reach. Above them, several colourful species of birds soared overhead or ruffled their feathers atop the houses and trees. Mitra stared at them with fascination.

"Do you have birds in your world too?" Abel asked.

"We do," said Mitra. "But I did not expect to find them here. I did not see any while we were out in the forest."

"They prefer to stick to the Village," said Abel. "Their nests are easy prey for ratri rakshas."

"I see," said Mitra, his gaze falling to the buildings in their vicinity. "Are those walls made of bamboo? They are the only plant I recognize so far in this world."

"They are," Abel confirmed. "Bamboo is a sturdy material and easy to harvest so we use it for many of the buildings. But that isn't their only use. Come, why don't we head over to Mrs. Sumi's stall and get something to eat? She sells bamboo shoots and other things that you might recognize."

Mrs. Sumi was a round old woman with wrinkled, tawny skin, and gray hair tied into a neat bun atop her head. She worked at her stall with practiced precision, pounding a sticky wad of rice on a chopping board with a bamboo stick. Mitra took in the potent scents wafting over, a strong, fermented aroma mixed with a faint sweetness.

"Is that *akhuni*?" He asked. "Fermented soybeans?"

"Oh ho, it sure is," Mrs. Sumi smiled. "You must be that outworlder I've been hearing about. Tell me, how are you familiar with our cuisine if you've just arrived in Shambhala?"

"Soybeans are a common crop on my home world," Mitra explained. "So are bamboo and rice. These are familiar ingredients."

"I see, I see," the old woman nodded. "Well, how about I whip you up something that'll remind you of home?"

"That would be lovely," Mitra said. "But I would also like to sample some of your local cuisine."

Mrs. Sumi grinned. "What'll it be? We've got starflower syrup, starflower juice, duskroots, and hkaru. I make recipes with dawnflowers, but I'm usually out of stock by the time Night falls. You'll have to wait until Dawn for a fresh batch."

Mitra eyed the slimy blobs of white flesh laid across the chopping board. "Is that what you and Esta were harvesting when you found me, Abel?"

"Yes," said Abel. "That's hkaru."

"These just arrived fresh from the forest," Mrs. Sumi beamed.

"In that case, I'll try some," said Mitra.

"Excellent!" Mrs. Sumi clapped.

"Why don't we get a little bit of everything?" Abel suggested. He pulled out a pouch of currency. "Don't worry, it's on me."

Mrs. Sumi smiled. "Such a sweet boy. I'll prepare some rice and curry dishes for you two to enjoy."

The Tales of Abel and Mitra

Abel handed over several small green and blue shells from his pouch.

"Is that currency?" Mitra wondered.

"Yes," Abel said. "They're from a species that's been extinct for ages. Blue shells are common so they're worth the least. Green ones are rarer so they're worth more. Red shells are the rarest of all."

"Abel! There you are!" Avi came racing toward them from across the square, carrying two empty baskets in tow. He tossed one into Abel's arms as he skidded to a stop. "I dropped off our harvest already. So, *this* is why you ditched me, huh? Left me to finish the shift on my own while you were off with the new guy."

"S-sorry," Abel stammered.

"It's fine, don't sweat it," Avi sighed, throwing an arm over his friend's shoulder. "Usually, *I'm* the one who gets distracted while *you* cover for me. So…" he glanced at Mitra with curiosity. "What's so interesting about this new guy that you left me hanging?"

Abel fidgeted under Avi's arm. "Avi, this is Mitra. He's an archivist. Mitra, this is Avi—my best friend and former Night Mission partner."

"It is a pleasure to meet you, Avi," smiled Mitra. "I was told you were the one who discovered that hkaru colony out in the forest."

"Yeah, that's right," Avi beamed. "And *I* heard that you're an excellent storyteller."

"Oh?" Mitra cast a subtle glance in Abel's direction.

"Well?" Avi said, crossing his arms. "Let's hear one then! Abel always came to me for stories when we were kids, but he got sick of them after a while. I need some new inspiration."

"It wasn't that I got sick of them," Abel muttered. "You just always told the same stories over and over again."

"How?" Avi gasped. "There was the *Legend of the Shadow Men*, *The Legend of the Shadow Men Part Two*, *The Prequel of the Legend of the Shadow Men*, *The Tale of Makarasa-man*, *The Tale of Makarasa-man Part Two*, *The Tale of Makarasa-man Part Three*…"

"Every single one of them was about some damsel in distress getting kidnapped by ratri rakshas out in the woods," Abel said with a tone of amusement. "Then the hero would embark on a grand adventure with his trusty sidekick to rescue her."

"What's wrong with that?" Avi crossed his arms defensively.

"The characters, climax, and conclusion of your stories were always the same."

"Fine," Avi huffed, leaning back against Mrs. Sumi's stall. "Let's hear a story from Mister Falling Star over here and I'll judge if his stories are better than mine."

"Very well," a faint smile tugged at Mitra's lips. "But let us enjoy our meal first. Mrs. Sumi just prepared something. Would you care to join us?"

Abel decided it would be best for them to retreat into the canopy rather than remain in the square. There were too many onlookers, too many unwanted stares and whispers, that made him uncomfortable to stay in public. There was a private treehouse nestled in the upper branches that he and his friends had constructed when they were children. It was a quiet place of retreat, situated at one of the highest points in the Village and shielded from the rest of the settlement by a thick layer of foliage. Abel often retreated there when he

The Tales of Abel and Mitra

wanted time to himself, gazing up at the Night sky and imagining worlds far beyond Shambhala.

They spread their meal across the table and began digging in. Mitra scooped up a fried piece of hkaru, inspecting it briefly before taking a bite.

"What do you think?" Abel wondered.

"It has an interesting texture," Mitra said as he savoured the dish. "Its flavour reminds me of oysters."

"Oysters?" Asked Avi.

"A delicacy on my world," Mitra explained.

"Huh," Avi chuckled. "I can't imagine anyone considering *hkaru* a delicacy."

Mitra glanced up as several meteors streaked across the Night sky. "It's a lovely view."

"Eh," Avi shrugged, shoving a piece of curry-soaked duskroot into his mouth. "It gets boring after a while with the same old view every Night. I could draw a map of all the stars with my eyes closed. But Abel never seems to get bored of it. I find him up here at least a couple times a Night."

Abel's face flushed with a rosy glow in the dim lighting. "It makes me feel at peace."

Mitra's attention shifted to the lower third of the sky off to their right. A dark arch rose from one end of the horizon to the other. Below that arch, there were no stars at all, only pitch black.

"What is that over there?" Mitra wondered.

"Blue Sky," said Abel. "It's what keeps Darkside shrouded in eternal Night."

"I see," Mitra nodded. "What is it like on Darkside? Without sunlight, I imagine the ecosystems would be quite different than here in the Valley. It must be quite cold.

Yisei Ishkhan

Though, I must say, the Valley is warmer than I would expect, considering you never experience Day."

"Noa says the trees incubate the Valley and keep it warm," said Abel. "The temperature doesn't fluctuate much between Night, Dawn, and Dusk. As for Darkside, not much is known about those parts. The Elders don't allow us to travel beyond the Purvanchal Range, and anyone who has ever ventured there hasn't come back."

"That's not *entirely* true," Avi objected. "Granny Inali told me that one of her friends went to Darkside when she was a kid. He only stayed a few hours, but he came back with stories about the strange creatures and eerie landscape on the other side.

"Auntie Inali told you that?" Abel asked. "Why did you never tell me *those* stories?"

"Because that's classified information," Avi flashed a cocky grin. "But where do you think I got the inspiration for *The Legends of the Shadow Men* and *The Tales of Makarasa-man*?"

Abel's expression lit up with newfound wonder as he recalled the fantastic tales Avi used to tell him growing up.

"But enough about Darkside," Avi said, stuffing a spoonful of rice into his mouth. "We're here for Mister Falling Star to tell us a story about *his* world!"

"Very well," Mitra said, turning his gaze up to the Night sky. "Let me tell you a story—a story of forgiveness and trust…"

The Tales of Abel and Mitra
II. The Tale of Áedán and Ingvar
January 12, 806 AD
Iona Abbey, Muile, Kingdom of Dál Riata

Áedán shivered as the icy winter air breezed across his skin. But it wasn't the cold that sent a chill down his spine—it was the blood-curdling shrieks echoing along the halls of the abbey. His fellow monks were being slaughtered one after the other at the hands of the heathens. Hidden in the shadows of a quiet corner, Áedán clutched his cross tightly, its sharp edges biting into his palm and drawing blood. But he felt no pain. The faint sting was drowned out by the rage bubbling up inside him. His breathing became ragged. He wanted to scream.

"Áedán, be quiet," Colmcille urged with a hiss. The older monk pressed a bony hand over Áedán's mouth. If it weren't for him holding the boy back, Áedán would've burst forth from their hiding place by now. Colmcille trembled as the thumping of steps drew near. "They're coming…they're coming…"

Áedán leaned forward, struggling against Colmcille's grip as he peered through a crack in the door they were crouched behind. His heart raced in his chest. It was one of *them*—one of the heathen Northmen. The towering brutes with golden hair and ruddy faces stormed through the abbey like wolves through a sheepfold.

Their leader barked orders in a tongue Áedán didn't fully understand, but he could still make out the meaning: *Search everywhere.*

He had seen their kind once when a small raiding party landed on the island four years prior. They had killed a couple of monks and stripped the abbey of its treasures before returning to the seas. Since then, the monks had anticipated that the northern barbarians would one day return. But nothing could've prepared them for this.

Áedán stiffened as he glimpsed what the approaching Northmen held in their hands: severed heads. Mutilated and dripping with blood, he couldn't tell whose heads they were. Perhaps it was better not to know.

"These men and their ugly haircuts!" One of the Northmen jeered, shaking the tonsured head like a grotesque trophy. "Makes them hard to carry!"

The other men erupted into coarse laughter. Áedán's fingers clenched tighter around his cross.

"P-please! P-please, don't do this!" A quivering voice pleaded through the jeers. Áedán glanced further to the right, past the cluster of Northmen and severed heads. On the ground lay a frail, trembling monk–Ælfgar, one of the few Saxon monks at the abbey. Ælfgar spoke in his native Englisc tongue, allowing a degree of mutual intelligibility between himself and the barbarians. "L-let me give them a proper Christian burial!"

"Alright," the leader of the Northmen grinned, bearing his fangs like a wild animal. "Ingvar! Get over here!"

From the back of the group, a young man emerged. His features were smooth and sharp, and he did not yet sport the thick facial hair that marked his comrades. His blonde, disheveled hair blew wildly in the wind. He glanced down at the trembling monk with his deep blue eyes, a glint of curiosity rather than malice in his gaze.

The Northmen's leader grabbed Ælfgar by the collar, dragging him to his feet and shoving him into Ingvar's hands.

The Tales of Abel and Mitra

"The Christian says he wants to bury his dead," the Northman sneered. "You know what their God teaches? That the *dead* should bury the dead!"

The heathens burst into jeers, calling for Æelfgar's head. The poor monk's eyes rolled into the back of his head, and Áedán thought he might've died of fright.

"Kill him!" One of the Northmen spat. "Slice his throat!"

"Batter his head in with your axe!"

"No, your fists! Use your fists!"

The Northman leader put a hand on Ingvar's shoulder. "Well, son. How you choose to kill him is up to you."

Ingvar didn't meet the gaze of any of the men in his group. His head was downcast as he studied Æelfgar's face intently.

"*Kyrie Eleison...*" the murmured prayer escaped Æelfgar's lips. "Lord have mercy…"

"He's asking for mercy!" The Northman gave Ingvar a heavy slap on the back. "So, give it to him!"

Ingvar turned, dragging Æelfgar along with him as he made his way to the edge of the terrace. The other men followed his movements, their brows furrowing as he pushed Æelfgar toward the ledge. On the other side, the cliff plunged down into the raging waters far below.

"Oh, c'mon!" One of the Northman shouted. "Don't tell me you're gonna throw him off the edge!"

"Where's the fun in that?" Another scoffed.

"Quiet," their leader ordered. "Let the boy make his decision."

As Æelfgar dangled there, his feet on the ledge and Ingvar gripping him by his collar, the monk seemed to regain his bearings. His eyes bulged in his head as he glimpsed the sea below him and he let out a harrowing cry.

"Save me, Lord! SAVE ME!"

There is no greater love than to lay down one's life for one's friends.

That verse suddenly rose to the forefront of Áedán's mind. It was one that Æelfgar often repeated to him and came back to him in the old monk's voice.

"Áedán, don't!" Colmcille warned.

But Áedán had already lunged forward. With sheer willpower, he broke free of Colmcille's grasp, bursting down the doors and bounding across the terrace. The Northmen froze as Áedán streaked past them, his face twisting with hatred and contempt.

Ingvar barely had the chance to glimpse the boy before the pointed tip of the cross was jabbed through his right eye. Blood splattered across the terrace and Ingvar stumbled backward, losing his footing on the ledge. He let go of Æelfgar, desperately reaching to grab onto anything to save him from falling. His fingers wrapped around Áedán's arm.

"Ingvar!" The Northman leader roared.

"Áedán!" Colmcille's anguished cry echoed from the distance.

The world tilted sideways, and wind tore through his ears as Áedán plummeted over the cliffside. The icy waters slammed into him like a stone, swallowing him up beneath dark waves.

***

It was white. Nothing but whiteness filled Áedán's vision.

I'm dead, he thought to himself. *This must be the gates of Heaven...*

The Tales of Abel and Mitra

He reached his hand forward, but as he did, the light began to dim.

No. Wait. Don't leave me behind. Wait!

The more desperate he grew, the quicker the light receded, slipping away like water through his fingers until it disappeared entirely. Darkness engulfed Áedán.

His eyes flew open. He lurched upright with a start, coughing a mouthful of water onto the ground. He gagged, choking to catch his breath as his chest heaved. Sharp pebbles dug into his palms and legs. He wasn't dead. He was on a beach. He pushed himself up to his feet and shivered. Frosty winter winds whipped their way across the shore, chilling Áedán to the bone as they froze the wet garments to his skin.

He surveyed the shore, spotting a cave at the base of the cliffside off to his right. There was no time to dwell on what had happened to Æelfgar or the others. If he didn't reach shelter soon, he'd catch hypothermia and freeze to death.

His boots crunched over the stony ground as he shuffled his way over to the cave. He ducked under the rocks, keeping close to the wall for support. It was cool, but not as frigid as out on the beach. A damp scent permeated the cave, and a melodic drip of running water echoed from somewhere in the distance. After a short descent, it was pitch black.

Áedán crouched against a boulder in a warm patch of the cave, teeth clattering as he peeled off his soaked garments.

Fire… he thought to himself. *I need to start a fire…*

He fumbled blindly along the ground, his fingers scraping across cold stone and gritty sand in a desperate search for something he could use to start a fire. Nothing.

Great, he thumped his head back against the wall, curling into a ball as he shivered uncontrollably. *Is this what you wanted,*

Yisei Ishkhan

God? You saved me from the depths of the sea only to watch as I freeze to death in a cave?

A faint click echoed from somewhere nearby. Something was scraping against the rocks. He figured it must be some sort of animal, but didn't concern himself with what it might be. There were no large predators on these islands, but for a moment, he wished there was. Better to have a wolf or bear end his suffering quickly than to spend the next few hours slowly freezing to death.

Just as his consciousness began to fade, a faint flicker of light appeared in the darkness. He thought he was imagining it, but the light grew steadily brighter until he could no longer look at it directly. Warmth spread throughout the cold chamber—a fire.

Dazed, Áedán's body moved on instinct, shuffling toward the light. He didn't stop to question how it had appeared. All he knew was he needed to be near it.

"You're still alive?" A weak voice pierced through the silence.

Áedán froze. That voice spoke in the tongue of the Northmen. Beyond the flames, he could just make out a figure lurking nearby. Ingvar leaned heavily against the wall of the cave, his once-handsome face marred by blood pouring down from where Áedán had driven the cross into his eye. The cross was gone, and so was the eye.

The front of Ingvar's shirt was cut open in what seemed to be a failed attempt to remove it. The Northman couldn't get his arms out of the sleeves. His pale chest rose and fell unevenly.

Áedán had stripped himself. Under most circumstances, he was ashamed to let others see him unclothed. But shivering on the brink of hypothermia left little room for modesty. He inched closer to the fire, keeping a careful eye on Ingvar. The Northman was weak and didn't make any threatening moves. Áedán stretched out his hands over the fire, staring through the flames at Ingvar on the other side. The fire was growing weak. With each passing second, Áedán found it more difficult to see the man.

"Get more fuel," Ingvar said. "Unless you want us both to freeze to death."

Áedán said nothing. After a few moments, Ingvar prodded at the fire.

"Fuel," he enunciated the word in his tongue. "Do you understand? For the fire."

"I understand," Áedán huffed in Englisc. "Shall I conjure it from thin air? There's nothing but rocks and sand here."

Ingvar gestured to a dark shape near the wall. "Use that."

Áedán followed his gaze. His eyes went wide in horror when he realized what he was looking at–Æelfgar's body.

"You killed him!" Áedán cried.

"He was already dead when I found him," Ingvar muttered. "Must've hit his head on the rocks on the way down."

"*You're* the one who pushed him down!"

"If I recall correctly, *you* ran into *me* and sent all three of us off that cliff. Now, are you going to rekindle the flames or not?"

Áedán peered over Æelfgar's corpse, his stomach twisting. The monk's cassock had been removed by Ingvar to start the fire and only his inner garments remained. Áedán performed the sign of the cross, leaning over Æelfgar as he muttered a silent prayer.

Yisei Ishkhan

"*Kyrie Eleison*. Forgive me, Father. Forgive me, Æelfgar. Rest in peace, my dear friend."

He removed the monk's top but kept his pants on to at least afford him some respect. He tossed the cloth onto the open flames, but it continued simmering out.

"It's not enough," said Ingvar. "You need to create another spark."

"With what?" Áedán snapped.

Ingvar nodded toward the ground near the dwindling flames. Áedán detected a faint glint of metal. He reached down to retrieve the object and gasped.

It was his cross!

The bloodied relic was cold in his hands, one end smeared with gore from the Northman's eye and the other dull from being scraped against the rocks.

Realization dawned on Áedán. "You used this to start a fire?! That's...that's *sacrilege*!"

"Sacrilege..." Ingvar repeated the word in Englisc. "Was it also 'sacrilege' when you stabbed that precious relic of yours through my eye?"

"Give me your knife," Áedán glared at the Northman, ignoring his comment. "I know you have a knife since you cut open your shirt. Give it to me!"

"Lost it," Ingvar said. "It fell into a crevice earlier. That's why your relic had to do the job."

Áedán's knuckles turned white as he clenched the cross in his fist. He closed his eyes, inhaling a deep breath as he fought the urge to stab it through the Northman's other eye.

Dona nobis pacem, he uttered a silent prayer. *Grant us peace.*

The Tales of Abel and Mitra

In the back of his mind, Áedán could almost hear Æelfgar's voice speaking to him.

This is not the will of the Lord. Remember what He taught? "You have heard that it was said, 'Eye for eye, and tooth for tooth.' But I tell you, do not resist an evil person. If anyone slaps you on the right cheek, turn to him the other cheek also. And if anyone wants to sue you and take your shirt, hand over your coat as well."

Áedán gritted his teeth.

"Well?" Ingvar broke the silence. "What's it going to be? Do you want to freeze to death?"

"Fine," Áedán mumbled. "I'll do it."

Kyrie Eleison. Lord have mercy.

He drew the edge of the cross against the rocks, flinching at the grating sound. It took several tries before sparks appeared.

Kyrie Eleison. Lord have mercy.

The fire flared up weakly and he was forced to try a few more times before the cloth was aflame. Áedán breathed a sigh of relief and sat back. He laid out his clothes by the fire, and once they had dried, threw them back on.

Ingvar remained slumped against the rocks, his one eye closed. Blood had ceased flowing from the wound, drying in streaks that caked his face. Áedán averted his gaze, focusing his attention on Æelfgar's body. He murmured the last rites before beginning to gather stones from the floor of the cave.

"What are you doing?" Ingvar croaked.

"Giving him a proper Christian burial," Áedán said.

"Why not just burn him?"

"Heaven forbid!"

Ingvar scoffed. "It's a waste of fuel–"

Yisei Ishkhan

"Absolutely not!" Áedán fumed. "Cremation is a *heathen* ritual! I will not treat a good Christian like Brother Ælfgar with such disrespect!"

"Suit yourself," Ingvar shrugged. "That just means you'll have to spend more time scrounging the beach for other scraps to burn."

"I will. For *myself*. You can rot in this cave for all I care."

Áedán was caught off-guard as a chuckle echoed through the darkness.

"Has anyone ever told you that you've got quite the temper?"

Áedán bit his tongue. Ælfgar had told him that countless times. So had Colmcille and the other monks. They warned that if he continued to sow the seeds of negativity, that was exactly what he'd reap. He hated hearing such remarks, but from his fellow brethren, he could tolerate the advice. But he refused to take such words from a heathen.

"What do *you* know about *me*?!" Fury consumed him. "*Of course* I have a temper! After you heathens ransacked my home and slaughtered my brethren, who *wouldn't* be angry?! For all I know, I'm the only monk left! You and your kind can burn in Hell!"

"*Hel*..." Ingvar tilted his head, unfazed by Áedán's venomous remarks. "Yes...Helheim is where I'll end up if I don't die in battle. Though, it's a cold place, not hot. Your Hel sounds like a nicer place. I'd rather be burning now than freezing..." he chuckled to himself. "I wonder if being stabbed through the eye by a holy man counts as a death in battle? What do you think? Maybe the Valkyries will let me into Valhalla after all..."

The Tales of Abel and Mitra

"You bloodthirsty heathens," Áedán spat. He turned on his heel and stormed out of the cave. Outside, the bitter wind clawed at his skin, but he barely felt it.

I'm sorry, Æelfgar. I'll finish burying you later.

Night had descended upon the beach, though Áedán couldn't be sure if it was the same day as when the Northmen had laid siege to the monastery. He wasn't particularly hungry, so he assumed that not much time had passed. Not that it mattered. He suspected there wouldn't be anything left when he returned.

He squinted at the stars, trying to orient himself. Based on their positioning, he determined that the shore ran north to south and that he was currently facing westwards as he looked out over the sea. That meant he was no longer on Ì Chaluim Chille but had drifted to another island. Perhaps this was Oileán Muile or one of the smaller islands scattered between the two. Across the water loomed another island in the distance but he doubted it was home. It seemed too far away for him to have floated across the straits without drowning or freezing to death.

Wonderful, he thought to himself. *Stranded on some godforsaken rock with a half-dead heathen for company.*

He couldn't worry about that for now. His first priority was finding food and water.

A flock of seabirds circled overhead but he only saw them perch along the upper portions of the cliff, never venturing down to the beach. Áedán made his way along the shore, discovering clumps of seaweed and what looked to be oysters. He grimaced. It was hardly a feast, but it was his only option. Gathering them up in his cassock, he returned to the cave. He recalled the sound of running water echoing faintly in the

Yisei Ishkhan

cavern earlier and hoped it would lead to an underground spring.

Ingvar was right where he left him, lying by the fire as he took shallow breaths. The flames had dimmed to little more than embers, and Áedán tossed some dried bark he'd scavenged on the beach to rekindle the fire. Then, he set to work roasting the seaweed and bashing the oysters with a stone, hoping to crack open their firm shells.

"I thought you weren't coming back," Ingvar murmured after a while.

"You're still alive?" Áedán muttered, a trace of disappointment in his tone.

"If you want me dead, you could always finish the job," Ingvar said. "I can't put up much of a fight in this condition, though if I want a chance to reach Valhalla, I should at least put in some resistance."

Áedán glared at the Northman with a look of disgust. "Is that how you get to paradise in your religion? By killing or being killed?"

"More or less. Those who die bravely in battle are rewarded with feasts and glory among the gods. Heroism is one of the greatest aspirations in our culture."

Áedán scoffed. "Slaughtering your enemies on the battlefield isn't heroic."

"No?" Ingvar asked. "And what do your people consider heroic?"

"Self-sacrifice. To lay down one's life for one's friends. Not brutally charging into a battle for the thrill of bloodshed."

"So," said Ingvar, "when you charged at me, was that to save your friend, or for the thrill of bloodshed?"

The Tales of Abel and Mitra

"It was desperation," Áedán muttered, casting a glance at the body of the monk lying nearby. "And utterly pointless, since he's dead anyway. Ælfgar would condemn me for my actions. I know he would. Not because I laid my life on the line to try and save him but because I attacked you." He squeezed his cross in his palm, drawing blood. Áedán sucked in a breath. "On the night our Lord was betrayed, he said to his followers 'Put away your sword, for those that live by the sword will die by the sword.' We Christians—especially monks like me who are bound by vows—are called to spread peace, not war. Love, not hatred. In a moment of wrath, I gave in and attacked you. Not that you don't deserve punishment for your actions, but that punishment is not mine to give." He let out a sigh. "Ælfgar would've died regardless of my interference. God holds our lives and deaths in His hands. Because I gave into temptation, I'm stuck here with you, paying the price for my sins. *Kyrie Eleison. Dona nobis pacem.*"

A wry smile tugged at Ingvar's lips. "So, you holy men are called to a life of pacifism? No wonder you never fight back. Surrendering to your fate isn't exactly heroic if you ask me. It sounds more like cowardice."

"You confuse restraint with weakness," Áedán said mockingly. "But I wouldn't expect a heathen to understand. Your people only think of worldly things. Even in your Valhalla, the gods reward you with pleasures of the flesh."

"Enlighten me, then. What does your god reward you with in the afterlife?"

"Peace, hope, love, unity with God—these are higher rewards than worldly pleasures could offer."

"And your god came to bring these to his people?" Ingvar asked. "Is that why he sacrificed himself and died on that cross? Well, what did his sacrifice accomplish? Where is there peace, or hope, or love in this world? It doesn't exist. There is only war, despair, hatred, and suffering. That's the reality of this existence. Your god seems weak. And weak gods have weak followers who surrender in the face of danger instead of fighting to live."

"You're wrong," Áedán said. "True, there may not be much peace, hope, or love in this world–not yet. But it exists in the world to come. Even now, God works to bring it forth here in this world. It starts in the hearts of men. When a man's heart is transformed, he transforms his community. When a community is transformed, it transforms the kingdom. When a kingdom is transformed, it transforms a civilization. When a civilization is transformed, it transforms the world."

"That's a lovely idea," Ingvar said wistfully. "But it's naive. While you work to change the world from the bottom up, those who wield true power crush them from the top down. The strong rise and the weak fall. That's the way of the world."

"No," Áedán pushed himself to his feet. "You're wrong."

"How so?"

"Because history proves it! When God's people were enslaved in Egypt, they had no earthly power on their side, only the power of God! And God led them out of captivity, out of their wanderings through the desert, and into the Promised Land. They were later conquered by the Assyrians, then the Babylonians, the Persians, the Greeks, and the Romans. Again, they were enslaved and cast into exile. And yet they endured. They outlasted all the empires that had conquered and enslaved them and live on today through the Church. Our Lord had no kingdom, yet they called Him King. He had no slaves, yet they called Him Master. No education, yet they called Him Teacher. No medicine, yet they called

The Tales of Abel and Mitra

Him Healer. No army, yet His message conquered the hearts of all those who had oppressed His people. The Egyptians, Assyrians, Babylonians, and Greeks abandoned their old gods and today follow Him! Since then, His message has spread across the world, from Éire to India, not through violent conquest, but through the message of love and peace!" Áedán took a deep, shuddering breath. "It was not armies and kings who brought His message to these distant shores. It was the poor, the enslaved, the women, and the outcasts. Even the mightiest of empires, from Rome to Ethiopia, bowed before him."

"Rome..." Ingvar mused. "I have heard of this Rome. They abandoned their old gods, and their empire came crashing down."

"Only because it was invaded by heathen barbarians like you," scoffed Áedán.

"Perhaps they grew weak when they started worshiping your god," Ingvar shrugged. "Had they stuck to their old ways, perhaps they wouldn't have fallen."

"Rome was merely a kingdom of this world," Áedán said. "*All* kingdoms of this world have their days appointed by the Lord. None will last forever. But the Church will. The Church outlasted the fall of Rome, and even the barbarians who brought Rome to her knees eventually bowed before the True Living God–the Angles, the Saxons, the Burgundians, the Franks, the Lombards, the Ostrogoths, the Vandals, the Visigoths. All have since become Christian. One day, I imagine that the Bulgars, Slavs, and even you Northmen will be welcomed into the fold of the Church. And the message of Christ will spread to far-off lands we've never dreamed of until finally, the Gospel has reached all the world."

Áedán huffed to catch his breath. He'd spoken with such zeal that he barely registered the weight of his own words.

"We'll see about that," a flicker of amusement flashed through Ingvar's eyes. "We'll see."

The Northman burst into a violent fit of coughing. For a fleeting moment, Áedán's expression softened as concern washed over him. He quickly masked it.

"Finally kicking the bucket?" He huffed.

Ingvar wiped his mouth with the back of his hand. "I don't know that expression. I'm just thirsty. My throat feels like sand."

Áedán ceased hammering away at the oyster shell he'd been trying to pry open. He cocked his head, straining to catch the faint *drip, drip, drip* of water. It came from somewhere in the distance, deeper within the cave, tantalizingly close yet still elusive.

He rose to his feet, lighting a piece of driftwood to use as a torch before heading in the direction of the water.

"Finally offering me a branch of Yggdrasil, huh?" Ingvar croaked.

Áedán paused. "I don't know what that's supposed to mean."

"Extending a peace offering."

Áedán snorted. "Don't flatter yourself. I'm thirsty too. I'm getting water for myself, not for you."

He strode off. The sound of the water came from somewhere to the right. He headed in that direction, sticking close to the wall of the cave. The *drip, drip, drip* never grew any louder, remaining as distant as when he first detected it. He decided to step away from the wall, into a more open space

The Tales of Abel and Mitra

where the chamber opened ahead of him. He waved his torch back and forth, but the roof and walls of the cave melted into the shadows.

With a startled cry, Áedán slipped. The rocks gave way beneath his feet, crumbling underfoot and cascading down a steep slope. He hit the ground, the torch spinning out of hand before he went tumbling over the edge.

Something caught his arm.

Áedán's head snapped upward, heart pounding in his chest. Ingvar's face loomed above him, blurred by the dim light. Objectively, the young Northman had handsome features. But with his blood-streaked face and a gaping hole where his eye should've been, he looked more like a ghost than a man at that moment.

"What are you doing?!" Áedán cried.

Ingvar's grip around him tightened. "Saving you from falling to your death. I came this way earlier and nearly made the same mistake as you."

He huffed, struggling to pull Áedán back from the edge. The young Northman had broad shoulders and the well-built upper body one would expect of a warrior. Under ordinary circumstances, he should've been able to hold Áedán's thin frame with ease, as he had with Æelfgar. Yet now, Ingvar trembled, a tense grimace etching itself on his face.

Áedán grabbed hold of the ledge and pulled himself up the rest of the way, his thin arms burning with effort. Once he was convinced that the rocks wouldn't crumble beneath him again, he shook himself free of Ingvar's grasp.

"That was your chance to let me die," Áedán mumbled. "Why would you save me? You didn't save Æelfgar from

Yisei Ishkhan

falling off a cliff—you were the one who tossed him over yourself!"

"These are different circumstances," Ingvar said. "If you haven't noticed, I'm injured. I must've broken a rib or two when we first fell. I'll never make it down this slope to find that source of water. I don't even know if I can get back out to the mouth of the cave. You're my only chance at finding food and water. So no, it's not in my best interest to let you die." A glimmer of amusement crossed his face. "Besides, if I'm going to die down here, I'd rather not do it alone. Even a stuck-up monk like you makes better company than none."

Áedán shook his head, turning his back on the Northman as he began a cautious descent down the slope. "Even if I find water down here, I have no means of bringing it back to you."

Ingvar's hand fell to his side. Áedán froze, irritation bubbling over when he saw what the Northman held—an oyster shell.

"You stole my oysters?!" Áedán snapped.

"I opened them for you," Ingvar corrected. "All that hammering wasn't getting you anywhere. I wouldn't expect someone with such dainty hands to manage, so I pried them open with my knife. You can thank me by bringing me back some water."

Áedán snatched the shell from Ingvar's hand. "I knew you had your knife all along."

"Who says I did?" Ingvar said innocently. "Found it while you were gone."

"Stop talking and I might consider fetching some water for you," Áedán grumbled.

Ingvar smiled, deciding not to push further.

The Tales of Abel and Mitra

Torch in hand, Áedán slid down the slope. It wasn't as steep as he'd feared and seemed manageable for the climb back. The sound of dripping water grew louder, guiding him forward. His pulse quickened as he lit the path ahead. A tiny stream trickled from a crack in the cave wall, forming a shallow pool.

He knelt beside the pool, holding the oyster shell aloft like a chalice. This was the moment of truth. He dipped the shell in the water and took a cautious sip. A sigh of relief escaped his lips–it was fresh! He drank himself to his heart's content, savouring each mouthful. For a blissful moment, he forgot his predicament, until Ingvar's faint voice echoed from up ahead.

"Don't tell me you drowned in a puddle! You better hurry back up here before I decide to eat the rest of your oysters."

Áedán groaned. He scooped up some water with the shell and stared at it in dismay. It barely held a mouthful and now he'd have to climb back without spilling it.

It took a few attempts before he was successful. He shoved the shell into Ingvar's waiting hands.

"Enjoy this," Áedán huffed. "You don't know how much trouble it was just to get that back for you."

Ingvar threw his head back and downed the water in a single sip. He let out a contented sigh before holding out the shell again. "More?"

Áedán's eyes narrowed. "Absolutely not. Do you know how many trips it would take to satisfy your thirst? I'm hungry. I'm eating my oysters first."

When they returned to the fire, Áedán found that four of the eight oysters had been cracked open.

"You ate *half* of them?!"

Yisei Ishkhan

"I'll eat the other half too, unless you promise to bring up more water for me."

Áedán scowled. "No wonder you're thirsty. Oysters are salty!"

"Then maybe next time you can bring back something else."

Áedán threw up his hands. "There's nothing on that beach except oysters and seaweed!"

"That's not true," Ingvar said. "I saw birds circling over the cliffs when I arrived. And there's bound to be fish in the water."

"Do I *look* like I can hunt or fish?"

"No. Which is why it's a shame I'm the injured one and not you."

Áedán shook his head in disbelief. He plopped down by the fire, continuing to hammer away at the oysters. After ten minutes of trying, he'd gotten nowhere.

Ingvar shifted over to the young monk's side, pulling forth his dagger and prying it between the oyster's shells. It popped open with ease.

"It looks like we'll need each other to survive," Ingvar said, extending the oyster to Áedán. "So how about a deal? You bring me food and water, and I'll crack open these oysters for you. I might even teach you how to hunt and fish."

Áedán crossed his arms. "We don't need each other. If I leave you here, you'll die alone. I can make it out myself."

"Then I suppose you won't be needing this," Ingvar shrugged, tilting the oyster shell against his lips and slurping up the flesh.

"Hey!" Áedán fumed.

The Tales of Abel and Mitra

Ingvar smacked his lips. "I got a good look around the beach earlier. It doesn't extend far to the north or south before running into cliffs. Those cliffs are impossible to climb, and swimming against those waves isn't an option, especially at this time of year. There's a reason all three of us wound up at this cove–you, me, and the body of your friend. The currents brought us here, which means you won't get far if you try to swim against them."

"Then what?" Áedán mumbled. "We're stuck here forever?"

"I can craft a boat," Ingvar said. "Or at the very least a raft."

"A raft?" Áedán asked skeptically. "Out of *what*? There's hardly anything on that beach."

"Then you'd better start scrounging," Ingvar grinned.

Áedán shook his head in exasperation. "You've lost it if you think I'm going to climb down to the bottom of the cave dozens of times a day to fetch enough water to keep you alive. It'd be better if you just rolled down the cliff and stayed there."

"No need for that," Ingvar chuckled. "If you find some more wood, I can carve out a bucket for you to carry. Then you can bring back enough in one trip for the both of us."

Ingvar grabbed another oyster, prying open its shell with his knife and extending it to Áedán. "Do we have a deal?"

Áedán let forth a deep sigh, snatching the shell from Ingvar's grasp and wolfing it down. "I can't believe I'm agreeing to work with a heathen."

***

After about a week, they had settled into a routine. Áedán rose early, descending to the bottom of the cave with their makeshift bucket to fetch water. He'd spend as much time as he pleased by the pool, quenching his thirst and occasionally wandering further to explore the cave's depths. He hoped he would find something of value: materials, or better yet, another way out. Alas, nothing came of his efforts.

Later, he would scour the shoreline, tirelessly pacing back and forth. As Ingvar had noted, the beach didn't extend very far before it ran into the cliffsides. Áedán had made a couple of attempts to climb the rocks, but they were too slick and sharp to make it far.

Most days, the debris that washed ashore was of little use to them. Occasionally he would recover pieces of driftwood, though even that was scarce. Sometimes, he returned to the cave with nothing at all.

Their diet consisted solely of oysters and seaweed for the first week, but Ingvar was working on a fish trap from the materials Áedán brought back. On the seventh day, while Áedán was out on his routine patrols, Ingvar emerged from the cave.

"What are you doing?" Áedán scolded him as he raced over. "You'll catch a cold out here!"

They had used the tattered remains of Ingvar's clothes to bind his ribs and wrap his face injury, so the Northman had little more to wear than his trousers. His golden hair hung in wild tangles past his shoulder, the right side of his face was discoloured, and he sustained a cut on the lip. He was filthy, covered head to toe in grim. Yet even in this disheveled state, something was striking about him.

For the first time since they'd met, Áedán was seeing Ingvar in full daylight. His features were striking, like busts of old Roman deities he'd seen on a visit to Northumbria—

The Tales of Abel and Mitra

Bacchus perhaps, or Apollo. His emerald-green eyes, framed by golden lashes, held an almost childlike gentleness to them that Áedán found difficult to look away from.

"What?" Ingvar's lips curled into a playful smirk. "I know I look awful, but you don't need to stare. You don't look much better yourself, you know."

"I wasn't staring," Áedán huffed. "What are you doing out of the cave?"

Ingvar placed a hand on his ribs and winced slightly. "My injuries are healing, thanks to the healthy diet of shellfish and seaweed you've been bringing back. But I think it's time to supplement our diet." He held up the fish trap he'd been painstakingly working on all week.

Áedán was unimpressed. "It looks like something a child slapped together with reeds."

"It'll do the job," Ingvar chuckled. "I know it's a simple design but sometimes it's the simplest designs that are most effective. It's shaped like a funnel, with wood protruding inwards on the interior. Once fish swim in to get the bait, they'll get stuck. That's the idea, at least."

Ingvar carried the trap to the far side of the beach, where the sun glinted off tidal pools nestled in the rocks. Most of the food Áedán had brought back was from this pool, but he had yet to capture anything larger than a crab.

Ingvar lowered the trap into the pool and fastened it in place. "We'll see what we catch when the tide comes in tonight."

"It better work," Áedán muttered.

He crouched by the pool, glimpsing his face in the shallow waters. For once, it was still enough that he could see his reflection. He was paler than usual, his dark curls tumbling around his face as he ran his fingers through them with disdain.

"My tonsure is gone," he mumbled. Back at the monastery, he had to shave the top of his head almost daily to keep up the expected appearance of a monk.

Ingvar patted the young monk on the head and gave his hair a ruffle. Áedán yelled at him, and Ingvar laughed. "Why do monks wear their hair in such a ridiculous fashion? You look better like this."

Áedán shot him a sharp glance. "We aren't supposed to take pride in our appearance. The tonsure is symbolic of renouncing worldly pride and vanity, something I wouldn't expect a heathen to understand."

"True," Ingvar grinned, running a hand through his golden locks. "I'm glad *I'm* not a monk. How does one end up in your position anyway?"

"Some choose it. Others don't. Sometimes an orphan will be brought to an abbey, or unwanted children if a family has too many to take care of. That was what happened to me."

"You're an orphan?"

"I may as well be. My father is Maelchon mac Cináed, a chief on the mainland and a relative of the king. My mother was a slave from Éire, which makes me the bastard son of a chief. Mother did her best to care for me, but when she passed, I ended up at the local church. Ælfgar was a deacon at the time, and he took me under his wing. I traveled with him throughout Dál Riata and down to Northumbria. That's how I picked up the Englisc tongue. When Ælfgar decided to retreat to the monastery, I came with him."

Ingvar's expression softened. "I'm sorry. It's my fault your friend is dead."

The Tales of Abel and Mitra

Áedán scoffed. "Don't apologize if you don't mean it. You've probably killed dozens of people without remorse. Spare me your feigned guilt."

"You're wrong," Ingvar said. "Æelfgar was the first person I'd ever killed."

"You expect me to believe that?" Áedán snapped. "I know what your people are like. You looted the monastery a few years back, and probably countless others on your way here."

"This was my first raid," Ingvar admitted. "My father forced me to come. He's the chief—the one who ordered me to kill Æelfgar. I didn't want to do it. That's why I hesitated. But I knew if Æelfgar didn't die by my hand, one of the others would kill him."

An image of Ingvar's father surfaced in Áedán's mind: a towering figure with golden hair and a flowing beard, his faded green eyes cold and unyielding.

"Ingvar Sigurdsson," the young Northman said. "That's my name. The bastard son of Chief Sigurd Thorsson. My mother was a Slav captured during a raid somewhere in the east. What do you know? We're both bastard sons of chiefs and their slave girls."

"That's nothing to bond over," Áedán scoffed. "We're nothing alike."

"No," sighed Ingvar. "I suppose not. You were adopted by a monk and raised in a monastery where you were taught pacifism; I grew up with a sword in hand, taught that the greatest glory in life was dying on the battlefield so I could feast in Valhalla until Ragnarok."

Áedán folded his arms. "If you think your upbringing excuses your actions, you're mistaken."

Yisei Ishkhan

"I know. At the end of the day, the choices I made were my own. My path was shaped by those around me, but I was still the one who walked it. To be honest, I thought it was the only path available for me. My father never treated me like my brothers because I was a bastard. He always said I had more blood of a slave running through my veins than a Viking–weak and submissive like my mother and her people. I thought that if I could kill Æelfgar, I would prove him wrong. I see now how foolish I was. I was willing to kill a defenseless man just to impress my father. There is nothing that can excuse that, nothing that can atone for my mistakes."

Something stirred within Áedán. Was he hearing this right? A heathen Northman was confessing his sins. It gnawed at Áedán. He'd grown up steeped in teachings about grace and forgiveness, yet here he was, too consumed by pride and bitterness to offer them. Worse, instead of admiring Ingvar's honesty, he was envious that he couldn't do the same. He couldn't help but feel a loathing for the Northman bubbling up inside him.

Áedán sneered. "You sound more Christian than me."

He had meant for the words to come off as condescending, but the moment they left his mouth, he realized how ridiculous he sounded. He flushed, turning red from ear to ear as he silently cursed himself for not keeping his mouth shut.

Ingvar's lips twitched in amusement. "Did I hear that right?"

"Hear what?" Áedán muttered, turning his gaze away from the Northman.

"That *I*, a *heathen* Norseman, exemplify the values of your religion better than *you*, a Christian monk?"

The Tales of Abel and Mitra

"You stupid oaf!" Áedán fumed. "Why would I say that?! Stop twisting my words and pretending like you understand the grammatical complexity of the Englisc tongue! I...I said no such thing!"

"If I recall correctly," Ingvar smirked, "lying is a sin."

Áedán flew into a rage, his fist swinging toward the Northman. "You're insufferable!"

But even in his injured state, Ingvar was quicker and stronger than him. He caught Áedán by the arm, twisting it with ease and shoving the monk onto the sand. With his knee firmly pressed into Áedán's back, he pinned the monk down effortlessly.

Áedán let out a frustrated cry, thrashing against Ingvar's weight. "Get off me, you brute!"

Ingvar chuckled. "You know, I think you would've made a fine berserker if you'd been born a Norseman. You've certainly got the spirit for it–more than I do at least. It took me months before I was comfortable wielding a weapon in combat. You, on the other hand, improvised with your cross and jabbed me through the eye without a second thought."

Áedán flailed, kicking his legs against the sand, but he couldn't shake himself free.

"I have a confession to make," Ingvar leaned closer, his voice dropping to a whisper. "I lied to you too. The truth is, I can get to the pool at the bottom of the cave and back just fine on my own. I never needed your help fetching water."

Silence hung in the air for a moment before Áedán erupted. "You bloody bastard! You had me running up and down like your slave!"

"I needed the rest," Ingvar said, removing his knee from Áedán's back and letting the young monk wriggle his way out.

Yisei Ishkhan

"And *you* needed the exercise. Did you really think you'd be able to take me on in a fight with these tiny arms?"

Áedán swatted his hand away, pushing himself to his feet. His face burned bright with embarrassment as he stared up at the Northman with daggers in his eyes. "You're unbelievable." He dusted the sand from his robes and stormed off to the cave.

Ingvar chuckled as he followed closely behind.

The tide was beginning to roll in.

***

Áedán rose early the next day, already in a foul mood as he stumbled out of the cave and onto the beach. To his surprise, the trap had caught not one fish, but two. They were small, but enough to sustain them for the day.

"See? Told you it would work," Ingvar gleamed, stoking a small fire as they cooked up the fish.

"Barely," Áedán grumbled. "We can't go on like this forever. "We need a boat, or rope–*something* to get us out of here."

Áedán prayed that night for a miracle, as he did every night since washing up on these shores. But this time, his prayers were answered. The next morning, the shore was littered with more debris than he'd seen in all their previous days combined.

"Thank you, Lord, for bringing these materials to us," Áedán uttered a quick prayer as he set out onto the beach.

"Are you sure this is a gift from *your* god?" Ingvar said. "I prayed last night too, to Ægir, Rán, and Njörðr–the gods of the sea. It seems more likely *they* were the ones who answered."

The Tales of Abel and Mitra

Áedán snorted. "My Lord was a fisherman before He began His earthly ministry. *He's* the one who answered our prayers, not your false idols."

Ingvar shrugged. "Well then, let's see what your god has brought us."

The debris appeared to be wreckage from a ship. Several of the wooden planks were long enough to be pieces of a ruined hull, and they even managed to retrieve a couple of oars and a shield. Ingvar frowned when he spotted Áedán hauling the shield over to him.

"What is it?" Áedán asked.

"That symbol on the shield is Mjölnir, the hammer of Thor. My father had a shield with a similar design…"

Half a dozen snide remarks about Ingvar's father being dead came to mind. But for once, Áedán held his tongue.

"Do you think these came from his ship?" Áedán wondered.

"It was likely one of ours," Ingvar said. "Our fleet was the only one to set out on an expedition this far to the west."

"How many ships did you sail with?"

"Ten."

"Then I'd say there's a low chance that your father was on this one," Áedán said.

Ingvar managed to smile. "Are you trying to console me?"

Áedán scowled. "Don't get used to it."

As they continued scouring the beach, it didn't take long to confirm that the wreckage was indeed from one of Sigurd's ships. They came across a table, a couple of candelabras, a chalice, and a bell–all items that Áedán recognized from the monastery. They even found the carved wooden head of a dragon that once decorated the helm of a Viking ship.

Yisei Ishkhan

But the most remarkable find was tucked away in the drawer of a wooden table—an illuminated manuscript. The interior of the drawer was miraculously dry, and Áedán was grateful that the book remained undamaged. His heart skipped a beat as he recognized the cover of the codex. It was an unfinished work that Colmcille had been labouring over for years, with vibrant and colourful Celtic knotwork surrounding images of saints and angels. At the center, a figure with a thick beard and curly red hair sat enthroned—Christ, exalted and divine.

Áedán's face lit up. "Looks like *my* God was the one who answered our prayers after all!"

"What is it?" Ingvar wondered, peeking over Áedán's shoulder.

"An illuminated manuscript Colmcille was working on."

"And…what is it used for exactly?"

Áedán flashed him a confused glance. "It's a codex, for reading. Do you Northmen not have codices where you come from?"

Ingvar shrugged. "We carve runes into stone on wood. Not…" he brushed his fingers across the pages of the manuscript, "whatever this material is."

Áedán swatted his hand away. "Truly barbaric."

"Who are these?" Ingvar wondered, pointing to the figures that surrounded Christ on the cover. "I thought you only had one god."

"These are the patron saints of Éire," said Áedán. "We call them *Naomh* in our tongue." He pointed out the figures on the cover one by one. "This is Naomh Pádraig, born in Britannia in the last days of the Roman Empire. When he was young, he was captured by pirates and sold as a slave in Éire.

The Tales of Abel and Mitra

At the time, Éire was pagan. But Pádraig introduced them to our faith, and the island became a bastion of Christianity even as Britannia and Rome fell to the barbarian hordes. This man is Naomh Colmcille. He was born in Éire but crossed the sea and came to these islands. He was the one who founded our monastery. And this woman…" Áedán's voice grew quiet as his fingers traced over her fiery-red locks, "this is Naomh Brighid. She was born to a chieftain and a slave girl and raised by druids at a time when there were still pagans in the land. When she grew up, she founded an abbey in Éire. She was my mother's favourite saint."

He flipped carefully through the thick parchment with reverence. Each page contained both Latin and Gaelige text surrounded by religious motifs and iconography that weaved together a story. The text had been filled in from the Gospels of Matha to Eoin, but most of the imagery remained uncoloured.

"It's a shame that you heathens would steal something you can't understand or appreciate," Áedán huffed. "I'm glad the Lord returned this to my hands. I hope Colmcille and the others are still alive. If we ever make it off this cursed island, I'll return it to him so he can finish this masterpiece."

They gathered their wreckage at the mouth of the cave, where Ingvar went to work assembling the materials into a makeshift raft. There still wasn't enough to support their weight on water, but it was a start. Ingvar hammered away at the planks, disassembling pieces of furniture and struggling to tie them together with rope and seaweed.

"Need a hand?" Áedán offered without a trace of enthusiasm in his tone.

Yisei Ishkhan

"I think you'd only get in the way," Ingvar chuckled. "Why don't you read a passage from me from that codex? I'm curious to hear what your stories are like."

Áedán raised an eyebrow. "You want me to read to you from a Christian holy text?"

"Why not? It's better than hammering away in silence."

"Alright," Áedán said, unsure if the Northman was being serious. He pored over the pages until he happened across one of his favourite stories. "This one is from the Gospel of Lúcás–the *Parable of the Lost Son*. Try to keep up."

He cleared his throat, translating the text from Latin and Gaelige into the simplest Englisc he could manage so Ingvar could follow along despite the language barrier.

"There was once a man with two sons. The younger son said to his father, 'Give me my inheritance.' So, the father divided his property between the two sons. The younger son went off into a distant land, spending all his money on worldly pleasures."

"Sounds like he had a good time," Ingvar grinned.

Áedán glared at him before continuing. "He squandered *everything*. When the land was struck by famine, he had nothing left. He was forced to work in a field, envying even what the pigs were given to eat. One day, he realized that even his father's servants had food, while he was starving. So, he decided to return home and beg for forgiveness. He planned to say to his father, 'I am no longer worthy to be your son. Let me be your servant instead.' And so, he set out for his home."

"But while he was still a long way off, his father spotted him in the distance, and ran to him, throwing his arms around him, and kissing him. The son said, 'Father, I have sinned

The Tales of Abel and Mitra

against heaven and against you. I am no longer worthy to be called your son.' But the father said to his servants, 'Come and bring the best robe for my son; put a ring on his finger and sandals on his feet. Let us have a feast in celebration!' And so, the celebration began."

"Meanwhile, the elder son was in the field. When he came near the house, he heard music and dancing. When he asked what was going on, the servants replied, 'Your brother has returned, and your father has thrown a feast in celebration!' But the elder brother became angry and refused to go in, so his father came out and pleaded with him. The elder brother said, 'Look! All these years I've been serving you and never disobeyed their orders. Yet you never threw me a feast! But when this son of yours who has spent his inheritance comes home, you throw a celebration for him!' The father said, 'My son, you are always with me, and everything I have is yours. But we had to celebrate today because this brother of yours was dead and is now alive again. He was lost, and now he is found.'"

Áedán set down the book. "Well, how was that? Simple enough for a barbarian like you to understand?"

Ingvar chuckled. "That's the end?"

"It's just one short story contained within the narrative."

"There was less glory and adventure than our sagas," Ingvar smiled. "There weren't any dragons or giants, dwarves or elves. It was a rather simple story with simple characters. It wasn't even about your god, just normal people."

"The father in the story was an *allegory* for our god," Áedán huffed. "Clearly the story wasn't simple *enough* for a barbarian to understand–"

"I liked it."

Yisei Ishkhan

Áedán froze. "You…you *liked* it?"

Ingvar nodded. "Sometimes the best stories are the ones about average people like us. It's a reminder that we don't have to be perfect. We can't live up to the glory of the gods or heroes, and maybe that's fine. We're merely human, after all."

"*That's* what inspired you about the story?" Áedán stared at him. "I think you missed the message it was trying to get across."

"No, I understand," Ingvar smiled. "Your god offers redemption to the ones that have gone astray, isn't that right?"

"Well, well, so you *do* have a brain in there after all," Áedán leaned back.

"You remind me of the elder brother in the story."

Áedán stiffened. "*Excuse* me?"

"See?" Ingvar chuckled. "You're only proving my point."

Áedán rolled his eyes. "The point of the story is that we're *all* like the lost son. None of us are perfect. We've all fallen astray at some point and need the forgiveness of the Father."

"Even a righteous holy man like yourself?" Ingvar teased.

Áedán grit his teeth. "Yes."

Ingvar clapped lightly but dropped the rock he'd been using as a hammer as it slipped from his grasp. He reached down to retrieve it, wincing as he gashed his arm on the sharp edge of the boulder he was leaning against, leaving a deep cut on his forearm. Blood dripped down and stained the sand below.

The Tales of Abel and Mitra

Áedán jumped to his feet and rushed over. "Are you alright?!"

"It's just a scratch," Ingvar winced.

Áedán whipped out a cloth and took hold of Ingvar's arm, wiping away the blood and beginning to wrap the wound.

Ingvar glanced up at him in surprise. "I've never seen you so concerned for my well-being."

Áedán flushed but kept his eyes fixed on the task at hand. "You need your arms to finish building the raft. You're no use to me if you catch an infection and die."

"You didn't seem concerned that my eye might have an infection," Ingvar noted.

Áedán glanced up at the Northman's face. Ingvar had kept a bandage over his eye since their first day together, and while he cleaned the wound twice a day, he never removed the cloth in Áedán's presence. Áedán hadn't come this close to Ingvar's side, despite spending more than a week stranded together. For the first time, he noticed a putrid smell wafting from beneath the cloth.

"Take your bandage off," Áedán demanded.

Ingvar tilted his head. "Are you sure you want to see what's underneath?"

"No. But I have to see how bad it is. Now take it off."

With a sigh, Ingvar untied the cloth from his head. Áedán recoiled as the injury was revealed. The skin around Ingvar's right eye was swollen and black, with a jagged scar running across it. Dry scabs crusted over some areas, while others were raw and oozing with pus and rot. Áedán gagged but forced himself to stay composed.

"Why didn't you tell me it had gotten this bad?!" He demanded.

Yisei Ishkhan

"What would you have done about it?" Ingvar shrugged. "I can't see it, so I don't know how bad it is."

"Can't you *feel* it?!"

Ingvar shrugged again.

"Wait here," Áedán muttered. "I'm going to get some water and clean it for you. *Clearly,* you haven't been doing a good job of that yourself."

He rushed back into the cave, snatching up the bucket, and heading down to the pool. As he descended, a strange stillness struck him. It was quiet–*too* quiet. When he reached the pool, he saw that the stream of water that had bubbled forth from the wall since their arrival had stopped running.

"Just one more thing to deal with," he muttered.

He dipped the bucket into the water, filling it to the brim before rushing back to join Ingvar on the beach.

"Hold still," Áedán ordered.

Ingvar obediently tilted his head back, his one eye watching Áedán with quiet amusement. He winced as the young monk dabbed at the infected wound with a cloth. Áedán worked methodically, cleaning away the pus. But there was little else he could do.

"You seem worried," Ingvar smiled. "But I feel fine."

"For now," Áedán mumbled. "If that infection spreads, you'll be dead within days."

"Guess I'd better finish the raft soon then. Can't leave you stranded on this island with a second corpse."

"Don't say that sort of thing," Áedán snapped. "Don't joke about your death."

Ingvar shrugged. "Death isn't such a bad thing, is it? At least in your worldview. It's an end to suffering. I like your

The Tales of Abel and Mitra

idea of an afterlife more than the thought of fighting endless battles in Valhalla until the day of Ragnarok."

Áedán shook his head with a sigh. His eyes drifted to the tattoo on Ingvar's chest–a sprawling tree etched just below the collarbone. Its roots twisted downward as the branches stretched up, weaving together in a pattern that reminded Áedán of the Celtic knotwork that adorned Colmcille's illuminated manuscript.

"What does that symbol mean?" Áedán asked. He'd noticed the tattoo since the day they'd met, but it hadn't interested him until now."

"This?" Ingvar glanced down at his chest. "This is Yggdrasil–the World Tree. Its roots reach out and bind all the Nine Worlds together, from Asgard to Helheim. Everything is connected through it."

Áedán's gaze lingered on the design, its intricate beauty sparking a begrudging admiration.

"I was glancing through the manuscript when you were gone," Ingvar admitted, drawing Áedán's attention to the codex as it lay open on a wooden plank. It was flipped open to the Gospel of Lúcás. "I was trying to understand this story through the pictures, but I couldn't figure it out." He pointed to an image of a man with golden locks bandaging the wounds of a frail figure with dark curls. "This looks a bit like you and me, don't you think?"

"It's the story of the Good Samaritan," Áedán said flatly. But as he scanned the accompanying text, he quickly realized that there were slight deviations from the version he knew. Colmcille had reimagined the cultural context to suit a modern interpretation.

"Can you read it for me?" Ingvar asked. "It looks interesting."

Yisei Ishkhan

"One day," Áedán began, "a monk came to ask Christ, 'What must I do to inherit eternal life?' Christ replied, 'What is written in the law?' The monk said, 'Love God with all your heart, and love your neighbour as yourself.' Christ told him, 'Do this, and you will live.' But the monk wanted to justify himself, so he asked, 'Who is my neighbour?'"

"Christ said to him, 'A man was traveling from Armagh to Lundenwic when he was attacked by robbers. They stripped him of his clothes, beat him, and left him for dead. An abbot happened to be traveling along the same road. But when he saw the man, he passed by on the other side. Later, a bishop came down the same road. But when he saw the man, he too passed by on the other side. But then came a Northman. When he saw the man there, he took pity on him. He went to him, bandaged his wounds, and brought him on his horse to an inn. He took out two coins and gave them to the innkeeper, saying, 'Look after him. When I return, I will reimburse you for any extra expenses.'"

"Finishing his story, Christ asked the monk, 'Which of these three do you think was a neighbour to the man who fell victim to the robbers?'"

Áedán turned to Ingvar expectantly.

Ingvar smiled. "The one who helped him out?"

Áedán nodded his head slightly as he closed the cover of the book. "Go and do likewise."

On the rear cover was etched the design of a tree, strikingly similar to the one tattooed on Ingvar's chest.

"You've got your own Yggdrasil," Ingvar chuckled.

"The Tree of Knowledge," Áedán said. He traced a finger along the branches. "The Forbidden Fruit, through which evil entered into the world when Ádhamh and Éabha defied God."

The Tales of Abel and Mitra

His finger traced down the length of the tree to a serpent encircling the base of the trunk. "And the serpent who tempted them."

"Huh," said Ingvar, a glimmer of curiosity in his eyes. His finger traced along his tattoo. "There's a serpent that lives in Yggdrasil too. Níðhöggr. He gnaws at the roots of the tree, leading to its decay and eventual destruction on the day of Ragnarok."

Áedán furrowed his brow, flipping the book around to the front cover as he inspected it more thoroughly. He gleamed in satisfaction as his finger fell to the bottom of the image. "Christ crushes the head of the serpent underfoot. He has already triumphed over your Níðhöggr."

***

Ingvar's condition worsened over the coming days. The infection on his face must've spread throughout his system. He soon fell ill and was unable to continue venturing out of the cave to assemble the raft. Not that it mattered anyway—after that day of collecting scraps across the beach, no new material drifted ashore. To make matters worse, the spring deep in the cave never started to flow again. At first, Áedán wasn't too concerned by this. The pool that remained seemed vast enough to last for months. But soon, he realized that the water was disappearing faster than he'd anticipated.

"I don't understand where it's all going," he grumbled one evening. "There's no way it could've all evaporated that quickly!"

He sulked by the fire, his fingers busy weaving dried seaweed together into the swastika-like shape of Naomh Brighid's cross. His mother had taught him the craft when he was a child, hanging the crosses over their doorway in the hope of invoking the saint's protection and blessings. Áedán knew it was a quaint superstition. But as his desperation grew, he found himself reviving the tradition, hanging the crosses at the mouth of the cave. He didn't expect to receive any blessings from Naomh Brighid; he only hoped the makeshift symbols might catch the eye of a passing ship.

"Maybe it isn't evaporating," Ingvar murmured, his voice thin and raspy. He was pale and trembling, his breathing uneven. Even sitting upright seemed to drain him. "Maybe it's draining somewhere deeper. Maybe there's another cavern below."

"Another cavern?" Áedán frowned. "I know this cave like the back of my hand. I think I would've noticed if there was another cavern."

"Maybe you just need a fresh pair of eyes?" Ingvar said. "Or eye, I should say."

Áedán stared at him in disbelief. "You want to go down there?"

Ingvar shrugged. "I haven't been much use these past few days. It's the least I can do."

"How will you get back up the slope after?"

"Look," Ingvar sighed. "You said we only have a couple of days left of water. We'll both be dead within a week. Forget about the raft or my infection. Finding water is our top priority."

"Fine," Áedán sighed. "But don't blame me if you get stuck down there."

He was forced to help the Northman to his feet, struggling to support him as they hobbled toward the slope. While Ingvar had visibly thinned from their meager diet, he was still far heavier than Áedán.

"Are you sure about this?" Áedán asked skeptically.

The Tales of Abel and Mitra

"I'll be fine," Ingvar assured.

Áedán nodded. "Just slide down slowly. The path is covered in rocks, but it isn't far to the bottom. Try not to get any more injuries along the way."

Áedán waited until Ingvar made it to the bottom before following him. He led them over to the pool. It was even lower than when Áedán had stopped by this morning.

"Where was the water coming from?" Ingvar asked.

"There," Áedán pointed to a crack between two rocks. "It was just a trickle, but it stopped flowing on the day the wreckage washed up."

Ingvar whipped out his knife as he approached the wall.

Áedán frowned. "What are you doing?"

"The water had to be coming from somewhere," Ingvar said. "There must be another cavern where the pool originated from, or perhaps a source of water outside the cave."

"You think we'll find an exit if we break down the wall?"

"It's worth a shot." Ingvar jabbed the knife into the hole. He strained, sweat trickling down his face as he tried to wriggle it through.

"Let me try," Áedán said impatiently.

Ingvar smirked. "You? With those dainty hands of yours?"

Áedán rolled his eyes. "I think I have more strength in me than you do at this point."

Ingvar stepped aside as he let Áedán take hold of the hilt. He jammed it forward, throwing his weight against the wall. Cracks spread along the wall. Áedán scooped up a stone from the ground, bringing it down hard against the rocks. The cracks splintered upward. He hit the wall again, harder this time. On the third strike, the wall crumbled inward. A sudden flash of blinding light burst through the opening, illuminating the cavern for a moment before disappearing behind the dust and debris.

"Did you see that?" Ingvar's voice beamed with excitement. "Or am I losing my mind?"

Áedán began to dig, scoping aside the pebbles and dirt as he cleared out the hole. After a few minutes, the light broke through once more.

"You were right!" Áedán exclaimed. "There really *is* an exit on the other side!"

"Step aside," Ingvar said.

Áedán did as he was told as Ingvar threw his full weight against the wall. It came crashing down, sending a billow of dust into the air. They shielded their eyes as an intense white light spilled into the chamber. Once the dust had settled and their eyes adjusted, they stared in awe at the space revealed before them—an expansive chamber far larger than any of the other sections of the cave. Its walls stretched up to a dome-shaped ceiling high above. One section of the roof had collapsed at some point, leaving an opening to the sky. Sunlight poured down from above, illuminating the debris that tumbled down, forming a sloped pathway from the cavern floor to the opening. The incline seemed no steeper than the entrance to the cave back on the beach.

But what stole their breath was the pool of water stretching across the cavern floor. It was so pristine and crystalline that it perfectly mirrored the ceiling above, creating the illusion of an endless abyss. At its center, a solitary tree rose from a rock, its branches stretching toward the cavern roof while the reflection extended downward like roots into the pool's depths.

The Tales of Abel and Mitra

Áedán's gaze shifted to the tattoo on Ingvar's chest. "It almost looks like–"

"The Tree of Knowledge?" Ingvar offered.

A smile tugged at Áedán's lips. "I was going to say Yggdrasil."

Before Áedán could stop him, Ingvar stepped forward, wading into the shallow pool. Ripples cascaded out from his steps to the other shore, distorting the mirror-like surface.

"What are you doing?" Áedán called out.

"Don't you see!" Ingvar laughed, pointing up at the hole in the roof of the cave. "That's our way out! We're not trapped anymore!"

"We still don't know what's up there," Áedán said. "It might not lead anywhere."

"Well, there's only one way to find out."

He knelt, scoping water into his hands and splashing it onto his face. The bandage on his head came loose, sinking to the bottom of the pool.

"Ingvar!" Áedán snapped. "You'll contaminate it!"

"*Hm?*" Ingvar turned to face him.

Áedán's scowl vanished in an instant. His breath caught in his throat. Was he imagining things? The pallor that had dulled Ingvar's face was gone. The infection, scabs, and even the jagged scar cutting across his eye had all disappeared. Ingvar's hand flew to his face, his fingers tracing the now smooth skin around his right eye. His golden lashes fluttered open, revealing a deep, vibrant blue eye, whole and unmarred.

"Can you…see…?" Áedán dared to ask, his voice barely more than a whisper.

A radiant smile lit up Ingvar's face, his blue eyes gleaming with new life. "I can see."

Yisei Ishkhan

The Tales of Abel and Mitra
The Tale of Abel and Mitra

"That's the end?!" Avi exclaimed, jumping out of his seat. "That can't be the end! They didn't even make it out of the cave! What was out there? Did it lead off the island? Or did they just find themselves stranded at the top of the cliff, with nowhere else to go?"

Mitra smiled. "I'll leave that up to your imagination."

"Huh?" Avi blinked, his expression blank for a moment before a spark of realization lit up his eyes. "Ohhh! I get it! It's one of *those* stories–the ones full of symbolism but with no clear answers. That's why you threw in both the Tree of Knowledge and Yggdrasil, isn't it? That tree at the end can be interpreted as either one! Maybe the whole point of the story was that the two trees are the same! Or maybe...maybe that tree at the end was just some random tree after all! Wait, wait, I've got it! The entire story never even happened at all! Áedán and Ingvar were dead all along! The cave represents Hell, or maybe Purgatory. Yes, that must be it! And the light at the top of the cave symbolizes their arrival at the Gates of Heaven!"

Abel let out a soft sigh. "I think you're overthinking this, Avi. Not every story has to be so complicated."

A flicker of amusement danced in Mitra's eyes. "I like Avi's interpretation, but I can assure you that Áedán and Ingvar were very much alive at the time. Had they been dead, their tale would never have entered my archives."

"What, so this was a true story?" Avi asked in amazement.

"Very much so," Mitra assured. Reaching into his pockets, he produced two items. One was a cross, decorated with intricate Celtic knotwork; one end was dull, and the other stained dark red. The other item was an ivory dagger, with the carving of a serpent weaving its way around the hilt.

Abel's jaw dropped. "Are those—?"

"Áedán's cross and Ingvar's dagger," Mitra confirmed.

"Whoa!" Avi beamed, taking the blade from Mitra's hand and studying its design. "Why do you have them?"

"They fell out of the boxes when Miss Nineveh was loading the crates, so I took them with me."

"Are all those crates from your vessel filled with relics from your world?" Abel wondered.

"For the most part."

"I'd like to see what other things you have in your collection," Avi said, passing the dagger from one hand to the other.

"So," said Abel, "did you find Mitra's story interesting?"

"Interesting?" Avi considered that thought. "Yeah, sure, I guess. But it was a bit anticlimactic if you ask me. I was hoping for a story with some more action and adventure, maybe with a little romance thrown in."

"As Ingvar said," Abel spoke up, "'sometimes the best stories are the ones about average people like us.'"

"Yeah, yeah," Avi waved his comment aside. "I still prefer my *Legends of the Shadow Men* and *Tales of Makarasaman*."

Mitra chuckled. "I would like to hear your stories."

"Yeah? Maybe another time," Avi stretched. "My shift is over. I think I'll be headed to sleep soon."

The hundred and twenty-fifth hour of Night was approaching, and they bid Avi farewell as he returned home.

The Tales of Abel and Mitra

The Elders hadn't assigned Mitra a place to stay, and so Abel offered for him to come back to his home.

"We only have three bedrooms," Abel explained. "You can take the bed if you'd like."

"Thank you, but the floor will suffice for me," Mitra assured. "Besides, after the extended hibernation I had on my journey, I doubt I will require rest anytime soon." He cast a glance out of Abel's small window. The Night was just as dim as when he'd arrived, despite the countless hours that had passed. "It must be confusing to determine when to sleep and when to rise when you spend two hundred hours in the darkness of Night."

"You'll get used to it," Abel said. "Everyone has a different sleep schedule depending on when their shifts are. Avi should've headed off to bed right when his shift ended, but he has a habit of staying up later than he should."

"Do you have another shift at the farm when you awake?"

"At the hundred and fortieth hour," Abel nodded. "Then another at the hundred and sixty-fifth hour. After that, I'm free until Dawn. Everyone will gather at the Church for a Dawn Service. Then we watch the silver phoenixes as they migrate back to Darkside. It's a beautiful sight, you should see it."

Mitra smiled. "I look forward to it."

***

Abel set out in the coming hours to show Mitra around the farms in the lower layers of the forest. He taught Mitra everything from the delicate process of harvesting duskroots without damaging the plants, to the proper method of extracting nectar from starflowers. Around them, villagers cast curious glances at Mitra, but few dared to approach him.

Yisei Ishkhan

Mitra seemed disappointed by this, expressing a desire to get to know more people. But Abel didn't mind–he preferred not to make small talk.

At around the hundred and seventieth hour of Night, they were joined by Avi, Esta, and Noa as their shifts overlapped in the lower branches where the starflowers bloomed.

"Since we're all here," Avi beamed, "how about I tell you all *The Third Legend of the Shadow Men?*"

"Oh, please," Noa groaned. "I'd rather not hear it."

"I wanna hear it," Esta piped up. "I didn't know there was a third story; you've only ever told me the first two–and that weird prequel."

Avi puffed with enthusiasm. "Well, the third legend is the most suspenseful of all! Our protagonist's village is ransacked by the Shadow Men, and his beloved–who he heroically saved in the first two legends–gets captured. Naturally, he has to set out on another dangerous adventure to rescue her!"

Noa crossed his arms. "And how exactly is this any different from all the other stories you tell?"

"Well, you see, Noa, in *this* story our protagonist is faced with greater perils than in the first two stories *and* the prequel combined!"

Noa was unimpressed, but Esta leaned in with interest.

"Well, now I *have* to hear it."

Abel glanced at Mitra. "I'll let you be the tiebreaker."

"I would like to hear one of Mister Avi's famous legends," Mitra smiled. "Though, I may struggle to fully appreciate the story without having heard the previous parts."

The Tales of Abel and Mitra

"No problem!" Avi beamed. "I'll give you a quick recap before we dive in!"

"Here we go," Noa muttered.

What followed was a dramatic recounting of *The Legend of the Shadow Men*, from the prequel to part two. Then began *The Legend of the Shadow Men (Part Three)*. Avi's tale didn't disappoint when it came to throwing every possible threat one could face at the protagonist. Our hero outran a kamkara, outwitted a pack of makarasa, barely escaped the web of an oyeba, and narrowly avoided falling into a lukano den. The story climaxed with a confrontation with the Shadow Men, leading to his triumphant rescue of his beloved.

When the tale concluded, Noa was the first to speak. "You recycled half of those fight scenes from *The Tale of Makarasa-man Part One*, didn't you?"

"What?" Avi bristled. "No! Well...maybe I borrowed *some* elements. But I added twists!"

"Uh-huh," Noa nodded. "Your so-called 'plot twists' are predictable. I saw every one of them coming."

"Maybe you've just gotten too familiar with my *genius storytelling*!" Avi declared.

"Maybe *too* familiar," Noa sighed. "You've told me these same stories a dozen times."

"Alright," Avi slapped Noa on the back. "I've heard enough of Noa and his negativity. I wanna hear what Mister Falling Star thinks."

They all turned to Mitra expectantly.

"I quite enjoyed it," Mitra said. "Your story reflects a classic use of character archetypes. Though I am curious—why did you decide not to give any of the characters names?"

Esta snorted. "Because Avi's terrible at coming up with names." She gestured to a nearby branch, where the pku were nibbling away at some ganaan. "Have you heard what he calls his pku? Spinner."

"Because he spins webs!" Avi protested. "It's a practical name!"

"Exactly," Esta said. "Uncreative."

"I always thought he left his characters unnamed so that anyone could imagine themselves in the story," Abel said earnestly.

"Or," Noa offered, "Avi just likes to imagine *himself* as the hero. Though we all know he'd be the first to run screaming if he ever met a real Shadow Man."

"Hey!" Avi flushed. "I will not take this slander!"

"Slander?" Noa scoffed. "Did you tell them how you screamed like a baby and fell from your branch after spotting a lukano? That was on our last Night Mission."

"I was...trying to scare it off," Avi said defensively.

"Right."

Before Avi could tell his side of the story, a voice called out from one of the nearby trees.

"Noa! Are you down there?"

Noa glanced up and spotted his sister Nineveh hanging from one of the branches overhead.

"Yeah?" He called out. "What is it?"

"Head to bed," Nineveh ordered. "I'm sending out a team in eight hours to investigate an anomaly in the forest. You're coming with me."

Noa sighed. "Do I have to?"

The Tales of Abel and Mitra

"We need a team that's both experienced and agile. You fit both those requirements, so I need you out there. Off to bed. Now."

"Fine, fine," Noa sulked. He turned to the group. "Catch you later. We probably won't be back at the Village until Dawn."

Avi gave his friend a pat on the back. "I wish I could come with you."

Noa smirked faintly. "I'd switch places with you, but you don't have enough experience yet. One day. See you at Dawn."

As Noa departed, Nineveh dropped from her branch, her eyes locking on Mitra.

"The Elders have reviewed most of the crates we brought back," she said. "Ninety percent of the items have been deemed harmless, but a handful require further investigation. They'll meet you at the storage facility at the hundred and ninety-eighth hour, just after the Dawn service."

Mitra nodded. "I will be there.

"Good," Nineveh turned her attention to Abel. "You seem to have become his chaperone. I can arrange a team to watch the outworlder."

"Oh…" Abel glanced from Nineveh to Mitra. "I don't mind his company. That is, as long as you're fine with sticking by me?"

"I quite enjoy having Abel by my side," Mitra smiled.

"Very well," Nineveh nodded. "See you at Dawn."

***

The Dawn service was one of the few occasions when everyone in the Village synchronized their schedules to assemble in one place. The Church, perched on one of the largest trees at the Village Center, resembled an oversized hut with a sloping roof and a circular design. Inside, its amphitheater-style layout ensured that everyone had a clear view of the altar. Unlike most of the Village's structures, the Church's walls were bleached white, giving the illusion that it was crafted out of marble rather than wood. Ornate carvings adorned its pillars and ceiling, depicting stories Mitra found vaguely familiar.

One of the most prominent carvings depicted a boat carrying eight individuals and an array of creatures, few of which Mitra recognized other than a pair of pku and a couple of bird species. At the forefront of the vessel, a young man stretched out his hands. A bird with a large, curved bill topped with a horn-like protrusion flew toward him with a leaf clutched in its beak.

"What is that story?" Mitra gestured to the carving.

Abel followed his gaze. "That's the story of how our ancestors arrived in Shambhala—*The Journey Across the Sea of Darkness*. Near the end of the story, the boy named Noa sends off Hayainu to search for dry land. Hayainu returns with a leaf in her mouth, and the people follow her into the Valley of Shambhala.

"Fascinating," Mitra said. "Is Hayainu a hornbill?"

"She is," Abel nodded. "Hornbills are the most sacred animals in our culture. Do you have them in your own world?"

"We do," Mitra nodded. As he glanced about the chamber, he noticed other depictions of the species along the walls and pillars. Down below, four carvings of hornbills supported the altar on their massive bills.

The Tales of Abel and Mitra

Most days, Abel and the others sat near the front of the Church. But today, hoping to avoid drawing attention to Mitra, he steered them toward the uppermost balcony at the back of the building.

"Ugh, all the way up here?" Esta groaned. "I can barely see from this far back."

"Just sit," Abel muttered.

As they settled in, Avi scanned the crowd. "Has anyone seen Noa anywhere? He should've been back by now."

"He's probably exhausted from his Night Mission," Esta noted. "I wouldn't be surprised if he went home to take a nap."

Avi frowned. "I don't see Nineveh either. She's never missed a service before."

Before they could say anything more, a gong rang out, signaling the start of the service. Vishel appeared, making his way down the aisle as he was flanked by altar servers holding large leaves like umbrellas over his head. Others tapped bamboo staffs along the ground in a rhythmic manner, creating a lively tune that echoed through the chamber. Despite his hunched posture and stoic expression, Vishel carried himself with an air of authority. He and the other members of the clergy were adorned in beaded skirts, colourful shawls, and feathered headdresses that were both regal and intimidating.

On either side of the altar, the choir began chanting a hymn in a language that sounded like an archaic form of the common tongue heard throughout the Village. They sang in polyphony, their melodic voices both haunting and beautiful:

The Lord is my Light and my salvation.

Yisei Ishkhan

Whom shall I fear?
The Lord is the stronghold of my life.
Of whom shall I be afraid?

Your word is a lamp for me,
Your word is a light on my path.
For you are the fountain of my life,
In your Light, we see Light.

Your life is the Light of mankind.
The Light shines in the darkness,
And the darkness has not overcome it.

The people walking in the darkness
Have seen a great Light,
On those living in the valley of the shadow of death
A Light has dawned.

Vishel reached the altar, spreading his arms over the congregation. "May the Light of Dawn shine forth on your path as this Night comes to a close."

"And also on your path," the congregation responded.

Vishel's eyes swept across the crowd. "I'm sure you've all heard about the unusual Night we've had here in Shambhala. For the first time in our history, an outworlder has arrived in our Village."

Murmurs rippled through the congregation as heads turned in Mitra's direction.

Abel winced. *So much for keeping a low profile.*

The Tales of Abel and Mitra

"Ah," Vishel nodded. "There he is. We hope that your time with us has been pleasant thus far and will continue to be. As we welcome the Light of Dawn, let us also extend a warm welcome to our visitor from the stars!"

Applause erupted. Abel shrank back in his seat as Mitra bowed his head and gave the crowd a polite wave.

"As it is written," Vishel continued, "'The foreigner must be treated as one of your own. Love them as yourself, for you too were once foreigners in exile.'"

He began to preach his sermon, beginning with a story of exile, and how their ancestors had followed the Light into the Promised Land of Shambhala; he then told of how the Light of Dawn would one day drive out the Darkness and vanquish Night from the world.

Mitra listened intently, absorbed by every word that the priest spoke.

When the Dawn Service ended, the tension in the air seemed to ease. For the first time, some of the villagers dared to approach Mitra. A handshake here, a bow there, even a few smiles.

Abel did his best to steer them out of the crowd. "You have a meeting with the Elders at the storage facility soon," he reminded Mitra.

"Yes," Mitra nodded. "We should head down there."

"We'll save you a seat in the starflower fields!" Avi called out as he and Esta departed. "The silver phoenixes migrate at Dawn. You won't want to miss it!"

"We'll join you if we can," Abel promised. As he and Mitra descended to the forest floor, Abel asked Mitra his thoughts on the Dawn Service. "You seemed interested in what Vishel was saying."

Yisei Ishkhan

"Indeed," Mitra nodded. "Your stories and theology bear greater similarity to the cultures of my home world than I expected."

"There are many different beliefs in your world, aren't there?" Abel wondered. "Nezahualatzin worshiped different gods than Domingo. So did Áedán and Ingvar."

"Your God seems to be the same as the God worshiped by Domingo and Áedán," Mitra noted. "To be more specific, your Church shares many similarities with a movement called the Church of Heavenly Light in my world. Both emphasize the image of God as a divine Light–in your case, the Light of Dawn. Of course, this may simply be a reflection of the cultural context your people find themselves in. Any culture engulfed in prolonged periods of darkness would naturally emphasize the salvific nature that Light brings to the world."

"You seem to know a lot about these sorts of things," Abel noted.

Mitra smiled. "I am, after all, an Archivist."

By the time they reached the storage facilities, several Elders, including Inali and Vishel, were already waiting for them. The storage facility was a chamber hidden beneath the roots of a tree, connected to the broader tunnel system that ran beneath the Village.

"Shall we begin?" Vishel asked, gesturing to the entrance.

The crates were brought out, half a dozen of them, and placed carefully before Mitra. Each one contained items the Elders had deemed to be of concern. Their wary eyes flicked between the alien artifacts and Mitra, hoping for an explanation.

The Tales of Abel and Mitra

"Could you tell us the function of these items?" Inali wondered.

Mitra stepped forward as he examined the relics, his expression calm. "Most of these are indeed weapons."

Vishel narrowed his gaze. "Why were you carrying such things aboard your vessel?"

"They are relics of my world's history and culture," Mitra said, unbothered by the Elders' growing discomfort. "Few are still functional, and those that are were secured to prevent misuse. Their purpose is purely educational."

He began to point out the relics, one by one. "This is a grenade from the First World War—just the outer shell, so you need not worry about it detonating. This is a *sarissa*, a pike that would have been used in the phalanx formations employed by Alexander the Great; the tip is brittle and would likely shatter if you attempted to use it. This is a cannonball from the Dardanelles Gun, the massive cannon the Ottomans used to batter the walls of Constantinople; it is useless without the cannon. This is a drone employed in the Melekhite Siege of Rome; it's been decommissioned. This is a Mongol bow that was likely used in the conquest of the Song Dynasty; I have no arrows in my collection."

"What about this one?" Abel wondered, eyeing a handheld device.

Mitra smiled. "You already know what this one is. It is Domingo de Granada's–the very arquebus he carried during the Fall of Tenochtitlan."

"No way!" Abel gasped. "This was really his?"

"I'm afraid we'll need to hold onto most of these items," Inali said. "Even if they are no longer functional."

Yisei Ishkhan

"I understand," Mitra nodded. He reached down into the crate containing Domingo's gun, retrieving a smaller box within.

"What is that?" Vishel eyed him.

Mitra opened the lid with care, revealing two wooden bracelets, their beads tainted with a deep crimson hue. "These items were stored together with the gun, since both hail from the same historical event. They are not weapons–merely prayer beads."

Abel's eyes sparkled with curiosity. "Domingo and Sandoval's bracelets?"

Mitra nodded.

Vishel examined the bracelets for a moment before grunting. "You may take them with you. The rest of the items will be stored here."

"Thank you," Mitra bowed his head. Then, he held out one of the bracelets toward Abel.

Abel blinked in surprise. "Are you…giving this to me?"

"They were meant to be worn, not hidden away in a box."

Tentatively, Abel extended his hand, allowing Mitra to slide the bracelet around his wrist. He turned it over, feeling the rough texture of the beads against his fingers. "This must've been Sandoval's," he murmured.

"Originally," said Mitra. "If you recall the end of my first story, it later ended up on Nezahualatzin's hand. It remained with him before finding its way back to Spain. Eventually, it ended up in my collection."

Abel's fingers lingered on the worn beads. He could almost feel the weight of history that this tiny relic bore.

The Tales of Abel and Mitra

"Well," Mitra smiled, "shall we head over to the starflower fields to join the others?"

***

As they set out to search for Esta and Avi, the number of villagers stopping to greet Mitra only seemed to grow. Each interaction carried an awkward undertone, as if no one knew quite how they should act around the man. While they smiled and waved warmly enough, their eyes betrayed uncertainty.

Abel found this rather annoying and did his best to steer his friend away from the crowds.

"It's ironic," he muttered. "Everyone's suddenly so friendly to you *after* Vishel's sermon about welcoming foreigners. It's like they're only doing this because they feel obligated to."

Mitra chuckled. "It is understandable. Your people have never encountered an outsider before. Fear is a natural response in such circumstances. It is a common human reaction, not limited to the people of your Village."

They found Esta and Avi lounging with Akavi and Spinner on one of the lower branches overlooking the starflower fields. They joined them, dangling their legs over the edge, the vast expanse of golden blossoms shimmering below them like a sea of stars. Here and there, silver phoenixes flitted lazily from flower to flower.

"Noa still isn't here?" Abel asked.

Avi shook his head, frowning. "No sign of him, or Nineveh for that matter. I think their party is still out in the forest."

"Nineveh *did* say that they were investigating an anomaly," Esta pointed out. "Any idea what it might be?"

Yisei Ishkhan

"No idea," said Avi. "Noa didn't say much before he left, but it seemed like they were headed back to Mister Falling Star's vessel."

They turned to Mitra expectantly.

"I was not informed of their plans," Mitra said. "Most of my relics have already been brought back, so I am unsure what purpose they would have in revisiting the site."

Abel sighed. "They'll be fine. They have the most experienced members of the *Makarasa Morung* out there. Besides, it's almost Dawn. The ratri rakshas will be retreating to the shadows soon."

"Ugh!" Avi groaned. "It's the waiting that's killing me! Abel, once Dawn arrives let's head out into the forest to search for them."

"Is that even *allowed*?" Esta asked.

"Sure it is!" Avi exclaimed. "There's no rule against going into the forest at Dawn. The restrictions only apply at Night."

"Fine," Abel said hesitantly. "I'll come with you. I know you'll go even if I don't, but I don't trust you on your own."

"Great!" Avi cheered, clapping him on the back. He turned to Esta with a sly grin. "Hey, you wouldn't mind covering our shift, would you? Abel and I usually harvest dawnberries at the tenth hour of Dawn."

"No way!" Esta huffed. "I have my own responsibilities, thank you very much! Why don't you ask Mister Falling Star to cover for you? He's so perfect at doing *everything*; he could probably finish the harvest in half the time."

"I would, but I'd rather he come with us," Avi said. He turned to Mitra. "What do you say?"

The Tales of Abel and Mitra

"I can certainly come along," said Mitra.

"Perfect," Avi beamed. "Ugh, I wish Dawn would come already! We've still got another hour to wait!"

"Mitra, why don't you tell us another one of your stories while we wait?" Abel suggested.

Esta raised an eyebrow. "Oh, so Mister Falling Star is a storyteller too?"

"Yeah!" Avi gleamed. "He tells quite good ones too."

Esta smirked. "Better than *The Legend of the Shadow Men* and *The Tales of Makarasa-man*?"

"Well, not quite," Avi faltered. "But he's not bad. He could give me a run for my money!"

Mitra chuckled. "On the topic of money..." he slipped out a small circle from his pocket that flickered in the faint glow of the starflowers. With a flick of his fingers, he tossed it in Avi's direction.

The boy fumbled to catch it. "What is this?" Avi turned the circle over in his hands, examining it curiously. It had a square hole in its center and faint inscriptions etched around the edges.

"A bronze coin," Mitra said, "from the reign of Toghon Temür–also known as Emperor Huizong, the last ruler of the Yuan Dynasty."

"I'm guessing this coin has a story behind it," Abel gleamed with excitement.

"Of course," said Mitra. "Let me tell you a story–a story of learning to accept the whims of the world..."

Yisei Ishkhan

III. The Tale of Nayan and Anahit
January 13, 1356 AD
Korean Quarter, Zaitun, Jiangzhe Province, Yuan Empire

The bronze coin spun through the air, catching the glint of the setting sun as the young man who had tossed it grinned with exaggerated flair. Nayan caught the coin, slapping it onto the back of his hand. He sucked in a deep breath, a bead of sweat tracing its way down his temple as he anticipated which side the coin had landed on.

"Enough of your games!" Bellowed one of the three men across the table from Nayan. His thick Xiang accent echoed throughout the teahouse. "Show us what it landed on already! C'mon!"

"Patience, my friend," Nayan quipped, masking his nerves under a dazzling smile. He unveiled the coin. The side inscribed with characters bearing the emperor's regnal name was side up.

"Hah! You lost!" Jeered man. He laughed, clapping his two buddies on the back. "Looks like our drinks are paid for tonight!"

A nervous laugh escaped Nayan's lips. "About that…"

"What?" Growled the man on Nayan's left, speaking broken Hokkien with a heavy Jurchen accent. "You don't have money?"

"Let me see…" Nayan feigned innocence, hands darting to his pockets. In one swift motion, he grabbed hold of the legs of the table, flipping it forward. Platters of dumplings, bowls of rice, and cups of wine rained down on the trio. The

The Tales of Abel and Mitra

Xiang lost balance, falling back in his chair as the table crashed down on him.

"After him!" Shrieked the Jurchen.

But Nayan was already vaulting over the balcony railing. "Sorry, gentlemen!" He called out over his shoulder, his laughter trailing behind him. "I'll pay you back…someday!"

Nayan landed gracefully on the bustling street of the Korean Quarter below, nearly trampling a young woman in the process. He grabbed her by the waist, saving her from her fall as he swept her into his arms.

"Miss Gyeonghwa!" Nayan beamed when he saw that she was his favourite courtesan at the establishment. "Tell the boss I'm sorry for the mess up there."

"A-Khoang!" Gyeonghwa flushed, pressing her body closer to his. She, like most, only knew Nayan by his alias. "You're leaving already?"

Nayan dodged as a porcelain cup smashed onto the ground at his feet.

"There he is! Stop him!"

Nayan flashed a cheeky grin at the men still up on the balcony before turning back to Gyeonghwa with a polite bow. "I'd love to stay, my dear. But maybe next time."

Gyeonghwa giggled. "Come back soon!" She called out as Nayan disappeared into the crowd.

He weaved through the maze of alleyways, left, right, then another left, until he was sure he'd lost his pursuers. Leaning up against the side of a stall, he huffed to catch his breath. His head wrap had come undone during his escape, and his braids tumbled loose over his shoulders.

"Hey!" A shrill voice interrupted his moment of rest. An elderly woman appeared, wagging her finger at him as she berated him in Persian. "I recognize you! You're trouble! Now scram!"

"Oh, *Baklava Lady*!" Nayan flashed a charming grin as he responded in her tongue. "Long time no see! Since when did you expand your business to the Korean Quarter?"

"Someone had too much to drink this evening," the woman scowled at him. "This is the *Persian Quarter*."

Nayan's eyes darted around as he took in his surroundings, suddenly realizing that he'd crossed from the Korean to the Persian Quarter.

"You're right," he laughed. "My bad! Been a while since I've come this way."

"And you better not come again!" Baklava Lady screeched as she began beating him with her cane. "You thieving bastard!"

Nayan dodged her cane, throwing up his hands in mock surrender. "I didn't steal from you last time, I swear! It was that gang of delinquent Sogdian kids!"

"Oh, sure. You're no better than they are! Everyone on these streets knows you're a thief. Scram!"

"I only steal from those who scam and cheat others," Nayan assured. "I'm an *honest* thief! And I know that *you're* an honest businesswoman, so you needn't worry about me, Baklava Lady."

"An honest thief is still a thief!" She spat, raising her cane for another swing.

Nayan ducked out of the way and slipped down another alley before the old woman could bring the cane down on his head. "Catch you later, Baklava Lady!"

The Tales of Abel and Mitra

After another block, he slowed to a halt as he considered his next moves. *Looks like I'll have to avoid both the Korean and the Persian Quarters for a while*, he sighed to himself. *But where to next? Somewhere I haven't completely ruined my reputation yet...*

His thoughts wandered to the Uygur Quarter. He hadn't stayed there for a couple of years but remembered it fondly. They were less strict than some other neighbourhoods in the city when it came to restrictions on alcohol, gambling, or women. Plus, he was nearly fluent in their tongue, and thanks to his Keraite ancestry could blend in seamlessly with the locals.

And so, he made his way across town.

"Ah, how I missed this place!" Nayan spread his arms wide as he entered the central bazaar of the Uygur Quarter. The district was alive with sights and sounds that stimulated every one of his senses. He salivated as he took in the aroma of roasted lamb kebabs, fried noodles, meat dumplings, and yogurt dishes, mixed with the exotic fragrances of fruit wines and fermented milk. Men and women haggled for prices in Uygur, Sogdian, and other tongues, as the lively rhythm of drums and stringed instruments from a celebration in the distance echoed through the streets.

Nayan fingered the bronze coin in his pocket. It was the last and only one he'd had for the past two weeks, and he'd been reluctant to depart with it. He felt a stab of guilt for scamming those men in the Korean Quarter, but after two days without food, he'd been desperate for a meal. His gambles in prior weeks had kept him well-fed as he convinced others to pay for his meals. But today, his luck had finally worn thin.

The bronze coin was enough to buy him a hot meal or a bottle of alcohol, but what would he do then? It wasn't enough to rent a room at an inn for the night, and after more than a month of sleeping in dingy alleyways, he preferred a warm bath and a bed to sleep in over food or drink.

He glanced at the food stalls nearby, tempted to snag a lamb kebab from one of the glistening racks. The vendor was distracted by a customer, and he knew he could get away with stealing without being noticed.

No, he knocked himself on the head. *No more stealing. I came to the Uygur Quarter to start fresh. I don't need to ruin my reputation in another district.*

Besides, stealing wouldn't fix the root of his problem. He flipped the bronze coin between his hands. He had to find a way to make money.

To his left, an old man slouched against a wall, his unkempt hair falling over his face. A dirty bowl sat before him with a few pitiful coins inside. Nayan's gaze lingered for a moment.

I can't stoop to begging, he thought, his pride recoiling at the idea. *Besides, who's going to take pity on a young, healthy, ridiculously charming young man like myself?*

His attention was drawn to a melody off to the right. In the square, a dark-skinned man tapped rhythmically against a handheld drum, singing in a tongue that vaguely reminded Nayan of Persian. Beside him, a woman who must've been his sister danced in circles, her colourful dress fanning out around her, and bells tied to her ankles chiming as she tapped her feet in tune with the music. A few onlookers clapped and tossed coins at them.

Nayan chuckled to himself. *Nobody's going to pay to see me dance.*

The Tales of Abel and Mitra

Further down the street, incense wafted from the windows of a brightly lit building. Music and the laughter of women spilled into the night air. A gilded sign above the door proclaimed in both the Chinese and Uygur scripts: *Golden Pleasure House.*

That's always an option, Nayan sighed. Selling his charm to a wealthy patron in exchange for food or a roof over his head wasn't a bad deal. He'd dabbled in similar arrangements before, though he preferred long-term relationships over fleeting romance.

His thoughts drifted to Soraya bint Hitham, one of the daughters of a wealthy Baghdadi merchant in the Arab Quarter. Their fiery affair last year had ended in disaster when her family learned of him. Nayan had been forced to fake his death, shave his mustache and beard, and take on a new alias to avoid being cut down by Hitham ibn Sulaiman's men in the streets.

Ah, Soraya, Nayan reminisced. *Your laugh, your touch...a whole year has passed, and I still miss you. I swore I'd never set foot in the Arab Quarter again, but maybe I'll return just to get one last glimpse of you...*

"Hey, watch where you're going!" A vendor snapped at him in Uygur.

Nayan had stumbled into a noodle stall at the edge of the bazaar. *That drink from the teahouse must've finally hit me*, he chuckled to himself. He muttered a quick apology before weaving down a nearby alleyway.

His legs gave out as he rounded the corner. He fell sprawled across a set of steps, the world spinning around him before fading into black.

He wasn't out long before being rudely awakened by the whack of a whisk against his face. His eyes fluttered open as

Yisei Ishkhan

he sat up in surprise, finding himself face-to-face with two figures clad in red robes. White veils covered their faces, leaving only their beady eyes visible as they glared down at him.

"You're blocking the entrance to our temple," one of them grumbled in Uygur.

Nayan pushed their whisks out of his face, jumping to his feet as he dusted off his robes. He glanced up, reading the plaque above the door–*Guangming Manichean Temple*.

"Keep your unclean flesh off our sacred spaces," the second parishioner huffed.

"A thousand apologies," Nayan offered a dramatic bow, a sheepish grin spreading across his face. "It won't happen again."

He sauntered down the street, flipping the lone bronze coin between his fingers. His stomach growled.

How can I be hungry already after just having a whole meal in the Korean Quarter?! He sighed to himself, flipping the coin another time. *Blank side up, I steal.*

It landed with the characters facing up. He sighed again, slumping to the ground with his back against a wall. As he lamented his plight, the voice of a woman interrupted his thoughts.

"Hetoum, give this man some spare change."

Nayan glanced up in surprise. He understood the tongue she spoke in, but it took him a moment to place it. Armenian! Yes, it was definitely Armenian, though a different dialect than what he was familiar with.

A striking pair stood before him. The boy, Hetoum, was draped in a plain black cassock, his youthful face flushing with nervous energy. Beside him stood a woman who radiated

The Tales of Abel and Mitra

authority. She was adorned in purple and gold silk robes, with an ornately embroidered shawl pulled over her head. She looked about twice the boy's age, and Nayan stared at them in confusion as he wondered what their relation might be.

"Yes, my lady," Hetoum replied. He pulled out a sachet of coins and dropped it at Nayan's feet.

Before Nayan had the chance to register what had happened, the two continued down the street, disappearing around the corner. Nayan poked his finger into the sachet and felt around. There were at least ten bronze coins inside! He could hardly believe it. It had been at least a year since he'd had his hands on this much money.

"Wait!" He called out after the pair, snatching the sachet from the ground and racing after them.

Dammit, did this lady really give me pity *money?! Unbelievable! I've never begged for money before! And who leaves* this *much change for a common beggar, anyway? Unbelievable! This woman must be loaded!*

"Hey, lady! Wait up!"

He turned the corner, catching a glimpse of purple silk disappearing into a lavish establishment. His heart sank when he glimpsed the plaque over the building's entrance–*Cardamom of Qocho*.

"Great," he sighed. "The fanciest restaurant in the Uygur Quarter. No way they're letting someone like *me* inside."

He glanced up. The building was three stories tall, with balconies along the second and third floors where patrons dined. He spotted the pair arriving at the top floor, joining a table alongside an older Uygur gentleman.

His gaze shifted. The building next to the restaurant was a Buddhist shrine with a five-story pagoda. Nayan's lips curled into a mischievous grin. *If I can't* walk *in, I'll drop* in.

Yisei Ishkhan

It pained him to even think about parting with the ten bronze coins, but he knew he had to. He might be a thief, but he wasn't a beggar!

He approached the pagoda. The building's tiered roof was low, so he scaled it with ease, hauling himself onto the second story. From there, he squeezed through an open window, winding his way up the flights of stairs until he reached the fourth story. He poked his head out over the restaurant balcony below.

Perfect, he beamed. *She's right there. Now all I have to do is toss the sachet onto the table…*

He scrambled as a few of the coins fell loose. As he clambered to retrieve them, the tiles on the roof suddenly slipped, and Nayan lost his grip. Several patrons at the restaurant screamed in surprise as he came crashing down on the table, right on top of a platter of roasted lamb.

The Uygur gentleman shot to his feet, his red face brighter than the wine now spilled across the floor. "What on Earth–?!"

"My bad," Nayan groaned in Uygur as he lay sprawled out across the table. He lifted the sachet of coins in the air, glancing at the wealthy Armenian lady. Switching to her tongue, he continued, "I came to return this to you. Sorry for dropping in like this."

The woman's sharp gaze appraised him in silence, her expression unreadable. Finally, she spoke. "You're that beggar from the street. A Uygur who knows our tongue? I'm impressed."

"I'm neither a Uygur nor a beggar," Nayan said defensively. "Now, are you gonna take back your money or what?"

The Tales of Abel and Mitra

"Not a Uygur?" The woman asked, ignoring his question. "Then what are you? You don't look Han."

Nayan flashed a dazzling grin, pushing himself into a seated position, though remained on the table. "I, my lady, am a prince of the Keraite Clan! Ever heard of Princess Sorghaghtani, also known as Empress Xianyi Zhuangsheng?"

"Of course," the woman replied. "Who hasn't? She was the mother of Kublai Khan and one of the most powerful women in history."

"Well," Nayan puffed out his chest. "I'm her great-great nephew!"

The woman looked him up and down. "And the descendant of such a noble lineage spends his days crashing into high-end establishments?"

"I told you–I came to return your money!" He thrust the pouch out to her.

The woman cocked her head, and Hetoum stepped forward, accepting the sachet on her behalf.

"I suppose this would cover the cost of the meal you just ruined," the woman said. "Or half of it, at least."

"Half?!" Nayan cried in disbelief. He turned to the older gentleman, switching over to speaking Uygur. "How expensive is the food here?!"

"More than your life is worth," the man spat.

"Gentlemen," the woman interrupted with a sly smile. "There is no need for insults. I have a proposition."

Nayan leaned in, worried about what she might suggest.

The woman gestured toward the young Armenian by her side. "Hetoum seems to have difficulty translating the nuances of my conversation with Mister Tursun."

Yisei Ishkhan

"I'm sorry, my lady!" Hetoum stammered. "I only learned the Turpan dialect of Uygur, but this man is from Kashgar!"

"No need to apologize," the woman smiled warmly. "You've done well, but why don't you take a break. Our Keraite friend here has, quite literally, fallen into our laps at an opportune moment." She turned to Nayan expectantly. "If you can help me strike a deal with our business partner, I will consider the cost of this meal covered."

"Fine, fine," sighed Nayan. "I'll do it."

"Excellent," the woman clapped. "Mister Tursun, shall we proceed?"

The Uygur gentleman was less than enthused to have their uninvited guest remain at the table with them. But as Nayan went to work, effortlessly translating their conversation, the tension eased. Mister Tursun ran a silk factory in a nearby town, and the wealthy businesswoman hoped to buy a portion of his goods to sell to the West. Nayan skillfully managed to navigate negotiations until the two came to an agreement that benefited both parties.

By the end of the evening, Mister Tursun had his arm over Nayan's shoulder, shoving a cup of alcohol in his face. For the first time in his life, Nayan thought he'd had too much to drink.

The Armenian woman raised a toast. "To a successful business venture."

"Yes!" Mister Tursun bellowed, raising his cup. "More to drink!"

Nayan shook his head with a chuckle as he rose from the table. "As tempting as that sounds, I'd better be on my way. Pleasure doing business with you."

The Tales of Abel and Mitra

"Wait a moment," the businesswoman interjected. "You never told me your name. I might wish to employ your services in the future. Translators of your skill are rare to come by, even in a city like Zaitun."

"The name's Nayan," he gave a dramatic bow. "But most know me by my Chinese alias, Ke Khoang-wen. No fixed address, but if you ask around for the dashing young Keraite, someone's bound to point you in the right direction."

"No fixed address?" The woman mused. "So, you *are* a beggar after all?"

"I prefer 'vagabond.' There's a difference."

"Of course," a flash of amusement crossed the woman's face. "How about I make you an offer? Work for me, and I'll give you pay. I assume you're fluent in Mongol and Hokkien as well, which puts at least four languages under your belt. I'll need a translator next week for negotiations with a Mongol nobleman. What do you say?"

"Pay is nice," Nayan nodded as he considered the offer, "but I'd prefer a roof over my head."

"That can be arranged."

Nayan took out the single bronze coin he'd been holding onto, giving it a flick into the air. It landed blank side up on his hand. He smiled.

"Deal."

"Wonderful," the woman folded her hands together. "Hetoum, why don't we escort our friend to his new living quarters?"

"Of course, my lady," the boy replied.

"And what should I call you, boss?" Nayan wondered. "Now that we'll be working together."

Yisei Ishkhan

"You may call me Anahit," smiled the woman. "Anahit Hovhannisyan."

***

The living arrangements Anahit had in mind happened to be an abbey at Surb Grigor Cathedral in the Armenian Quarter. Nayan recognized the building from the time he'd spent in the district a couple of years earlier, but the abbey was a new addition.

After bidding farewell to Anahit for the night, Hetoum led Nayan to meet his uncle, an abbot by the name of Vartan Nazaryan.

"So, Lady Hovhannisyan sent you here, did she?" Vartan stroked his long, white beard. "You know, she was our generous benefactor who made the construction of this abbey possible. Without her charitable donations, we never would've been able to afford such an expansion."

"I knew that woman was loaded," Nayan muttered to himself in Mongol.

"What was that?" Vartan wondered.

"Nothing," Nayan replied in Armenian. "I'm just impressed, that's all. I remember when this space behind the church was just an empty lot."

"Yes," Vartan said in disapproval. "It was a squatting ground for beggars and delinquents. By the way, how is it that you came to speak our tongue? Typically, it is us Armenians who pick up the tongues of the lands we travel to. It is rare to hear a foreigner speak our language so fluently."

Nayan shifted uncomfortably, recalling how he spent his youth among the very squatters that Vartan had derided a moment ago. His gang had been a wild mix of Armenians, Alans, Persians, Sogdians, and Syrian youths.

The Tales of Abel and Mitra

"Oh, you know," Nayan beamed. "I've had friends from every corner of this city. Armenian is just one of the many tongues I've picked up over the years."

"You said you were a Keraite, didn't you? One of the Christian tribes? They are followers of the Church of the East, if I'm not mistaken."

"Indeed," said Nayan. "I was brought up in the Church, but you know how us Mongols are when it comes to religion. My uncle was a follower of Tengri who had a Christian wife and a Manichean mistress; his sons grew up to be Buddhists and Muslims, and no one batted an eye."

Vartan nodded knowingly. "Surb Grigor is an Apostolic church. We are not in communion with Catholicos in Baghdad. Nevertheless, I hope you feel welcomed during your stay with us."

"Don't worry about me," Nayan smiled. "I don't get hung up on doctrinal differences."

Vartan gave him a tour of the abbey, pointing out their many facilities: a chapel, dorms for the monks and nuns, a soup kitchen, an orphanage, a school, and even a small hospital.

"You've got quite the operation here," Nayan noted.

"Indeed," sighed Vartan. "There is much work to be done to serve the needs of the community." They came to a room at the end of the corridor. "These will be your quarters."

Now this is what I've been craving, Nayan sighed to himself. He fell asleep as soon as his head hit the pillow.

Over the next week, as he awaited his meeting with Anahit, Nayan busied himself helping in the soup kitchen and orphanage. While the food was bland–no alcohol, roasted lamb, or fried desserts in sight–he wasn't complaining. Three solid meals a day was a luxury for a man who had grown used to going to sleep hungry.

Hetoum, who turned out to be one of the monks residing at the abbey, showed Nayan the ropes around the place.

"How long have you been a monk at this abbey?" Nayan asked him one day.

"Three years," the boy replied. "I've been here since it first opened. I had no other family, so Uncle Vartan took me in from off the streets."

"Were you born in Zaitun?"

Hetoum nodded. "So were my parents and grandparents. But our ancestors came from Antioch before the city was destroyed."

"Antioch," Nayan mused. "I had a friend that we called Antioch when I was younger. Actually, he's the one who taught me Armenian. I can't recall what his actual name was…"

"My brother used to be called Antioch by his friends," Hetoum piped up. "And since I was his younger brother, they would call me 'Little Antioch.'"

"No way!" Nayan's face lit up. "You're Little Antioch?!"

Hetoum pulled back from the man in surprise. "That's just what they called me…"

"We all used to call one another by nicknames in our gang," Nayan laughed. "There was Tarson, and Tabriz, and Shiraz, and Samarkand. They used to call me Khanbaliq, even though I've never been to the capital and doubt I have any relatives there."

"You're Khanbaliq?" Hetoum's eyes sparkled.

"So, you remember me!"

The Tales of Abel and Mitra

"Vaguely..." said the boy. "I was still just a child back then."

"It must've been five or six years since I last saw that group..." Nayan mused. "How's your brother? What's he up to these days?"

Hetoum shook his head. "It must've been *eight* years since you last saw him. He died eight years ago."

Nayan froze. "No...he's dead? I'm so sorry, I didn't know. What happened?"

"He got mixed up with the wrong people," Hetoum said. "They...they never found out who did it. The gang broke up soon after. Samarkand and Shiraz looked after me for a while before passing me onto Uncle Vartan."

"I must've left just a few months before he died..." Nayan said. "I remember your brother started hanging out with the wrong crowd. I warned him against them, and we had a huge fight about it. I stormed off to the Uygur Quarter for a while, just to take some time alone. When I returned, everyone was gone. No names, no leads–I couldn't track any of the gang down. Eight years...I can't believe it..."

"My brother really looked up to you," Hetoum said suddenly. "After you left, he realized you were right. He tried to break off from those gangs, but one of them came after him."

"I'm sorry..." Nayan muttered. "I shouldn't have run off."

"It isn't your fault," Hetoum murmured.

"It is, in a way," Nayan sighed, running his hand through his hair. "Whenever things don't go my way, I run off on my own. It's a bad habit. Even when I bumped into you and Lady Hovhannisyan the other day, I was only in that part of town because I'd cheated a couple of guys in the Korean Quarter out of a meal. I'm terrible, aren't I?"

"My brother always said you were a bit of a lone wolf," a small smile flashed across Hetoum's lips. "He said you had trouble trusting people and felt like you could only depend on yourself."

Nayan shrugged. "I can't say he was wrong. But those days I spent with you guys were the closest I've ever felt to having a family."

"My brother would've said the same thing."

"What was his real name?" Nayan asked. "We only ever called him Antioch."

"Davit," Hetoum replied. "Davit Nazaryan."

"Davit," Nayan chuckled. "He didn't look like a Davit. If you ask me, *he'd* make a better Hetoum, and *you* a better Davit."

Hetoum flushed. "W-what's *that* supposed to mean?"

"Nothing," Nayan laughed. "I just think the name would suit you better."

"Well…well, *you* don't look much like a prince!" Hetoum shot back.

Nayan burst into laughter. "I can't argue with you there."

***

Nayan met up with Anahit later that week just outside the Mongol Quarter.

"Before we go," he said, "I have a request to make. Don't tell anyone who I am. If they ask, you can call me Ke Khoang-wen. But I'd rather they didn't know I'm a Keraite prince. Or a Mongol, for that matter."

The Tales of Abel and Mitra

Anahit crossed her arms. "I would have thought that your status as a prince might benefit us in dealing with a Mongol nobleman."

Nayan grinned sheepishly. "Let's just say I don't have the best reputation around the Mongol Quarter."

"Is there anywhere you *do* have a positive reputation?" Anahit chuckled. "I don't care about your background. As long as you do your job, I won't ask questions."

Nayan hadn't stepped foot in the Mongol Quarter for over a decade and couldn't help but feel nervous as he strolled through the familiar streets. He'd only been a boy when he was last here and doubted anyone would recognize him. Still, he kept his head down.

Much to his relief, their destination was only a couple blocks away. The nobleman, Qurchaquz, was a Naiman who hailed from the capital. Rather than the local Hokkien, he spoke in the formal, northern dialect of Chinese, a tongue Nayan hadn't used since his youth. Luckily, Nayan retained command of the language.

Anahit's discussions with Qurchaquz involved dealings with the import of ivory from Aden. It was a lucrative business that Anahit was only just getting involved with, and Qurchaquz promised her a loan in exchange for a discounted rate on ivory imports. Anahit agreed, and they signed a deal the same day.

As they departed the Mongol Quarter, Nayan had regained his usual swagger. "You seem to have connections all over the city," he remarked. "How long have you been in Zaitun?"

"About five years," said Anahit.

Yisei Ishkhan

"Five years!" Nayan gasped. "And you still don't speak any of the Chinese tongues?"

"I have no need," Anahit replied. "There are Armenians all over the world. Everywhere I have gone, I can find someone to translate the local tongue for me. Originally, I hail from Constantinople, but I've spent time in Persia, Syria, Yemen, and Malabar before coming to Zaitun. Imagine how much time I'd waste if I tried to learn the native tongue of every land I visited. I'd have learned half a dozen by now."

"Amateur," Nayan laughed. "I know at least *twice* that many tongues, and I've spent my entire life here in Zaitun!"

Anahit flashed him a skeptical glance, but soon, the young man was speaking in a dizzying array of languages: the local Hokkien dialect, Armenian, Mongol, Arabic, Persian, Sogdian, Greek, Uygur, and several other Turkic languages Anahit didn't recognize. He even tossed in a couple of words in Frankish for good measure.

"Perhaps God has graced you with the gift of tongues," Anahit mused. She pulled forth the contract she'd signed with Qurchaquz. "But this is where *my* gifts lay."

"Money is great," Nayan admitted, "but it isn't everything. You might be a woman who has traveled the world, but *I'm* a man who has actually *lived* in those worlds! You can't truly understand someone unless you're immersed in their culture. When I stroll through the Persian bazaars or the Arab souks, I feel I'm walking the streets of Isfahan or Baghdad. When I haggle with the Sogdian and Greek merchants, I get a small taste of life in Samarkand and Constantinople!"

"Have you really never lived outside the city?" Anahit wondered. "I find that difficult to believe."

The Tales of Abel and Mitra

"Why is that?" Nayan smirked. "What *I* find difficult to believe is a woman as well-traveled as yourself can only speak her native tongue. You said you hail from Constantinople, didn't you? Surely you at least know a bit of Greek."

"I resided in Constantinople's Armenian Quarter," she admitted. "I know the basics, but you sound like you have a better command of the language than I do. I don't have time to immerse myself in local cultures; not when I'm the one running my business."

"Oh?" Said Nayan. "Are you the one running Lusavorich Imports?"

"Who else would be?"

Nayan shrugged. "I assumed your husband was in charge."

"I don't have a husband. He passed away a decade ago. I inherited his company and turned it into Lusavorich Imports."

"Ten years? I'm sorry to hear that. Was it during the Great Plague?"

"It was just before the Great Plague struck," Anahit clarified. "He was already an old man by the time we married. He knew he only had a few years left, and he had no family of his own. He was a friend of my father and wanted to pass on the business to someone he could trust. Our marriage was purely transactional."

"I see. And you never had children?"

"We couldn't," she said briskly. "Well, I suppose that isn't *exactly* true. But neither of us had an interest in consummating our marriage. Though, I wouldn't have minded children."

"I see…" Nayan blinked, trying to process her words. "Then who will inherit Lusavorich Imports when you can no longer run it?"

Yisei Ishkhan

She shrugged. "The Nazaryans are distant relatives of mine, and there's plenty of them scattered all over the world. I suppose I'll pass it on to one of them."

"Must be nice to have something to pass on to your descendants," Nayan sighed. "I've always wanted a family of my own, but what's the point if I can't give them a decent life? I wouldn't want them to struggle to get by like I have."

Anahit furrowed her brow. "I don't mean to pry, but if you're truly a Keraite prince as you claim, what are you doing on the streets? The Keraite nobles have a grand estate in the Mongol Quarter. Are you not welcome there?"

"It's a long story," Nayan flashed a wry smile. "To put it simply, I was disowned."

"Oh? And what did you do to deserve that?"

"Have you heard of Prince Shiktur?"

"Well, of course. He's one of the most prominent nobles in the city."

"He's my father."

Anahit frowned, a flicker of curiosity flashing through her eyes. She shook her head. "I don't follow. Care to enlighten me?"

"During the reign of Kublai Khan, our family took part in a rebellion led by a prince named Nayan."

"Your namesake?" Anahit guessed.

Nayan nodded. "Prince Nayan rebelled against Kublai Khan because he was disillusioned with Chinese influence in the Mongol court and wanted to preserve our traditional ways. My grandfather took part in this rebellion as a young man. After they were defeated, Prince Nayan was executed, and my grandfather exiled here, to Zaitun. You can imagine how

The Tales of Abel and Mitra

terrible a fate that would've been for a man like him. He wanted nothing more than for our people to return to traditional life on the steppe. Instead, he was banished to the most cosmopolitan city in the world. He isolated himself within his estate, raising his family to detest everything and everyone who wasn't Mongol. I grew up in that gilded cage, cut off from the rest of the world. I'd never even met someone who wasn't Mongol before I snuck out at age thirteen."

Nayan beamed. "Imagine my shock when I stepped into the real world and discovered how different the world was from the one I knew. There were people who spoke different tongues, ate different foods, wore different clothes, and even looked completely different from me. I started to sneak out regularly, making friends with all sorts of different people. Eventually, I met a girl…"

"Anahit chuckled. "I was wondering when romance would come into this."

"She was Southern Han from a prominent family," Nayan said, a wistful smile creeping across his face. "You've probably heard of them, so I won't mention them by name. But I'm sure you can imagine how taboo our relationship was. Mongols are the highest caste. Beneath us are the *Semu*–Turks, Persians, Arabs, and others who surrendered early in the Mongol conquests. Below them are the Northern Han, descendants of the Jin Dynasty. But the Southern Han…" Nayan shook his head, "they're the lowest caste. They descend from the Song Dynasty, the last to surrender to the Mongols. My family had disdain for all who were not Mongol–and for the Southern Han most of all."

"My servants knew that I'd been sneaking away from home. When my parents found out, they began to say all sorts

Yisei Ishkhan

of nasty things about everyone who wasn't Mongol. They thought that their fearmongering would persuade me against interacting with outsiders. It had the opposite effect. Now that I had met people on the outside, I knew that everything my parents said was nonsense. Sure, perhaps there's a bit of truth to any stereotype. But that's just what they are—stereotypes. It isn't fair to paint an entire group of people with a negative brush because of what a handful of them are like. But that's exactly what my parents were doing, and I'd had enough of it. I told them I was in love with a Southern Han girl. It was more to spite them than anything else. You can imagine how the rest of the story goes."

"And the girl?" Anahit pressed. "Was she worth all the trouble?"

"Hardly," Nayan laughed. "She couldn't have left me any quicker once she learned I wouldn't inherit anything from my family."

Anahit's expression softened. "It's a shame that 'love' often goes no deeper than wealth or status."

Nayan shrugged. "She taught me an important lesson about the world—you can't rely on anyone but yourself. I suppose that's why I don't easily place my trust in others."

"You seem to trust me well enough," Anahit pointed out.

"Well, sure. I knew you were dependent on me for my translation skills, so you wouldn't be so quick to abandon me. If I found out you were a shady character, I could always bail on you with nothing to lose. I'd just end up back on the streets where I started."

Anahit smirked. "Even if I no longer had need of your services, I'm sure Vartan and the abbey would continue offering you a place to stay."

The Tales of Abel and Mitra

"So, what you're saying is that I'm essentially working for you for free?"

Anahit shrugged. "I offered to pay you, didn't I?"

"Perhaps I'll take you up on that offer then," Nayan grinned. "How much are we talking?"

She produced a sachet and tossed it at him. "Would that suffice for each time I commission your services?"

Nayan peeked inside. His eyes widened. "This much for *one* meeting? This could get me through a *month*!"

"I can reduce the pay if you insist."

"Nope, I'll take it," Nayan stashed the sachet in his pocket. "When's our next meeting?"

Anahit chuckled. "Three days from now, in the Korean Quarter."

"Korean?" Nayan shrunk. "That's just about the last place in the city I'd like to be."

"Let me guess–bad reputation?"

"Something like that."

"Well," Anahit pulled out a coin from her pocket, flicking it in Nayan's direction. He caught it in his palm. Blank side up. "Maybe you should start cleaning up that reputation."

***

Over the next few months, Nayan and Anahit fell into a comfortable rhythm. Twice a week, she'd commission him for his translation services, paying him generously each time. Instead of squandering his newfound income on alcohol and fancy meals as he did in his youth, he saved up enough money to rent a small room. His new place was just down the street from Surb Grigor Cathedral, at the crossroads between the Armenian, Sogdian, and Uygur Quarters. It wasn't much, but it was the first place he could call his own.

Yisei Ishkhan

Ever since he'd met Anahit, things looked to be making a turn for the better. He had a stable income, a comfortable place to live, and people he could rely on. He took her advice, going about the various districts he'd spent time in over the years and making atonements for his past where he could. He paid back the three men in the Korean Quarter for the meal he'd cheated them out of and gave Miss Gyeonghwa enough money that she could buy her way out of servitude and return to Korea like she'd always wanted. He even introduced Anahit to Baklava Lady, and Anahit offered the woman a loan to open her own shop in the Persian Quarter.

But across the empire, dark clouds were gathering on the horizon.

"Did you hear the news from the north?" Anahit whispered under her breath as she and Nayan strolled through the Uygur Quarter one day. They were on their way to the Indian Quarter for another business deal.

"You have more connections across the empire than I do," Nayan said. "What happened?"

"Zhu Yuanzhang seized control of Jiankang a few days ago."

Nayan frowned. "Never heard of him. Is he someone important?"

"A peasant boy turned Buddhist monk turned rebel insurgent. He's only a couple of years older than you."

Nayan scoffed. "So, he's gone from rags to riches, while I've gone from riches to rags. Why are you telling me this?"

"They say this could be the founding of a new dynasty."

Nayan brushed her comments aside. "They've been saying that for years. Rebellions pop up like weeds every other month–seizing a city here, getting crushed there. Often the

The Tales of Abel and Mitra

government doesn't even need to step in to deal with them; the movements tear themselves apart from within. I give this Zhu Yuanzhang two weeks before he loses control of Jiankang."

"This isn't like the other rebellions," Anahit said, her voice falling to a whisper. "They say Zhu joined forces with the Red Turbans and the White Lotus Society. Discontent is growing across the empire, not just in one or two provinces. Even here in Zaitun. If Zhu gains enough support, he could pose a serious threat to the Yuan Dynasty."

Nayan chuckled. "I never took you to be the type to lose sleep over politics."

"This isn't just politics. Rebellions and dynastic changes affect trade. This could be bad for business."

"Or," Nayan countered, "it could be ripe with opportunity. I'm sure an innovative woman like you could find a way to turn war into profit."

"This is serious," Anahit hissed. "The Mongol nobility comprises one or two percent of the empire's population. Do you know what could happen to someone like you if a Han-led dynasty takes the throne?"

Nayan gave a nonchalant shrug. "I'll worry about that when the time comes. Who knows? It might not even be in my lifetime."

"No dynasty lasts forever," Anahit muttered.

But as they made their way deeper into the Uygur Quarter, even Nayan couldn't ignore the shifting atmosphere. They passed by the Guangming Manichean Temple, where a group of *Semu* soldiers speaking in Arabic raided the premises. Icons and sacred texts were scattered across the courtyard, and trembling worshipers in their red robes and white veils didn't resist as the soldiers dragged them out and lined them up for interrogation. The Manicheans kept their gazes lowered, muttering silent prayers to themselves.

"Who leads this temple?" One of the soldiers barked in Persian with a thick Arabic accent.

Two terrified monks pointed their fingers at an older priest.

"Take him," the soldier ordered.

"Wait, please!" The priest pleaded in broken Persian. "I did nothing wrong!"

"What's going on here?" A voice echoed from down the street.

Before the soldiers could drag him away, a second group of *Semu* soldiers emerged from around the block. Their leader, a young man, spoke in clear Persian with a Bukharan accent. Something about the man seemed familiar–Nayan was sure he'd seen him patrolling these streets before.

"None of your business, Shiite," spat the Arab.

The Persian bristled. "It very much *is* my business. I'm Faisal al-Bukhari, and my contingent oversees security in the Uygur Quarter. Under whose authority are you harassing worshipers here?"

The Arab unfurled a scroll. "The *governor's* authority. You and your men are dismissed."

Faisal stiffened. His eyes went wide as he glanced over the scroll in disbelief. "That...may be. But you still can't arrest civilians without evidence!"

"Oh, but we *do* have evidence," the Arab sneered as he rolled up the scroll. "The Guangming Manichean Temple

The Tales of Abel and Mitra

harbours sympathizers of the White Lotus Cult and the Red Turban Insurgents."

"Lies!" The Manichean priest cried. "We would never associate with *heretics*!"

The soldier's lips curled. "Save it for the interrogators." Turning back to Faisal, he added, "As for you, Shiite, I'd be on my way if I were you."

Faisal hesitated, glaring down at the other man. After a tense moment, he cursed under his breath, motioning for his men to fall back.

Anahit and Nayan watched in silence as the soldiers dragged the priest and several other Manichean worshipers into custody.

"What was that?" Anahit demanded, turning to Nayan expectantly as she waited for him to translate what they'd just witnessed.

"I…have no idea…" Nayan muttered.

As they continued toward the Indian Quarter, Anahit's words from earlier echoed in his mind: *No dynasty lasts forever.*

***

Nayan was distracted during their meeting in the Indian Quarter later that day. The rich aroma of sandalwood incense filled the air, causing his mind to drift. His thoughts still lingered on what he and Anahit had stumbled across in the Uygur Quarter on their way there.

"Nayan?" Anahit's sharp voice pierced through his reverie. She leaned closer, snapping her fingers in front of his face. "Nayan!"

He blinked, sitting up straighter as he came back to focus. "Sorry, what was that?"

Yisei Ishkhan

Anahit cleared her throat. "You haven't translated what Mister Soroushian just said."

Nayan flushed. He turned to their host, a Parsi incense merchant from India, and bowed his head. "I apologize," he said in Persian, "could you repeat that?"

"Of course," Sohrab Soroushian offered a forgiving smile. "I was saying that I have a facility down in Kochi. If Lady Hovhannisyan is interested, we could discuss adding the city to her trade route."

Nayan quickly translated the offer into Armenian.

"Kochi?" Anahit nodded. "I have connections there. It's a possibility I'm open to exploring."

"Excellent," Sohrab said. His attention shifted to Nayan. "Lady Hohvannisyan isn't the only reason I requested this meeting. Ke Khoang-wen, yes? I've heard much about you these past few weeks. They say you can speak a dozen languages."

Nayan leaned back in his seat, counting on his fingers. "More or less," he beamed. "I wouldn't say I'm *fluent* in them all, but I know enough to get by."

"Fabulous," Sohrab bobbed his head. "I could use someone with your talents. Over the coming months, I will require a translator familiar with Armenian, Greek, Mongol, and Uygur. You happen to know all four of them. What do you say?"

Nayan flashed a glance at Anahit. "I'll consider it."

"Lovely," Sohrab clapped. "You look pale, Mister Ke. Would you like some tea?"

"That'd be lovely."

The Tales of Abel and Mitra

Sohrab called out to the next room, and a moment later, a young woman emerged with a tray of tea. She moved with grace, her striking features catching Nayan's attention: fair skin, dark almond-shaped eyes, rose-petal lips, and silky black hair. Nayan studied her intently, unable to determine what her ancestry might be.

"Thank you," Nayan said as she placed a cup in front of him. For a fleeting moment, their eyes met. A soft blush crept up her cheeks before she averted her gaze and retreated to the other room.

"My daughter," Sohrab beamed. "Nasrin."

"Oh?" Nayan nodded, taking a sip of his tea. "I would've never guessed."

Sohrab chuckled. "We get that a lot. Her mother is a native of Zaitun, a Southern Han woman. Nasrin doesn't resemble either of us."

"She is lovely," said Nayan. "Does she speak Persian?"

"Fluently. She knows Gujarati and Hokkien as well."

"Impressive," a playful smile tugged at Nayan's lips. "Is she married?"

Sohrab chuckled at his boldness. "My wife and I have been searching for a suitor, but she's turned down all our suggestions."

"Well," Nayan beamed. "I happen to know a bachelor or two."

Anahit cleared her throat. "It seems the two of you are having an interesting conversation without me. Care to translate?"

Nayan faltered, hastily switching back to Armenian. "Mister Soroushian says he's in need of my services," he lounged in his seat, twirling his lucky bronze coin between his fingers. "What do you think? Should I take him up on his offer?"

"That depends. Are you looking to make extra money?" A look of amusement crossed Anahit's face as she glanced at the door Nasrin disappeared behind. "Or do you have other intentions?"

Nayan shrugged. "That remains to be seen."

"The choice is yours to make," said Anahit. "You aren't bound to my services."

"In that case..." Nayan straightened, the coin still twirling between his nibble fingers. He tossed it into the air, its metallic gleam catching the light. It landed in his palm, blank side up. He turned to Sohrab, switching back to Persian. "I'll take you up on your offer."

***

Anahit's concerns regarding the political stability of the empire began to materialize over the following years. However, it wasn't the Red Turbans rebels led by Zhu Yuanzhang in the north that posed the most immediate threat to her business. In 1357, war erupted closer to home as Zaitun found itself at the heart of a new rebellion.

The seeds of this unrest were sown the day Nayan and Anahit witnessed *Semu* soldiers ransacking the Guangming Manichean Temple in the Uygur Quarter. Unlike the northern rebellions linked to the White Lotus Society, the Zaitun uprising was rooted in an entirely different sectarian conflict. It was sparked by the replacement of Persian soldiers with Arabs by the governor. This shift in power ignited tensions that had long been simmering beneath the surface.

Zaitun's Persian community had been established in the city in the early years of Mongol rule following the conquest

The Tales of Abel and Mitra

of the Song Dynasty. The Mongols employed a strategic policy of relocating soldiers and officials from one disparate part of the empire to the other, ensuring their loyalties lay with the emperor rather than local populations. Thus began Zaitun's emergence as a bustling port city. From its harbours, goods ranging from ivory, incense, precious metals, silk, ceramics, and ore flowed between China and distant lands. So too did people. From Japan to Java, India to Europe, foreigners flocked to Zaitun, drawn by the allure of wealth and opportunity.

Eventually, the city's Arab community rose in influence, unsettling the Persians, who feared losing their long-held dominance. Violence swept the city in waves of interethnic strife. In one instance, an Arab garrison was attacked, leading not only to the deaths of the soldiers stationed there but hundreds of innocents in the neighbouring districts. The Arabs retaliated by burning down half a dozen Shiite mosques and schools in the Persian Quarter. This rising tension escalated into a full-scale rebellion when a Persian faction calling themselves the Ispah seized control of Zaitun, massacring the city's Mongol nobility and their allies.

Nayan had learned that the Keraites had fled the city early in the conflict, escaping the massacre. The irony wasn't lost on him–his ancestors' anti-Chinese rebellion had driven them into exile in Zaitun, and now an anti-Mongol rebellion had driven them out. To survive, Nayan was forced to conceal his heritage. He abandoned his Mongol braids, adopting a Chinese-style topknot instead, and was careful to only go by his Chinese alias, Ke Khoang-wen.

Once the Persians solidified their control over Zaitun and the surrounding regions, the violence subsided. But the city remained cloaked in uncertainty. The surviving Mongols had fled, and while some of the Arab officials and soldiers had departed for trade ports in Southeast Asia, most of Zaitun's population remained. Many of the common folk had resided in Zaitun for generations, and while they adjusted to life under their new Ispah overlords, Zaitun's position as a central hub for global trade quickly waned.

The Ispah continued expanding their influence across Jiangzhe Province, but how long would their success last? It was only a matter of time before the Yuan rallied a counteroffensive, or Zhu Yuanzhang's Red Turban rebels swept south.

By the third year after the Ispah takeover, Zaitun's fortunes had waned. Trade dried up, and those who could afford to leave did so while they still had the chance. Soon, Nayan found that the once bustling streets he'd been so familiar with growing up were unrecognizable. Whether in the Armenian, Korean, Uygur, or other districts, shops were shuttered, places of worship abandoned, and markets emptied as the once-great city fell to decay.

***

"Our meeting today is with the head of the Franciscan Order in the Latin Quarter," Anahit said. She and Nayan cut through the Armenian Quarter, keeping their eyes fixed ahead as they passed through the dilapidated streets. "In addition to his native tongue and Latin, he also speaks Frankish, Greek, Mongol, and Hokkien. You may choose whichever tongue you'd like to converse with him."

"Ah, the Latin Quarter," Nayan mused. "Now *there's* one district of the city I don't yet have a negative reputation in– only because I've hardly spent any time there."

The Tales of Abel and Mitra

"I'm surprised," Anahit said. "How did you manage to pick up Frankish?"

"There was a Frankish priest who used to linger around the Armenian Quarter back in the day. He wanted to convert me; I wanted to learn his tongue. A mutually beneficial agreement, though I must say I got more out of it than he did. He went back to Europe eventually."

"More might soon follow," said Anahit. "The Franciscans seem eager to leave the city as soon as possible. Most of them came here as missionaries, not merchants, so they have no ships of their own. They sent me a letter requesting that I offer them passage aboard one of my vessels bound for Constantinople."

"What about you?" Nayan tilted his head. It wasn't a discussion that he and Anahit had often, but as Zaitun's prospects continued to decline, the question became inevitable. "Are you considering leaving the city?"

Anahit paused for a moment. "Business has slowed under the Ispah, but leaving now would be premature. This current situation cannot last forever. When a new regime comes to power, trade may once again flourish. Besides," she gestured to the abandoned buildings, "with most of the competition gone, this may be the *best* time to be in business."

"Have you had any leads on the Arab merchant I asked you about?" Nayan wondered. "Hitham ibn Sulaiman?"

"Ah, yes. He and his family departed Zaitun about a year ago, resettling in one of the Majapahit vassal states."

"And his daughter?" Nayan pressed. "Soraya bint Hitham?"

"She was married to a wealthy spice merchant."

Yisei Ishkhan

"I see…" Nayan said with a wistful look in his eye. "I'm glad she's safe."

"An old lover?" Anahit wondered.

"The first woman I ever truly loved…"

Anahit chuckled. "I'll be sure not to share that with Nasrin Soroushian. How is your courtship going?"

"Splendid. Nasrin is perfect in every way, and I intend to marry her. But you know what they say—one never forgets their first love."

Anahit raised an eyebrow. "I never took you to be a hopeless romantic. So, when are you and Nasrin getting married? You've been courting for what—three years now? Most men have already been married by your age."

"Timing is everything," Nayan grinned. "After my experience with Soraya, I've learned how crucial it is to get a father's blessing before proposal."

"Oh, please. Everyone knows Sohrab adores you. If you put this off for another month, it might be *him* who comes to *you* first."

"These are complicated times," Nayan flipped his bronze coin in hand. "Sohrab's been talking about returning to India with his family. I'm not sure I'd want to follow them there. I've never left the *city*, let alone the *country*. This is the only place I've ever called home."

"There's an Armenian saying: 'It's better to be a poor man in your homeland than a king in a foreign land.' I don't entirely agree, but I understand the sentiment."

They arrived in the Latin Quarter. The Franciscans' cathedral was modest compared to Surb Grigor. Its design was simple but employed a blend of Western and Chinese architecture that Nayan found pleasant.

The Tales of Abel and Mitra

Before he could comment, the head of the Franciscans stepped out to greet them, a pale man with a large nose and a balding head.

"Greetings," he said in fluent Hokkien. "You must be Mister Ke and Lady Hovhannisyan? I'm Alessandro d'Aquila, the head priest here. Please, come in. Mister Ke, which tongue would you prefer to converse in? I've heard that you speak Frankish and Greek?"

"It's been ages since I've used either of them," Nayan chuckled. "Your Hokkien is fluent, so why don't we stick with that?"

Their meeting with the Latin priest was brief. With fewer than two hundred Europeans remaining in Zaitun, most of them Franciscan missionaries, it was easy for Anahit to arrange their passage on one of her ships back to Europe.

As they departed the cathedral, Anahit paused, spotting familiar faces in the courtyard. Nayan overheard a couple of women speaking in Armenian.

"Those are some old friends of mine," Anahit said. "Go ahead of me, I think I'll catch up with them."

"I promised to treat you to that Javanese restaurant tonight," Nayan said. "You said you wanted to try it."

"Ah, that's right."

"I'll wait for you here," Nayan said. "I've never been inside a Latin church before. I think I'll look around."

"Don't get too comfortable," she called out, disappearing into the courtyard to join her friends.

The cathedral's interior was dim, its narrow nave lit only by faint candlelight as night set in. By the altar, a lone figure knelt, lighting a candle before an icon of Christ painted in a

Yisei Ishkhan

Chinese style. The sight intrigued Nayan; the parishioner didn't appear to be a foreigner.

"I hear your priests will all be returning to Europe within the next few weeks," Nayan said in Hokkien. "Will you be returning with them?"

"I'm native to this country," the man responded in Hokkien, speaking with a heavy northern accent. "There's no other place I'd rather be." The man rose, turning to face Nayan.

"You're Han?" Nayan wondered. "I don't see many Han attending Christian churches."

"I'm from Chang'an. My family comes from a long line that has practiced Jingjiao since the Tang Dynasty. But unfortunately, all the Jingjiao Churches have been closed in recent years. The Keraites were our patrons, but with the Mongols driven out of the city, there is no one left to keep them running. I decided that this Latin Church was the best alternative."

"Jingjiao..." Nayan repeated. "You mean the Church of the East? Well, what do you know! I too come from a family that follows that tradition."

"Oh, really?" The man's eyes lit up. "You don't look Han...are *you* a Keraite?"

Nayan ran his hand through his hair. "I tend not to boast of my heritage–especially in times like these."

"Of course," the man's voice fell to a whisper. "Forgive me for prying. My name is An Yu-sin. My wife is a native of Zaitun, but if the situation continues to deteriorate, we'll likely seek refuge in the north with my family back in Chang'an."

They continued to converse as Nayan awaited Anahit's return, discussing family, faith, and the challenges of their

The Tales of Abel and Mitra

uncertain times. When Anahit finally returned to fetch him for dinner, she had trouble pulling him away from his new friend. Nayan and Yu-sin bid one another farewell, promising to meet again.

"Fruitful discussion?" Anahit asked as they made their way to dinner.

"He's an interesting man," Nayan nodded. "He was brought up in the Church of the East like me, but recently converted to the Latin Church."

Anahit scoffed. "Those Latins are always stealing everyone else's flock."

"And how did your little reunion go?" Nayan asked.

"Delightful," she said, a trace of sarcasm in her tone. "Like your new friend, they're converts to the Latin Church. Of course, any *true* Armenian like myself can only be a follower of the Apostolic Church. *Our* Catholicos sits in Cilicia, not *Rome*."

Nayan chuckled. "The Latins seem to be the only ones interested in gaining converts. I don't think I've ever seen a Han or Mongol at Surb Grigor. As for followers of the Church of the East–they mostly inherited their faith from their ancestors, like me."

"We Armenians came here as merchants," said Anahit. "The Latins came as missionaries. I am in Zaitun to make money, not disciples."

"Those seem like reversed priorities," Nayan smirked. "To be honest, I find the Latin Church rather intriguing. Based on my conversation with An Yu-sin, they seem to have more theological overlap with the Church I grew up in than with yours."

Yisei Ishkhan

"Naturally," Anahit waved her hand dismissively. "Latins and Nestorians—you're both heretics. You divide Christ's nature in two, and then wonder why your churches divide into endless schisms."

"I don't know much about theology myself," Nayan admitted. "But if you ask me, it seems like the churches divide from one another over minutia. I think politics and culture have more to do with it than actual theology."

"You might be right about that," Anahit mused. "That's another strength *our* Church has over the Latins and Nestorians. The Latins want their Pope to be based in Rome; the Nestorians want their Catholicos to be based in Baghdad. You both forget that it isn't these men who are the head of the Church—it is Christ himself. We Armenians can have our Catholicos based Cilicia, and still be in full communion with the Syrian Patriarch and the Coptic Pope."

"Coptic?" Nayan repeated. "Who are they?"

Anahit turned to him. "You haven't met any Copts? There's a small community of them in the city. I'll introduce you to them sometime. They're the natives of Egypt, before the Arabs came in."

"I see. Then they have their own tongue, distinct from that of the Arabs?"

"They do. But Coptic is a dying language. Most of the Egyptians are still Copts, but Arabic has become the language of governance, trade, and education since the time of the Arab conquests. The Egyptians haven't been ruled by a native dynasty in nearly two millennia. First, they were conquered by the Persians, then the Greeks under Alexander, then the Romans, followed by the Arabs. The current rulers of Egypt are the Mamluks—Turkic slaves from the steppe."

The Tales of Abel and Mitra

Nayan grinned. "We steppe nomads rule almost the whole world, don't we?"

"I don't know if you could still consider yourself a steppe nomad," Anahit scoffed. "You speak Chinese, dress Chinese, have a Chinese hairstyle and a Chinese lifestyle."

Nayan puffed out his chest. "I'm still a Mongol by blood and a Mongol at heart."

"Perhaps," Anahit shrugged. "But the woman you're courting is half-Chinese, and if you raise your children here, they will likely grow up speaking Chinese. In a couple of generations, your descendants might forget they had Mongol ancestors at all."

A wry smile spread across Nayan's face. "Maybe my family wasn't wrong to fear that our culture would die out. Chinggis Khan set out to conquer China. But in the end, China will conquer us."

***

Over the next few years, the Ispah began losing ground as Yuan forces pushed them back. Their movement fractured into infighting, and as they lost their grip on power, anarchy ensued. Zaitun's fortunes continued to decline, with trade drying up as famine and disease struck the city. One night, a massive fire broke out, consuming large parts of the foreign quarters. The blaze was blamed on Han loyalists of the Yuan, sparking a wave of brutal retaliation as Han homes and businesses were looted and destroyed.

Amid the chaos, Nayan had grown close to An Yu-sin, even beginning to attend the Latin Church with him and his wife. When their neighbourhood was engulfed in violence, Nayan offered them and their newborn son refuge. He'd recently moved into a new residence in the Armenian Quarter, with more than enough room to accommodate them.

Yisei Ishkhan

"It's awful out there!" Cried Kong Thai-cheng, An Yu-sin's wife. The woman clutched their young son as the family settled into Nayan's home for dinner on the night they moved in with him.

"I know," Nayan said gravely. "Sohrab is planning to leave the city. So is Anahit."

"Surely they'll at least wait until after your wedding," Yu-sin said. "It's less than a month away."

"They will," Nayan nodded. "But after that…they may only be around for a couple more weeks."

"Won't Sohrab want his daughter to leave with him?" Thai-cheng wondered.

"Of course," Nayan sighed. "But I'm not sure I want to leave China. I know you understand my sentiment. This is the only place in the world I could ever feel at home. Nasrin said she'd leave the decision up to me. I still don't know what we should do."

"You could come with us to Chang'an," Thai-cheng offered.

Nayan turned to him in surprise. "Are you leaving too?"

Yu-sin glanced at his wife. "We're planning to leave the week after your wedding."

Nayan sank back in his seat with a wistful smile, turning his cup of wine in his hand. "So, everyone's abandoning ship. I might be the last man left standing in Zaitun."

Shouts suddenly erupted from the street outside–a cacophony of voices screaming in several different tongues. Thai-cheng flinched, clutching her son closer to her chest. A violent knock echoed through the house from the front door.

"Stay here," Nayan hissed. "I'll see what's going on."

The Tales of Abel and Mitra

He rose from the table, slipping a knife into his hand as he inched his way down the corridor. These days, one could never be too cautious when answering the door to a stranger.

He froze. Blood was seeping through the cracks of the door. He threw it open to find three *Semu* soldiers on the other side. They fell over the threshold. Two were already dead, but the third was breathing faintly, barely clinging to life. Blood poured from a deep wound as a blade remained embedded in his side, splattering across Nayan's robes as he collapsed atop the prince and knocked them both to the ground.

Tai-cheng shrieked as she glimpsed the scene from down the hall. Yu-sin rushed over, rolling the injured *Semu* man off Nayan and slamming the door shut.

"What in Heaven's name is going on?!"

"I have no idea," Nayan pushed himself to his feet. "But this man needs to be treated, or he'll bleed out."

"I'll handle it," Yu-sin assured. "Just keep my family safe."

Nayan nodded, taking Tai-cheng and their son back to the dining hall.

Tai-cheng's sobs filled the room as she clung to her child. "What happened to this city? When I was a girl, Zaitun was the greatest city in the world! People came here from all over to build a better life for themselves! How did it come to this?"

Nayan paused, leaning in the doorway as he muttered to himself. "Every Golden Age comes to an end. The only certainty in life is uncertainty."

***

Yu-sin had managed to stabilize the man's injuries by morning and even arranged for the two corpses of the dead *Semu* to be sent off to the morgue. Nayan remained by the injured soldier's bedside for most of the day, until finally, the man's eyes fluttered open that evening.

"Where am I?" He groaned in Persian. He was around Nayan's age, with a short black mustache and beard, and thick lashes. His features would have been handsome if it weren't for the cuts and bruises he'd sustained and his pale complexion from blood loss.

"You're in my house," Nayan said. "You're safe here. Can you tell me what happened? You were banging on my door last night with two other men. Both of them are dead now."

"Salim and Farid," the man murmured, his voice heavy. "They were good men...loyal soldiers..." He clenched his jaw, struggling to hold back tears.

Nayan placed a comforting hand on his shoulder. "Are you with the Ispah?"

The soldier's eyes narrowed. "So what if I am? Are you going to kill me like those thugs in the street killed my men?"

"No. I'm not taking any sides in this conflict."

The soldier studied him warily before sighing. "Faisal al-Bukhari. That's my name. Thank you for taking me in. I'd be dead if I was left out in the streets."

"Faisal al-Bukhari...?" Nayan repeated. "Have we met before? Wait...yes. Didn't you patrol the Uygur Quarter before this chaos began?"

Faisal furrowed his brow. "Do I know you?"

"No, no. I was just passing by in the street that day. You're the one who confronted those soldiers who ransacked the Manichean temple!"

The Tales of Abel and Mitra

"No," Faisal interrupted. "I *do* know you! That voice, that accent. You're a Mongol, aren't you?"

Nayan froze. "How did you know?"

"Khanbaliq?" Faisal asked cautiously.

Nayan's eyes went wide. Then it hit him. "Shiraz?!"

The soldier's face broke into a grin. "It's really you?!"

"I can't believe it!" Nayan laughed. "You *actually* became a soldier like you always wanted!"

"And you…" Faisal glanced around the room. "You went from a scrappy street urchin to living in a place like this."

"I always said I was from a noble family, didn't I?" Nayan beamed. "I'm just returning to my roots."

Faisal pulled his old friend into a hug. "It's been so many years. I can't believe we ran across one another again."

"*I'm* surprised we didn't recognize one another sooner!" Nayan chuckled. "Now that I'm getting a better look at you, you really haven't changed much since we were kids."

"Nor have you," Faisal agreed. "It must be the beard. I grew mine out; you cut yours off."

"Last I remember, you *couldn't* grow one out," Nayan gave him a nudge. "Finally became a man, huh?"

Faisal slapped him on the shoulder. "I see that your banter hasn't changed."

Nayan smiled. "So, Faisal al-Bukhari, was it? Shiraz suits you much better. But why did you go by that name if you're originally from Bukhara?"

"Because Bukhara sounds lame," the Persian scoffed. "And your real name was…?"

"Nayan."

Yisei Ishkhan

Faisal nodded. "You look like a Nayan. It's a better name than Khanbaliq, at least."

Nayan sighed and shook his head. "I always *told* you guys I hated Khanbaliq, but you insisted? Speaking of the others, what happened to them? Tarson? Tabriz? Samarkand?"

"We disbanded after what happened to Antioch. Did you ever hear about him?"

"I did," Nayan said. "I reconnected with Hetoum–Little Antioch–just before the rebellion broke out."

"Little Antioch…" Faisal mused. "I haven't seen him in years. He must be all grown up now."

"He's a monk at Surb Grigor Cathedral," Nayan said. "Got a beard thicker than yours, too."

"Oh, shut up."

"It's true! So, about the others, did you lose touch?"

"Tabriz returned to Persia before the rebellion broke out. Samarkand became a traveling merchant along the Silk Road a couple of years ago. Tarson…I don't know what became of him, but I heard he was killed in the war."

"I see…" Nayan's shoulders slumped. "I always held onto the hope that we'd all be reunited someday…"

Faisal placed a hand on his friend's shoulder. "Maybe not all of us. But running into you again is still a miracle. That counts for something."

"I'm getting married in a month," Nayan blurted out. "Hetoum will be there, if you'd like to attend."

Faisal raised an eyebrow. "You? Married? Who's the unlucky lady?"

The Tales of Abel and Mitra

Nayan scoffed. "I always had better luck with women than you did. Actually, she's a Persian like yourself. Or half Persian, at least. Nasrin Soroushian."

"The daughter of the Parsi merchant from India?" Faisal's eyes went wide. "You're kidding. How'd you manage to snag a beauty like her?"

Nayan leaned back with a smirk. "Like I said, better luck with women than you."

They both laughed, the camaraderie of their old friendship rekindling. The night was filled with conversation as Nayan introduced Faisal to Yu-sin and Thai-cheng. Eventually, Faisal confessed that he'd been part of the Ispah movement but deserted after the original commanders were assassinated. He and his comrades had been ambushed in the street the previous night when their identities were discovered.

With nowhere else to go, Nayan offered his old friend refuge while he healed from his injuries. By the time Nayan's wedding came around, Faisal had recovered enough to attend the ceremony.

The ceremony was intimate, a gathering of close family and friends. From Nayan's side, Anahit, Vartan, Hetoum, and Yu-sin's family were the only ones in attendance. Nasrin had her parents and a couple of friends invited, but no more than two dozen were present for the service. They held the ceremony at Surb Grigor, with Vartan presiding over the vows.

The feast in the cathedral's courtyard was a joyous occasion but tinged with bittersweet farewells. As the guests dined under the glow of lantern light, Nayan stood to raise a toast.

Yisei Ishkhan

"To friends, old and new. To family, whether by blood or by choice. And to Zaitun, the city that brought us all together!"

"To Nayan and Nasrin," Anahit raised her cup. "After six years of waiting, I wasn't sure I'd live to see this day finally come."

The guests laughed, but a subtle melancholy hung in the air. Anahit and Sohrab had both decided that they would be leaving Zaitun in two days' time, departing south for the Majapahit Empire and eventually India.

As the festivities continued, Nayan rose from his seat and leaned toward Nasrin, his voice dropping to a whisper. "Go spend some time with your parents."

Nasrin looked up at him, her dark eyes glistening in the moonlight. "Where are you off to?"

Nayan smiled, his expression softening as he glanced across the table at Anahit. "To say farewell to someone without whom none of this would've been possible."

Nasrin nodded knowingly as she and her husband parted ways.

"To think," Nayan smirked as he approached Anahit, "that I'd find a wife before you found yourself a new husband."

Anahit chuckled. "I told you, I have no interest in men. Besides, I've built up Lusavorich Imports just fine without a man, wouldn't you agree?"

"You forget," Nayan gestured to himself, "how much *this man* contributed to cementing your trade deals."

Anahit smirked. "If only I hadn't tossed that sachet of coins to you that day."

The Tales of Abel and Mitra

"The Lord works in mysterious ways, doesn't he?"

Anahit took a sip of her wine, her smirk fading into a contemplative smile. She gazed up at the moon, luminous as it hung low in the night sky.

"Have you decided?" She asked gently. "Will you remain here, or will you head to India with Nasrin's parents?"

"Let's see," Nayan pulled the bronze coin from his pocket and held it up, its surface glimmering in the moonlight.

Anahit rolled her eyes. "You're not leaving your fate up to a coin toss, are you?"

"No," Nayan chuckled. "I've already made up my mind. But for old times' sake..." he gave the coin a toss, watching as it spun through the air. It landed blank side up.

"So?" Anahit asked. "What's the verdict?"

"I'm heading to Chang'an with Yu-sin and his family," said Nayan. "We're set to leave at the end of the week. Vartan plans to return to Constantinople with you, but Hetoum and Faisal both agreed to join me. It'll be like having my old gang back together again."

"Chang'an, huh?" Anahit mused. "It's the former capital of previous dynasties and the final stop along the old Silk Road. I suppose it's a fitting destination for you."

"You're always welcome to join us," said Nayan. "The land routes aren't as prosperous as they were in ancient times, but you can still make a profit."

"I appreciate the offer," Anahit smiled. "But I think it's finally time I returned to Constantinople. I've been gone for almost two decades, and I'm not young anymore. I'm thinking of retiring and passing on Lusavorich Imports to the Nazaryans."

Yisei Ishkhan

"*Retire?*" Nayan shook his head. "I can't imagine what you'd be doing if you weren't working."

"Who knows? Perhaps I'll become a nun."

"You? A nun?" Nayan laughed. "After all this time toiling away to amass wealth, and you plan to spend the rest of your years rejecting worldly fortunes?"

"What else would I spend it on?" Anahit shrugged. "I should found my own abbey in Constantinople–a proper, *orthodox*, *Armenian Apostolic* abbey–not a heretical Latin or Nestorian one." She flashed Nayan a grin.

Nayan tilted his head back, his eyes tracing the weathered roof of Surb Grigor Cathedral. "I wonder what will become of this place when all its worshipers are gone."

"Who can say?" Anahit shrugged. "It will likely fall into ruin, but it wouldn't be the first time our faith has died out in this land. The first missionaries reached China centuries ago at the height of the Tang Dynasty. But after the Great Tang collapsed, it vanished, only to return one day with you Keraites riding down from the steppe alongside Chinggis Khan."

"It never fully vanished," Nayan noted. "An Yu-sin and his family have been followers of Jingjiao since the time of the Great Tang, even after all the churches were destroyed and the priests scattered."

"Then perhaps," said Anahit, "the faith will endure, waxing and waning like the cycles of the moon. Who knows? Maybe one day, new missions will revitalize the Church in this country. I only hope that when the time comes, it'll be missions sent by the *Apostolic* Church, and not the Latins or Nestorians."

The Tales of Abel and Mitra

"Only time will tell," Nayan chuckled. "We won't be around to see it, but our descendants might. Or *my* descendants, at least."

Anahit scoffed lightly. "If you ever have a daughter, I expect you to name her after me."

"*Hmm...*" Nayan grinned, pulling out the bronze coin from his pocket once again. "I'll consider it."

He gave the coin a flip.

Yisei Ishkhan

The Tale of Abel and Mitra

"What kind of story ends like that?" Esta rolled her eyes. She leaned back against the moss of the tree trunk, flicking pebbles down into the pools of water below.

"Where would you prefer that I end the story?" Mitra asked, the glint of a smile behind his eyes. "With Nayan and Anahit's deaths? Or shall I continue the narrative through Nayan and Nasrin's descendants?"

"Not with their *deaths*!" Esta exclaimed. "But you could at least give them a happier ending. Why do they have to part ways?"

"I am simply relaying their tale as it is recorded in my archives."

"All of Mitra's stories end like this," Abel chimed sheepishly. "Still, I'd like to know what happened to them after they left Zaitun–unless it's some tragic ending where they both die before even making it out."

"They left as planned," Mitra assured. "Anahit journeyed south to India before continuing to Constantinople. Nayan traveled north with his wife and the others. It is thanks to Nayan's meticulous records, passed down through his descendants, that their story found its way into my archives."

"And what happened to Zaitun?" Avi piped up. "Were the rebels successful?"

"Four years after Nayan and the others departed, the Yuan Emperor dispatched an army that recaptured Jiangzhe Province. The Ispah were crushed, and nearly all foreigners in the city were massacred. Had they stayed, Nayan and Anahit would've met the same fate, and their story would have died with them."

The Tales of Abel and Mitra

"So, Anahit was right," Avi muttered. "The Golden Age of Zaitun came to an end."

"It was not only Zaitun's time that came to an end. Two years after retaking the city, the Yuan were overthrown, and a new dynasty rose to power–the Great Ming. Zhu Yuanzhang, the peasant-turned-rebel leader of the Red Turbans, took the throne as the first Ming Emperor. He reunified the country, driving out the Mongols. In the coming generations, China became isolationist and closed off from the outside world, never again witnessing a period as cosmopolitan as Zaitun had been under the Yuan."

"What was it that Anahit said at the end of the story?" Abel ventured. "'Waxing and waning like the cycles of the moon'? What is a 'moon'?"

"Ah," Mitra chuckled, glancing up at the sky. "I suppose you would not understand the saying, seeing as your world lacks a moon of its own. Her analogy reflects the transient nature of all things in the world. They rise and fall in cycles, much like Dusk in your world gives way to Night, and Night gives way to Dawn."

As he spoke, rays of light cascaded across the sky: sapphire, lilac, cyan, and amber blended together in a manner reminiscent of the Aurora Borealis.

"Beautiful…" Mitra whispered.

Abel tugged at his sleeve. "Don't miss what's happening below!"

Mitra turned his gaze downward. Along the forest floor, a dazzling display of light unfolded. The golden glow of starflowers burned with an intensity surpassing that of their nocturnal brilliance. Around them, silver phoenixes flapped their wings lazily, their scales reflecting the iridescent hues in the sky above as they ascended.

Yisei Ishkhan

"Where are they going?" Mitra asked.

"They only spend the Night in the Valley to feed," Abel explained. "After that, they return to Darkside to lay their eggs. We'll see them again in six hundred hours when Night falls again."

"They won't be *these* ones," Avi said. "The ones that come back the next Night will be their offspring. Silver phoenixes don't live for more than one Cycle. When they fly back to Darkside, they're heading to their deaths."

"That's just a theory," Abel frowned. "No one's ever seen the full life cycle of a silver phoenix before, so it hasn't been confirmed."

Avi shrugged. "Noa did. Once, he found a silver phoenix that got trapped and couldn't make it back to Darkside before Dawn. He brought it home and took care of it, but it died after less than ten hours."

"Maybe they can't survive in the light," Esta suggested, twirling her finger through her hair.

Avi shook his head. "He kept it in a pitch-black room."

"That doesn't prove that *all* silver phoenixes die after returning to Darkside," said Abel. "There could be other factors at play–it could've been injured, or died of starvation, or maybe they can't survive the temperature change between Night and Dawn. Even a subtle change in temperature might be enough to affect them."

"Who knows," said Avi. "All we know is that once Dawn breaks on the horizon, they don't stick around in the Valley. Whatever the reason, they need to be on Darkside once Night ends." He pushed himself to his feet, giving Nayan's bronze coin a flip as he tossed it back to Mitra. "And now that it's

The Tales of Abel and Mitra

Dawn, *we* need to be out in the forest. C'mon, let's find Noa and the others."

***

While Esta headed off to begin her shift, Avi, Abel, and Mitra made their way to the storage facility to retrieve one of the hovercycles brought back from Mitra's vessel. Four of them had been brought back, but three were taken out by Nineveh and her team on their Night Mission.

"Do you think the Elders would permit us to take it?" Mitra wondered.

The facility was quiet and unguarded. Most of the villagers were still at the starflower field.

"Why not?" Abel said. "They belong to you. Besides, the Elders only confiscated the weapons in the other room. They said nothing about the items in this area."

"Very well," Mitra nodded. "This hovercycle supports up to three passengers. I will be the one steering, so one of you will sit in the front, and the other will hold onto me from behind." He glanced at the two of them expectantly.

"Abel's the smallest," Avi said quickly. "I might block your view, so he should sit up front."

"S-sure..." Abel said. "That works for me."

He climbed into the front seat. Akavi and Spinner each took a spot on his shoulders. Mitra positioned himself behind him, sliding his arms under Abel's as he gripped the handles. Avi swung onto the back, holding onto Mitra's waist.

"Hold tight," Mitra warned. "We should reach the crash site in half an hour."

He hit the engine, and the hovercycle roared to life, lurching forward as it floated slightly off the ground. The sudden acceleration caught Abel off-guard, his head knocking back against Mitra's chest. As they zipped along, debris bounced off the windshield. The vehicle rose and fell like a boat traversing the waves as they navigated the forest floor, avoiding rocks and roots. Abel grew dizzy as he watched the world blur past them. He was grateful that Avi had suggested he sit in the front–he wasn't sure he'd have been able to hold on for long had he been at the back. He glanced down, constantly checking to see that Avi's arms were still wrapped around Mitra's waist and that his friend hadn't fallen off.

"Does everyone in your world travel like this?" Abel wondered.

"This kind of hovercraft is a relatively recent invention," Mitra replied. "It did not exist during the eras of the stories I told you."

The canopy above them was dense, allowing little light from the sun to filter through. But occasionally, they could catch glimpses of the sky. Dawn shone with a deep violet hue that shrouded the valley in an eerie aura. Most nocturnal creatures had either returned to Darkside or gone into hibernation. The starflowers closed their petals, their golden light dimming to a pale glow.

"I didn't expect Dawn to be just as dark along the forest floor as Night," Mitra mused.

Just then, a faint glimmer appeared in the distance, slightly to the right. It flickered unnaturally, catching their attention.

"Is that…a fire…?" Abel asked.

"It appears so," said Mitra.

"A fire? Where?" Avi craned his neck. "That must be them!"

The Tales of Abel and Mitra

Without hesitation, Mitra steered them in the direction of the flames. As they neared, the destruction became evident–several trees were scorched black, their bark charred as high as twenty meters. Debris from one of Mitra's hovercycles littered the swampy terrain and smoke curled into the sky. A small fire smoldered along some of the roots and lower branches.

Mitra brought them to a halt. Avi leaped off before they'd come to a full stop, anxiously scanning their surroundings.

"Search for survivors!" He raced off toward the wreckage.

Abel headed in the opposite direction, while Akavi and Spinner hopped down from his shoulders and went their own ways, disappearing into the underbrush. Mitra approached the main husk of the wreckage.

"I have never known one of these to explode before," he furrowed his brow.

Abel moved carefully through the swamp, his feet sinking into the terrain. The dense shrubbery and massive roots winding their way around the forest floor made it difficult to spot anything on the ground. He hopped onto one of the lower branches to get a better view of the area.

"Noa! Nineveh!" Abel's voice echoed through the trees. "Is anyone there?!"

Something caught his eye by one of the roots–a lump on the ground vaguely resembling the shape of a body. He leaped down, dread washing over him as he raced over.

"Hey! Is someone there? Are you alright?!"

There was no response. As Abel drew near, he saw why–the lower half of the body was missing.

Abel let out a strangled cry, stumbling backward and landing hard in the shallow water.

Yisei Ishkhan

"Abel?" Mitra called out. The man was at his side in moments, pulling him to his feet.

Abel could barely breeze, his petrified gaze fixed on the corpse. "He's…he's…"

"He is dead," Mitra placed a firm hand on Abel's trembling shoulder, turning him away from the scene. "But it is not Noa."

"I know…but still…" Abel quivered. He recognized the man's face from the village, but the shock prevented him from recalling his name. The pool the man lay in was thick with blood, while his face had gone cold and gray, staring into the void.

"There is nothing we can do for him," Mitra said gently. "We need to continue searching for the others."

Before Abel could respond, Avi's panicked voice rang out from the distance.

"Oh God! Guys! Come quick!"

By the time Mitra and Abel reached Avi, Akavi and Spinner were already by his side. Avi was pale, frozen in place as he stared up at the lower branches thirty meters overhead.

"What is it?" Mitra asked.

Avi raised a shaking arm, pointing at a white blob hanging between the branches.

Mitra frowned. "What is that?"

"The web of an oyeba," Abel gasped. "Something's caught inside it…"

"*Someone*," Avi said in horror. "We've gotta get them down!"

Mitra didn't waste a second. In a blur, he leaped onto a root five meters above the ground, swinging his way up into

The Tales of Abel and Mitra

the lower branches. The pku were right on his tail while Abel and Avi struggled to catch up to them. By the time they reached the web, Mitra had already severed the blob–a cocoon-like mass of oyeba silk–from the rest of the webbing. Akavi and Spinner went to work, peeling away the outer layers of silk with their mandibles.

"Look out!" Cried Avi.

Abel barely registered the warning before a dark shadow dropped onto them from above. The attacker was swift, a hulking form that descended on them with terrifying precision. The monstrous oyeba unfurled its ten spindly legs, each tipped with sharp, claw-like edges. Oyeba had a similar physiology as pku, but were far larger, at about half the size of a grown man.

Mitra's back was turned, yet he was unfazed by the beast's sudden appearance. He spun around, his hand clamping down hard against the narrowest segment of the oyeba's thorax just as its mandibles parted to reveal a grotesque, gaping maw. The creature grunted, startled by its prey's reflexes. Mitra paused, holding the creature in mid-air as he studied its features for a moment. The oyeba squirmed, stretching its legs toward Mitra's face. But before it could cut Mitra with its claws, he brought down his arm in a controlled arch, slamming the creature hard into the branch they were standing on. The oyeba let out a guttural screech before its legs fell limp. The thread attaching it to a higher branch snapped. As Mitra released his grip, its lifeless body tumbled to the forest floor below, splashing into one of the pools.

Mitra turned to the others calmly. "I assume that was an oyeba?"

Abel and Avi both stared at him agape.

Yisei Ishkhan

"You…you just *one-handed* that thing," Avi said in disbelief. "How did you do that?!"

"As Esta would say," Mitra smiled, "I am a man of many talents."

"Are you alright?" Abel asked in concern. "It didn't bite you, did it?"

"No. Why? Are oyeba poisonous?"

"They're not. I was just worried."

"I am fine," Mitra assured.

Their attention shifted to the sticky blob Akavi and Spinner were still working on. With each strand of silk peeled away, it became clear that the blob wasn't just a shapeless mass, but a human.

"Please don't let it be too late," Avi whispered.

He and the others knelt next to the pku, carefully helping them tear away the rest of the webbing. When they uncovered the head, a pale face emerged, covered in a viscous substance. Abel's breath caught in his throat.

"It is Nineveh," Mitra said.

"Is she…?" Avi didn't dare finish his question.

"I sense a heartbeat," Mitra assured.

Without hesitation, he cleared her nostrils, scooping away the silk with his fingers. Nineveh's chest heaved. Her eyes shot open, and she jerked upright, coughing out blobs of the liquid.

"What–?" She gasped between breaths. "What are you doing here…?"

"What are *we* doing here?!" Avi cried. "You didn't come back to the Village, so we came looking for you! And it's a

The Tales of Abel and Mitra

good thing that we did! Another hour longer in that web and it would've started dissolving your flesh!"

"She needs to be cleaned off," said Abel.

Mitra scooped Nineveh into his arms, descending to the forest floor where they washed her in one of the pools. Nineveh winced as the sticky liquid came off, leaving patches of raw, reddened skin.

"What happened out here?" Avi demanded, barely waiting for her to catch her breath. "Where are the others?"

"We were attacked," Nineveh rubbed her temples. "I barely escaped. The others…are gone…"

"No!" Avi's voice cracked. "What about your brother? Where's Noa?!"

"Noa is alive. At least, he was when I last saw him. They took him."

"Who?" Abel pressed. "Who attacked you?"

Nineveh's face darkened. "The makarasa."

Silence fell over the group. Abel and Avi shared a glance, their faces going pale.

"Makarasa," Mitra repeated. "As in the namesakes of *The Tales of Makarasa-man*?"

"Yes," Avi gulped. "Only the *real* makarasa aren't as friendly as Makarasa-man."

"They're intelligent," Abel's voice trembled. "The most intelligent of the ratri rakshas. They're the only ones that hunt in packs."

"Which makes them the most dangerous," Nineveh said.

"What are they doing in the Valley?" Avi started to pace. "They rarely venture this far, especially this close to Dawn."

"It seems we weren't the only ones interested in the crash site," Nineveh said. "They ambushed us while we were inside, killing Longchar and Dhara. The rest of us tried to flee, but they caught up to us here. One of the vehicles exploded during the fight, and they took the other two with them. Noa was captured. As for Visha and Pekru…"

She glanced across the pool, to where a charred body lay against the trunk of a tree.

"They are dead," said Mitra.

"Damn it!" Nineveh slammed her fists into the dirt. "We don't have time to mourn. We have to go after my brother!"

"You are in no condition to go anywhere," said Mitra. "You need to return to the Village and recover." He turned to Avi. "Do you think you can drive the hovercycle?"

"I…think so…" Avi stammered. "Yeah, I've got this."

"What about you?" Abel glanced at Mitra.

"I will go after Noa."

Nineveh stared at him in disbelief. "*You?* You don't know what you're up against. No one's ever gone to Darkside and made it back."

"That's not true," Avi piped up. "Granny Inali told me—"

"Even *if* that story that Inali told you is true, so what?" Nineveh scoffed. "That man who supposedly went to Darkside way back when never encountered any ratri rakshas—let alone the makarasa. If Mr. Falling Star wades into their territory alone, he won't last five minutes." Her voice cracked. "None of us will. Even if I manage to convince the Elders to assemble a rescue team, what good will that do? We don't know what the terrain is like beyond the Purvanchal Range. We have no idea how many makarasa might be out there…"

The Tales of Abel and Mitra

"Miss Nineveh," Mitra said gently, kneeling at her side, "I will find your brother. I promise."

Nineveh's flickered with a momentary glimmer of hope, but doubt soon set in. "I appreciate your…enthusiasm. But if you're willing to risk your life for my brother, you're either immensely naive or immensely foolish."

"Mitra took down that oyeba in one hit!" Avi interjected. "If anyone can take on the makarasa, it's him!"

Nineveh raised an eyebrow, glancing past them at the dead oyeba in the other pool. "In one hit? *You* did that? That's…impressive. Still, a single oyeba is nothing compared to a swarm of makarasa."

"I will be fine," Mitra insisted.

Nineveh hesitated. "Let's at least return to the Village first. We should consult the Elders. I doubt they'll agree to send out a team to save Noa, but it's worth a shot."

***

There wasn't enough room on the hovercycle for all of them, so Nineveh and Avi took it while Mitra carried Abel through the trees. Despite traveling on foot, leaping gracefully from branch to branch, Mitra somehow managed to keep pace with the vehicle below.

Abel clung to Mitra's back, his nerves getting the better of him. "Were you serious about going after Noa on your own?"

"He is in danger," Mitra said matter-of-factly.

"Exactly, which is why you can't save him by yourself!"

"As Nineveh said, your Elders are unlikely to send out a rescue team. I estimate there is less than a 0.5% chance of that occurring. And I agree with their decision–it is too dangerous to risk the lives of others to save one man from Darkside. Which is why *I* must go."

"But you'll be killed!" Abel cried. "You don't know what you're up against! The makarasa are more intelligent than any of the other ratri rakshas–maybe even as intelligent as *we* are. No one who's ever faced them has survived!"

A slight smile spread across Mitra's lips. "Then I suppose I will be the first."

Abel could hardly believe the certainty in his voice. He squeezed his arms tighter around the man. Esta had been right. Mitra's skin was soft–unnervingly soft–like polished silk. Despite the pace at which they moved, he hadn't even broken a sweat.

Abel laid his head against the man's back. He was unable to detect a heartbeat. He wasn't even sure if Mitra was breathing.

"Mitra…" Abel said in a quiet voice, his voice almost drowned out by the rushing wind. "Are you…are you really human?"

For a moment, there was no response. Abel wondered whether he had spoken too softly for Mitra to hear. He was about to let the matter drop when Mitra spoke, his voice as calm as ever.

"Why do you ask?"

Abel hesitated. "It's just…you're not like everyone else. Not only are you stronger and faster than the rest of us, but you don't seem afraid of anything."

Mitra didn't answer immediately, his silence heavy as he considered Abel's words. Finally, he said, "As an archivist, it is not only my duty to preserve stories and relics from the past but also to protect and defend humanity."

The Tales of Abel and Mitra

"Is that why you want to save Noa?"

"If I have the power to do so, then is it not my responsibility?"

"That doesn't mean you need to risk your life!"

"My life is not at risk. I can assure you of that."

"How can you be so confident?!"

Mitra smiled. "Because I may not know what I am up against, but neither do the makarasa."

"You sound like you've gone insane," Abel whispered. "But you still haven't answered my question. Are you human? You've shared so many stories from your world, but I still don't know anything about you."

"My story is complicated," Mitra chuckled. "There is no time to tell it before we return to the Village. But I could tell you a shorter story in the meantime."

Abel let out a deep sigh. "Fine. But you have to promise me that the next time we get the chance, you'll tell me more about yourself."

"Certainly," Mitra agreed.

"So," Abel huffed, "what's this other story that you want to tell me?"

"It is one of my favourites," Mitra gleamed. "Let me tell you a story–a story of loss, and heroic sacrifice…"

Yisei Ishkhan

IV. The Tale of Hikaru and Shirō
April 15, 1638 AD
Hara Castle, Shimabara Peninsula, Hizen Province, Tokugawa Shogunate

The acrid taste of smoke hung heavy in the air as thick, black plumes blotted out the sun above Hara Castle. Beneath the suffocating darkness, the faint metallic scent of blood lingered–the charred bodies of ten thousand men, women, and children lay strewn across the stretch between the castle's inner and outer walls. For months, these grounds had served as the last refuge for the desperate people of the Amakusa Islands as they sought sanctuary from the Shogun's forces. Now, they were a killing field.

Kirishima Hikaru stumbled through the gates of the castle's main keep, his breath ragged and heart pounding.

"The inner wall has been breached!" The young rōnin cried. "Prepare our defenses! Where is Commander Masuda?!"

"H-he's at the chapel!" One of the soldiers stammered. "He refuses to come out!"

Hikaru stormed past them, pushing his way through the dim corridors, and weaving through the masses of survivors huddled inside. Their gaunt faces and hollow eyes stared up at him, pleading for salvation. He could do nothing for them. Months of siege had drained their hope as they were ravaged by hunger and disease. If they by some miracle survived the Shogun's forces, starvation would claim them within days.

Hikaru reached the chapel doors, where two rōnin stood guard.

"The Commander is inside," one of them muttered, his gaze fixed on the floor. "He said no one is to disturb him."

The Tales of Abel and Mitra

Hikaru hesitated, but only for a moment. He calmly slid the doors open, stepped over the threshold, and closed the doors behind him. He was careful to adhere to the proper etiquette, removing his shoes and katana, and bowing his head as he entered the room. The stillness of the chapel was suffocating. Thick incense wafted through the air, clouding his senses. Only the dim flicker of candles lit the room, their glow casting wavering shadows across the wooden beams. Along the walls, Western-style portraits of saints, angels, Seibo Maria, and Iesu Kirisuto passed down for generations since the time of the Jesuits stood in silent witness. At the far end of the room, above the white stone altar, hung Commander Masuda's banner:

LOVVADO SEIA O SĀCTISSIMO SACRAMENTO

Praised be the most holy sacrament

The Portuguese inscription crowned an image of two angels kneeling before the Bread of Life and the Chalice of Salvation.

Hikaru's gaze fell to the figure leaning before the altar, only his black hair tied in a high ponytail visible from this angle. Dressed in dirt-streaked white robes, Masuda Shirō Tokisada–known by his baptismal name Hironimo to his followers–clutched a rosary in his hands, its beads clicking softly as he murmured a Latin prayer.

A heavy feeling weighed on Hikaru's heart as he approached the Commander. Shirō, barely more than a boy, had in only a matter of months become the prophetic leader of the Shimabara Uprising. But the burden of leadership had taken its toll on him. For the past few days, he'd locked himself within the main keep of the castle. His youthful features that once shined with radiance had been carved with deep lines of weariness, and he had grown thin from the rationing. Hikaru had been drawn to his master's otherworldly charisma, but now he could hardly recognize the frail figure before him. The zeal with which Shirō had inspired their movement had vanished.

Hikaru folded his hands together, knocking his head against the wooden floorboards as he lay prostrate before the boy. "Commander Masuda…"

Shirō made no response, continuing to mutter his prayers.

Hikaru, still prostrated, closed his eyes. He let Shirō's voice pull him away from the cacophony of crackling flames, clashing blades, and desperate cries in the distance. For a moment, a memory overtook him—a scene from their first battle together at Shimabara Castle in the winter. Shirō had stood tall atop a hill overlooking the battlefield, clad in a white kimono with a cross painted on his forehead. In one hand, he held a *gohei*, a wand used by the Shinto priests. Its zigzagging streamers caught the light as he waved it over the battlefield, commanding his legions of rōnin and peasant farmers. His voice carried over the chaos as the rally cries of his men shouted in response: *Santiago!*

At that moment, the sun's rays had fanned out behind Shirō's head like a halo. To Hikaru, the young commander appeared as more than a man—he was the embodiment of Sei Mikaeru, commanding his legions of angels.

Reality snapped back to Hikaru as the crack of a sword against splintering wood and the thundering of steps grew louder. The chapel doors flung open. Hikaru spun around, his hand instinctively reaching for the hilt of his katana. He cursed silently to himself. He had left it at the door.

Three rōnin stormed into the room.

"The castle is on fire!" One of them cried.

The Tales of Abel and Mitra

Another raised his blade, jabbing it accusingly in Shirō's direction. "This is *his* fault! He fooled us with his magic tricks and promises of salvation! God has abandoned us! Perhaps he was never on our side to begin with!"

"Ibaraki!" Hikaru urged. "The Commander is in prayer! Lay down your weapon!"

"Step aside, Kirishima," Ibaraki said. "That boy dragged us into this hell. He must pay for what he's done!"

"Please!" Hikaru pleaded. "This is not the time to turn on one another!"

"It's too late!" Ibaraki spat. "The Shogun's forces breached the keep! We'll be slaughtered like everyone outside!"

A wave of despair washed over Hikaru. Were they all going to die here, cut down in a bloody massacre as their bodies were desecrated by flames and their heads lopped off by the enemy? An image flashed through his mind, one he'd been suppressing, but could no longer ignore. When the Shogun's forces first breached the outer wall earlier that day, Hikaru had watched helplessly as his father was cut down with the other rōnin. His father had been a retainer of the Arima Clan and was one of the most skilled samurai Hikaru knew. But weakened by the weeks of starvation, he was barely able to stand as the Shogun's army descended on him.

At that moment, Hikaru's remaining hope of survival had evaporated. As he joined the panicked fray retreating behind the castle's inner wall, he soon learned of the fate that had befallen the rest of his family. His cousins were burned alive as their tents were set alight. His younger brother was trampled to death amid the chaos. His mother and older sister threw themselves over the castle walls into the sea. His younger sister had already died from starvation days prior. Everyone he cared about was gone–everyone except Shirō.

Yisei Ishkhan

He would do anything to protect the boy.

"Stand down, Ibaraki!" Hikaru ordered. His eyes scanned the room. There was an old samurai blade on a display stand to his left.

"No, *you* stand aside, Kirishima!" Ibaraki retorted. "Or we'll cut you down along with him!"

Hikaru lunged for the blade, taking a fighting stance as he pointed it at the men. "I won't let you harm him."

Ibaraki sneered. "So, that's how it is?"

The three soldiers lunged simultaneously. Hikaru's body was heavy from malnourishment and lack of sleep, but a sudden rush of strength drove him forward. He swerved, dodging a strike from the first soldier and coming down with an attack of his own as he slashed the man across the arm. The man yelped, dropping his weapon. Hikaru delivered him a kick to the chest and sent him crashing through the door. The second soldier's blade swung forward, but Hikaru intercepted him, pushing him back.

But as Hikaru was distracted by these two men, Ibaraki slipped past him.

"Commander Masuda, run!" Hikaru cried. He pushed his opponent to the ground, turning to go after Ibaraki.

Shirō hadn't moved. He remained kneeling in prayer, his head bowed, seemingly oblivious to the battle raging behind him. He didn't make a sound, even as Ibaraki's blade sunk into his side.

"NO!" Hikaru shrieked.

He lurched forward, his katana arching through the air in one fluid motion. Ibaraki's head went flying, hitting the ground with a thud. A moment later, the rest of the man's body collapsed. Blood splattered forth from the gaping hole in his neck, staining the wooden floor and rice paper walls.

The other two attackers regained their senses, bearing down on Hikaru. But the young rōnin felled them both in a single strike.

Drawing a steady breath and lowering his blade, Hikaru knelt at Shirō's side.

"Commander...?" His voice wavered.

Shirō was hunched over, his head resting against the floor. Blood seeped through his white robes as he clutched at the wound in his side. He was still breathing, but barely. He coughed up a mouthful of blood.

"Kiri...shima...?" He whispered, as if only just noticing Hikaru's presence. "Was he...right? Has God...abandoned us...?"

"No!" Hikaru exclaimed, tears stinging his eyes. "No! Of course not!"

The battle grew louder in the distance. Blood-curdling shrieks echoed from the corridor before they were abruptly cut off. A burning beam from the roof collapsed over the doorway to the chapel.

"We can't stay here," Hikaru said. He put one of Shirō's arms over his shoulder to help him to his feet.

Shirō let out a sharp gasp. "Leave me..."

"No!" Hikaru cried. "I won't leave you behind! I *can't*!"

"We're all going to die here..." Shirō whispered. "You...and me...everyone..."

"We can still make it," Hikaru insisted, hobbling toward the back of the chapel as he half-carried, half-dragged Shirō. "There's a tunnel in the storage room—it leads out of the castle. Remember?"

Yisei Ishkhan

Shirō shook his head. "Even if we make it out…we have nowhere to go…"

"We can worry about that later!"

He used the katana to slash through one of the thin rice paper walls, exposing the corridor beyond. The air was thick with smoke, stinging Hikaru's eyes and throat. Flames roared above them, popping and crackling as they burned through the upper floors of the castle.

As they limped down the hall, a commotion down an adjacent corridor caught Hikaru's attention. Several people raced toward a room engulfed in flames, tossing themselves into the fire. Their shrieks sent a chill up Hikaru's spine.

"What…are they doing…?" Shirō's breath caught in his throat.

Hikaru glanced away. "They'd rather die by their own hand than face the Shogun's army."

They shuffled past the burning room. The bodies were already blackened beyond recognition. Hikaru turned Shirō's face away from the sight.

They reached the storage room, and Shirō collapsed as soon as they made it inside, his breaths shallow and laboured. Hikaru rushed over to the far wall, shoving aside crates and weapon racks as he cleared the floorboards that covered the entrance to the tunnel. He jammed the tip of his blade under the wood, prying open the hole. He breathed a sigh of relief, rushing back to fetch Shirō. But just then, a loud crack sounded above him. He barely managed to leap out of the way before the ceiling beams came crashing down, burying the tunnel beneath smoldering rubble.

"Damn it!" Hikaru cursed, slamming his hands into the ground.

The Tales of Abel and Mitra

"Aren't you always telling the soldiers to watch their language…?" Shirō said weakly.

Hikaru glanced in his direction. The boy was slumped over on his side, his eyes barely open as a pool of blood formed around him. Hikaru hurried to his side, cutting some of the fabric loose from his sleeves and trembling as he struggled to wrap the boy's wound.

"Tell me…Kirishima…" Shirō murmured. "Is this what Hell looks like…?"

"Don't say such things," Hikaru chided. "That's not for you to worry about."

Shirō's eyes flicked upward, his gaze distant. "What if…what if Ibaraki was right…? Maybe this *is* my fault. Maybe I deserve to be punished…"

"No!" Hikaru cried. "Ibaraki chose to join this cause, just like the rest of us! None of this is your fault. It's the Shogun's oppressive taxes and persecution of our faith that drove us to revolution. You didn't ask to become the leader of our movement!"

A faint chuckle escaped Shirō's lips. "The people said I was sent by God to deliver them. I let them believe it. Tell me, Kirishima…do you think God truly sent me?"

"Of course," Hikaru insisted. "God has a plan for us all. The poorest peasant has no less worth than the Emperor. You're the one who taught me that. Your words have inspired so many, giving us hope and purpose–to fight to create a better world for our descendants."

Shirō shook his head, his gaze unfocused. "If God has a plan for all of us, that includes the Shogun, doesn't it?"

Yisei Ishkhan

Hikaru hesitated. "Yes. But that doesn't mean the Shogun is following God's will. God sent you to deliver His suffering people from the Shogun's grasp."

Shirō grimaced, shifting uncomfortably. "If that is my purpose in this life, then I have failed. All I've achieved is leading God's people to their deaths."

"We can't say what the outcome of this will be. Even in our failures, God brings about His glory."

Shirō flashed him a skeptical smile. "The scriptures say that everyone who rules is appointed by God, and that we should not oppose those authorities. 'Give to the Emperor what is his, and to God what is God's.'"

"And let the Shogun bleed the people dry until they starve?" Hikaru shot back. "The Shogun has taken more than what belongs to him—not just our taxes but our *lives*! He kills those of us who refuse to renounce God! Does God expect us to sit idly by and watch as the Shogun commits such injustice against His people?"

"I don't know..." Shirō whispered. His breath was growing faint. "My father told me stories he'd heard from the Jesuits. They said that back in Europe, many of their nations were once part of the Roman Empire--the same empire that Iesu Kirisuto was born into. At first, few followed our Lord. They were persecuted by their emperor as we are by the Shogun—thrown to beasts and torn apart for entertainment, dragged naked through the streets, burned alive, sawn in half. Yet they never fought back. They accepted their deaths, becoming martyrs. Their blood was the seed of the church, and it grew, like the tiny mustard seed, until it encompassed the whole empire. Without raising a sword, their emperor bowed before God."

The Tales of Abel and Mitra

"That was Rome," Hikaru murmured. "This is Nippon."

"Is there a difference? The priests said that the Church has grown faster in the past half-century in Nippon than it did in the first three centuries in Rome."

Shirō's voice grew faint with each word, his breath growing laboured. He burst into a fit of coughing, splattering a mouthful of blood across the floor.

"You need to conserve your energy," Hikaru warned. "Don't exert yourself. Do you think you can make it to the tunnel? It's safer there."

"I'll only slow you down," Shirō muttered. "Go on without me."

"I'm not leaving you behind!" Hikaru cried, his voice cracking. "You're all I have left in the world!"

Shirō's lips curled into a faint smile. "That isn't true. Even when you walk through the valley of death, God is still with you. And I will be too…even when I'm gone."

The door behind them burst open with a crash. Hikaru spun around, katana raised, as a figure stepped into the room from the smoke-filled corridor. It was one of the Shogun's men, his blade dripping with blood as he raised it to them. Two severed heads, grim trophies, hung from his waist.

"Well, well, well," the man jeered. "What do we have here?"

"Stay back!" Hikaru warned, stepping between the man and Shirō.

A weak tug at the hem of his robes drew Hikaru's attention.

"Kirishima…" Shirō whispered. "Don't fight him. I must bear the punishment for my sin…the sin of leading you all into this hell…"

Yisei Ishkhan

"Kirishima?" The Shogun's man spat. "The former retainer of the Arima Clan?" He narrowed his eyes as his gaze shifted from Hikaru to Shirō. "Then *you* must be…"

"Masuda Shirō Tokisada," Shirō said, rising to his feet. "I take it that I'm the man you're looking for."

"Commander Masuda," the soldier snickered. "The boy prophet. Is it really you? Look how far you've fallen! The Shogun will be most pleased to have your head!"

The soldier lunged, and Hikaru moved to intercept his attack. But before their blades could meet, a blow struck Hikaru from behind. Pain erupted in his back as he was sent sprawling sideways across the floor. He gasped, disoriented, as a figure shot past him. He realized the blow had come from Shirō, knocking him aside as he rose to take on the man himself.

The young commander stood tall and erect, showing no signs of injury. His skin had returned to a healthy complexion, and his robes shone with dazzling brilliance as white as snow, without a speck of blood staining them.

Then, the ceiling above them gave way. Flames roared as fiery beams crashed down and engulfed the room. Hikaru's vision blurred as the world went dark.

***

When Hikaru awoke, the fire still raged around him. His eyes watered as heat and smoke pressed in from every side, yet he barely noticed the pain.

"Shirō…?" He groped around in the haze. There was no sign of the commander or the man who had attacked them, only piles of flaming debris from the collapsed ceiling. No. There *was* something–a lump on the ground that he realized was a mass of white robes.

The Tales of Abel and Mitra

"No…" Hikaru choked as he crawled over to Shirō's side, clutching the body in his arms. A thick stream of blood splattered across Hikaru's robes, pouring from the boy's neck—or where his neck would've been. Shirō's head had been cut clean off his shoulders.

Hikaru's voice caught in his throat. Hot tears spilled down his cheeks, evaporating before they touched the blood-soaked floor.

"I'm sorry…" Hikaru wept. "I'm sorry…I'm sorry…"

Shirō's head was nowhere to be seen, nor was the soldier who had infiltrated the room. He must've made his escape with the young commander's head just before the beams above them came crashing down, blocking the exit.

There was a thump. Shirō's right arm had fallen limply to the ground. Clasped between his fingers was a pristine white feather, untainted by the blood and ash that coated the room. As Hikaru took the feather into his hands, he detected movement nearby. Nearby, a dove lay trapped with one of her legs under the burning debris, flapping her wings in a desperate bid for freedom. Next to her were the cracked remains of an egg, its contents oozing across the floorboards.

Hikaru was transfixed by the sudden appearance of the dove. He recalled how early into the campaign, Shirō would summon doves from the sky that would lay an egg in his hand. When the egg was cracked open, its inside would be revealed to contain a slip of paper bearing a verse from scripture. Curious peasants and rōnin would flock to their gatherings to witness the miracle. The doves Shirō summoned were said to be more than mere birds, but angels descending from Heaven, delivering a message to the people from God Himself.

Hikaru held his breath as he reached out, poking his fingers through the shattered pieces of eggshell. He pulled out a rolled-up slip of paper from within. With trembling hands, he unfurled the slip:

Put away your sword. For those who live by the sword will die by the sword.

Hikaru fell to his face, lying prostrated before the young commander.

"I hope you're at peace…" he whispered.

Carefully, he lifted the beam pinning down the dove. The dove flapped free, flinging herself into the air as she darted past Hikaru and disappeared out a window at the back of the room. Hikaru squinted as he watched her disappear into the light. Had that window always been there? He pushed himself to his feet, staggering over to the ledge, the slip of paper still clasped tightly in his hands.

I'm sorry, Shirō. Please, forgive me.

He leaned back over the edge, basking his face in the warm glow of the sunlight. Then he shifted his weight, tumbling off the ledge, and down toward the crashing waves far below.

***

The soft, golden glow warmed Hikaru's face, gently rousing him back to consciousness. He stirred, his eyelids fluttering as he struggled to adjust to the light. The warmth cradled him like an embrace, pulling him from the cold, dark abyss he had sunken into. He sat up with a start.

"Ah…" a croaky old voice broke the silence. "You're finally awake."

A wrinkly old woman sat beside a fire, its flames casting dancing shadows along the walls of the small hut. Hikaru was lying on a bed that was too small for him, draped in a coarse blanket that covered his otherwise naked form.

The Tales of Abel and Mitra

"Who are you?" He asked, shifting uncomfortably in the bed. "Where are my clothes?"

The old woman chuckled. "They're out back drying. You were soaked to the bone when you washed ashore here. We had to strip you of your robes, or you'd have caught a cold."

She handed him a bowl of soup, which he readily accepted.

"And where exactly are we?"

"A small island in Amakusa."

Amakusa. The name sent a ripple through Hikaru's chest. These islands were Shirō's home.

The woman studied him for a moment before continuing. "You're fortunate you washed up here, child, and not one of the other islands. They're less hospitable to people like us. They would've turned you over to the authorities to have you crucified or burned in the hot springs."

"'People like us'?" Hikaru repeated tentatively.

The woman hobbled over, pressing something into his hand. Hikaru glanced down to find the slip of paper he'd retrieved from the egg.

"You were clutching this when you washed ashore. It was all you had, other than your soaked clothes. I can't read, but my nephew can. He said it's a verse from our holy scriptures. You must share our faith to have held onto it so dearly. I'm surprised it wasn't damaged by the water. Tell me, where did you drift here from?"

"Hara Castle."

The woman gasped. "From across the strait? We saw the smoke for days after its fall. They say there were no survivors. They took the heads of those they'd executed and displayed them on pikes in Nagasaki as a warning to us. Even the young commander was killed. The poor boy. He was barely more than a child."

A pit sank in Hikaru's stomach.

"We must exercise the utmost caution in preserving our faith," the woman's voice dropped to a whisper as if the walls had ears. "Even on these islands. If word got out that we continue to hold to an outlawed faith, the Shogun's forces could have our entire village sentenced to death. Now that the revolution has been crushed, there will be no one coming to our aid. Our only hope is to hold fast to God's promise that He will deliver His people. We must be like our forefathers, who hid in the catacombs of Rome to worship God in secret."

Hikaru unfurled the slip of paper in his hand, his breath catching. For the first time, he noticed that there wasn't just one verse inscribed on the paper, but another on the reverse side.

There is no greater love than to lay down one's life for one's friends.

The Tales of Abel and Mitra
The Tale of Abel and Mitra

Abel said nothing as Mitra's story came to a close. They were nearly back at the Village, and the weight of his tale lingered in the silence between them.

"So?" Mitra asked after a while. "What did you think?"

"How can that be one of your favourite stories?" Abel whispered. "It was the saddest one you've told yet."

Mitra shrugged. "You asked for a shorter story."

Ahead, the glow of lights from the Village pierced through the darkness. Below them, Avi and Nineveh's hovercycle wound its way through the forest, heading toward a docking station. As Mitra adjusted their course, he reached into his pocket and handed a slip of paper over his shoulder to Abel.

Abel accepted it, examining the strange characters written on both sides. "Are these the versus Hikaru found in the egg?"

Mitra nodded. "*'Put away your sword. For those who live by the sword will die by the sword.' 'There is no greater love than to lay down one's life for one's friends.'* They are wise words, don't you agree?"

Abel's heart sank. "You're not planning to sacrifice yourself to save Noa, are you?!"

Mitra chuckled. "As I told you earlier, my life is not at risk."

He landed at the docking station, dropping Mitra off with the others. He turned to Nineveh. "I will bring your brother back soon. I promise."

Before anyone could say anything, he was off again.

"Wait!" Abel shouted. "We haven't even spoken to the Elders yet!"

"They aren't gonna help us," Avi muttered.

Nineveh sighed, her gaze fixed on Mitra as he disappeared in the distance. "That man must have a death wish. Come. Let's see what the Elders have to say."

***

To none of their surprise, the Elders refused to offer any assistance.

"I'm sorry," Inali said gravely. "Sending a team to Darkside is too dangerous, especially against the makarasa. We have a poor understanding of those creatures–their biology, their population, or how intelligent they truly are. We cannot risk provoking them further."

"So, we're just supposed to let them take Noa?!" Avi cried in disbelief. He turned to Vishel with a desperate plea. "How can you agree to this?! Noa is your grandson!"

Vishel's face hardened. "We have no choice. We've followed the exact same protocol in the past when *anyone* has been attacked by the makarasa. This time is no different."

"It *is* different!" Avi protested. "We have Mitra! You didn't see him out there, but he took down an oyeba in one strike! We should give him backup!"

Inali's gaze narrowed. "Speaking of the outworlder, where is he?"

Avi clammed up. "He–"

"He'll be back soon," Nineveh interjected, placing a steady hand on Avi's shoulder.

Avi flinched but held his tongue. He responded with a simple nod.

Inali sighed deeply. "I know how important Noa is to you all. But we cannot risk more lives to save him. I am sorry."

The Tales of Abel and Mitra

Nineveh bowed her head. "I understand. Thank you for hearing us out."

Avi looked ready to argue, but Nineveh pulled him out of the chamber before he could. Abel followed them outside. Once they were away from the Elders, Avi exploded.

"I can't believe those old dirtbags! Vishel would really abandon his own flesh and blood to the makarasa?! What kind of grandfather is he?!"

"We shouldn't be surprised," said Nineveh. "If we want to save Noa, we have to do it ourselves."

Avi's frustration melted into an eager grin. "Alright! We should catch up to Mitra before he gets too far ahead!"

"No," said Nineveh. "I'm going alone. You two are staying here."

"No way! You can't just leave us behind! What kind of friends would we be?!"

"Getting yourself killed out there won't help Noa. I'm the leader of the *Makarasa Morung* and have more experience in the field than both of you combined. You'll only slow me down out there."

"But–!"

"You two will cover for me when I'm gone. Is that understood?"

Abel stepped between the two of them. "We understand." He shot Avi a firm glance.

"Fine," Avi scowled. "We'll cover for you."

"Good," Nineveh said. "If we're not back within twelve hours, assume we aren't returning. But don't come after us. Inali is correct–we can't risk more lives to save one person." She flashed them a smile when she saw their anxious faces. "Mitra seems pretty confident that he can rescue my brother.

Yisei Ishkhan

For his sake, I hope he's right. But if we don't return, it was a pleasure knowing you."

***

Abel's windows were tightly sealed to block out the relentless light of Dawn, but even in the darkness, sleep eluded him. He tossed and turned under his covers, clinging to the faint hope that when he awoke, Mitra and the others would be back safe and sound.

His fingers traced along the ancient beads of the bracelet Mitra had given him. It had once belonged to Sandoval, then Nezahualatzin, and now it was his. In his other hand, he held tightly to the slip of paper Mitra had passed to him just before leaving. He couldn't read the strange characters on it, but just holding it gave him a sense of comfort.

Shirō's words from the story echoed in his mind: *Even when you walk through the valley of death, God is still with you. And I will be too, even when I'm gone.*

Please, come back safely, Abel prayed in silence.

A gentle knock at the door startled him. He sat up in bed. His parents and Esta rarely disturbed him when he was sleeping unless it was urgent. Could it be news regarding Noa?

"Abel?" Kitoli's voice called out from the other side. "Sorry to wake you, but your friend is here."

"My friend?" Abel sprang out of bed and threw on his clothes. Had Mitra and the others returned already?

"I told him you were resting, but he insisted on coming in."

Abel threw open the door and rushed into the kitchen. "You're back–!" His words caught in his throat as he saw Avi sitting at the table with a cup of tea in hand. He was dressed in his slick forager uniform, bearing a serious expression on

The Tales of Abel and Mitra

his face that Abel rarely saw from him. Akavi and Spinner were on the table, nibbling away at some ripe, violet dawnberries Kitoli had set out for them.

"Avi...?" Abel asked. "What are you doing here?"

Avi set his cup on the table and approached Abel, his voice dropping to a whisper. "Let's talk in your room." He turned to Kitoli, flashing her his usual, friendly grin. "Thanks for the tea, Mrs. Imsong. It was great."

Kitoli smiled. "Let me know if you boys need anything."

"We will," Avi assured, already steering Abel into the room. Akavi and Spinner scurried after them as they shut the door.

"You're dressed for a Night Mission," Abel remarked. "Don't tell me you're planning on following them to Darkside. We promised Nineveh we would stay here."

"*You* can stay, but I'm not just gonna sit around here and do nothing. The waiting is killing me. I just thought I'd let you know, in case you wanted to join me. Look what I found down in storage." He swung a bag off his shoulder and dropped it onto the floor. From inside, he pulled out two short staffs with pointed tips.

"What are those?" Abel asked.

"Some kind of weapon from Mitra's vessel," Avi said. As Abel reached for one, Avi yanked it away. "Careful. I almost blasted a hole in the wall when I retrieved them."

"You *stole* them?" Abel hissed. "The Elders confiscated them for a reason!"

Abi shrugged. "They're Mitra's, not the Elders'. I doubt he'll mind if we use them to lend him a hand. I also found another hovercycle down there. It's not the same model as the others we drove, but it should work the same way.

Yisei Ishkhan

Nineveh took the other one with her, so we'll have to make do. So, what do you say? Are you in?"

A look of determination gleamed in Avi's eyes, one Abel hadn't seen in his friend before. Abel's gaze dropped to the slip of paper Mitra had given him, recalling the verse written on it:

There is no greater love than to lay down one's life for one's friends.

He let out a long sigh. "I'm in.

***

Abel had felt cold before–the biting winds that whipped their way across the upper canopy, or the frigid pools hidden deep beneath roots and caves along the forest floor. But this was different. The freezing chill of Darkside seeped into his bones, unlike anything he'd experienced before. As Avi steered their hovercycle through the winding passes of the Purvanchal Range, Abel clung tighter to his friend, trying to absorb what little warmth he could. Luckily, their uniforms were equipped with internal temperature regulators. He pulled his hood over his head and covered his face in a mask and goggles, leaving not an inch of skin exposed. Without them, Abel was sure he wouldn't have lasted a minute. Akavi and Spinner buried themselves in his pockets.

"I didn't think it would be *this* cold," Abel's teeth clattered. His breath froze into tiny crystals.

"Of course it is," Avi said. "Darkside never gets sunlight."

They reached the end of the mountain pass, and Abel glanced up as he took in their new surroundings. The warm glow of Dawn disappeared behind the Purvanchal Range behind them, shrouding the land in perpetual darkness. Overhead, even the light of the stars disappeared. In the Valley, the looming shadow of Blue Sky blocked out a third

The Tales of Abel and Mitra

of the sky. But here, more than half the sky was swallowed up, and the darkness would grow even more oppressive the further they advanced.

What caught Abel's attention most, though, were the trees. He wasn't even sure they *were* trees. Unlike the towering trees in the Valley, the tallest plants on Darkside rose only a couple dozen meters. They had no branches, only thick trunks that fanned out at the top into broad, umbrella-like structures that blotted out the sky as they passed under them.

"Are these...trees...?" Abel asked

Avi gave the plants a wary side-eye as he navigated the vehicle. "What else would they be?"

"I don't know," Abel said. "Some kind of strange rock formation?"

"Have you ever seen rocks like this?" Avi wondered. He pointed to the base of one of the nearby structures as they passed by. "Look closer, they have roots. They're trees, or some kind of living organism. Keep your eyes out. Granny Inali told me that even the plants on Darkside are predatory."

Abel shivered. "Did she say anything about these?"

"She mentioned similar plants, but none that were this large. We've already traveled further into Darkside than anyone else has before."

The realization that they were in uncharted territory began to set in. He'd imagined that their journey to Darkside would've involved more challenges–treacherous terrain and winding paths through the mountains–but the alien landscape had appeared suddenly, after less than two hours since they departed from the Village. It felt surreal that such an exotic, haunting world could exist just a stone's throw from the idyllic valley he called home.

Yisei Ishkhan

"Are you sure this is the way Nineveh and Mitra went?" Abel asked.

"I may or may not have had Spinner attach some threads to Nineveh's vehicle before she left," Avi replied with a sheepish grin. "He's leading us right to her."

Spinner replied with a click of affirmation from Abel's pocket.

"But how do we know that Mitra and the makarasa went this way?" Abel pressed.

Avi shrugged. "Nineveh said her hovercycle could track the two vehicles the makarasa stole from us. Following those coordinates should lead us straight into their den. And Mitra? That guy's smart. I'm sure he's figured out a way to follow their trail."

As they advanced deeper into Darkside, they noticed signs of the makarasa's presence. Deep gouges marred the trunks of the strange trees, unmistakable claw marks of the beasts. Sticky splatters of green liquid coated the ground, perhaps the blood of some unfortunate animal that had been ambushed by the creatures and dragged into their lair. Abel shuddered at the thought that they were now headed into those very same depths to retrieve their friend.

The undergrowth thickened as they ventured further, a dense tangle of unfamiliar flora stretching in all directions. Abel marveled at the strange plants—stalks that curled into spirals, clusters hanging like glowing strings from above, vines that coiled tightly around the trunks of the trees and ran across the forest floor. Most of the plants resembled the trees in some form, with cap-like tops perched on long stalks. Some were massive, with thick trunks and wide umbrella-shaped

The Tales of Abel and Mitra

caps, while others were clustered in tiny colonies, with thin stalks tipped with tiny pinheads.

But it wasn't just their shapes that caught Abel's eye–it was the colours. Nearly every species glowed with bioluminescence, flashing and pulsating in dazzling patterns as if communicating with one another. The forest floor was alive with a symphony of colour as if putting on a show just for them. Who needed stars when the forest floor glowed brighter than any Night sky?

There was noise too. The air thrummed with clicks, hums, chirps, buzzes, and deep reverberations. One of the most common animals were four-legged critters that reminded Abel of the gubara he was familiar with. The gubara on Darkside were twice the size of their cousins in the Valley, glowing with a deep violet hue as they inflated their sacs atop their heads and floated into the canopy. But other than the violet gubara, the other fauna on Darkside seemed elusive. Abel caught brief glimpses of the occasional flicker of wings, or the scurry of something along the mossy ground, but these disappeared into the shadows before he had the chance to get a good look at them.

"There's so much life here," Abel noted. "But I've hardly seen any animals."

"They're hiding," Avi whispered. "I would be too if I lived in a place like this."

Abel instinctively reached for the staff clipped at his waistband–the weapon Avi had handed him before they left the Village. Along with these, they had a dozen light grenades on them, concoctions of starflower pollen mixed with duskroot extract that could be used to scare off ratri rakshas. It wasn't much to calm Abel's nerves, but at least it was something.

Yisei Ishkhan

Spinner let out two sharp clicks.

"Here?" Avi said in surprise.

Abel braced himself as his friend slammed on the brakes. They ground to a halt under the shadow of one of the massive trees. Akavi and Spinner leaped out of Abel's pockets.

"We're stopping here?" Abel asked, nervously glancing around. The elevated terrain looked out over the forest floor, but they were still only a couple of meters up. They were far too low in the forest for comfort, but there were no branches higher in the forest for them to rest on.

"Spinner said she should be around here," Avi explained. He turned to the pku. "Well? Lead the way."

Spinner gave another click, flashing a pattern along his back as he gestured for them to follow. They cautiously made their way through the undergrowth, careful to avoid the strange flora. But it was impossible not to brush up against the dense foliage. Something tugged at the bottom of Abel's pants. His heart leaped into his throat, and he whipped around in a panicked gasp, expecting to find some creature sneaking up on him. Instead, he found the thin tendril of a plant prodding at him.

"I-is it moving?!" Abel yelped, jerking away.

"Quiet," Avi hissed. He shot a glance at the plant. "Yeah, it is. I told you some of the plants out here are predatory. Careful of what you touch. And keep it down. The last thing we need is to advertise that we're here."

Abel swallowed hard, his gaze flickering nervously around them. "If the creatures here are anything like the plants, they probably already know we're here."

Avi tapped the staff and light grenades hanging at his belt. "That's what these are for. Stay sharp."

The Tales of Abel and Mitra

Abel unclipped his own staff, gripping it tightly in his trembling hands.

Spinner's clicks echoed from up ahead.

"This way," Avi whispered, motioning for Abel to follow.

They descended the slope, the forest growing darker and more suffocating as the plants loomed like a wall around them. The ground sank underfoot with each step they took, covered in a thick blanket of spongy moss.

"There!" Avi's voice cut through the silence as he pointed ahead. His earlier warnings to keep quiet were entirely forgotten in his excitement.

Up ahead, Abel spotted Nineveh's vehicle–or at least part of it. The front looked like it had been swallowed up by a mound of Earth. No, not Earth. As they drew closer, Abel realized that the "mound" wasn't a boulder at all, but two enormous shells. The massive creature clamped down on the hovercycle like the jaws of a giant predator.

"Is that…a giant hkaru?" Abel asked in disbelief.

"Looks like it, or a related species at least," Avi said.

Abel swallowed hard. "I don't see Nineveh…"

Avi dropped to the ground, brushing his hand over the mossy surface. "Footprints. These are big strides. She was running. C'mon! She might be in danger!"

They took off, following the prints toward the crest of another hill. But they stopped abruptly when Akavi and Spinner let out sharp, synchronized clicks–a warning signal. There were ratri rakshas nearby.

Abel grabbed Avi, pulling him to the ground. They kept their heads low, crawling the rest of the way to the top of the hill. As they peered cautiously over one of the roots, they caught a glimpse of movement below. There, suspended a few meters off the ground, was a human figure caught up in a dense web of glistening silk, struggling to break free. Abel's heart raced. It had to be Nineveh.

"She's alive!" Avi whispered, jumping to his feet.

Abel yanked him back down. "It could be a trap. Akavi and Spinner signaled that there was danger nearby."

"Then we have to get her out!"

Abel raised a finger to his lips. "We don't know what we're walking into. Be ready for anything. Akavi, Spinner, scout ahead."

He waited for their response, but none came. Abel frowned. "Akavi? Spinner? Are you there?"

"They were right behind us..." Avi's voice trailed off.

That was when Abel saw it. Four massive, glowing orbs loomed in the shadows just a few meters overhead. At first, he thought they were fruit dangling from the tree above. But as the orbs shifted, his blood ran cold. They weren't fruit. They were eyes.

"Avi..." Abel's voice cracked as he tugged at his friend's sleeve, prepared to make a run for it.

As soon as their pursuer realized it'd been spotted, it lunged. Abel barely managed a strangled scream before the monster descended on them. Eight colossal legs slammed into the ground like falling tree trunks, encircling them. Abel's vision blurred as he took in the beast—it stood nearly twice as tall of a grown man, most of its height consisting of its legs and thorax. Its body curved up to a head that was disproportionately small for the creature's size, dominated by four globular eyes that pierced through the darkness. Two blade-like forelimbs, larger than the other eight limbs, stretched out from the thorax and slashed through the air.

The Tales of Abel and Mitra

Avi was nearly crushed underfoot. He stumbled forth, crashing into Abel. The two boys fell to the ground.

"What the—?!"

"MAKARASA!" Abel screeched. He scrambled to push Avi off him and jump to his feet. He'd heard stories of the beasts, but nothing could prepare him for the terror of facing one in person.

Avi lay face-first on top of Abel and hadn't spotted the makarasa yet. As the creature came bearing down on them, Abel scrambled to retrieve the light grenades from his belt. He rolled out of the way just as the makarasa sunk its claw into the ground, barely avoiding being sliced in half.

Abel tossed one of the grenades. It exploded above them in a blinding flash of light. The makarasa shrieked, turning on its heel and in the process knocking Avi down the hill.

Abel reached for his staff. After a couple of clicks, it hummed to life, flickering with a violet light. He had no idea how to wield the weapon. He jabbed it up as the makarasa bore down on him again. A powerful blast shot from the staff, throwing him backward down the hill to where Avi had fallen. He lost his grip on the staff as it clattered onto the rocks further down.

Another shriek escaped the makarasa's mandibles. Abel glanced up to see that one of the beast's legs had been blasted off, leaving a steaming hole where a stream of thick liquid gushed forth. For a moment, Abel thought he'd taken down the beast. Then the makarasa let out a deafening screech, slamming its forearms into the ground and sending up a shower of debris. His attack hadn't deterred the beast—it had riled it up.

Abel scrambled to retrieve the staff, but before he could aim it at the makarasa's head, the beast descended on them.

Yisei Ishkhan

Everything went black.

***

A tickling sensation brushed across Abel's face, rousing him awake. He sneezed, sitting upright with a start. His head throbbed and his limbs felt heavy. How long had he been out? He blinked, trying to adjust to his surroundings. It was dark—far darker than it had been in the forest. The ground beneath him was no longer blanketed in soft moss, but slick and warm.

"Akavi?" Abel croaked.

He spotted Akavi and Spinner perched nearby, only visible due to the turquoise patterns glowing on their backs. Akavi flashed a welcoming pattern and waved his tiny limbs. Spinner was at work, unraveling the sticky threads of a cocoon-like lump.

"Ah, finally awake," a soothing voice echoed from the darkness.

"Mitra?" Abel gasped in disbelief. As his eyes adjusted, he spotted the figure of a man hunched over two other lumps further away. Abel glanced around, realizing they were in a cavernous chamber. Steep rock walls loomed around them on all sides, trapping them at the bottom of a deep pit.

"Akavi, Spinner, please finish unwrapping the others," Mitra said. He rose to his feet and approached Abel, placing a steady hand on the boy's forehead as he checked his temperature.

"What's going on?" Abel wondered. "What are you doing here? How did we get here? The makarasa—?"

"They brought you here," Mitra said. "I followed them inside to rescue Noa. Imagine my surprise when I found the three of you dangling alongside him, wrapped up like prey."

The Tales of Abel and Mitra

He gestured toward the three other cocoons. Spinner and Akavi had already uncovered the faces of Avi, Nineveh, and Noa. The pallid visages of his friends spooked Abel.

"Are they...?"

"They are alive," Mitra assured. "Simply unconscious. You do not look much better yourself. Are you the only ones who followed me here?"

Abel nodded, his face flushing. "The Elders refused to send a team. I know you said you could handle this alone, but Nineveh insisted on following you. And then Avi. I couldn't let them go alone."

Mitra's lips twitched into a faint smile. "Your concern is appreciated, but unnecessary. As I told you, I can handle this on my own. As you can see, I am the only one who made it into the depths of the makarasa hive while evading capture."

"The hive?" Abel echoed. "Is that where we are? Where are the makarasa? How did you find this place?"

"I followed their tracks," Mitra said simply. "As for the makarasa..." he glanced up the wall of the chamber, to where several dark shapes perched high above. "They are keeping watch. They only seem to enter this chamber to store or retrieve their prey."

Abel noticed countless silk-wrapped masses hanging from the chamber walls. There were hundreds of them, stretching as far as the eye could see into the gaping black abyss above them.

Abel's stomach churned. "Are those all...?"

"Prey," nodded Mitra. "Unfortunate creatures that were captured like the rest of you." He wiped the sticky silk residue off Abel's face. "Their silk traps dissolve prey into liquid, much like the oyeba webs. I opened a couple of the others only to find digested remains of unidentifiable origin." He glanced at Akavi and Spinner, still at work as they unwrapped the others. "Tell me, do all creatures in your world spin silk?"

"Many do," Abel said. "Especially the predators. Do you not have such creatures where you come from?"

"We do," Mitra said. "But none are as large as the species here. The predators of your world are far deadlier than any that exist on mine."

"We should leave," Abel shuddered.

"Soon," Mitra nodded. "But not yet. The others need time to recover. Besides, I am awaiting our diversion."

"Diversion?"

"On my way here, I encountered another predator," Mitra explained. "It resembled a pku in form, though was a million times larger than your friends. It far exceeds the size of the largest creatures to have walked on my world. It crossed paths with the makarasa I was pursuing. A battle ensued. Despite the beast's lumbering movements, it killed several of the makarasa without sustaining injuries."

"A kamkara..." Abel whispered.

"So *that* is a kamkara," Mitra mused. "The namesake of your *Kamkara Morung*?"

Abel nodded. "They feed primarily on makarasa and have no predators of their own. At least, none that we know of."

Mitra nodded. "The makarasa fled without much resistance, which gave me an idea—why not use the kamkara to our advantage? As the saying goes, 'The enemy of my enemy is my friend.' The kamkara will provide the perfect distraction to occupy the makarasa while we make our escape."

"You *lured* it here?" Abel asked in disbelief. "How?"

The Tales of Abel and Mitra

"That was quite simple. In fact, I learned the trick from the makarasa themselves; I noticed that they were leaving out bait to lure the kamkara *away* from their nest. I decided to do the reverse. It should arrive within a couple of hours. On my way, I encountered a second kamkara. Two is better than one, don't you think? I timed their bait, so both should arrive within minutes of each other."

"Kamkara are territorial," Abel warned. "They get aggressive, even around their own kind. *Especially* around their own kind."

"Even better," Mitra said. "Two kamkara fighting for dominance just outside the makarasa hive sounds like the perfect distraction. Should everything go according to plan, we will be able to sneak out one of the secondary tunnels undetected."

Abel let out a sigh. "I don't know how you do it."

Mitra cocked his head. "Do what?"

Abel chuckled. "*Everything*. You've only been here a few dozen hours, and you've already faced the most dangerous ratri rakshas on Darkside. None of our people dare to cross the Purvanchal Range. You've seen more of our world than any of us, and you're not even afraid. You don't even look tired! You ran for hours by foot, and somehow had the time to lure two kamkara here before coming to save us! How do you do it? You haven't even broken a sweat!"

Mitra chuckled. "I promised you my next story would be about myself, didn't I?"

Abel blinked at him in surprise. "Now? I'd like to know, but I don't know if this is the time for a story."

Yisei Ishkhan

"Why not? We have two hours before the kamkara arrive. I could tell you a story while we get the others cleaned up and wait for them to awaken. What do you think?"

"I'm not complaining," Abel said with a shrug. "I've been waiting to learn more about you since you arrived."

"Very well," smiled Mitra. "Then let me tell you a story–a story of learning from the mistakes of the past."

The Tales of Abel and Mitra
V. The Tale of Ismail and Mihai
May 8, 2123
Shores of Lac Lunaire, Alpine Republic

The crescent moon hung over the crescent-shaped lake. Its silver glow reflected in the tranquil waters below.

Ismail Ouali-St. Laurent descended the steep cobblestone steps of Lac Lunaire, his flowing golden locks whipping up in the crisp mountain breeze. Despite the uneven terrain, he could traverse this route with his eyes closed. It was a path he'd walked a thousand times, bringing him down the hillside village to Signora Lombardi's cottage by the lake.

Lac Lunaire was a secluded haven nestled deep in the Swiss Alps. With only a few thousand residents, the idyllic paradise had become a refuge for those escaping dramatic upheavals that gripped the rest of the continent in recent decades. Sticking to a tradition of unyielding neutrality, the Alpine Republic remained an ideal destination–a calm in the storm. From the sleepy village, it was difficult to believe that one was at the heart of a continent undergoing the greatest turmoil it had faced in two centuries.

For Ismail, Lac Lunaire was a sanctuary. From his chalet in the hills, he often gazed over the picturesque village, the rolling green hills, and the crystal blue waters of the lake as towering mountains soared into the clouds overhead. He could almost imagine that he was in another world.

Dawn was yet to break across the horizon, and most of the village remained asleep as he reached the lake's edge. Here was the cottage of Signora Maria Lombardi. She was a supercentenarian, and like most of her generation, never married or had children. Thus, she lived alone. For most of her life, that had suited her just fine; but as she was getting on in years, she found herself increasingly isolated as most of her friends and family died off.

Ismail had first run into the old woman when he moved to Lac Lunaire a couple of years prior. She'd been in the market, seated on her levitating E-Chair as she argued with one of the vendors.

"You call that a fair price?!" Maria snapped in Italian. "In my day, we were allowed to bargain!"

Her E-Watch quickly translated her words into German for the vendor.

"I'm sorry," grumbled the vendor in his native tongue. "This isn't Italia, and we're not in the 20th century. My price is fixed."

"Ridiculous!" The old woman spat. "I'll have you know that I was born in the *21st* century!"

"If you aren't buying, move along."

Observing from a distance, Ismail had decided to step in. It wasn't something he would normally do, but this time he felt called to help the old woman.

"Pardon me, Signora," he greeted her in Italian. "Perhaps I can make you an offer."

Maria's face lit up. "Finally, someone who speaks Italian around here! What are you proposing? I don't recognize you. Are you new in town?"

"I am," Ismail flashed a charming smile. "I simply noticed your attempt to negotiate a deal for Kavkazian wine with that vendor. If you're interested, I have a few bottles in my chalet. I'd be happy to pass them along.

The Tales of Abel and Mitra

The old woman narrowed her gaze. "Kavkazian wine doesn't come cheap. I don't think I have anything to offer you in return."

"You needn't offer me anything," Ismail assured. "You see, I have an old friend down in Habisha who's been generous enough to send me the best delicacies from around the world. Every month, I receive a delivery from somewhere new–Aotearoa, Malabar, Qocho. This month's shipment was from Kavkazia and included several bottles of local wine. Unfortunately, I forgot to relay to my friend that I'd given up drinking some time ago. I'd rather give the bottles to someone who can enjoy it than let it go to waste."

"'Some time ago'?" Maria scoffed. "How old are you? Twenty?"

"Twenty-five."

She chuckled. "Even if you gave up drinking when you were an infant, you're not old enough to say, 'some time ago.' I've lived more than four times as long as you! Talk to me when you get to my age!"

Ismail chuckled. "So, is that a deal?"

Maria cocked her head. "Your friend must be rich to send such extravagant gifts each month."

"She's interested in some of my research," Ismail said. "Her generosity is a way of expressing appreciation for my work."

"I see. Well, only a fool would turn down an offer of free Kavkazian wine!"

And thus, an unlikely friendship began. Ismail didn't know anyone else in town, and Maria didn't get along with most–yet somehow, their friendship worked. Ismail would visit her almost every morning, escorting her to the market, strolling along the shores of the lake, or simply sitting with her for tea while she recounted stories from her youth. Her company was a much-needed distraction for Ismail—an excuse to come into town and avoid becoming a recluse in his chalet consumed by his work.

Besides, her stories fascinated him. There were still many people old enough who remembered what life was like before the Great Collapse, but few with memories stretching as far back as Maria. Born in an era when digital forms of record-keeping dominated, the memories of people like her were the best sources of information for early-21st-century life. Most digital records had been lost in the Great Collapse.

Ismail listened intently, carefully jotting down notes from Maria's stories. Someday, he hoped to compile them into an archive, preserving them for future generations.

As his heels clicked along the cobblestone path on the way to Maria's home, he noticed an unusual light coming from her windows. She normally preferred to keep her house dark to conserve energy.

He rapped lightly at the door.

"*I kimm!*" An unfamiliar voice called out from the other side. The door creaked open, revealing a middle-aged woman with short blonde hair. She smiled politely, switching over to Universal English with a heavy Bavarian accent. "Can I help you? Oh! You must be Ismail!"

"Yes," Ismail furrowed his brow. "Is Maria home?"

"Yes, yes. She's told us all about you. *Kumm nei, kumm nei.*"

Ismail smiled, tentatively stepping foot into the cottage. Three children—two girls and a boy—caught him off guard as

The Tales of Abel and Mitra

they burst from a room to the right, shrieking with laughter as they raced past him down the hallway.

"Ariana! Leo! Watch where you're running!" The woman cried in German. When she turned, Ismail realized that she was pregnant with another child. "I'm sorry, they're just excited. Oh, I forgot to introduce myself! I'm Kristen Tiedemann. My husband is the grandson of one of Maria's old friends. We live in Innsbruck but decided to pay Maria a visit on our way to Geneva. Maria is just in the kitchen with my husband."

Ismail followed Kristen down the corridor and saw that the children were already there, chasing each other around the table. Maria and Kristen's husband sat in deep conversation, unfazed by the chaos.

"Ariana, drop the spoons," Kristen hissed. "Leo, don't stand on the chair. Angelina, take your siblings outside to play. But stay away from the lake."

"*Ja, Mama,*" the oldest girl said, taking the other two children by the hands. They giggled as they shuffled past Ismail and disappeared out the door.

"Ah, Ismail, you're here!" Maria's face lit up. "We were just talking about you!"

"Only good things, I hope," Ismail smiled, taking a seat at the table. He reached out, giving Kristen's husband a firm handshake. "Ismail Ouali-St. Laurent."

"Fabio Belini," the man replied.

"Belini," Ismail repeated. "I recognize that name. Maria has shared quite a few stories about the wild escapades she and your grandmother had in their youth."

Fabio raised an eyebrow. "*Nonna* never mentioned those. I've always known her as a proper lady."

Maria waved his comment aside. "She liked people to see her that way. But she wasn't always so proper. She changed after meeting your *Nonno*...and after the Great Collapse."

A heavy silence followed her comment.

"In any case," Fabio broke the tension. "Maria was just telling me how you've been sharing your wine shipments with her. We were about to crack open a bottle of Aquitanian Chardonnay. Care to join us?"

"Fabio!" Kristen scoffed. "This early in the morning?"

"What?" Her husband shrugged. "*Sono Italiano!*"

Maria chuckled. "Ismail doesn't drink."

"A Frenchman who doesn't drink?" Fabio laughed. "What a pity!"

"It interferes with my work," Ismail smiled.

"Ah," Fabio nodded. "And what work would that be?"

Maria leaned in toward him with a whisper. "*Classified*. He hasn't even told *me* yet."

"Oh?" Fabio folded his hands together. "Now I'm intrigued."

Maria turned to Ismail with a frown. "I'm sorry for not telling you that Fabio and his family were coming to visit. I thought it was next week. They'll be staying here for a few days."

"No need to apologize," Ismail said. "I was just planning to visit the market this morning. I'll let you catch up with your guests."

"You won't be staying?" Fabio asked.

"I have work to attend to," Ismail offered a faint smile. "*Classified* work."

The Tales of Abel and Mitra

Fabio chuckled. "Of course. Perhaps you'll join us for dinner? We made reservations at the Spanish restaurant in town."

"My favourite place," said Ismail. "I'll give Maria a call later and let you know if I'm available. In any case, it was a pleasure meeting you."

"The pleasure is ours," Fabio said.

Kristen echoed her husband's sentiment as Ismail rose from his seat to leave.

"Ismail," Maria called out, steering her E-Chair over to him. "Before you go, there's something I must tell you. Early in the morning, I heard a violin playing in the distance. At first, I was irritated at being woken up, but then they started playing *our* song. It was the most beautiful rendition I've ever heard."

Ismail's heart skipped a beat. "*Roma?*"

She nodded.

Roma: The Second Fall of the Eternal City, was the *magnum opus* of the legendary Floriano. The famed musician was hailed as the greatest living composer, standing alongside Bach, Tchaikovsky, and Vivaldi. The symphony was a melancholic composition, a haunting requiem for a bygone era.

"They might still be out there," Maria said. "I heard them by the lake, just a few minutes before your arrival."

Ismail nodded. "Thank you for telling me."

He stepped outside, almost tripping over the children as they dashed through the garden, waving sticks in hand as they engaged in an imaginary sword fight. He followed the shore of the lake. The waters were clear, the glasslike surface perfectly reflecting the clouds and towering mountains overhead.

Yisei Ishkhan

A single note rang out from ahead, long and drawn out as it echoed through the stillness. The familiar tune of *Roma*'s overture followed, drawing him forward. The tune led him to a stone bridge spanning the village creek. At the crest of the bridge, he saw her–a slim frame wrapped in a floral petticoat, her straight black hair cut into a short bob cut. Though her back was to him, Ismail recognized her instantly. He felt a sudden urge to leave, but as the music shifted into the first movement, he was drawn to stay.

He leaned against the ledge of the bridge, closing his eyes as he took in her performance. She didn't acknowledge him directly as she stared out at the lake, but he knew she was aware of his presence. She always had keener senses than most.

For nearly an hour, he stood transfixed. Maria hadn't been exaggerating–listening to her play was otherworldly. It stirred memories in him, not all of which he wanted to recall. By the final note, his chest felt tight. He quickly wiped the tears from his face.

"Your playing has improved," he said in a low voice.

"Well, I'd hope so," the woman said with a light chuckle. She set down the violin and turned to face him. Her almond-shaped eyes were bright and warm, and she had a small, curved nose over her thin lips. "I've had three years of practice since we last met. It's good to see you again, Ismail. You haven't changed much, though I think your hair is a bit longer now."

Ismail gave a faint smile. "You haven't changed at *all*. Tell me, Natsuki, what brings you to Lac Lunaire?"

The Tales of Abel and Mitra

"I came to visit an old friend," she mused. "It was difficult to track you down after you disabled your *Aeterna* ID."

"How *did* you track me down? I thought I was off the grid."

"A mutual friend tipped me off."

"Professor Solomon," Ismail sighed and shook his head. "She's the only one who knows I'm here. She still sends me gifts every month."

"Of course she does," Natsuki chuckled. Her tone shifted. "Did you hear that Floriano passed away?"

Ismail's heart sank. "No. When was this?"

"Just the other day. Some say it was poison, others suicide." She shrugged. "I'm surprised you didn't know. He was your favourite composer, wasn't he? Unless things have changed since Rome?"

"They haven't," said Ismail. "*Roma* is my favourite piece by him. But I don't keep up with news of the outside world. Life in Lac Lunaire is quiet. Most people come here to escape, to leave the rest of the world behind."

"I hope I haven't disturbed your tranquil abode."

"You haven't," Ismail assured. "I'm just surprised, that's all. Are you and Nuwa–?"

"Engaged," Natsuki raised her hand. Her ring shimmered in the light of dawn. "He proposed a few weeks ago."

Ismail blinked in surprise. "Congratulations."

Her laughter bubbled up. "You don't sound very enthusiastic."

"Sorry," he said sheepishly. "I just wasn't expecting that response. I'm surprised he's allowed you to visit me. Does he even know you're here?"

"Of course. He's at the lodge right now."

"The lodge?" Ismail paled. "You mean he's *here*? In Lac Lunaire?"

"He was the one who wanted to see you," said Natsuki. "I just came along as his mediator."

"You're joking," Ismail let out a laugh, but when Natsuki's expression didn't waver, he realized she was being serious. "Why would *Nuwa* of all people want to see me?"

"I know it might be hard to believe, but he's changed in the past few years," she flashed him a smile. "And so have you, it seems."

Ismail crossed his arms. "And how would you know that?"

Natsuki tilted her head to the south. "That old woman you've befriended—she's Italian, isn't she? From Rome?"

He stiffened. "So, you've been spying on me?"

"I wouldn't say '*spying*,'" she chuckled. "Nuwa is the Apostle of Light. He has connections all over the world, even here in your quaint little village."

"Why am I not surprised," Ismail sighed. "Yes, Maria is from Rome."

"I thought so. Does she know about your past?"

Ismail narrowed his gaze. "No. And I intend to keep it that way. Do you think anyone here would tolerate me if they knew who I was?"

"If even Nuwa has changed his mind about you, anything is possible."

"I find it hard to believe that he *has* changed his mind."

"I'm sure many would say the same about you. Why did you choose to befriend that old woman? Did you feel guilty about what happened in Rome?"

The Tales of Abel and Mitra

"I can always rely on you to psychoanalyze my every action," Ismail smirked. "I suppose you can say that. But if by 'changed' you mean I'm no longer the reckless idealogue I was in college, then you'd be correct. As for the way I was born..." he shrugged. "I'm afraid that won't ever change."

"Well," Natsuki said gently. "Nuwa had a change of heart on those matters since you last saw him."

"Has he?" Ismail huffed. "I'll believe it when I see it."

"He's more open-minded than he was before. Our time in Naga-Zo changed him."

"Naga-Zo, huh?" Ismail nodded knowingly. "Are you referring to the incident where civilians were deported off-world? Surely that's a crime against humanity."

"It is," Natsuki sighed. "The High Council is convening an emergency meeting. Unfortunately, not all nations adhere to the terms of the Treaty of Ntu, so there is little that can be done about the matter."

"Are you coming directly from Naga-Zo?"

Natsuki nodded. "We were fortunate to get out. We managed to smuggle out a few refugees, including a little girl. She's an orphan. The rest of her family was deported off-world, so we're considering adopting her. She's at the lodge with us. Actually, she is the reason Nuwa had a change of heart."

"Oh? How so?"

Natsuki smiled knowingly. "Perhaps if you agree to meet him, you can find out for yourself."

"Classic Natsuki," Ismail chuckled. "Offering just enough information to entice me, only to keep the answers out of reach."

Natsuki laughed. "So, will you meet him?"

"I'll consider it."

"Don't keep him waiting too long," Natsuki urged. "We can only stay in Lac Lunaire for a few nights. He'd truly appreciate it if you met with him. We'll be at the Heavenly Light Church tomorrow morning if you'd like to join us."

"The one at the top of the hill at the edge of town?"

"That's the one."

"I haven't stepped foot in a church since San Pietro," Ismail mused. "I'm not sure I'd be welcome there."

"Even Paul of Tarsus started as a prosecutor of the Church," Natsuki noted. "And look what he became–the greatest Apostle in history."

"If you're expecting such a transformation in my life, prepare to be disappointed."

Natsuki shrugged. "The Lord works in mysterious ways. I believe He has great plans for you, and that you will do far more to advance His kingdom than Nuwa and I will ever accomplish."

"Sure, *Prophetess* Natsuki," Ismail said.

"Please," she scoffed. "They call me that all the time, but I don't like that title. I'll see you tomorrow morning at church, then?"

"Tomorrow morning," Ismail bid his friend farewell. He made his way back to his mountain chalet, his thoughts swirling at the encounter. Upon reaching home, he sighed, collapsing in a heap on the couch.

Welcome back, sir, the soothing voice of his virtual assistant came from overhead. *You appear exhausted. Shall I prepare some tea?*

"Yes, please. Thank you, Aida."

The Tales of Abel and Mitra

No problem, sir. A few moments of silence passed. *Your tea is brewing in the kitchen. It will be ready in three and a half minutes. Would you like me to bring it to you?*

"No need. I'll make my way over to the kitchen."

As you wish, sir.

He pushed himself up from the couch, sauntering over to the table and sinking into his chair. He felt as if he were carrying a heavy weight on his back. He gazed distantly out the floor-to-ceiling window at the valley below.

Is everything alright, sir? Aida wondered. *You appear fatigued. Would you like me to conduct a health assessment?*

"That won't be necessary," Ismail sighed. "Tell me, Aida, do you remember Nuwa Yuen-Serwanga?"

You told me never to mention that name to you, sir.

"Of course I did," Ismail muttered. "I would've rather forgotten about him. But it seems *he* hasn't forgotten about *me*. I ran into Natsuki this morning in town. She told me that Nuwa is here, in Lac Lunaire, and wants to meet me."

Will you agree to his request?

"I'm debating it. I'd prefer to never see him again. That being said, *he* always despised me more than I despised him. Natsuki said he's had a change of heart these past few years. I'm curious to find out whether or not that's true."

You've always been a reserved individual, sir. Ever since moving to Lac Lunaire, you've further isolated yourself, clinging onto fragments of your past while simultaneously running from it. Perhaps it would be best to confront a part of your past you've been suppressing for a long time— Nuwa Yuen-Serwanga.

"You're probably right," Ismail grumbled. "As much as I hate to admit it. That might be for the best."

Yisei Ishkhan

Of course I'm right, sir. After all, you programmed me to deliver only objective insights. She paused for a moment. *Your tea is ready, sir.*

Ismail rose, making his way over to the counter to retrieve the steaming cup. He blew lightly on the rim before taking a sip. "I suppose I'm meeting Nuwa in the morning, then. Aida, please set my alarm for 9:30."

Alarm set, sir.

***

St. Mauritius Heavenly Light Church sat atop a steep cliffside, offering a beautiful view of the lake below. The parish was a whitewashed building with a red-tiled roof and a bell tower that summoned the faithful to worship. It was large enough to hold a couple dozen parishioners in its central nave. Once a Reform parish, it had recently been converted into a Heavenly Light congregation. These days, it seemed most of the churches had, regardless of their denominational background.

Ismail kept his head low, tucking his golden locks into a woolen scarf that he'd wrapped around his neck. He averted his gaze from everyone he passed, hoping they wouldn't notice him as long as he wasn't looking at them. His hopes were quickly dashed.

"Ismail? What are you doing here?"

He glanced up in surprise at the sound of Maria's voice. The old woman was seated in the pews at the back, together with Fabio, Kristen, and their three children. Kristen held one of her squirming daughters in her lap as the other two children scurried about, climbing over and under the pew.

"Maria," Ismail said in surprise. "And Fabio and Kristen. A pleasure to see you again."

The Tales of Abel and Mitra

"Couldn't make it for dinner last night?" Fabio asked. "The paella was delicious."

"Ah, yes," Ismail flushed. "I apologize for not getting back to you. I was…distracted by other matters. I completely forgot about your invitation."

"No worries," Fabio chuckled. "We were planning on taking Maria out again tonight. Do you have any recommendations?"

"To be honest, I haven't been to many places in town," Ismail said. His eyes shifted nervously about the room, scanning for Natsuki or Nuwa. He spotted plenty of familiar faces–the elderly Spanish couple who ran the restaurant seated next to the pretty Hungarian florist; the burly Greek man in the back who ran a gyro shop chatting with a Frenchman; a young Turkish couple with two children; the German librarian and his young daughter who ran the bakery.

It struck Ismail that despite seeing their faces regularly throughout town, he couldn't recall their names. He'd introduced himself to most of them when he first moved into town but hadn't made an effort to get to know them.

"I'm surprised to see you here," Maria remarked. "I didn't know you were a churchgoer."

"I'm not," said Ismail. "And what about you? I thought you were an agnostic."

"Back in my day everyone was an agnostic," she admitted dismissively. "It was the status quo, and I never gave it much thought. Fabio and Kristen invited me to the service, so I decided to come along. I must admit, I'm not familiar with these Heavenly Light churches. When I was a girl, the Catholic Church was the biggest in the world, especially in Italy. No one had heard of the Church of Heavenly Light back then. Now, it seems to be the opposite. Especially after what happened in Rome."

Ismail's stomach churned at the mention of the city.

"It's remarkable how much the world can change in a century," Fabio noted.

"Oh, certainly," nodded Maria. "My oldest memory is of my *Bisnonna* scolding me for always being glued to my phone. She was born exactly a hundred years before me, and told me that when she was young, people didn't even have home telephones."

"*Mama*, what's a phone?" Asked Fabio and Kristen's eldest daughter.

"I...don't know," Kristen admitted sheepishly.

"Oh, of course you don't know," Maria laughed, waving the E-Watch on her wrist. "Nowadays we use *these*. I'm still getting used to them myself. I took for granted the technology I had as a kid. After the Great Collapse, we didn't even have electricity to light our homes for a few years! I bet you can't imagine living in a world like that..."

As she rambled on, Ismail began tuning out her words. He'd already heard it all before.

Fabio glanced at him with a smile. "Is this your first time attending a Heavenly Light service?"

"It is," Ismail admitted sheepishly.

"And what made you decide to come today?"

"I happened to run into an old friend yesterday who invited me. Speaking of which..."

"Ismail Ouali-St. Laurent."

The low voice was unmistakable as it echoed from behind him. Ismail turned around. Nuwa Yuen-Serwanga stood out

The Tales of Abel and Mitra

amid the crowd– a tall, imposing figure clad in saffron robes that contrasted with his dark skin and even darker curly hair that cascaded past his shoulders. His expression, as usual, was unreadable. He stared at Ismail with a narrow gaze.

"Nuwa Yuen-Serwanga," Ismail nodded slightly.

Behind Nuwa stood Natsuki dressed in a violet kimono, the gentle smile on her face contrasting sharply with her fiancé's gaze. Between them was a young girl, staring up at Ismail in silence.

"Natsuki," Ismail bowed to his old friend.

"Ismail," Natsuki greeted him. She gestured to the girl. "This is Eli."

"A pleasure to meet you, Eli."

Eli shrank back, ducking behind Nuwa's robes.

"She's shy," Natsuki chuckled.

Nuwa glanced at Maria, Fabio, and Kristen. "Am I interrupting?" He asked in Italian.

"Not at all!" Fabio assured. "Ismail was just telling us how his old friends invited him here today. That would be you, I assume?"

"'Friends,'" Nuwa repeated, glancing at Ismail. "Yes, that would be us."

"You never told me you had *friends*," Maria nudged Ismail. "And ones who speak Italian, no less! Who is this tall, handsome fellow?"

"Natsuki and Nuwa are old classmates from college," Ismail explained.

"Wait," Fabio interjected. "Did you say Nuwa Yuen-Serwanga? As in *the* Nuwa Yuen-Serwanga."

"Yes, that would be me."

Yisei Ishkhan

Fabio's face lit up. "Ismail, you didn't tell us you were friends with the Apostle of Light himself! Why didn't you tell us he was here in Lac Lunaire?"

"I only found out yesterday," Ismail said.

"If you'd excuse us," Nuwa placed a firm hand on Ismail's shoulder. "It's been years since we've seen each other. I'd like to take some time to reconnect with Ismail."

"Of course, of course," Fabio said. "It was a pleasure to meet you."

Ismail flinched under Nuwa's grip as he was steered away from the group, down the aisle toward the front of the church. Ismail glanced back to see if it was really Nuwa's hand on his shoulder. It was. Ismail could hardly believe his eyes. In all the years they'd known each other, Nuwa had refused to make physical contact with Ismail. Most of the time, he wouldn't even cast a glance at him or utter his name.

Ismail flashed a look of disbelief in Natsuki's direction. She shrugged as if to say: *See? I told you he changed.*

Nuwa directed Ismail to the very front row of the church. The pews were nearly empty, save for a lone woman in her late twenties with a distant look in her eyes. Her gaze shifted to Ismail as they approached, her face brightening with a warm smile.

"Shpresa Arumugampillai," she extended her hand in greeting. "I'll be leading the service today."

"Ismail Ouali-St. Laurent," he shook her hand. He recognized the woman from around town but couldn't remember where he'd seen her before. "I didn't realize that you were a preacher."

"Oh, I'm not," Shpresa chuckled. "Lac Lunaire is a small village, so we don't have full-time clergy. Members of the

The Tales of Abel and Mitra

congregation take turns leading the service. My profession is typically selling parts."

It dawned on Ismail. "You're the one who delivered the NeuroSynth Core Processor to my chalet last year!"

"Oh?" Shpresa raised an eyebrow. "So, you *do* remember me."

"You were so persistent about delivering it personally, and I didn't understand why," Ismail shook his head as he glanced at Natsuki and Nuwa. "Let me guess, Shpresa is your 'connection' in town?"

"I cannot disclose that information," Nuwa said flatly.

Ismail turned back to Shpresa, but the woman had already risen from the pews.

"Would you look at the time," she glanced at her E-Watch. "It's already eleven. Time for the service to begin."

She took her place at the front of the church as a small choir assembled. They began with hymns, singing in French, German, Italian, and Turkish, the dominant tongues of the town, as well as Universal English. Most of the songs felt distant to Ismail, but the final hymn struck a chord with him. It was one of Floriano's compositions, a piece from *Roma*:

In the shadow of the seven hills,
Babylon trembles, prophecy is fulfilled.
Kingdoms rise and kingdoms fall,
But Heaven's Light shines on it all.

Trumpets sound, the angels weep,
Rome descends to eternal sleep.
Upon the Eternal City has fallen Night,

Yisei Ishkhan

As we await the coming Light.

A new Jerusalem, a transformed world.
The Light of Dawn shall be unfurled.
His grace shall come to every nation,
A promise fulfilled, divine salvation.

"Are you crying?" Nuwa muttered under his breath.

Ismail blinked. It was only then that he noticed the warm tears streaking down his face. Flustered, he pulled a tissue from his pocket and wiped them away. "I didn't expect to hear a piece by Floriano."

"Floriano was a devoted follower of Heavenly Light," Nuwa pointed out. "Most of his compositions contain religious themes and imagery, so it's unsurprising that many have found their way into the church."

Ismail shifted uncomfortably in the pews as Shpresa began preaching her sermon. He found himself glancing down at Nuwa's feet. Though there was a gap between them large enough for another person to squeeze in, this was the closest he'd ever sat to the man.

"What?" Nuwa scoffed. "I'm not going to bite."

"Are you sure you're comfortable sitting this close to me?" Ismail asked.

For the first time since they'd met, Nuwa's expression softened. "You're not contagious."

"You sure acted like I was in the past."

A flash of embarrassment crossed Nuwa's face, but it was gone as quickly as it appeared. "I'll admit I had prejudices against people like you back in college. I realize now that I

The Tales of Abel and Mitra

was wrong. I understand if you can't forgive me for that, but I'm glad that you at least agreed to meet me."

Ismail turned to him in surprise. He could see pride in Nuwa's eyes, but also sincerity. For a man like Nuwa to admit his faults was no small feat.

Ismail chuckled. "The fact that you're willing to admit that I'm a *person* really shows that you've changed."

The tension between them dissipated, and for the rest of the sermon, Ismail's mind was at ease. He leaned back in the pew, the weight of old grievances fading away.

When the sermon came to a close, Shpresa stepped down from the pulpit, her face glowing. "How did I do? It was only my second time preaching."

"You were wonderful," said Natsuki.

Shpresa blushed. "Thank you. Will you be sticking around? I was thinking of grabbing a bite in town."

"We have some catching up to do with Ismail," said Nuwa. "But we'll join you for dinner at that Turkish place."

"Lovely! Would you care to join us, Ismail?"

"I'll have to check my schedule."

"You're always welcome to join us!" She took Ismail's hand in hers, giving him a firm shake before heading off to chat with the other congregants.

"So," Ismail said, turning to Natsuki and Nuwa, "where should we begin?"

"May we visit your place?" Nuwa asked. "It's the chalet overlooking the village, isn't it?"

"I don't often have guests," Ismail said, unnerved by the thought. "It's a mess."

"We don't mind," Natsuki said. "Besides, the matter Nuwa is interested in is up there."

Yisei Ishkhan

"Professor Solomon," Ismail sighed. "She told you about my work, didn't she?"

"Truth be told," said Natsuki, "we aren't just in town to see you. Professor Solomon asked that we check on your progress."

"Of course she did," Ismail grumbled. "I finished it weeks ago, but I have yet to activate it. I'm not sure what will happen when I do."

"If your previous projects are any indication, I'm sure it will exceed expectations," Natsuki said.

"I appreciate the flattery, but this project is on a completely different scale than anything I've built before. Hold on…" Ismail paused, "how do you know of my other projects? Everything I've put out into the public has been anonymous."

"Oh, come on," Natsuki laughed. "You're one of the most sophisticated AMI engineers in the world! Who else could it be?"

"Besides," added Nuwa, "Your last project was called an *Artificial Intelligence Documentary Assistant*. Aka 'AIDA.' That was the same name you gave your virtual assistant back in college. Not exactly subtle if you were trying to cover your tracks."

"I'm surprised you remember that," Ismail huffed. "But what surprises me more is that you pay attention to the field of AMI. I thought you were against it."

"Nuwa was," said Natsuki. "But Eli changed his mind on that matter."

Ismail glimpsed the girl's face peeking out from behind Natsuki's kimono. She had been so silent and still during the

The Tales of Abel and Mitra

service that he'd nearly forgotten she was there. Her wide eyes stared up at him.

"As I mentioned yesterday," said Natsuki, "Eli lost her family back in Naga-Zo."

"Deported off-world," Ismail recalled.

"We heard about AIDA while in Kochi. Eli asked us to let her communicate with her family using it, but Nuwa was opposed to the idea."

"To no one's surprise," Ismail said.

Nuwa shook his head. "But Eli was persistent."

Natsuki gave him a nudge. "He has a soft spot for children."

"So," Ismail concluded, "you had a change of heart after realizing the wonderful capabilities of my work? That still doesn't explain why you changed your mind on *me* specifically."

"You're a gifted individual, Ismail," Nuwa grumbled. "I won't deny that. Engi or not, it shouldn't matter. The circumstances of your birth are beyond your control and shouldn't define your worth. It was wrong for me to condemn you for something beyond your control. In the end, you are still created in the image of God."

"What was that?" Ismail raised his hand to his ear. "Can you repeat that, I didn't quite catch it."

"No," Nuwa grumbled. "Now, will you permit us to see your current project, or not?"

"It's a private matter," Ismail said. "Professor Solomon should've informed you that it isn't for public use."

"I'm aware of that," said Nuwa.

"But Nuwa and I aren't exactly the public, now are we?" Natsuki added with a smile.

265

Yisei Ishkhan

Ismail sighed. "If you're expecting a similar experience to your encounter with AIDA, I must warn you that this project operates on a completely different level. The two cannot be compared. AIDA compiles data from video feeds, sound recordings, photographs, and manual inputs to recreate a simulation of what a person would've looked, sounded, and acted like in life." He glanced at Eli. "It isn't solely used to 'communicate with the deceased,' but that is what most consult it for. With all that said, it's still an imperfect system. It can convince its client that they're interacting with their loved ones, but all it's doing is mimicking the appearance, gestures, tone of voice, and personality of the deceased."

"And how does that differ from your current project?" Natsuki wondered. "Other than the fact that you can communicate physically rather than through a simulated projection?"

"The difference is this project exercises its own agency. It isn't intended to convince the observer that it's a real person. It is, in essence, a person itself."

A still silence fell upon them.

"Who do you think you are?" Nuwa scoffed. "God?" Despite his skepticism, his tone betrayed a hint of unease. "It's impossible to create life from nothing. Much less *human* life."

"Perhaps," Ismail admitted. "But it wasn't created from nothing. I used stem cells to recreate the body–"

"You *cloned* him?" Natsuki gasped.

"I suppose you could say that. But his body has been augmented with synthetic parts. That's what I needed the NeuroSynth Core Processor for–to upload a Memoria Chip. It should hold all the same memories and personality stored

The Tales of Abel and Mitra

on the chip, which theoretically, would make him the same person. Of course, I haven't implanted the chip yet, so I have yet to determine whether it will be successful."

Nuwa shuddered.

"You said you finished weeks ago," said Natsuki. "Why haven't you implanted the chip yet?"

"I couldn't bring myself to," Ismail hesitated. "I'm afraid what it...what *he* might say to me."

"Then shall we find out together?" Said Nuwa.

Ismail sighed. "I never thought the two of you would be the ones giving me this final push."

***

Ismail was uncomfortable having visitors in his chalet. Other than Shrepa's brief visit months ago, no one had stepped foot in his home since he'd moved in. He had no idea what the proper etiquette was for hosting guests.

"Can I get you something?" He asked. "Tea? Coffee? Something to eat? The restroom is just down the hall to the right."

He glanced at Eli. The girl stared back at him with her large, almond eyes. She still hadn't said a word since they'd met, clinging to the fringes of Natsuki's kimono.

"I can project something onto the holograph, if you'd like. What do kids watch these days?"

"What do you think, Eli?" Natsuki asked. "Do you want to tell Uncle Ismail what you'd like to watch?"

Ismail flinched at being called 'uncle.' Eli said nothing, continuing to cling to Natsuki's side.

"She'll stick with us," Natsuki said.

Ismail nodded. "Right this way, then."

Yisei Ishkhan

He led them to his study, a space littered with books and loose pages, some stacked into neat piles and others scattered across the floor. Scribbled notes, equations, and sheets of music were pinned across the walls. In the corner of the room sat a flamenco guitar, shiny and spotless, and the only object that looked like Ismail took care of. Along the side of the guitar were the letters P+M faintly carved within a heart.

Natsuki smiled as her gaze rested on it. "When did you start playing?"

"Shortly after we parted ways," Ismail said.

"Can you play us something?"

Nuwa scoffed. "Ismail never had an ear for music."

Ismail approached the guitar, and for a moment the others expected him to pick it up. Instead, he reached for a box on the shelf resting above the guitar. He popped open the lid–inside was a Memoria Chip.

Nuwa's expression darkened. "I never understood why anyone would implant one of those into their brain."

"I know your faith generally prohibits the use of this kind of technology," Ismail held up the chip between his two fingers, inspecting it carefully. "But without this, my project would've been impossible."

He approached a metallic cylinder along the glass wall overlooking the valley. As he drew near, lights illuminated the device, revealing its true function–a containment pod. Inside, a man's figure lay in suspended animation.

Natsuki gasped, and Eli withdrew behind her, poking her head out as she stared at the man in confusion. Nuwa stiffened, his eyes locked on the pod.

"It looks just like him..." he murmured in disbelief.

The Tales of Abel and Mitra

"That's the point," Ismail said. He entered a code on the control pad, unlocking the pod. The screen slid open. Ismail glanced back at the others. "If you've changed your mind, we don't have to go through with this."

"Please continue," Nuwa said.

Ismail stood next to the body, combing his fingers through its black locks. He sought the precise spot above the ear for the Memoria Chip's insertion. *Click.* The Memoria Chip fell into place.

"Aida, initiate reanimation," Ismail commanded.

Initiating...

The body began to stir. One finger twitched, and a moment later they all began to curl. The man raised his head, eyes fluttering open as if he'd awoken from a deep sleep.

Nuwa stepped back, his composure slipping. Ismail held his breath.

The man sat upward, flexing his fingers as he studied his hands. His bronze skin was flawless, his nose perfectly straight, his lips full and his jaw chiseled. He resembled a living masterpiece, like something sculpted by Michelangelo or a Classical artisan.

His hazel eyes flicked toward them, studying each of them intently. A gasp escaped Nuwa's lips. Those eyes were unmistakably human. There was more life in them than in the eyes of most people.

"Do you know who we are?" Nuwa asked tentatively.

"I...recognize you..." a slight smile spread across the man's face. His voice was smooth and melodious.

"Do you know who *you* are?" Ismail asked.

Yisei Ishkhan

"Who I am...?" The man repeated the question as if testing the words. A flicker of understanding spread across his face. "I am Mihai. Mihai Aslan Ionescu-Amaya."

Natsuki's hands flew to her mouth, tears welling in her eyes. "I can't believe it! It's really you!"

"It's not him," Nuwa interjected, though his voice wavered as he spoke. "He doesn't have a soul. He's just accessing Mihai's memories through the chip."

"The memories..." Mihai murmured. "They're blurry. I recognize your faces, but I can't recall who you are..."

"Aida, initiate *Recuperatio memoriae*," Ismail said.

Of course, sir.

As Ismail approached Mihai, the man's eyes tracked his every movement, his expression unreadable.

"You recognize my face," Ismail said. "Now, it's time for you to recall your memories."

Mihai stared at him for a long moment. "Will it be painful?"

Ismail's expression softened. "Some of it will be. But it won't last long."

He took Mihai's hands in his. As their eyes locked, a glimmer of recognition flashed through Mihai's eyes. "I know you...you're Icarus..."

"Icarus?" Natsuki asked in confusion.

Ismail blushed. "It was the alias I used when we joined the Melekhites. They called me Icarus, and Mihai was known as—"

"Mitra," Mihai said, the name rolling off his tongue.

Before they could say another word, Aida's voice echoed through the chamber.

The Tales of Abel and Mitra
Initiating Recuperatio memoriae.

***

The *Instituto d'Arte e Technologia di Roma* was a prestigious institution, among the top centers of study in the fields of art and technology in the Post-Collapse Era. For Ismail, it represented the culmination of a lifelong aspiration. Both his parents were alumni–his mother, a renowned soprano blending folk music with operatic grandeur, and his father, a master sculptor and painter whose works evoked classical styles. But unlike his parents, Ismail wasn't here to pursue the arts. His interests lay in the sciences–the field of Artificial Mobile Intelligence Engineering.

Despite this, he'd been forced to enroll in electives outside his field of study. He reluctantly selected a course called *The Rise of New Religious Movements in the Post-Collapse Era*. On the first day of classes, he sat at the back of the lecture hall, quietly flipping through his syllabi for his *Introduction to Applied AMI Development* class as he tuned out the professor's words.

"Now, would everyone please get into groups and introduce yourselves to your peers," the professor's voice rang out.

Ismail, lost in his thoughts, continued glancing through his syllabi until he felt a hand on his shoulder.

"What is it?" Ismail glanced up in irritation.

When he saw the man standing there, his voice caught in his throat. He had bronze skin, wavy black hair, and striking hazel eyes that almost appeared golden in the light. His features were flawless, like those of the sculptures of Eros or Apollo his father had carved–only *alive*.

Yisei Ishkhan

"Are you part of our group?" The stranger asked, holding up a card labeled D1.

It was only then that Ismail realized a card labeled D4 had been placed on his desk. In the row ahead of him, a girl with perfectly straight black hair turned to smile at them, waving a card labeled D2. Next to her, a guy with dark, curly locks and a serious look in his eyes held up a card labeled D3.

"What are the groups for?" Ismail muttered.

"Were you not paying attention?" The guy in front rolled his eyes.

"We have to work together on a research project this semester," smiled the golden-eyed stranger, taking a seat next to Ismail.

"Professor Solomon asked us to introduce ourselves," the girl piped up. "Name, major, where you're from, and a fun fact about yourself. Who wants to go first?"

"Nuwa Yuen-Serwanga," muttered the man in front. "Political Science Major. From Ukerewe."

"And a fun fact?" Asked the golden-eyed man.

"I don't enjoy icebreakers. That's my fun fact."

"Pleasure to meet you, Nuwa," the golden-eyed man extended his hand in greeting. "I'm Mihai Aslan Ionescu-Amaya. I was born and raised here in Rome, but my parents are from Paris. I'm majoring in Classical Music and Traditions, with a focus on dance."

"Ooh," the girl's eyes lit up. "That sounds interesting! What kind of dance?"

"Ballet and flamenco are my specialties, but I dabble in tango and folk styles. Lezginka and prisiadki are two of my favourites. I suppose that can be my fun fact."

The Tales of Abel and Mitra

"You'll have to show us sometime!"

"With pleasure," said Mihai. "Now, tell us about yourself."

"Hello everyone," the girl waved both of her hands, then bowed her head to them. "I'm Kirishima Hoa Natsuki. I'm originally from Nippon, but I grew up in New Seoul. My major is Post-Collapse Era Studies, so this course is part of my program. And a fun fact, I play the violin and shamisen. Music has always been a big part of my life."

Finally, all eyes turned to Ismail. He hesitated a moment before speaking. "My name is Ismail Ouali-St. Laurent. I'm studying Artificial Mobile Intelligence Engineering. My family is also from Paris, but I was born in the Alpine Republic and grew up moving between different cities."

"And your fun fact?" Mihai prompted.

"That *was* my fun fact."

"Oh, that doesn't count," Natsuki chuckled. "Tell us something else."

"You didn't make Nuwa give you a fun fact."

"Technically, he *did* give us one," Mihai noted with a smile. "It just wasn't very *fun*."

"Fine," Ismail sighed as he racked his brain. "My mother is an opera singer, and my father is a sculptor. Both are alumni from this institute."

"Interesting!" Natsuki beamed. "Did she also take ballet?"

"She focused on music, specifically opera and Amazigh folk music."

"Wait," said Mihai. "Did you say your surname was Ouali? Your mother wouldn't happen to be Louna Ouali, would she?"

Ismail turned to him in surprise. "You know her?"

Yisei Ishkhan

"Who doesn't!" Mihai said. He glanced at the others expectantly, but they both shook their heads. "Oh, come on. She performed in *Carmen* and *Die Zauberflöte*! But my favourite has to be her legendary performance in *Un inno all'alba e al tramonto*. Combining ballet and opera? Simple genius!"

"I don't watch opera," mumbled Nuwa.

"I've only seen *Le nozze di Figaro*," Natsuki piped up.

"She played the lead role in that!" Mihai laughed.

"Oh, *her*," Natsuki nodded, turning to Ismail in surprise. "She's your mother?"

"Wasn't that opera involved in a controversy for only having Engi performers?" Nuwa narrowed his gaze. "Your mother is an Engi?"

Natsuki winced. "Isn't that a derogatory term?"

"Why?" Nuwa huffed. "It's descriptive–easier than saying 'biologically *engi*neered'. If your mother is one, that makes *you* one."

"Yes," said Ismail indifferently. "Both of my parents were bioengineered as embryos. So was I, before the practice was outlawed. You're right. That makes me an 'Engi,' as you people like to call us."

"'*You people*'?" Nuwa fumed. "You see how they denigrate us? Engis are the epitome of privilege–born to wealthy parents who predetermined their success by engineering them to have the best intelligence, health, and beauty. Everything is handed to you from conception, while the rest of us have to earn our place in the world."

"Do you think life is easy for us?" Ismail scoffed. "We're burdened with impossible expectations while simultaneously demonized for existing. I didn't choose to be born this way.

The Tales of Abel and Mitra

Do you know how disappointing it was for my parents when I didn't become a skilled musician?"

"Easy to say that when everything has been handed to you," Nuwa sneered. "It's ironic that you're majoring in Artificial Mobile Intelligence Engineering when your *own* intelligence has been artificially engineered through gene editing."

"I think that's enough," Mihai said in a firm voice.

Professor Solomon's voice called out from the front of the class. "What's going on back there?"

"Nothing," Ismail grumbled.

"As I was saying," the professor continued, "you'll be dividing into pairs to focus on a particular area for this project, before coming together as a group to synthesize your research. Numbers One and Two will form one pair, and Numbers Three and Four the other."

Ismail stiffened as he glimpsed the number on his card– D4. Nuwa was D3. Without a word, he rose from his seat, grabbed his belongings off the table, and slipped out of the back of the class.

"Hey," Mihai hissed. "Where are you going?"

When Ismail didn't reply, he followed him out. He found Ismail in the restroom, leaning over the sink as he stared at his reflection in the mirror.

"Why are you here?" Ismail mumbled, still staring into the mirror.

"I just wanted to check on you," said Mihai.

"I'm fine. If you aren't here to take a piss, go back to class."

Yisei Ishkhan

"Professor Solomon asked us to brainstorm ideas," said Mihai. "I thought you might want to be there to discuss with us."

"I'm dropping the course."

Mihai frowned. "Because of Nuwa?"

Ismail straightened, meeting Mihai's gaze in the mirror. "I can't work with someone who despises my existence. Trust me, I've met plenty like him before. They both envy and despise Engis like me."

Mihai approached the sink, pulling out his card–D1. "Then let's switch. I'll pair with Nuwa, and you can team up with Natsuki. It's a win-win for all of us."

Ismail eyed him with skepticism. "Except for *you*."

Mihai shrugged with a playful grin. "I get to see you in class twice a week for the rest of the semester."

"Oh, I see how it is," Ismail said, a trace of amusement in his tone. "Because my mother is Louna Ouali, you're hoping to get on my good side so you can meet her someday."

"No," Mihai laughed. "But now that you mention it, I wouldn't mind that. That's not why I'm doing this. This is about *you*, not your mother. You need an elective, and last I checked most of the others are full. Unless you were planning to sign up for *Underwater Basket Weaving 101* or *The Art of Left-Handed Puppetry*, I'd recommend sticking with this course."

"Fine," Ismail snatched the D1 card from Mihai's hand. "I'll stay. But don't come complaining to me if you can't stand being Nuwa's partner."

Mihai laughed. "I won't. I promise."

The Tales of Abel and Mitra

As Ismail handed Mihai his D4 card, he studied him carefully in the mirror. "You wouldn't happen to be an Engi yourself, would you?"

"Me?" Mihai flashed a charming grin. "Nah. I'm 100% *au naturel*. Well…" he tapped the side of his head, just above the ear, "except for the Memoria Chip. Why do you ask?"

Ismail hesitated, his eyes darting away. "I was just curious. Sorry if it came across the wrong way."

"No worries," Mihai chuckled. "I get asked that question all the time."

"Really? Why?"

Mihai shrugged, leaning against the sink as he and Ismail made eye contact in the mirror. "You tell me. *You're* the one who asked."

Ismail shifted uncomfortably, his face flushing. "Well, I don't know. Why don't you take a look at yourself in the mirror?"

Mihai smirked. "Are you saying only Engis can be this dashingly handsome?"

"People who bioengineer their children try to max out their traits. Not just in terms of skills and intellect, but also physical appearance. Who wouldn't want their kids to be good-looking? Still, I've never come across someone as striking as you–Engi or otherwise."

Mihai laughed. "I'll take that as a compliment. But you know, I'd rather be judged for my character than my genetics. Wouldn't you agree?"

Ismail's face burned even brighter. He cleared his throat and muttered, "If only everyone thought that way."

***

Yisei Ishkhan

Ismail remained in the course, partnering with Natsuki while Mihai teamed up with Nuwa. Their group settled on researching the paradigm shift in the Church of Heavenly Light during the decade following the Great Collapse. Both Natsuki and Nuwa were followers of the Church, so they had an intimate understanding of the subject.

While Ismail found the Melekhite movement more intriguing, he didn't object to the group's choice. He and Natsuki would explore the lives of two of the Church's most pivotal figures of that era–Jiao Tianguang and Gulifar Tursun. Mihai and Nuwa focused on other key figures from the Church's history outside China.

Working alongside Natsuki was a breeze. Her fascination with Tianguang and Gulifar bordered on obsession; she was even taking an entire course dedicated to them. She practically begged Ismail to let her do most of the work. Ismail obliged without complaint.

Nuwa, as it turned out, held the title of "Apostle of Light," and was recognized as a spiritual successor to Jiao Tianguang within certain branches of the Church. While the details of what that title entailed escaped Ismail, he wasn't inclined to delve into the ecclesiastical structure of the Church, particularly where Nuwa was concerned. All he knew was that Nuwa hailed from a prominent lineage. To Ismail's relief, Nuwa didn't flaunt his position and seemed uncomfortable discussing it. Despite his disdain for Engis, at least he wasn't *completely* an elitist.

As the months passed, the group grew closer. Though Mihai and Ismail weren't paired together, they spent more time with each other than their official partners, both in and out of class. Natsuki didn't mind when Ismail opted to spend

The Tales of Abel and Mitra

a day working alongside Mihai instead of her. She took the opportunity to pry into Nuwa's life, eager to understand more about his role in the Church. Nuwa, initially distant from the group, gradually warmed up, and even ceased his habit of glaring at Ismail every time they crossed paths.

The semester came to an end faster than they expected. To celebrate the success of their research project, Mihai invited Ismail to his performance of *The Nutcracker* on Christmas Eve. He'd been preparing for the ballet the entire semester.

"Your parents are invited too, of course," Mihai beamed, slipping three tickets to Ismail. "I'd love for them to attend, but I understand if they're busy. I imagine your mom's schedule is packed this time of year."

To Ismail's surprise, his parents enthusiastically accepted the invitation.

"Of course we'll be there," smiled his father, Auguste St. Laurent. "*The Nutcracker* was the first date your mother and I went on when we were your age."

"How *poetic*," Louna purred, her crystal-blue eyes shining with excitement. "And just *look* at these tickets—why, they're the best seats in the house!"

She wasn't kidding when she said that. On Christmas Eve, the family found themselves seated in a private booth with a perfect view of the stage. Even when he and his father would attend his mother's operas, Ismail rarely had a seat as good as this.

Ismail had seen *The Nutcracker* several times as a child but had never truly paid attention. Growing up with a mother like Louna Ouali, he'd been dragged to countless performances a week for as long as he could remember and had grown sick of them. But ever since befriending Mihai, he'd gained a newfound appreciation for the arts.

In the months since they'd met, Ismail had yet to see Mihai dance. When Mihai finally appeared onstage playing the Nutcracker Prince, Ismail was mesmerized. Mihai moved with grace and charisma, each leap and spin seemingly effortless.

"Is that your friend?" Auguste remarked. "You didn't tell us he had the role of the Nutcracker Prince!"

"How did you know it was him?" Ismail furrowed his brow. "You've never met Mihai before."

Auguste chuckled. "The look on your face when he first came out. He has an exquisite figure! His visage strikes a perfect balance between masculine and feminine–like a modern Antinous or Björn Johan Andrésen. Simply stunning! I must get a closer look at him after the performance. Do you think you could introduce us? He'd make a perfect model for a classical sculpture."

Ismail's face flushed red. "You're here to watch him, not recruit him. Just enjoy the rest of the show."

When the performance came to a close, Louna was the first to rise from her seat, cheering enthusiastically with tears in her eyes. "Bravo! That was the most beautiful rendition of *The Nutcracker* I've ever seen!"

Considering how many times she'd attended the ballet, that was high praise.

"What was your friend's name again?" She asked.

"Mihai," said Ismail.

"Yes! Mihai. Didn't you say that he's a fan of mine?"

"A little more than a fan, if you ask me."

The Tales of Abel and Mitra

"Well, I'd love to meet him!"

"There's a reception afterward, but don't you have a show tonight?"

"Yes," Louna sighed. "*Un inno all'alba e al tramonto*. I need to be there in an hour. Say, why don't you tell Mihai we're looking for someone to take on one of the lead roles for the opera? Some of our actors are retiring soon."

"He's a dancer, not a singer," Ismail said. Then turning to his father, he added, "Or a model."

"*Un inno all'alba e al tramonto* incorporates elements of ballet," Louna said. "If you ask me, Mihai would be perfect as Aamu. Even if he's not a singer, that face alone will draw a crowd!"

"*Vraiment!*" Auguste beamed. "I'd love to do a sculpture of him. I'd even do it for free!"

"Alright, alright," Ismail said, shuffling his parents to the exit. "I'll mention it to him. But you two should get going, or you'll be late for your show."

He bid his parents farewell before heading down to the reception hall for the afterparty. The ballroom was elaborately decorated, with dazzling gold trimmings along the walls and a grand crystalline chandelier.

He spotted Mihai instantly, with a high-collared black suit and his hair now hanging loose over his shoulders. Surrounded by the other performers and a swarm of paparazzi, he flashed Ismail a look of relief when he spotted his friend, excusing himself from the others as he made his way over.

"You made it!" Mihai beamed, handing Ismail a glass of champagne. "What did you think of tonight?"

Yisei Ishkhan

"I've seen *The Nutcracker* before, but your performance was something else. Even *Maman* was impressed."

"*Ta mère?!*" Mihai exclaimed. "She was here?!"

"Both my parents were."

"Best night *ever!*" A squeal of delight escaped Mihai. "I can't believe I got to perform for Louna Ouali! Where is she now?"

"She had to leave for her own performance. *Un inno all'alba e al tramonto* is playing tonight."

"*Zut alors,*" Mihai sighed. He threw back his head, downing the rest of his champagne.

"I'll introduce you to them some other time," Ismail said. "Preferably when there *isn't* paparazzi around."

He shielded his face as a swarm of media drones circled about, snapping pictures of them for the press.

"Were you one of the performers tonight?" A voice echoed from one of the drones, pushing itself in front of Ismail's face.

"This is Ismail," Mihai stepped in, "he's my friend, just here as a guest."

"*Boyfriend?*" Gasped another drone. "Ladies and gentlemen, you heard it here first!"

"I said *friend,*" Mihai shook his head. "I'm very much single."

"Well, chat says you'd make a *stunning* couple!"

"Alright," Mihai chuckled, taking hold of Ismail's hand and dragging him away, "I think that's enough paparazzi for today."

"W-wait!' Ismail cried as he realized he was being pulled toward the dance floor. "Where are we going?"

The Tales of Abel and Mitra

"The drones aren't allowed on the dance floor," Mihai said. He signaled to the orchestra, and they began playing a tune. "So, shall we?"

"You're joking. There's no way I can keep up with a professional like you."

"Relax," Mihai chuckled. "It's just a waltz, not ballet."

"Do I *look* like I can dance?"

"Well," Mihai grinned, taking Ismail by the hand and wrapping his other arm around his waist. "I suppose we'll have to find out."

Before Ismail could object, he found himself pulled along the dance floor to a cheering crowd of onlookers.

"This is a *terrible* idea," Ismail muttered.

"Just follow my lead," Mihai beamed. "Forward, back. Forward, back. Now a spin–perfect! See? You're getting the hang of it."

"I'm getting *dizzy*," Ismail huffed. "Is this composition one of Tchaikovsky's?"

"*The Sleeping Beauty Waltz*," nodded Mihai. "Don't get me wrong, I love Tchaikovsky. But after listening to the soundtrack of *The Nutcracker* all semester, I need something other than Classical Romantic composers. I'm thinking something along the lines of Celia Cruz or Shakira. Do you have any suggestions?"

"I don't know who they are," Ismail admitted. "I don't listen to much other than Floriano."

"Floriano is great, but his style is similar to Tchaikovsky. Let's spice it up! How about jazz? Or maybe disco? Duke Ellington and ABBA, perhaps?"

Ismail frowned. "Never heard of them."

"What?" Mihai gasped. "How about The Chainsmokers or BTS?"

"BS what?"

Mihai stared at him, dumbfounded. "Elvis Presley? Michael Jackson? You must at *least* know them."

"I...don't know very much about Pre-Collapse Era pop culture," Ismail admitted. "You take your pick. You mentioned before that flamenco was your other specialty, didn't you?"

"Flamenco is far more complex than the waltz," Mihai said. "It's not a dance form a beginner can just pick up on the first attempt."

"Who said I'd be dancing?"

"I know!" Mihai's eyes lit up. "Tango."

"No way."

"Don't worry, I'll guide you through it. I'll ask my parents to play a slow and simple tune."

"I'm not dancing the tango. Wait...*tes parents*?"

"Oh, did I forget to mention it?" Mihai grinned. "My parents are part of the orchestra for tonight."

Ismail glanced at the musicians at the far end of the ballroom, suddenly overcome with discomfort.

"My father is Zhan Ionescu, the one on the violin," Mihai explained. "And the woman next to him in the red dress is *mi mamá*–Miranda Amaya. She's more of a vocalist than an instrumentalist, but dance is her real passion. She's the one who taught me flamenco."

"Mihai Aslan Ionescu-Amaya," Ismail mused. "'Mihai' and 'Ionescu' are Romanian, correct? And Amaya is Spanish?"

The Tales of Abel and Mitra

"Gitano."

"Ah, *bien sûr*. Flamenco. As for 'Aslan'–is that Turkish, or just a C.S. Lewis reference?"

Mihai chuckled. "Nakh, actually." He gestured to his suit, where cartridge ornaments were stitched into the fabric around his chest. "You see this outfit? It's a *chokha*, the traditional attire of men in Kavkazia. My grandmother was Nakh, but her family left Kavkazia back when they were still ruled by the Russians. After the Paris Revolts, my family resettled here. You also have Parisian roots, don't you?"

Ismail nodded. "The Oualis are Amazigh and the St. Laurents are Quebecois who escaped to France during the Great Collapse."

"Remnants of the New Worlders," Mihai mused. "Does your family preserve any Quebecois heritage?"

"*Un peu*," Ismail replied in a heavy Quebecois accent. "When they first moved to France, my family settled in a village in Normandy primarily inhabited by other Quebecois refugees. The Quebecois have always had a strong desire to preserve their heritage–a desire that was only reinforced after the Great Collapse. Only a few thousand escaped before the Treaty of Ntu was signed. Naturally, my grandparents wanted to have as many children as possible and pass on only the best of our genes to preserve the legacy of our people. That's why my mother is an 'Engi.' But the French have always been opposed to bioengineering, so it wasn't long before it was banned."

"Do you agree with the idea of banning it?" Mihai wondered.

Ismail paused for a moment. "It's a controversial subject. I understand why people like Nuwa dislike us–the idea that some genes are superior to others is difficult for people to accept. But I'm not sure if hindering the progress of science is the solution."

"Perhaps progress isn't necessarily a good thing," Mihai suggested.

"Perhaps not," Ismail said. "But while the Society of Heavenly Light outlaws it, groups like the Melekhites, Nippon, and Xin continue making advances with the technology. If the Society of Heavenly Light adopts a technophobic path, they'll be outcompeted."

As Mihai adjusted their position, Ismail noticed a wooden bead bracelet around his wrist. A small cross dangled from it.

"I didn't realize you were religious," Ismail noted. "Catholic or Orthodox? Or do you follow Heavenly Light like the others?"

"None of the above," said Mihai. "This is just a family heirloom. My parents are both Melekhites. I'm not religious, but if I had to pick one, I might go with Tiberianism."

"You mean that misogynistic cult?" Ismail scoffed. "Aka Neo-Mithraism?"

"There isn't one stream of the religion," Mihai said. "Just like you have Catholics, Orthodox, Protestants, Heavenly Light, and other Christian denominations, there are different branches and sub-branches within Tiberianism. Some are misogynistic, others aren't."

"Fair enough. So, what's the story behind that family heirloom?"

"It belonged to a Spanish Conquistador who took part in the conquest of Mexico. Eventually, it found its way back to Spain and was passed down in the family. There's a matching one back at my parents' home. It's become a family tradition to give the second bracelet as an engagement gift."

The Tales of Abel and Mitra

"How romantic," Ismail mused. "I wish I had something like that to pass on."

"Speaking of Conquistadors…" Mihai signaled to the orchestra. They immediately switched from the *Sleeping Beauty Waltz* to a much livelier tune. Miranda Amaya had risen from her seat, smiling as she belted out a new song *en Français*.

"What song is this?" Ismail asked in surprise as their waltz faltered.

"*Conquistador* by Kendji Girac!" Mihai beamed with renewed energy. "Oh, we really need to brush you up on your 21st-century music."

Before Ismail could protest, Mihai pulled him close, his hands guiding them into the next dance.

"Wait–!" Ismail's face flushed red. "I'm *not* dancing flamenco!"

"This isn't flamenco," Mihai laughed. "It's tango!"

"I don't care *what* it is! I can't dance!"

Mihai ignored him, expertly leading Ismail across the dance floor. The crowd parted for them, clapping and cheering, but Ismail was too focused on keeping his balance to notice the audience. He had no idea what he was doing, but Mihai's guidance saved him from making a complete fool of himself. They weaved and spun about, Ismail's body moving in ways it never had before.

When the song ended, Ismail collapsed into a chair, panting and flushed. Sweat beaded his forehead. Applause erupted from the crowd as Miranda began a new song.

Mihai knelt by Ismail's side, extending his hand to him. "What do you say to another dance?"

"No way," Ismail struggled to catch his breath. "My legs are about to give out! I'm calling it a night."

Yisei Ishkhan

Mihai laughed. "Sorry for dragging you into that. But admit it–it was fun."

A faint smile tugged at Ismail's lips. "Just don't make me do that in front of an audience again."

***

The good times never last forever. Three years into their studies at the *Instituto d'Arte e Technologia di Roma*, the social upheaval that had gripped much of the world in the decades following the Great Collapse finally reached Rome. For more than a generation, Italy had stood as a bastion of stability and liberty amidst the chaos ravaging most of Europe. Refugees from across the continent flocked to Rome, especially after the Paris Revolts saw France overthrown by a Melekhite uprising. Italy remained one of the few places where dissenting political and religious beliefs were free to be practiced.

But that era of liberal tolerance was fast crumbling.

The increasingly militaristic Melekhite movement fueled unrest worldwide, toppling government after government. This created division between Rome's Melekhite community. A militaristic, millenarian Melekhite branch known as the Kampfists sought to overthrow the government and join in the global revolution. Meanwhile, those part of the pacifist Roohani sect like Mihai's parents emphasized self-cultivation and shunned political involvement.

As election year arrived, fears of the growing Melekhite movement led to their community becoming a key target of political campaigning. The *Renaissance Party*, backed by refugees from elsewhere in Europe, sat low in the polls; they saw it as Italy's responsibility to liberate the continent from Melekhite regimes. The Melekhites, meanwhile, had a party of

The Tales of Abel and Mitra

their own, and were polling at a couple points higher than *Renaissance*. The forerunners of the race, however, were the *Nationalists* and *Liberal Conservatives*. The latter had governed for decades, seeking to uphold the nation's status quo as a bastion of liberal values; the former sought to expel foreign influences–Melekhite, European, or otherwise–including the descendants of immigrants up to the third generation.

As tensions escalated, sectarian violence ensued. In retaliation for a Heavenly Light uprising in Egypt, radical Kampfist Melekhites bombed Rome's largest Heavenly Light Church with drones during Pasqua celebrations. Hundreds were killed and injured in the attack. Mass unrest ensued, with Melekhite communities–both Kampfist and Roohani–ransacked, injuring dozens more. The unrest in the streets of Rome spread nationwide, leading to a surge in the polls for both the *Nationalists* and *Renaissance* as support for the *Liberal Conservatives* plummeted.

The people were demanding change. But Ismail feared how much change they were willing to tolerate.

In the leadup to the election, the *Liberal Conservatives* bowed to pressure from the *Nationalists* and *Renaissance*, passing a motion that outlawed all political activity tied to the Melekhite movement. This marked the beginning of the end of the era of liberal democracy.

One day, Mihai burst into Ismail's dorm, his face ashen and his gaze distant. Ismail had never seen such fear in his friend's eyes before.

"What happened?" He asked, pulling up a chair for Mihai as he sent Aida to prepare a pot of tea.

"It's my parents," Mihai's voice trembled. "They've disappeared."

Ismail paled. "In the crackdowns?"

Yisei Ishkhan

"They were performing for a Melekhite worship service last night when the police came in and shut them down. I saw on the news that they were taken into custody, but I can't get into contact with anyone."

"Why would they target your parents?" Ismail furrowed his brow. "I thought they were only cracking down on the political factions."

"I don't know," Mihai ran a hand through his hair, breathing heavily. "I just don't know what to do."

Ismail took hold of his friend's hand and gave it a gentle squeeze. "We'll figure this out. I'll come with you to the police."

But the police proved to be a dead end. The officers claimed they were not involved with the operation, and rumors circulated that the military or even mercenaries might be behind the disappearances. But nothing was certain. Weeks went by, and they still found no leads on what happened.

Then came the elections. The *Liberal Conservatives* faced a resounding defeat, falling to a distant third behind the *Nationalists* and *Renaissance*. Alleging foreign interference, the outgoing government declared the results void and called for martial law. But the military backed the newly elected *Nationalists*. Tanks and drones were deployed into the streets of Rome, and the *Liberal Conservatives* were ousted from power.

The new regime wasted no time in quashing the opposition. The *Instituto d'Arte e Technologia di Roma* was branded a breeding ground for Kampfist extremists and other radicals. The institute was shut indefinitely, and Ismail and the others found their studies cut short. The Church of Heavenly

The Tales of Abel and Mitra

Light and Tiberianism were labeled 'dangerous foreign cults,' and added to the list of banned sects alongside the Melekhites.

Then came the purges. *Liberal Conservative* and *Renaissance* politicians deemed to be tied to these cults were sacked from parliament. Within weeks, the political opposition had been ousted in the name of 'preserving democracy.' Even the Catholic Pope, Augustine III, was deposed in favour of a *Nationalist* puppet–Clement XV.

Augustine's departure marked the beginning of the crackdown on foreigners. The government gave a week for foreigners to leave the country, vowing that those who remained after the deadline would be stripped of their rights and forcibly deported. They defined foreigners as not only those born abroad, but the children and grandchildren of immigrants. When Ismail heard the news, he pleaded with his parents to leave for his grandmother's chalet in the Alps.

"We'll send you there," said Auguste. "But your mother and I are staying."

"You have to come with me! Everyone knows who you are! It's only a matter of time before they come for you!"

"We are artists, Ismail," Louna said calmly. "It's our responsibility to inspire people and give them hope, and to oppose injustice and oppression. If we flee, what message does that send to the people who are left behind?"

"I won't leave without you!"

"You *must*," Auguste said in a stern voice. It was one of the few times in Ismail's life that he'd heard such a tone from his father. "You're the last of the St. Laurents and the Oualis. You must live on for the rest of us."

"Then come *with* me!" Ismail said. "Come with me so I *won't* be the last of our family line!"

Yisei Ishkhan

"We can't," said Louna. "We could only manage to get two tickets." She produced them from her pocket, placing them into Ismail's hands. "Go with Mihai and take the train up to Zürich."

Ismail knew that arguing with them was futile. He'd inherited his stubbornness from his parents; even if they'd managed to find more tickets, they'd already made up their minds to stay.

The next day, Ismail found himself at the station with Mihai, bidding his parents farewell.

"Take care of one another," Auguste said.

Mihai nodded. "We will."

Ismail remained silent

"Mihai," Louna said, stepping forward. "We will continue the search for your parents. I promise."

Tears welled in the corners of Mihai's eyes. "Thank you. You don't know how much that means to me."

"Of course," Louna said, taking his hands in hers. "You're like a second son to us. We'll do everything we can."

Mihai bowed his head. "I'm glad to have met you, Madame Ouali." He extended his hand out to Auguste, giving him a firm handshake. "I hope to see you again soon, Monsieur St. Laurent."

Auguste nodded. "As do I."

Both of his parents turned to Ismail expectantly. He didn't make eye contact with them as they took him into an embrace.

"Stay safe," Louna said.

"You too," Ismail whispered.

He watched as they disappeared into the crowd.

The Tales of Abel and Mitra
***

The train stationed was jam-packed, busier than Ismail had ever seen. Every train departing the city–bound for Nice, Zürich, Innsbruck, or Ljubljana–was beyond capacity. It had been a miracle that Ismail's parents managed to secure two tickets.

Ismail glanced up at Mihai as they shuffled their way through the crowd. "Are you really okay with leaving?"

"As long as I'm with you, I don't care where we go."

"Don't you want to keep searching for your parents?"

"What else can we do that we haven't already?"

"I don't know…but there must be *something*."

"They're dead."

Ismail froze. "What?"

"My parents are dead. I know they are."

"How?"

"I just know," Mihai placed a hand on his chest. "It's a feeling I've had for a while now. I can't explain it, but I know they're gone."

"A *feeling*?" Ismail repeated in disbelief. "That doesn't mean anything! You can't give up hope just because of that! There's no logic to it!"

"Ismail, please," Mihai said gently. "I know it doesn't make any sense to you, but I *know* it's the truth."

Ismail took a deep breath. "I'm sorry."

Before either of them could say more, their attention was drawn to a disturbance in the crowd. Overhead, drones zipped through the air, blaring messages in multiple languages.

"Libertà! Libertà! Join the *Songs for Freedom* rally at sundown tonight at Piazza di Spagna! *Libertà! Libertà!"*

Yisei Ishkhan

The crowd buzzed with murmurs of confusion and concern.

"What is that?!" Barked a soldier near the platform.

"SHUT IT DOWN! SHUT THEM DOWN!" Another roared.

Echoes of *Libertà! Libertà!* continued to echo above the chaos.

"*Libertà!*" A voice rang out from within the crowd.

"SILENCE!" The soldiers ordered.

But the cries only grew louder. A moment later came a second shout of *Libertà!* This was soon followed by a third. Then came cries of *Liberté* and *Libertad! Sloboda! Liria! Freiheit! Özgürlük! Wolność! Szabadság! Huriya! Azadi! Eleftheria!*

FREEDOM! FREEDOM! FREEDOM!

Impassioned cries, full of sorrow and anger, hope and fear, rose louder and louder into a symphony that drowned out the furious orders of the soldiers blasting over the intercoms.

A gunshot cracked through the cacophony.

Shouts for freedom turned into blood-curdling screams as the crowd scrambled in every direction. There was blood on the ground, but Ismail couldn't tell whether it was a soldier or a civilian who had fallen. The press of bodies knocked Ismail to the ground on top of a woman.

"I'm sorry!" Ismail cried, pushing himself to his feet as he helped the woman up. When their eyes met, his face lit up in surprise. "Natsuki?"

"Ismail?!" Natsuki gasped.

The Tales of Abel and Mitra

Nuwa emerged from behind her, taking her by the arm and leading her away. Mihai came up from behind Ismail, pushing him in the same direction.

"We need to get out of here," he hissed.

They ducked into a corner at the edge of the station.

"What are you doing here?" Ismail said in disbelief as they caught up to Natsuki and Nuwa. He hadn't seen either of them since classes had been suspended weeks ago. "I thought you already left the city."

"We tried," Natsuki sobbed, "but we haven't been able to purchase tickets."

"If the government wants us out of here, they should give us free passage," Nuwa grumbled. "We were planning to force our way onto the train."

Without hesitation, Ismail shoved his ticket into Natsuki's hand. "Take mine."

Natsuki blinked through her tears. "W-what? No, I can't! What about *you*?"

"I'll have an easier time than *you* passing as a native of Rome. Besides, I can't leave just yet."

He took off toward the exit.

"Wait!" Mihai shouted, grabbing him by the hand. "Where are you going?!"

"Didn't you hear the message on the drones? There's a rally at sundown at Piazza di Spagna–the *Songs of Freedom*. My parents will be there, I just know it! They're going to get themselves killed!"

Mihai cursed under his breath, handing over his ticket to Nuwa. "Platform 3, departure for Zürich. Go!"

Yisei Ishkhan

Natsuki opened her mouth to speak, but Nuwa took her by the hand and dragged her into the crowd before she had the chance.

"What are you doing?!" Ismail gave Mihai a shove. "You should've left with Natsuki! Why'd you give your ticket to that *prick?!*"

Mihai grabbed him by the shoulders, looking him in the eye. "What did I just tell you? As long as we're together, I don't care where we are. If you're going to Piazza di Spagna, I'm coming with you."

"Okay," Ismail inhaled a shaky breath. "Fine."

Checkpoints had been set up along most of the major intersections in the city, forcing Ismail and Mihai to weave through narrow alleyways. Every few minutes, drones would zip overhead, some ordering civilians to return home, and others blaring the same message from earlier: "*Libertà! Libertà!* Join the *Songs for Freedom* rally at sundown tonight at Piazza di Spagna! *Libertà! Libertà!*"

Soldiers scrambled to silence them, occasionally opening fire to shoot the drones out of the air.

By the time Ismail and Mihai reached Piazza di Spagna, the sun was dipping low on the horizon, casting long shadows over the crowd in the square. They pushed their way to the top of the Spanish Steps, scanning the sea of faces below in the hopes of catching a glimpse of Ismail's parents.

"Anything?" Ismail asked.

Mihai frowned and shook his head. "Have you noticed that there aren't any soldiers or drones around here?"

Ismail glanced up. Mihai was right. The skies were empty, and he didn't spot any military uniforms in the crowd. A pit formed in his stomach. Something wasn't right.

The Tales of Abel and Mitra

Libertà! Libertà! Libertà! Libertà!

The chant echoed across the square, gaining momentum as more voices joined in. From their vantage, Ismail spotted a couple of flags go up into the air–the *Liberal Conservative Party*'s flags. They were joined by more–flags of *Renaissance* and other outlawed parties, and banners bearing slogans of the Melekhites, Church of Heavenly Light, and even Tiberians.

"There!" Mihai shouted. "By the fountain!"

Ismail followed his gaze, spotting his parents amid the sea of flags and banners. He watched as a young man stepped forward, wearing the type of mask one would wear at a masquerade. As he addressed the crowd, their voices died down.

"They thought they could intimidate us into submission!" The man roared. "They thought they could divide us, that they could strike us down one by one, and that we would cower in fear and back down! But look around! We stand as one people tonight, gathered regardless of race or tongue, politics or faith. Too many times in history have the people kept silent, keeping their heads down in the face of oppression. But we refuse to submit! We will not back down! We will stand strong in the face of persecution! We will stand and fight for freedom! *Libertà! Libertà! Libertà!*"

"*Libertà! Libertà! Libertà!*" Echoed the crowd.

Ismail's stomach churned as he watched his mother step forward.

"And now let us sing!" Louna cried. "Let us sing the songs of freedom sung by those who came before us as they faced tyranny! *O bella ciao, bella ciao, bella ciao ciao ciao!*"

Yisei Ishkhan

The crowd surged forward, pounding their fists in the air as they burst into song. Louna and Auguste led the march westward.

"We have to stop her," Ismail said. He turned to a man in the crowd. "Where are they marching to?"

"Palazzo Montecitorio," said the man.

Ismail paled. He and Mihai attempted to push their way to the front of the crowd, but they were too tightly packed in the streets. As they moved deeper into the city, Louna led the crowd in songs of resistance–*We Shall Overcome, The Battle Hymn of the Republic, Baraye,* and even *Shinzō wo Sasageyo!*

Palazzo Montecitorio loomed ahead. As they drew near, a fleet of drones suddenly appeared in the sky, ordering the crowd to disperse. Despite the commands, the crowd pressed on.

Ismail spotted tanks in the street, lined up in front of the government buildings alongside infantry with raised weapons.

"Halt!" Ordered one of the soldiers. "You are ordered to disperse immediately, or you will be dealt with by force."

"We are exercising our democratic rights!" One of the protestors yelled.

The crowd roared in approval, but their voices ceased as Louna stepped forth with her arms raised. Even from this distance, Ismail caught a glimpse of her blonde locks as she slipped forth from the crowd, putting herself between them and the soldiers.

"What is she doing?!" Ismail hissed. He called out to her, but his voice was drowned out by the wind.

Louna pointed a finger at the sky and muttered a few words, though it was impossible for Ismail to hear what she

The Tales of Abel and Mitra

was saying from this distance. Whatever it was, it seemed to cause hesitation among the soldiers. Louna continued forward, unfazed by guns trained on her. She began to sing. At first, her voice was little more than a whisper, but the song grew louder as it spread through the crowd.

Do You Hear the People Sing?

Before Ismail knew it, he and Mihai had joined along, their voices trembling with defiance.

Louna reached the first soldier, the barrel of his gun nearly pressed up against her face. For a moment, the soldier hesitated. His hands shook, and it seemed he was about to lower his weapon.

Then gunfire rang out.

Louna's voice was silenced mid-note, just as the crowd reached the line *"The blood of the martyrs."* The song was cut short as panic ensued. Some screamed, scrambling to flee the square. Others surged forward in fury, only to be cut down by gunfire from the soldiers and drones overhead. Some in the crowd had come prepared for a fight. As banners and flags fell, guns were raised, returning fire and taking down several soldiers.

"Get down!" Mihai yelled.

His voice was cut short by a deafening explosion to their right. Blood and debris sprayed into the air as one of the tanks opened fire. Ismail's vision blurred, his ears ringing as a face loomed over him.

"Ismail…?" Mihai's voice echoed in the distance. "Ismail!"

"Mihai…?" Ismail murmured.

"I've got you," Mihai said, scooping Ismail into his arms and shielding him from the chaos.

Yisei Ishkhan

Ismail glanced around, searching in vain for his parents. He watched as hundreds of faces went by. Some were stained with blood and dirt, others missing an eye or part of their jaw. Some didn't have faces at all.

Mihai turned the corner, ducking into an alleyway. As the square disappeared behind them, Ismail caught a glimpse of a man kneeling on the ground in front of a line of fallen soldiers. He clutched the body of a woman in his arms, like Michelangelo's *Madonna della Pietà*.

Ismail couldn't make out any details about the pair. Their bodies were blackened and charred by the flames burning around them.

Soon, they would be nothing but ash.

***

"Ismail? Ismail!" Mihai's voice roused him from his slumber.

Ismail groaned, trying to open his eyes. His head pounded, but at least the ringing in his ears was gone. The silence was unnerving. The acrid stench of blood and smoke clung to his clothes, though another odor, damp and musty, now filled the air.

"Mihai...?" He managed, his voice hoarse. He sat up, glancing around. It was dark, with nothing but damp walls on either side.

Mihai sighed in relief. "Thank goodness you're awake."

"Where...are we...?"

"The catacombs under the city," came a vaguely familiar voice. A young man stepped into the faint light, his ruddy hair cropped short except for long bangs that fell over the left side of his freckled face. "I'd lay back down if I were you–you took a nasty blow to the head."

The Tales of Abel and Mitra

Ismail frowned. He recognized the man but couldn't place him. "Who are you?"

"Giovanni Ricci," the man smiled. "But in the Underground, I go by Gwydion."

"The Underground...?"

Giovanni cocked his head. "I assumed you'd know about us, considering your parents were involved."

Ismail's stomach clenched. "My parents! Where are they?!"

Mihai placed a gentle hand on his shoulder. "Ismail...I'm so sorry. They didn't make it."

"No...they can't be..."

"It's true, I'm afraid," Giovanni sighed. "I saw it for myself. Your mother was shot by the soldiers, and your father was consumed by the flames when he tried to save her."

The image flashed through Ismail's mind–the man holding a woman's lifeless body like the *Madonna della Pietà*.

"No..." Ismail's voice cracked as tears streamed down his face.

"I know it's no consolation," said Giovanni, "but their deaths weren't in vain. They've become martyrs for the cause, heroes to the people. Their legacy will live on for generations."

"What is this 'Underground' you're a part of?" Mihai asked.

"A resistance," Giovanni said. "An alliance of dissidents from all walks of life united against the Nationalist government. We fight for freedom, justice, and the rights that they're trying to strip from us. Louna and Auguste were key figures in the movement."

"They never told me," Ismail whispered.

"I see," Giovanni nodded. "I suppose they wanted to protect you from this. But we can't stay silent in the face of oppression."

It dawned on Ismail. He knew something about Giovanni seemed familiar. "You're the one who led the speech at the beginning of the rally–the one wearing the mask."

"So, you recognize me," Giovanni grinned. He pulled the mask from his bag and held it in front of his face. "Most in the Underground prefer to remain anonymous. That's why I wear this mask and go by Gwydion."

Ismail narrowed his gaze. "Then why did you tell us your real name?"

"Because I trust you," he said before glancing at Mihai. "Both of you. Mihai, I knew your parents from the Melekhite gatherings before the crackdowns. As for Auguste and Louna, they joined the Underground a few weeks ago. I didn't know them well, but if you're anything like your parents, I know you'll stand on the right side of history. I want you to trust me; that's why I'm showing you who I am. I won't lie, when I saw Mihai carrying you through the crowd, I wasn't planning on helping you escape. There were hundreds of people injured in the square. I could've chosen to help any of them. But I chose *you*." He leaned in, studying Ismail's face intently. "Has anyone ever told you that you have your mother's eyes? As soon as I saw your eyes, I knew you were Louna's son. You might be the son of a famous opera singer, but that isn't all you're known for. I've heard that you're an AMI engineer and have made significant breakthroughs in your field. Skills like yours are invaluable to our cause."

Mihai frowned. "Did you help me save Ismail just so you could recruit him?"

The Tales of Abel and Mitra

Giovanni shrugged. "As I said, there were countless others in the square I could've saved. I had to make a decision, and I chose Ismail because I knew he had potential."

"Ismail isn't a soldier," Mihai said.

"You're right," said Giovanni. "He's *more* valuable than a *thousand* soldiers. Did you see those drones over the city today? The ones calling for the rally at Piazza di Spagna? Those were government drones. I was the one who hacked into their systems and had them spread that message. But my skills are nothing compared to Ismail's. I could only override a handful of drones for a few minutes at a time. I'm sure someone with Ismail's skills could've hijacked every drone in the city and turned them to our side."

"I appreciate you helping me save Ismail," said Mihai. "But I think you're talking to the wrong people. Both of our parents were born abroad. We can't stay in the city."

"Well?" Giovanni said, turning to Ismail. "What do *you* have to say? Your parents had tickets for you to leave, and yet you chose to remain."

"Ismail," Mihai said gently. "Your parents wanted you to leave. There's a reason they didn't tell you about their involvement with the Underground. They didn't want you to get caught up in all this."

"It doesn't matter what they wanted," Ismail murmured. "They're dead now, and I *am* caught up in this."

"This is a chance for you to avenge their deaths," Giovanni said. "Not for the sake of vengeance, but for justice. The wicked cannot escape punishment for their sins. There must be retribution. I won't force you to work with us. If you decide you want to leave for the Alps, I can arrange that. But if you choose to work with us, you will be welcomed with open arms. We may come from different backgrounds, with different ideological and political beliefs. I know that your parents and I shared little in common. But that's the only way tyranny can be defeated–when people unite despite their differences to overcome it. Just consider my invitation at least."

Ismail nodded slowly. "I will. Thank you for saving me."

"Don't mention it," said Giovanni. He flicked his hand, passing a business card to Ismail. "Here's my contact if you wish to get in touch. We avoid using *Aeterna* servers; the government monitors them. Usually, we meet in the catacombs or sewers. I'd recommend using an alias if you don't want to be compromised. Remember, to everyone else, I'm Gwydion."

***

Thus began Ismail and Mihai's involvement with the Underground. Ismail adopted the alias "Icarus," while Mihai became known as "Mitra." To everyone except Giovanni and a select few leaders of the Underground, they were known only by those names.

Initially, the Underground didn't demand much of Ismail's time–he hacked into drone systems to broadcast messages or wiped incriminating security footage. But over time, his genius became indispensable. He developed advanced tools to hack into government systems, transferring sensitive files to the Underground's servers without detection, and devised methods of neutralizing high-tech military weapons. With these breakthroughs, the Underground's actions grew bolder–raids on military bases, sabotaging government facilities, and the acquisition of advanced weaponry.

The Tales of Abel and Mitra

Mihai was wary of participating in the movement, but refused to let Ismail attend their meetings alone. He hoped to convince Ismail to detach himself from the cause, but the more Ismail became involved, the more valuable he became to them. He was the linchpin of their operations. While Giovanni had initially given them the option to leave Italy, he doubted that offer still stood now.

Not that Ismail wanted an out. With each passing day, he spent more and more time working on assignments Giovanni gave him, readily accepting every task thrown his way. One day, he insisted on working overnight. Mihai had enough of it and decided to confront him.

"You spend all day cooped up down here! When was the last time you went outside?"

Ismail shrugged, hunched over the wires of his latest project. "Last week? Maybe two weeks ago?" He didn't even turn to face Mihai in the doorway.

"This isn't healthy!" Mihai threw up his hands. "You need to come up once in a while–at least once a day. You need fresh air. Sunshine. Human interaction that doesn't just involve Gwydion barking orders."

"I'm busy."

"On what?" Mihai paced over to the table, plopping down at the seat next to him.

"I'm developing an android, one that has a human mind, and doesn't just mimic human behaviour through a program."

"That's...impressive," Mihai admitted. "But why?"

"Because I've always wanted to," Ismail said, his tone somewhat annoyed. "This is my passion, Mihai. I've always wanted to work on a project like this, but it's expensive."

Yisei Ishkhan

"And now you have Gwydion to fund your research," Mihai scoffed. "Why do you think he's giving you money for these projects? Do you think he cares about advancing science and technology? He'll turn that thing into a weapon as soon as it's operational."

Ismail sighed. "Anything can be turned into a weapon. The Chinese invented gunpowder trying to create an elixir of life. Some used it for fireworks; others used it in warfare. What others do with my inventions is up to them. Besides, if I don't create this, someone else will."

"Are you serious?" Mihai gasped. "You don't feel responsible for how your inventions are used? What about those drones you repurposed last week? They *killed* people. *You* killed people!"

Ismail paused, but only briefly. "Soldiers and government targets."

"No!" Mihai cried. "*Civilians*! They bombed the home of a Nationalist politician and killed his wife and kids!"

Ismail clenched his jaw but hardened his focus as he continued fiddling with the wires. "We're at war, Mihai. There is always collateral damage. It's unfortunate, but inevitable."

He flinched as Mihai slammed his hands on the table.

"*Collateral damage*?!" Do you even *hear* yourself?! Those were innocent children! *Children*, Ismail!"

"I didn't kill them."

"Your weapons did!"

An abrupt cough came from the doorway. "Am I interrupting something?"

They both glanced up to where Giovanni stood leaning casually against the doorframe. He stared at them with a hint

The Tales of Abel and Mitra

of amusement in his eyes. Ismail turned away and went back to work.

"What do you want?" Mihai snapped.

"I know you're upset with that attack on General Bianchi's home," Giovanni sighed. "The deaths of his wife and children were…regrettable mistakes. They were mistakes due to compromised intel. But you must understand, Mitra–this is exactly why Icarus' work is so vital. Do you realize how many civilian casualties we've *avoided* thanks to his technology?"

Mihai narrowed his gaze. "Maybe we shouldn't be relying on violence to achieve our goals in the first place."

"There are other ways," Giovanni nodded. "The role you've played, Mitra, has been just as important for the cause as Icarus. Your voice inspires people, giving them hope when they need it most. If our message can sway enough people to our cause, we won't *have* to rely on violence to make a difference." He drummed his fingers along the table. "You know what day it is, don't you?"

"Pasqua," Mihai muttered.

Giovanni nodded. "We Melekhites don't celebrate the holiday, but it's still an important occasion for the people of this city. This is Rome, after all. Lend the people your voice. Give them hope that they can cling to."

"Fine," Mihai grumbled. "I'll do it."

"Good," Giovanni smiled. "People need to hear it."

He led Mihai out of the room, leaving Ismail behind to continue with his work. Mihai followed him through the catacombs, winding their way below the city. Even after so many months in these tunnels, he still didn't know his way around.

Yisei Ishkhan

"Poetic, isn't it?" Giovanni traced his fingers along the stacks of skulls lining the walls from floor to ceiling, the remains of those who'd been entombed here centuries ago. "Two millennia ago, the Christians hid in these passageways to practice their faith in secret, hiding in the shadows from their persecutors. Eventually, they rose to power–they even converted the emperor. But when they did, the persecuted became the persecutor. The pagans who'd oppressed them for centuries found themselves forced underground, until eventually they died out."

"Are you hoping to find your own Constantine?" Mihai scoffed. "Or Theodosius, perhaps?"

Giovanni chuckled. "Hardly. The Christians waited three centuries before Constantine came along and granted them rights. He could've just as easily chosen Mithraism, Manichaeism, or one of the countless other forgotten sects spreading in the empire at the time. But we're not waiting for a Constantine of our own to come along and grant us freedom. We'll seize that freedom ourselves." They arrived at the broadcasting room, and Giovanni turned to Mihai with a grin. "You know the routine."

"Do you have any requests?" Mihai asked.

"Just one," Giovanni mused. "*Dies iræ*. You know it, don't you?"

"Of course. Is that all?"

Giovanni waved his hand. "I'll let you choose the rest. Just keep it rolling. *Buona Pasqua.*"

Mihai settled into his chair as Giovanni departed, adjusting the broadcasting equipment. He picked up his guitar from the shelf, resting his fingers on the strings. It was his mother's guitar–one of the few reminders he had of her. He

The Tales of Abel and Mitra

traced his fingers along the carved initials on the edge–P+M within a heart. He didn't know who P or M were–some forgotten ancestors whose memory only lived on through those initials.

With a deep sigh, he activated the broadcast. Across the city, hundreds of drones would begin projecting his voice.

"Good evening, Rome. This is Mitra. Tonight, I will be singing a few songs for you. These are songs of lament, commemorating the victims of the massacres last year, the martyrs in the fight for freedom, and all who mourn for them. And of course, we remember the ultimate sacrifice–Christ's death on the cross for our sins."

He pressed a button, projecting a striking image through hologram broadcast by the drones: a stylized rendition of *Madonna della Pietà*. The image depicted a man cradling a woman's lifeless body as flames engulfed them both. Beneath it, the words *Libertà per Roma* glowed softly. The image was signed in the corner with *San Lorenzo*–St. Laurent. It wasn't just a reference to Ismail's father but to the historic San Lorenzo, Rome's patron saint who faced martyrdom by being burned alive all those centuries ago. The image had grown to become the most iconic symbol of the Underground's resistance.

Mihai strummed his fingers along the guitar. "I will begin with *A Vava Inouva*, an Amazigh folk song."

His voice wavered at first but grew stronger with each verse. Ismail had taught him the song, a lullaby that his mother had sung to him as a child. Though Mihai didn't understand the Kabyle tongue, he'd mastered the pronunciation. The melody flowed naturally from his lips.

Yisei Ishkhan

By the end of the song, tears were streaming down his face. He sniffled, wiping his eyes as he noticed movement and glanced up. Ismail was standing in the doorway.

"I'm sorry..." Mihai whispered, momentarily forgetting that his words were being broadcast to the city.

Despite the tears in his eyes, Ismail managed to smile. *That was beautiful*, he mouthed silently.

Mihai took a deep breath. "Next is *Dies iræ*."

Dies iræ, dies illa, (The day of wrath, that day)
Solvet sæclum in favilla: (Will dissolve the world in ashes)
Teste David cum Sibylla. (As testified by David and the Sybils.)

Quantus tremor est futurus, (How great will be the quaking)
Quando judex est venturus, (When the judge descends)
Cuncta stricte discussurus! (On whose sentence all depend!)

Lacrimosa dies illa, (Tearful will be that day)
Qua resurget ex favilla (On which the glowing embers arise)
Iudicandus homo reus: (The guilty man who is to be judged)
Huic ergo parce, Deus: (Spare him, O God)

Pie Iesu Domine, (Merciful Lord Jesus)
Dona eis requiem. (Grant them eternal rest)
Amen.

Mihai's voice trembled. He sang a couple more songs, but his voice was straining. He had a gift for singing, but he'd always

The Tales of Abel and Mitra

focused more on dance. He'd never exercised his vocals this much before.

"Lastly," he whispered, "I will sing *La Llorona,* a Mexican folk song about a mother mourning the loss of her children. This song is a tribute to my mother, who sang it to me when I was young."

Ay de mí, Llorona, Llorona (Alas, Llorona, Llorona)
Llorona de azul celeste (Llorona of the blue sky)
Ay de mí, Llorona, Llorona (Alas, Llorona, Llorona)
Llorona de azul celeste (Llorona of the blue sky)
No dejaré de quererte, Llorona (I won't stop loving you, Llorona)
Y, aunque la vida me cueste (Although it costs me my life)
No dejaré de quererte, Llorona (I won't stop loving you, Llorona)
Y, aunque la vida me cueste (Although it costs me my life)

Si al cielo subir pudiera, Llorona, (If I could go up to the Heavens, Llorona)
Las estrellas te bajara, (I'd bring the stars down to you)
Si al cielo subir pudiera, Llorona, (If I could go up to the Heavens, Llorona)
Las estrellas te bajara, (I'd bring the stars down to you)
La luna a tus pies pusiera, Llorona, (I'd lay the Moon at your feet, Llorona)
Con el sol te coronara. (And crown you with the Sun)
La luna a tus pies pusiera, Llorona, (I'd lay the Moon at your feet, Llorona)
Con el sol te coronara. (And crown you with the Sun)

¡Ay de mí!, Llorona, Llorona, (Alas, Llorona, Llorona)

Yisei Ishkhan

Llorona de ayer y hoy (Llorona of yesterday and today)
¡Ay de mí!, Llorona, Llorona, (Alas, Llorona, Llorona)
Llorona de ayer y hoy (Llorona of yesterday and today)
Ayer maravilla fui, Llorona, (Yesterday I was a wonder)
Y ahora ni sombra soy. (And today I am not even a shadow)
Ayer maravilla fui, Llorona, (Yesterday I was a wonder)
Y ahora ni sombra soy. (And today I am not even a shadow)

A un santo Cristo de fierro, Llorona, (To a holy crucifix, Llorona)
Mis penas le conté yo, (I told him my sins)
A un santo Cristo de fierro, Llorona, (To a holy crucifix, Llorona)
Mis penas le conté yo, (I told him my sins)
¿Cuáles no serían mis penas, Llorona, (What would not be my sorrows, Llorona)
que el santo Cristo lloró? (That the holy Christ wept?)
¿Cuáles no serían mis penas, Llorona, (What would not be my sorrows, Llorona)
que el santo Cristo lloró? (That the holy Christ wept?)

His voice resonated deeply, each line conjuring vivid memories from his youth. As his fingers strummed across the strings, his emotions swelled. It had been months since he'd danced–his final performance had been just before his parents' disappearance. But now, as he poured out his soul in the final verses of the song, he was overcome with a sudden desire to dance.

He swept his hand over the controls, punching in several commands.

Ismail leaped to his feet. "What are you–?!"

The Tales of Abel and Mitra

A warning flashed across the main screen: *Visual Broadcasting Live.*

Ismail paled. He raced forward, fingers flying over the buttons in an attempt to shut off the livestream. It was too late. Mihai's face was already being broadcast to the entire city. A wistful smile crossed his face as he set down his guitar, rising to his feet. He stomped a foot on the ground, synchronizing it with the clap of his hands. He closed his eyes, beginning to sing the remainder of the song as he danced one of his mother's favourite flamenco forms.

¡Ay de mí!, Llorona, Llorona, (Alas, Llorona, Llorona)
Llorona de un campo lirio, (Llorona of a lily field)
¡Ay de mí!, Llorona, Llorona, (Alas, Llorona, Llorona)
Llorona de un campo lirio, (Llorona of a lily field)
El que no sabe de amores, Llorona, (He who does not know love, Llorona)
no sabe lo que es martirio. (Does not know what martyrdom is)
El que no sabe de amores, Llorona, (He who does not know love, Llorona)
no sabe lo que es martirio. (Does not know what martyrdom is)

¡Ay de mí!, Llorona, Llorona, (Alas, Llorona, Llorona)
tú eres mi chunca, (You are my sweetheart)
¡Ay de mí!, Llorona, Llorona, (Alas, Llorona, Llorona)
tú eres mi chunca, (You are my sweetheart)
Me quitarán de quererte, Llorona, (They'll stop me from loving you, Llorona)
pero de olvidarte nunca. (But I'll never forget you)

Yisei Ishkhan

Me quitarán de quererte, Llorona, (They'll stop me from loving you, Llorona)
pero de olvidarte nunca. (But I'll never forget you)
Pero de olvidarte nunca… (But I'll never forget you)
Pero de olvidarte nunca… (But I'll never forget you)

His movements slowed, the last note lingering in the air as Ismail finally succeeded in shutting off the broadcast. The lights went out and the room plunged into silence. For a moment, only Mihai's heavy breaths filled the space.

"What have you done?" Ismail's voice trembled with fear and rage as he stormed over to Mihai. "You revealed your identity to the entire world! You just jeopardized the entire movement! You put your life in danger!"

"I know," Mihai muttered. "But maybe it's time to stop hiding."

"We have no *choice* but to hide!"

"No, we don't. We can leave this place. Come with me, Ismail. Let's leave this city together. I don't care *where* we go, as long as you and I are together."

"You just want to give up after everything we've fought for? What about finding justice for my parents? And for *your* parents?"

"Avenge not yourselves, for vengeance belongs to the Lord. Do not be overcome by evil, but overcome evil with good."

"What are you *talking* about?"

"A verse from the Book of Romans, a message from San Paolo to the people of this city."

The Tales of Abel and Mitra

"Oh," Ismail laughed. "So what? You're a Christian now?"

"That's not the point," Mihai sighed. "Look at yourself, Ismail. Ever since your parents' deaths, you've been consumed by anger, closing yourself off from everything else. I can't watch you destroy yourself for revenge. I want to see justice for what happened to our parents, and freedom for the people of this city. Believe me, Ismail, I do. But not at the cost of losing you."

Ismail scoffed. "Why do you care?"

"Because I love you, Ismail!" Mihai's voice broke. "If compromising myself is the only way to wake you up to reality, so be it."

"You idiot…" Ismail mumbled. His face burned bright red, though Mihai couldn't tell if he was embarrassed or angry. "*Love*? That's a stupid emotion that makes people do stupid things."

Mihai stepped toward Ismail, taking hold of his hands. "I'm not leaving without you. If you stay, I stay."

Ismail stared him down, his mind racing with words he couldn't quite piece together. As they stood locked together in silence, a sudden beep came from the monitor. An announcement crackled through the speakers:

All units report in. Simultaneous attacks have struck numerous military bases and government offices across the nation at 1800 hours. These are believed to have come from external sources, not internal militia. Reports suggest that the Melekhites in Anadolu, Ifriqia, Faransa, and Andalusia are responsible and are mounting a full-scale invasion in the coming hours. Top party and military officials, including President D'Amico and Pope Clement XV, have been taken hostage by Melekhite sympathizers and are being held at the Vatican. All available units are to rendezvous at Piazza San Pietro immediately. Curfew is now in effect. We are at war.

Mihai paled. "Attacks? What's going on?"

Ismail frowned, shaking his head.

"Ismail, where are Gwydion and the others?"

"They went out," Ismail said. "They had business to attend to."

Mihai slammed his hands on the table. "What *kind* of business?!"

Then it dawned on him as Giovanni's words from earlier came flooding back: *We're not waiting for a Constantine of our own to come along and grant us freedom. We'll seize that freedom ourselves.*

"He used my songs as a distraction to launch his attack!" Mihai fumed. "Did you know about this?!"

"I didn't!" Ismail cried. "He didn't tell me anything!"

"Of course he didn't," a bitter laugh escaped Mihai's lips. "Why would he? He doesn't trust us with his secrets. He's just been using us to exploit our talents."

"I can fix this," Ismail said.

"*Fix* it? He's taken *hostages*, Ismail! What are you going to do?!"

"I can disable the weapons he took with him if I get close enough. I just need to reprogram the system–"

"Forget about them. Did you hear the broadcast? This isn't just Gwydion's rebellion anymore. The Melekhites are launching a full-scale invasion on all fronts! We have to get out of the country. *Now!*"

But Ismail was already racing down the tunnels of the catacombs.

The Tales of Abel and Mitra

"Where are you going?!" Mihai shouted, chasing after him.

"The Vatican."

"I'm coming with you–!" As he approached the door, it suddenly slid shut. Mihai tried the handle, but it wouldn't budge. He slammed on the tiny window, peering out into the corridor. "Ismail! Open the door!"

"I'm sorry, Mihai. I know you'll follow me, and I can't let that happen. Everyone knows your face now. The streets aren't safe for you." His voice softened. "Just wait for me here. Once this is over, we'll leave the city together. I promise."

"Ismail! Wait! Don't go! It's too dangerous. We have to leave *now!*" He banged on the door, his voice faltering. But Ismail's footsteps were already fading into the distance.

***

As he raced up the dusty old steps, Ismail took a deep breath. *I'm sorry, Mihai. You were right. I've thrown away my humanity for the sake of vengeance. But I'll make things right. I'll stop Gwydion and his madness.*

A spring breeze greeted him as he stepped out into the street. He took a deep breath, inhaling the fresh air for the first time in weeks. He paused as he glimpsed the moon hanging in the sky. Its light was brighter than he remembered.

"I'll be back soon," he whispered, donning a white mask to conceal his identity before he disappeared into the night.

***

Getting to the Vatican was easier than Ismail anticipated, it was getting inside that was an issue. Though a curfew had been declared, the streets were eerily deserted of soldiers as units converged on Piazza San Pietro. Thousands of soldiers,

Yisei Ishkhan

tanks, and drones surrounded the city-state's borders, forming an unbroken perimeter that blocked any direct approach. Ismail's plan to shut down Gwydion's weapons from afar was thwarted. He had to get closer.

Luckily, he knew another way in. His father had been a member of the Swiss Guard in his youth and knew all the secret tunnels that led into the Vatican. Ismail found his way to one of them, slipping inside. It led directly to the Basilica di San Pietro, where he assumed the hostages were being held. There would be dozens, if not hundreds of top government and military officials gathered in the basilica for Pasqua Mass. It was the perfect opportunity for the Underground to launch their attack.

As he navigated the passage, he worked on recalibrating the switch to neutralize Gwydion's weapons. Each attempt ended with an *ERROR* message flashing across the screen. He cursed to himself. The signal couldn't penetrate the tunnel walls. His only option was to activate the command when he resurfaced.

He reached the end of the passage, where a ladder stretched into the darkness above.

This must be it. He took a deep breath.

He climbed cautiously, exiting under the floorboards of one of the balconies overlooking the central nave.

Keeping his head low, he peered out over the edge. Hundreds of parishioners sat in tense silence–priests, nuns, officials, and their families. Their heads were bowed, but not in prayer. At the altar stood a dozen masked figures wielding guns. But one man had his face uncovered. With a glimpse of his fiery red hair, Ismail recognized him at once.

The Tales of Abel and Mitra

Giovanni, Ismail thought. *What are you doing?!* He set to work, fine-tuning the programming on his switch. Just as he was prepared to activate the command, a voice echoed from below. Ismail inched closer to the edge, angling to get a clearer view of the pews.

Above the congregation, a hologram projected the stern visage of a military commander surrounded by soldiers, standing outside in Piazza di San Pietro.

"Giorgio, release the hostages at once, and we will lessen your sentence," the commander's voice boomed.

Giorgio? Ismail furrowed his brow. *Who is Giorgio?*

"I'm afraid I can't do that, *Papà*," Giovanni sneered. "*Everyone* here will pay the price for their sins."

Giovanni is Giorgio? So, he didn't even give us his real *name on the day we met?* Ismail glanced at the name beneath the hologram–Commander Claudio Rossi. Ismail reeled. Had Gwydion been the son of one of the nation's top military leaders this whole time?

The commander's eyes narrowed. "Dammit, son! You have no idea what you're up against!"

"No, *Papà*," Gwydion said, a malicious smile curling his lips. "*You* have no idea."

"You leave me no choice," Commander Rossi sighed. "Bring him here."

The screen shifted as three figures approached. Two were soldiers, and the third held restrained between them was…

"Mihai?!" Ismail hissed.

"Mitra!" Giovanni called out, his tone mockingly jubilant. "What a performance tonight! You've surpassed all my expectations. Revealing your identity to the world–how brave of you! And how foolish."

Mihai said nothing, his head lowered as he refused to bring his gaze to the camera.

Commander Rossi stepped back into view. "Mihai Aslan Ionescu-Amaya. He's a pawn in your game, isn't he? Your *Vox populi*. Release the hostages, and we'll hand him over to you. We'll even grant you safe passage out of the country."

Gwydion stilled, seemingly considering the offer. Then he laughed. "You don't get it at all, do you, *Papà*? We're *all* pawns here. Even me. Do what you want with him. I don't care."

"WAIT!"

Ismail's voice rang out, echoing across the walls of the basilica before he even knew what he was doing. Heads turned toward the balcony as he stepped into view. In the hologram, both Commander Rossi and Mihai noticed him. Mihai's face paled with fear.

"Icarus!" Gwydion exclaimed in delight. "Tonight is full of surprises. What brings you here?"

"Let them go, Gwydion!" Ismail demanded.

Gwydion smirked. "I'm sorry, Icarus. Did you forget how this works? *You* take orders from *me*, not the other way around."

"Fine," Ismail huffed, turning to the hologram. "I'll make you an offer."

"Icarus, don't!" Mihai's voice cracked.

"Icarus?" Commander Rossi frowned. "I'm sorry, who are you?"

"The brains behind the Underground's operations," said Ismail. "I designed the systems that hacked into your government files and military technology."

The Tales of Abel and Mitra

As proof, he pressed a button on his switch. In the hologram, the drones hovering in Piazza di San Pietro plummeted to the ground. Commander Rossi jerked sideways, narrowly avoiding being crushed by one.

"I'll surrender," Ismail said, "in exchange for Mihai's safety. Do we have a deal?

"No!" Mihai lunged forward. "Ismail wait–!"

With a wave of Commander Rossi's hand, the soldiers restrained Mihai. The Commander paused, considering Ismail's offer for a moment. "Very well. The exchange will take place on the steps of the basilica."

With that, the hologram flickered out.

Ismail raced down the balcony, finding a stairwell to descend to the basilica's ground floor. Emerging into the central nave, he was met with Gwydion, who stood waiting with an all-too-familiar smirk curling on his lips.

"Don't interfere," Ismail warned, his hand resting on the switch.

"Relax," Gwydion raised his hands in mock surrender, his tone amused. "I'm unarmed. I won't stop you. Go and sacrifice yourself for your beloved Mitra."

Ismail's gaze hardened. "You still need me. You won't make it out alive unless you accept the Commander's demands. I'm your best chance at escape. I can disable the weapons outside and know the secret passages leading out of the basilica."

Gwydion chuckled softly. "I appreciate your concern, but you are no longer of any use to us. You've already played your part, Icarus. I must applaud you–we never would've made it this far without you." His grin widened, a maniacal look flashing through his eyes. "But the time has come. Soon, deliverance will be upon us all."

Ismail shuddered, but he didn't have time to dwell on Gwydion's cryptic words. He shoved past the man, making a break for the main doors of the basilica. All that mattered was saving Mihai. He threw open the doors, the cool night air hitting him as he stepped onto the steps. Raising his hands in surrender, he moved slowly toward the top of the steps.

"Halt!" The soldiers barked. Their guns were trained on him. Below, thousands of others were gathered in the square. At the forefront was Mihai, being forced forward with the barrel of a gun pressed against his head.

"Let him go," Ismail called out, his voice calm but firm.

"Drop the device," the soldier ordered, "and any other weapons."

"Icarus, don't!" Mihai shouted. "Don't trust them! Get out of here! Please! Go!"

"If you move, we shoot," the soldiers warned.

"I'll drop it!" Ismail assured. He slowly lowered himself to the ground, setting down the switch before stepping back with his hands raised.

The soldiers nudged Mihai forward. He ascended the stairs, one step after another. When he reached the top of the steps, he mouthed two words: *Get down.*

Before Ismail could react, Mihai dropped, lunging for the discarded switch. Gunfire erupted. Ismail let out a sharp scream as the chaos unfolded. But as suddenly as it began, the gunfire ceased.

"He deactivated our weapons!" A soldier yelled. Another delivered a heavy kick to Mihai's stomach, sending him sprawling across the ground.

The Tales of Abel and Mitra

"Ismail, run," Mihai said weakly.

But Ismail couldn't move. There was blood pooling across the steps–lots of blood. Mihai had been shot in the back.

His mind raced, but before he could react, he was knocked off his feet. His eardrums rattled as the world lit up in a brilliant flash of white. Something exploded in the square.

No...not again...

Ismail groaned, struggling to regain his bearings as his head rang. He pushed himself to his feet. A sea of carnage had engulfed the square. Flames licked the basilica's stone steps as charred bodies lay scattered about. Thick plumes of smoke climbed into the sky, blocking out the moonlight.

A dark shadow zipped by overhead. Then another. Before Ismail knew it, there were dozens of them–hovercrafts. More explosions rang across the city as they rained down fire from above.

Ismail dragged himself to the edge of the steps where Mihai lay limp in a pool of his blood. He was alive–but barely. Blood soaked his clothes, and his pulse was growing faint. Ismail grabbed his friend under the arms, pulling him inside the doors of the basilica.

But the situation inside wasn't much better. The once-majestic nave of San Pietro had become a warzone. The explosions outside had toppled statues and relics, scattering debris across the blood-streaked floor. Some of the hostages had been executed. Ismail spotted the bodies of the president and Pope Clement XV slumped against the altar. The other parishioners had risen against their captors, overpowering them in a desperate bid to escape. But there was nowhere to run. An explosion struck the roof overhead, raining down debris. Horrified shrieks rang out, only to be abruptly cut off as a slab of stone slammed into the ground on Ismail's left. It barely missed him.

Ismail didn't look back, continuing to drag Mihai along. He made his way to the nearest alcove–a chapel off to the right. But he wasn't the only one seeking refuge in that corner.

"Still playing the hero, I see," Gwydion purred. "I thought you'd been blown to bits out there."

"We need to stop the bleeding!" Ismail cried.

Mihai had been faced down when Ismail found him on the steps, and Ismail had dragged him in that position the entire way. A dark trail of blood stained the pristine marble tiles of the basilica. Dozens of other bodies littered the ground beneath collapsed piles of debris, some dead, others dying.

Ismail tore at the hem of Mihai's shirt, hoping to access the wound. A thick gush of blood splattered out. Ismail tore off his own shirt, wrapping it as tightly as he could around Mihai's waist with the hope of stemming the bleeding. It leaked through.

"He needs proper medical attention…" Ismail's voice was quivering. He whipped around expectantly at Gwydion. "We need to get out of here!"

But Gwydion wasn't even looking at him. His gaze was upturned as he focused on the life-sized statue in the middle of the chapel. It depicted a young man, a soldier, with his hand outstretched to a dove that had come to rest in his palm.

"Do you know who this chapel belongs to, Icarus?" Gwydion asked calmly.

The Tales of Abel and Mitra

"Are you even listening to me?!" Ismail raged. "Mihai is *dying*! We need to get him help!"

"It's San Hironimo," Gwydion continued as if he hadn't heard a word. "Also known as Masuda Shirō Tokisada of Nippon. He was only recently canonized. After the new government came to power, they dedicated this chapel to him. You know, this formerly was the chapel of Michelangelo's *Madonna della Pietà*. But after that stylized image of your parents as the *Pietà* became the symbol of the Underground, they had it removed."

Ismail's heart sank. Gwydion was rambling, indifferent to Mihai's condition as bombs continued to rain down on them. The walls of the basilica trembled.

"San Hironimo was a military commander," Gwydion went on casually. "Some call him the 'Jeanne d'Arc of Nippon'—a charismatic young leader who fought for justice but met martyrdom before his prime. Perhaps it was his military background that made the authorities decide his statue was better suited here than the *Pietà*. Funny, isn't it? Symbols can so easily have their meaning changed over time. One generation's icon of resistance becomes the next generation's tool of authority. Michelangelo didn't anticipate his *Pietà* would inspire rebellion, nor could San Hironimo imagine being glorified one day by a military dictatorship centuries after his death in a land he'd never set his eyes on."

Mihai's skin was growing cold, his breath shallow and his pulse faint.

"If you ask me," Gwydion mused, "San Hironimo is better suited as a symbol for the Underground than for the government. He fought against oppression for the right to practice his faith, just as we do. In the end, his revolution was crushed, and the Christians of Nippon were forced to worship in secret for centuries. They became *Kakure Kirishitan*—the Hidden Christians. Sound familiar? But unlike them, I'm not waiting two hundred years for deliverance. And thanks to you, I don't have to."

He gleamed, turning to face Ismail. "Your tech, Icarus, made all of this possible. It disabled the military's defenses, allowing the Melekhites to liberate this country unimpeded! None of this could've been possible without you!"

The basilica shook as relentless bombing tore at its foundations. Much of the ceiling had already collapsed, and Ismail knew their alcove wouldn't hold much longer.

"'My name is Ozymandias!'" Gwydion laughed ecstatically. "'King of kings! Look on my works, ye Mighty, and despair!'"

"You're insane," Ismail spat.

Gwydion chuckled. "You have to be a little insane if you want to change the world."

A large chunk of the ceiling gave way, crashing onto the shrine and crushing the statue of San Hironimo. Only the dove perched atop its outstretched hand remained, sticking out of the rubble.

"History is written by the victors," Gwydion mused, barely avoiding being crushed as he sidestepped the debris. "One day, people will look back on this moment as a glorious triumph as legendary as the Greek conquest of Troy or Rome's destruction of Carthage." He chuckled. "Did you know that this basilica was built with stones from the Colosseum, which itself was constructed from the ruins of Jerusalem's Second Temple? Rome triumphed over the Jews, but the Jewish God triumphed over Rome. And now, we enter the dawn of a new era. This is not the end of the Eternal City; it is the beginning of the next chapter!"

He knelt by Ismail's side. "Before we attain our salvation, I must confess something."

Ismail ignored him, pouring all his focus into Mihai as he began administering CPR.

Gwydion leaned close, whispering into Ismail's ear. "On the day your parents were killed in the square, it was *I* who fired the first shot."

Time froze. Ismail's hands stilled as the world around him seemed to melt into silence. Even Mihai became a distant afterthought.

"You…" Ismail's voice trembled. "YOU KILLED THEM!"

He leaped from the ground, delivering a heavy blow to Gwydion's face. The crack of bone echoed through the chapel as both men collapsed to the ground. Ismail landed on top of Gwydion, pinning him down and continuing to pummel him.

"Sacrifice…is a necessary price to pay…for achieving greatness…" Gwydion rasped between the blows. Despite the broken nose and missing teeth, he grinned. "Your parents…shine brighter in death…than they ever could've imagined…in life…!"

"SHUT UP!" Ismail clamped his hands down on Gwydion's throat. He was so enraged that he failed to notice Mihai stirring behind him. Nor did he realize that above, cracks were snaking along the ceiling.

Though he was bloodied and bruised, Gwydion managed to turn his head up. His gaze grew distant. "Deliverance is upon us…"

Yisei Ishkhan

A hand gripped the back of Ismail's collar just as the ceiling gave out. The next thing Ismail knew, he was yanked backward and hurled onto a pile of rubble where the basilica's outer wall once stood. He rose to his feet, surveying the scene in a panicked daze as the dust settled. Most of San Hironimo's chapel was buried in rubble. A body lay on the ground–but it wasn't Gwydion's.

"Mihai!" Ismail cried, falling to his friend's side. "Say something!"

Mihai's figure was contorted, the lower half of his body trapped beneath the debris.

"You're alive…" Mihai whispered. Despite the twisted expression of agony on his face, he looked relieved. "You have to…get out of here…"

"I'm not leaving you!"

Mihai grabbed his arm with surprising strength. "I didn't pull you out so you could die here with me. Go! Before it's too late!"

Nearby, the glazed-over eyes of a mangled corpse stared back at Ismail from under the debris–Gwydion.

"I can't…" Ismail sobbed. Tears poured down his cheeks, dripping onto Mihai's face. "This is all my fault. I should've listened to you…I should've left when we had the chance…"

"You can still make it out…" Mihai's voice was eerily gentle. He fumbled, his shaky fingers gripping the beads of the Conquistador bracelet as he slipped it off his wrist. "Do me a favour. Pass this on for me…"

Ismail accepted the relic. He managed to nod but couldn't muster up any words.

Outside, explosions echoed in the distance as the Melekhite invasion shifted elsewhere in the city. Most of the

The Tales of Abel and Mitra

basilica had been reduced to ash and ruin. The destruction around them was finally beginning to register for Ismail. He was watching history unfold–the fall of a great city on par with Babylon, Constantinople, or Tenochtitlan. One day, future generations would look back on the ruins of the Basilica di San Pietro the same way they looked upon the Colosseum.

Yet Ismail felt nothing as he gazed upon the destruction. Everything he'd been fighting for these past months–the Underground, the people of this city, freedom, vengeance for his parents–none of that mattered now. All he cared about was the man who lay dying in his arms. He cradled Mihai's head, staying by his friend's side until the body had grown cold.

When he had no tears left to shed, he slid Mihai's bracelet onto his hand. A sudden urge overcame him.

"This isn't goodbye," he whispered. "Not yet."

His hand pressed against the side of Mihai's head, just above the ear. Sure enough, Mihai's Memoria Chip remained intact.

"I'm sorry," Ismail muttered. "But I'm keeping my promise to you. Let's leave this city together, Mihai."

He produced his pocketknife. Taking a deep breath, he prepared to salvage what remained of his friend, determined to preserve the bond that even death couldn't sever.

***

All at once, the memory shattered. When Ismail's eyes fluttered open, he found himself back in the study of his chalet at Lac Lunaire. Mihai stood before him, his hazel eyes studying Ismail intently. Their hands were still clasped together.

Yisei Ishkhan

"I remember..." Mihai whispered. "I remember everything..."

Tears welled in Ismail's eyes. He tried to speak, but his voice choked up. Instead, he leaned forward and enveloped Mihai in an embrace.

"I'm confused..." Mihai murmured. "Where are we? We were at the basilica and then...I don't remember." He glanced past Ismail, his eyes lighting up at the sight of the others. "Natsuki and Nuwa? What are you doing here?"

"That was three years ago, Mihai," Natsuki said gently tone.

"Three years...?"

"You died, Mihai," Ismail's voice quivered. "You died, but I brought you back."

Mihai froze. "I...died?" He glanced at his hands, studying their flawless design. "What happened? This body...it's different..."

"I cloned you," Ismail beamed. "I had to make some adjustments, but this *is* your body. As for your mind," Ismail tapped the side of his head, "everything is from your Memoria Chip."

Mihai's hand flew to the side of his head where the chip was implanted. His face filled with unease. "Why? Why would you do this, Ismail?"

"Why? Because I *had* to! I knew it was possible to bring you back!"

"No," Mihai flinched. "This isn't me. It can't be. I'm *not* Mihai."

The Tales of Abel and Mitra

"You *are*," Ismail insisted. "You have all the same memories and personality as you did when you were in your old body. I've just given you a new one."

"Just give him some time," Natsuki said. "It's a lot to process."

"No," Nuwa interjected. "Ismail's wrong. That isn't Mihai. It can't be. Mihai died that day, during the Siege of Rome. His consciousness ceased and his soul ascended to be with the Lord. This is just a clone of Mihai, processing his memories."

"Nuwa," Natsuki hissed. "You aren't helping."

Mihai's breathing quickened, his hands clutching his head. He let out a gasp as though in pain.

Sir, Aida's calm voice cut through the tension. *There's an issue.*

"I can see that, Aida!" Ismail snapped. "What's happening?"

The NeuroSynth Core Processor has entered overdrive. If this continues, it may cause irreversible damage to the Memoria Chip.

"Remove the chip," Ismail ordered. "Do it now!"

As you wish, sir.

From the pod where Mihai's body had been resting, several mechanical arms shot forth, two restraining Mihai while a third extended toward his head.

Panic flashed through Mihai's eyes. "What's going on?! What are you doing?!"

"Relax, Mihai," Ismail said, his voice calm but lacking in confidence. "Everything will be fine. I promise."

Natsuki covered Eli's eyes and ushered the girl out of the room. Nuwa remained nearby, silent in shock as he watched the scene unfold.

Yisei Ishkhan

Mihai strained against the mechanical arms holding his limbs in place, his body trembling with fear. The arm probing the side of his head latched onto him. Moments later, it withdrew, clasping the Memoria Chip. Mihai's body grew limp, his eyes fluttering shut.

"How is it?" Ismail asked with a shaky voice.

Aida extended the chip to him. *It's fried, sir.*

"No…"

"What does that mean?" Nuwa stepped forward. "Does that mean it can no longer access Mihai's memories?"

Not exactly. By my estimation, 75-80% of the Memoria Chip's data was imprinted into the NeuroSynth Core Processor.

A ray of hope flickered in Ismail's eyes. "Then he should still remember. That's more than the average person can recall on their own." He turned to Mihai expectantly. "Can you hear me, Mihai? You're still in there, aren't you?"

Mihai groaned, struggling to open his eyes. "Icarus…? Is that you…?"

"It's Ismail. Ismail Ouali-St. Laurent."

Mihai blinked in confusion. "Ismail? I don't recognize that name. You're Icarus, aren't you?"

A weak smile tugged at Ismail's lips. "Yes. I'm Icarus."

Mihai's eyes darted toward Nuwa. "And you're Nuwa. Nuwa Yuen-Serwanga."

Nuwa gave a slight nod, glancing nervously in Ismail's direction. "Yes."

Ismail frowned. "Aida, why does he recognize Nuwa but not me?"

The Tales of Abel and Mitra

As I mentioned, only 75-80% of the Memoria Chip's data was imprinted into the NeuroSynth Core Processor. It seems that most of Mihai's core memories have been erased.

"Mihai…" Mihai echoed. "Who is that?"

Ismail's heart sank. "*You* are Mihai. Mihai Aslan Ionescu-Amaya."

Mihai frowned. "But my name is Mitra."

"Mitra was your alias," Ismail said, his voice pained with regret. "It's the name you went by in the Underground. Do you remember that?"

"With Gwydion and the others…"

"Yes! Do you remember anything else?"

"Gwydion's real name was Giorgio, but he told us it was Giovanni."

"What about our time in the Underground?" Ismail pressed. "What are your most recent memories?"

Mitra strained. "They are all jumbled together. I cannot tell."

"Tell me what you remember about me," Ismail whispered.

"We had class together, at the *Instituto d'Arte e Tecnologia di Roma*. That is where I met you, and Nuwa, and Natsuki. We had that assignment together."

Ismail nodded. "You switched cards with me so I wouldn't have to partner with Nuwa. Do you remember that?"

Nuwa scoffed. "So *that's* what happened?"

Mitra shook his head. "I do not recall."

"What about our first dance, after your performance of *The Nutcracker* on Christmas Eve?" Ismail asked.

"I remember the performance…but not anything else."

"Your parents," Ismail said. "Do you know what happened to them?"

"My parents…?" Mitra repeated in confusion. "My mother was a flamenco dancer. My father was a musician…"

"But what happened to them?" Ismail insisted.

"I…do not recall."

Ismail slumped at his words, sinking into his nearby office chair and letting out a deep sigh. When Mitra spoke, it didn't sound like him speaking, but someone else recounting the details of his life secondhand.

"Well," Ismail muttered, glancing at Nuwa, "he seems to remember you, at least. What is it you wanted to say to him?"

Nuwa hesitated. "I just wanted to thank him. If he hadn't given me his ticket that day, I wouldn't have been able to leave Rome. So, thank you."

"You are welcome," Mitra said monotonously. "Yes, I remember that day. I was with Icarus, and we ran into you at the train station. We were preparing to board, but violence broke out. Suddenly, Icarus wanted to leave. He wanted to leave…but I do not recall where we went after that…"

"To find my parents, at the Piazza di Spagna," Ismail said.

"Your parents…" Mitra repeated. "Yes. It was your parents who got us those tickets. Nuwa, you should thank Icarus and his parents. They did not have to offer a ticket to me, but they did."

Nuwa shifted. "Thank you, Ismail."

"Is that all?" Ismail said with indifference. "You just wanted to say thank you?"

"Yes, but not just for the tickets," Nuwa glanced at Mitra. "Mihai had a profound impact on shaping who I am today,

The Tales of Abel and Mitra

even if I didn't realize it at the time. I don't know if you remember this, but on the day that Rome fell to the Melekhites, you sang a few songs as part of the Underground's final broadcast."

"Do you remember that?" Ismail asked.

"I remember you were working on a project," Mitra said, turning to Ismail. "I was upset. I wanted to leave the city with you."

A pained expression crossed Ismail's face. "Yes…"

"Gwydion came into the room," Mitra continued. "He asked me to sing a few songs. I followed him to the broadcasting room and sat on the chair with my mother's guitar in hand…" he shook his head. "I apologize. I cannot recall any of the songs I sang that day."

"That's alright," Nuwa said. "The songs themselves aren't what's important. What mattered was the emotions behind them. There was so much passion in your voice. I could tell how much you cared for the people of Rome when you sang. I took great inspiration from your voice. I'm not the type to easily be stirred by emotion. But that day, I felt something profound. Your songs made me want to become a better person—someone willing to sacrifice myself to serve others, as you had been willing to do."

Mitra cocked his head. "Can you tell me what songs I sang?"

"*Dies iræ*, *La Llorona*, and a few more," Nuwa said. "One was an Amazigh folk song, I believe."

"*A Vava Inouva*," Ismail said. "The one I taught you."

"Yes…" Mitra's eyes lit up. "Yes, I remember that song…" He began to hum the lyrics, but after a few moments, he faltered. "You said my voice inspired you because you could tell how much I cared for the people of Rome."

Nuwa nodded. "That's right."

A small smile spread across Mitra's face. "The thing is, I was not singing for Rome."

Nuwa furrowed his brow. "Then for what?"

"I remember now," a glint of realization flashed through Mitra's eyes. "I was singing for Icarus."

The Tales of Abel and Mitra
The Tale of Abel and Mitra

Mitra fell silent after those final words.

"What?" Abel piped up. "Is that the end of the story?"

"No story ever truly ends," Mitra said. "But it is impossible to go on forever telling them. Besides, our time is up." He gestured to the top of the cavern, where scuttling and screeching echoed from the makarasa. "Their sentries have been called off. They must be throwing in every soldier they have to fend off the kamkara. Which means this is our chance to escape."

As Mitra told his tale, Akavi and Spinner had managed to untie the others. Avi was stirring, but Nineveh and Noa remained unconscious. Mitra hoisted Nineveh onto his back, allowing the pku to seal her in place with their silk. He scooped Noa into his arms.

"Can you manage Avi on your own?" He asked. "He should be able to walk by now."

Abel nodded, slinging Avi's arm over his shoulder and hauling him to his feet. "C'mon. Time to go."

"*Mnn…*" Avi groaned. "Just…a little more sleep…"

"There is no time for that," Mitra said. "You can sleep all you want once we return to the Village." He glanced at the pku. "Akavi, and Spinner, can you lead the way?"

The pku responded with affirmative clicks, disappearing into the darkness as they scaled the wall. Moments later, silk threads descended from above. Mitra tested a strand with a sharp tug before wrapping it around his waist.

"Just follow my lead," he said to Abel, planting his feet against the wall and hauling himself up.

Yisei Ishkhan

Abel shot a wary glance up the cavern wall. "I don't think I can manage this with Avi."

Mitra nodded. "Very well. Wait here for me. I will be right back."

With an effortless leap, he scaled the wall, one hand holding Noa and the other gripping the threads. A few moments later, he dropped down to the bottom of the cave.

"Ready?" He asked, taking Avi off Abel's hands.

Abel laughed. "I can't believe I ever thought you were a normal human."

It wasn't long before they were all at the top of the wall. Akavi and Spinner had gone up ahead to scout the path. Abel struggled to keep up as Mitra navigated the tunnels. Avi dragged his feet, his head slumped forward. Abel feared he'd pass out again.

"I still have...so many questions..." Abel panted between his words.

"What do you wish to know?" Mitra's faint voice echoed from up ahead.

"I still don't understand...what you are. Are you human...? Or something else...?"

Mitra chuckled. "I suppose it depends on what you mean by human. Ismail cloned Mihai's genetic material to create me, but also used inorganic parts in my body. I lack many of the internal organs that most humans have. Ismail believed these were inefficient, and that he could create a stronger, more enduring body, with other materials."

"But how did Ismail bring you to life? I didn't understand all that stuff about Memori-whatever Chips and NeuroSomething Somethings."

The Tales of Abel and Mitra

Mitra chuckled. "I suppose it would be difficult for you to understand, coming from a world without such technological developments. You could say that I am like a sort of puppet."

"A puppet controlled by Mihai's memories? You and Mihai don't seem very similar. When you were telling me his story, I sometimes forgot that you were telling your own story. At the end of your tale, when Ismail reawakened you, it seemed like you'd forgotten too. But now you remember?"

"In a way," said Mitra. "But I do not recall those memories in the same way a human would. After Mihai's Memoria Chip was fried, Ismail uploaded some of his own memories into my NeuroSynth Core Processor. In a sense, I relived those memories, but through Ismail's eyes. It was like watching a film."

"What is a film?" Abel asked.

"Like a visual story," Mitra clarified. "You have memories of Ismail and Mihai's life through the story I told you, just as you do of the lives of Hikaru and Shirō, Nayan and Anahit, Áedán and Ingvar, and Domingo and Nezahualatzin. I am sure you even visualized these tales, imagining the scenery and characters, and what they may have looked and sounded like. Perhaps you pictured the vibrant pink hues of the Castile roses that Domingo saw on Tepayac hill, or imagined the scent of the salty sea breeze of the island that Áedán and Ingvar washed up on. Maybe you conjured up an image of what the exotic dishes that Anahit ordered at *Cardamom of Qocho* would have tasted like, or felt the heat of the flames that burned down Shimabara Castle. Or perhaps, when Louna Ouali sang the *Songs of Freedom*, you could almost hear what her voice might have sounded like."

"I did imagine some of those things," Abel admitted.

"Exactly. You were able to envision those memories, the people and places, despite never having laid eyes on them yourself. Perhaps the vision in your mind is far from what reality was, but you have still managed to capture a fragment of that memory nonetheless. Now, those memories live on in you, even if you never lived through them yourself. Does that make sense?"

Abel nodded.

"That is how Mihai's memories appear to me," Mitra continued. "Memories that I witness play out before my very eyes, but are not my own. That was why I became an archivist. Ismail and the others saw my potential to keep a record of history."

Abel instinctively felt for the beaded bracelet around his wrist, the very same one that Domingo had given to Nezahualatzin, and Mihai to Ismail. He wondered how much time had passed since then. Thousands, perhaps even tens of thousands of Cycles. How many countless generations and lifetimes had Mitra lived through?

"What happened to Ismail and the others?" Abel wondered.

"Ismail and I began compiling the archives and relics that you see in my collection. None of it would have been possible without Natsuki's assistance. She and Nuwa were married and spent most of their lives traveling, never settling in one place for long. They raised Eli as their own, and when the girl was grown up, she returned to Naga-Zo."

"Why are you talking…about my mother…?" Avi mumbled.

Mitra cocked his head. "Pardon?"

The Tales of Abel and Mitra

"Avi's mother is also named Eli," Abel explained. "No wonder that name sounded familiar."

"I see," Mitra nodded. "What is your family name?"

"Ao," Avi muttered. "The House of Ao."

"We inherit our family names from our maternal line," Abel said. "Avi's grandmother Inali is from the House of Ao."

"Intriguing," Mitra mused. "You know, the Eli from my story also bore the surname 'Ao.'"

"Really?" Abel said.

Before he could ask any further questions, the tunnel began to shake. Akavi and Spinner came racing in their direction, giving three sharp clicks and flashing the turquoise patterns along their backs—a warning signal.

"There are makarasa up ahead," Mitra whispered. "They are approaching."

Adrenaline coursed through Abel's veins. "What do we do?"

"Do not panic," Mitra said. He pointed toward the left wall. "There's a crevice. We can see if it leads us to another path."

They scrambled into the hole. It was narrow, barely wide enough for Mitra to pass through. He was forced to duck to avoid knocking his head against the ceiling, but they managed to make it through. The rumbling grew louder as a couple of makarasa scurried past, but soon faded into obscurity as they made their way deeper underground.

"Do you think they've already taken down the kamkara?" Abel wondered.

"We will soon find out," said Mitra. "Hopefully the makarasa fail to notice our absence."

Yisei Ishkhan

Abel shuddered at the thought of having to face the makarasa again, though having Mitra by their side made him feel slightly better.

Instead of retracing their steps to the main tunnel, they remained in the new passage. The incline rose steadily, a faint breeze coming from above that Abel hoped was a sign they were nearing the exit. After a few minutes of trudging through the darkness, they emerged in a cavernous space. The temperature dropped suddenly. Abel shivered.

"Is it safe here?" Abel's whisper pierced the deafening silence.

"It is safe," Mitra assured. He set Nineveh and Noa onto the ground. "I detect one other exit to this chamber, and it is too small for the makarasa to enter."

Abel blinked, straining to get a look around. "How can you even see anything? It's pitch black."

Mitra chuckled. "I was not relying on sight, but echolocation from your voice. But yes, I can see as well—both visible and infrared light. There is something ahead of us along the wall."

Abel set Avi alongside the others, taking Mitra by the hand as he was guided through the darkness. It was only then that Abel noticed that Mitra's hands were glowing slightly. Mitra raised them along the wall, illuminating strange lines etched in the stone. Mitra's hands grew brighter and brighter, allowing Abel to make out the strange designs.

Abel glimpsed several shapes carved near the top of the wall: a group of six-legged creatures with upright bodies and bulbous eyes. Mitra traced his hand across the image, revealing other drawings. There was a depiction of the

The Tales of Abel and Mitra

umbrella-shaped flora that covered the landscape of Darkside and other strange life forms that Abel didn't recognize.

"Is this a makarasa?" Mitra wondered, lowering his hand near the bottom of the wall to a depiction of a dark, foreboding decapod.

"I think so," Abel whispered.

As Mitra moved his hand along, more images of makarasa appeared while the smaller six-legged creatures vanished from the scene. The makarasa were depicted as violent beasts, devouring or hacking apart the other fauna with their terrifying claws.

Below the scene was a map of interconnected tunnels—a map of the underground caverns they'd traversed in the makarasa nest. At first, only the six-legged creatures were shown to inhabit the tunnels. But as Mitra continued to unveil more of the image, the makarasa appeared here as well.

When Mihai's hand reached the end of the wall, there was one final image engraved. It was less detailed than the others, with jagged lines of various depths, as if the drawing had been carved in haste or by a less skilled artist than the previous images. It depicted a lone, six-legged creature, huddled up in the tiny chamber.

"Do you recognize this species?" Mitra wondered.

Abel shook his head. "I've never seen any six-legged species in Shambhala before."

Mitra's attention drew away from the wall toward a nearby rock that jutted out. The surface of the rock was smooth—far too smooth to have been naturally formed. It looked like a ledge, with several oval-shaped objects resting on it. Mitra took one of the ovals into his hands—a carved statue with six legs and several globular eyes. The other statues appeared to be depictions of the same creature, but none were complete, missing an eye or a couple of legs.

"Do you think the makarasa made these?" Abel asked.

"They are too intricate for the makarasa to have carved," said Mitra. "Besides, the makarasa are too large to enter this chamber." He slipped the statue into his pocket. "Come. The exit is just behind the ledge. We should see where it leads before we bring the others with us."

Mitra dropped to all fours as he crawled into the narrow tunnel. Abel followed close behind him. The incline grew steeper until they emerged onto a rocky outcropping, halfway between the forest floor and the tops of the umbrella-shaped trees. From their vantage, they could gaze out over the unfolding battle raging beyond the makarasa nest.

Ahead of them, an enormous claw bore down on the swarm of makarasa below, crushing several at once. The ground splattered with their remains. One of the makarasa was seized by the kamkara, desperately writhing in a futile attempt to break free. But the more it struggled, the more the sharp edges of the kamkara's claw dug into its flesh, until one of its legs was severed. The kamkara brought the makarasa to its face, and the helpless creature disappeared down its gaping jaw like it was nothing more than a light snack.

Abel was awestruck at the magnitude of the kamkara's size. He'd encountered the beasts on several occasions when they crossed into the Valley of Shambhala, but only ever observed them from above and at a distance. Amid the backdrop of the Valley's towering trees, one couldn't fully appreciate the scale of just how monstrous kamkara truly were. Abel recalled his run-in with the makarasa earlier that day, and how the beast had towered over him and Avi. But

The Tales of Abel and Mitra

the kamkara dwarfed the makarasa. Its ten legs alone were each thicker and taller than a makarasa's entire body, but the bulk of the kamkara's size rested in their round thoraxes. Four eye stalks protruded from the top of kamkara's head, each easily the size of a grown man.

Dozens of makarasa swarmed the kamkara, attacking its legs with their claws. The kamkara barely noticed their presence. With each lumbering step, at least one or two makarasa were trampled.

The thundering rampage of a second kamkara echoed from nearby, but this was out of Abel's line of sight.

"It will not be long before the kamkara are overwhelmed," Mitra said.

"Really?" Abel asked. "It's already killed dozens of makarasa."

"Dozens in a swarm of thousands is nothing," Mitra said, nodding toward some of the umbrella-shaped trees. "Look. The makarasa are already making their move. They are climbing the trees to get on top of the kamkara's shell. The kamkara is a fortress covered in a thick exoskeleton, but their eyes are vulnerable."

"Kamkara may also rely on other senses," Abel pointed out. "Besides, a blind Kamkara may be more dangerous than one that can see."

"You might be correct, but I do not intend to stick around to find out. Wait here. I will be back soon."

"Where are you going?" Abel asked as Mitra began descending the slope.

"To retrieve the vehicles they stole from us. Go see if the others are awake." With that, he dropped off the ledge and disappeared into the darkness.

Yisei Ishkhan

Abel climbed back down the tunnel. As he neared the chamber, he heard voices up ahead, but they ceased as he exited the tunnel. Without Mitra's glowing presence, the cave was pitch black.

"Hello?" Abel called out tentatively. "Are you awake?"

"Oh, it's Abel," Nineveh's sigh of relief pierced the silence.

"Why didn't you say something sooner!" Avi cried. "We thought you were a makarasa."

"Glad to see you're alright," Abel huffed. "How's Noa?"

"Noa's here?!" Nineveh let out another relieved sigh. "Where? I can't see a thing!"

"He should be just next to you. Avi, you didn't tell her that we'd rescued her brother?"

"How was I supposed to know?" Avi retorted. "I don't remember anything after that makarasa ambushed us."

"Mitra saved us," Abel said. "We're safe from the makarasa in this room. Mitra just went to fetch the hovercycles for our escape." He dropped to his knees feeling around in the dark until his hand rested on Noa's clothes.

"How is he?" Avi asked.

"He's not responding," Nineveh said nervously. "Is he…?"

"He's alive," Abel assured. "He's just weak. He was trapped by the makarasa longer than we were, so it'll take him longer to recover. Come. Let's bring him to the exit. We should be ready to leave as soon as Mitra returns."

With Akavi and Spinner's help, they managed to drag Noa as gently as possible across the chamber and up to the outcrop overlooking the battle. Mitra's earlier prediction had

The Tales of Abel and Mitra

proven correct—several makarasa had scaled the kamkara's back and taken out one of its eyes. The other eyes had withdrawn into the creature's head for protection, leaving the creature to lash about in a blind rampage grabbing and gobbling up as many makarasa as it could get its claws on. But the beast was running out of steam, steering itself away from the makarasa swarm. It wasn't long before the creature began its retreat into the forest.

The forest floor was littered with the flattened remains of at least a hundred makarasa, but most of the swarm had survived the onslaught. They went to work, sweeping the battlefield and dragging away their fallen comrades. Abel watched with unease. None of the makarasa appeared distraught over what they'd just witnessed. They went about like it was just another day for them.

"There!" Avi's voice snapped Abel from his thoughts.

In the middle of the swarm, a streak of silver darted across the forest floor. It was a tiny speck from this distance, but Abel could just make out the figure of a man atop the vehicle as it weaved in and out between the makarasa. Several of the makarasa took notice of him, but by the time they reacted, he'd already zipped past them.

"C'mon!" Abel cried. "Let's meet him on the forest floor!"

"I still can't believe Mitra actually pulled this off," Nineveh said, helping Avi scoop up Noa.

Avi laughed. "Is there anything that man *can't* do?"

"Well, he's not exactly a *man*," Abel said.

"What's that supposed to mean?" Nineveh asked.

"Long story. I'll let him tell you about it later."

They landed next to the roots of a tree, keeping their heads down as Mitra approached. There were no makarasa in this area, but their screeches and thundering legs grew louder, seeming to come from every direction at once. Spinner clung tightly to Avi's head; Akavi buried himself into one of Abel's pockets and trembled.

"Get on!" Mitra yelled, jumping off the vehicle as it ground to a halt next to them.

"Just one?" Abel said.

"The others were damaged," Mitra said. "I will have to carry you on my back again."

The others had already piled onto the vehicle, with the still unconscious Noa up front, Nineveh behind him with her grip on the handles, and Avi at the back.

"Are you sure about this?" Nineveh called out.

"We will be right behind you," Mitra said. "Go."

Nineveh didn't need to be told twice. The hovercycle took off and they disappeared into the undergrowth. Abel hopped onto Mitra's back, and they took off after the others just as the makarasa bore down on them.

"Next time I ask you to leave something to me, I hope you will listen," said Mitra. Despite his words, his tone was gentle.

"I...was going to. But Nineveh and Avi insisted on coming after you. I didn't want to let them go on their own."

"I hope they have learned their lesson," Mitra said. "Tell me, what would you have planned to do had I not been there to save you? You were captured by the first makarasa you came across."

"I don't know," Abel flushed. "Thank you for rescuing us."

The Tales of Abel and Mitra

"You can thank me once we have safely returned to the Village."

After a while, the sound of makarasa pursuing them faded into the distance, leaving the forest still and silent. Abel took a deep breath, letting the chilly air of Darkside fill his lungs as his muscles relaxed. He hadn't realized how tense his body had been since they'd left the Village. How long had it been since then? A dozen hours? Most of that time had been spent unconscious, wrapped up in the makarasa den.

He closed his eyes, resting his head against Mitra's back. Mitra's body radiated warmth, but Abel couldn't detect the trace of a heartbeat or breathing.

"You said you have different organs than normal humans," he noted. "Do you have a heart or lungs?"

"Not exactly," Mitra said. "But my body can imitate the functions of most human anatomy. Ismail wanted me to be as lifelike as possible. For instance, I can eat, but my body does not digest food like yours does."

"But you need energy to function, don't you?"

"Of course, but far less than a human does. My body is more efficient in extracting energy from different sources. Most waste I produce takes the form of heat. My body absorbs oxygen and light directly, so I have no need to breathe. Though, I can mimic the function."

"Can you...do that now?" Abel asked sheepishly.

"You want me to breathe?" Mitra said with a trace of amusement.

"If that's not too much trouble. I find it comforting."

"Very well," Mitra smiled. He drew a long, deliberate breath. Abel felt the muscles along his back contracting. He exhaled. "How was that?"

Yisei Ishkhan

"It's nice," Abel said. "It sounds just like a human."

"Try not to fall asleep," Mitra said. "You might lose your grip and fall off."

"Akavi's silk should be enough to hold me in place," Abel mumbled. Already, he could feel his lids growing heavy as he started to nod off.

"Speaking of Akavi, we didn't leave the pku behind, did we?"

"No, he's right here," Abel said just as Akavi wiggled his way out of his pocket. The tiny pku hopped up onto Mitra's shoulder and responded with a couple of clicks.

"I am glad we all made it out in one piece," Mitra smiled.

"Do you think they'll come after us?"

"I doubt it. They were after the tech aboard my vessel, not us."

Abel frowned. "Why would they need it?"

"To study them, I suppose."

The thought unnerved Abel. "Do you think they're really that intelligent?"

"It is difficult to say. Intelligence can take many forms. Their form of intelligence may be incomprehensible to us, and vice versa."

"Do you think they'll be angry that you led the kamkara to their nest?"

"I doubt they will be able to trace it back to me. Besides, 'anger' is a human emotion. I am not sure the makarasa exhibit the same emotions as humans do."

"Do *you* feel anger…?" Abel wondered. "Or any emotions, for that matter?"

The Tales of Abel and Mitra

Mitra was quiet for a moment. "I believe I do. But I am not certain."

"Why not?"

"Can you be certain that you are awake now, and not dreaming?"

"I don't know," Abel admitted. "I usually can't tell when I'm dreaming until I wake up."

"That is how I regard emotion. They feel real to me, just as your dreams feel real to you. But how can I know they are genuine, and not an illusion created by my mind?"

"You could say the same thing about human emotions."

"I suppose you could," Mitra chuckled. "Perhaps I am not so different from a human after all."

"It's strange," said Abel. "Your body and mind aren't exactly human, but I can relate to you better than I can to other people."

Mitra shrugged. "That was Ismail's intention when he created me."

"Do you think those six-legged creatures were similar to us?" Abel wondered. "The ones we saw in the paintings and statues back in the chamber."

"Possibly. The makarasa, even if they are intelligent, do not seem to make extensive use of tools or create art. Those hexapods, if they indeed were the ones that created the art, might be just as creative as humans."

"What do you think happened to them?"

"You would know more than me," Mitra chuckled. "After all, this is your home world. But, if I had to guess, I would say they likely died out long ago. Species are not so different from civilizations. They rise and fall over time, struggling against nature and one another. Perhaps those hexapods were outcompeted by the makarasa."

He produced the statue of the six-legged creature from his pocket, handing it to Abel. Abel took the relic into his hands, brushing off the layer of grime to reveal its features. He stared into its bulging eyes.

"By my estimation, that statue is at least a thousand years old," Mitra said, before quickly clarifying, "approximately ten thousand Day-Night Cycles in your world. Perhaps your ancestors encountered them."

"I don't know," said Abel. "I've never heard any stories of six-legged creatures before. Ten thousand Cycles is a long time."

"It is. Entire civilizations on my world have been forgotten in much less time."

"Can you tell me about one?"

Mitra chuckled. "They wouldn't be forgotten if I had records of them, now, would they?"

"I guess not."

"But I can tell you the story of a civilization that few in my world remembered, despite being one of the oldest and most enduring."

Abel nodded, nuzzling his head into Mitra's back as he found a comfortable position. "I'd like to hear it."

"Then let me tell you a story—a story of the downfall of a great kingdom, of a civilization lost to the sands of time…"

The Tales of Abel and Mitra
VI. The Tale of Yusifina and Zakariya
October 5, 1516 AD
St. Nofer Cathedral, Daw, Kingdom of Dotawo

Dust danced in the moonlight streaming through the narrow windows of the ancient church. Princess Yusifina knelt at the altar in prayer, her white shawl draped over her curly black locks.

Though the hour was late, Yusifina had insisted on visiting the church for prayers. She needed solace, an escape from the suffocating drama in the court and infighting between various branches of the royal family. She'd summoned Bishop Botros from the rectory, who now stood before her at the altar, muttering prayers in Greek.

Yusifina's eyes flicked up to the dilapidated walls of the church. The icons of St. Nofer and St. Christophorus were faded and peeling. A third saint was depicted among them, but his image was so worn down that no one could recall who he was. All that was legible from the inscription under his image were the letters: ...*ius of Thebes*.

Despite being the center of worship in Dotawo, the cathedral was in decay from generations of neglect.

A microcosm for the kingdom as a whole, Yusifina thought to herself.

Dotawo was a kingdom in decline, a shadow of its former self. Gone were the days when Yusifina's ancestors ruled a vast land stretching the length of the Iteru, from the Sixth Cataract in the south to beyond the First Cataract in the north. Civil war, famine, plague, and invasions had ravaged the land, gradually reducing Nubia to ruin over the centuries until nothing but the rump state of Dotawo remained. The splendid cathedrals and opulent palaces fell to ruins, swallowed up by the desert or overrun by nomadic invaders.

The Golden Age of Nubia's glorious past was little more than a memory. As a child, Yusifina had heard tales of their legendary ancestors, the Empire of Kush, that once ruled over Egypt and expelled the Persian and Roman invasions. Now, they were a mere fragment of that once-great civilization, withering into obscurity and teetering on the brink of collapse. Even a small band of raiders out of the desert might be enough to topple the regime.

Bishop Botros finished his prayers with the sign of the cross. He turned to face the young princess, his dark features contrasting with his snowy-white beard. "*Kyrie Eleison.*"

"*Kyrie Eleison*," she repeated.

Lord, have mercy.

"This kingdom rests in the hands of God," said the bishop. "Do not be afraid. What will be will be, regardless of whether you worry."

"I know," Yusifina whispered. "I know."

The creak of the cathedral's doors echoed through the nave. Yusifina turned to see her attendant, Mariam, rush in with a frantic look in her eyes. She wasn't alone. Beside her stood a towering figure—a broad-shouldered man in a white tunic with a pelt draped over his shoulder and a bow strapped to his back. Yusifina recognized him as one of her husband's most trusted bodyguards—Zakariya.

"Mariam," Yusifina said, her voice tense, "what is this? You weren't supposed to tell anyone I was here."

But before Mariam could respond, Zakariya stepped forward. "Your Highness," he said calmly. "King Yuel is dead."

The Tales of Abel and Mitra

"No!" Yusifina sprung to her feet. "What happened to my brother?!"

"Prince Yudas has betrayed us," said Zakariya. "He has allied with the Mamluks. Prince Jirjis has sent me to fetch you. We must leave immediately."

The words struck Yusifina like a blow. Her brother was dead? And Yudas, his closest ally, was a traitor?

She would've collapsed had Mariam not rushed to her side. Zakariya hesitated as he offered his support as well, steadily holding her by the arm. The moment Yusifina found her footing, he stepped back and gave her space.

"My lady, we have to go!" Mariam urged. "Your husband is waiting for us."

"Jirjis…" Yusifina whispered. Her hand fell to her belly, where the faint stirrings of her unborn child drew her back to the present. She closed her eyes, her thoughts racing. She had to get back to Jirjis, not for her own sake, but for their child. "Take me to him."

Mariam nodded, and Zakariya rushed forward to lead the way. As Yusifina slipped through the doors of the cathedral, she stole one last glance at the altar. Something in her gut told her she would never lay eyes on it again. Her eyes met Bishop Botros, who watched her departure in silence. She offered a solemn nod of gratitude.

The bishop bowed his head.

"*Kyrie Eleison.*"

***

The streets of Daw bustled with life despite having been deserted just an hour earlier. Though it was still the dead of night, unrest brewed like a storm. Trouble in the palace seeped into the streets, and soldiers were on patrol, shouting orders for civilians to return to their homes.

Yusifina kept her head low, the folds of her shawl hiding her face as she walked beside Mariam and Zakariya. They rounded a corner, only to be stopped by a group of guards.

"Soldier!" One of them saluted Zakariya. "State your name and division."

"Zakariya," mumbled the man. "Royal guard."

The soldier glanced past him at Yusifina and Mariam, his eyes narrowing. "And these women?"

"Relatives," Zakariya said calmly. "I'm escorting them to safety. Is the palace secure?"

"Those traitors have locked us out," the soldier spat. "Send these women home and report to your Commanding Officer at once!"

Zakariya bowed. "Understood."

As soon as the soldiers moved on, Zakariya ushered Yusifina and Mariam into a shadowy alleyway. They continued along under the cover of darkness.

"Where are we going?" Yusifina whispered.

"Prince Jirjis is waiting at the city gate," Zakariya said. "He's securing a horse for you to flee."

"Flee?!"

"It isn't safe here, Your Highness," Mariam's voice quivered.

Before Yusifina could respond, the clamor of steel echoed from the streets ahead. Shouts followed, bouncing off the worn mudbrick walls of the city's perimeter.

Zakariya halted abruptly. "Stay here."

The Tales of Abel and Mitra

Mariam pulled Yusifina down behind a stack of crates as they peeked out of the alleyway. A group of men was fighting near the city gates, but the darkness obscured their faces.

Please, Lord, she prayed in silence. *Please protect Jirjis.*

Zakariya slung his bow from his back, his movements practiced and precise. He notched an arrow, taking aim, and firing. The snap of the bow echoed through the night, and one of the men in the distance crumpled to the ground. Zakariya shot another arrow, then another. Each found its target.

A lone figure remained by the gate, hunched as he staggered toward them. "Zakariya?!" The voice was hoarse but familiar.

"Jirjis!" Yusifina cried.

"Your Highness, wait!" Mariam protested.

But Yusifina was already running, pulling up the fringes of her robe as she raced across the square to her husband.

"Yusifina?!" A sigh of relief escaped Jirjis' lips.

Yusifina cupped his face in her hands, searching for his features in the faint moonlight. Her fingers brushed against something warm and wet trickling down his forehead.

"Jirjis, you're injured!"

"I'm fine, dear," he took her hands in his. "I'm glad you're safe."

Yusifina's voice quivered. "Is it true...? My brother...Yuel...?"

"He's dead," Jirjis said. "Yudas killed him."

"No..." Yusifina swayed, but she forced herself to remain composed. "I must go back. I must see for myself."

Yisei Ishkhan

"It's impossible," Zakariya said as he and Mariam approached. "You heard what those soldiers said—Yudas has sealed the gates of the palace."

"But my mother!" Yusifina cried. "And Dawid, Rehal, Istifan, and—"

"They're dead," Jirjis said. "They're all gone."

"No…" Yusifina's knees buckled. "No…no…" She fell to the ground, tears spilling down her face.

A sharp cry pierced the darkness. A moment later, Mariam collapsed to the dirt, an arrow protruding from her side.

Yusifina shrieked.

"Your Highness, we must go!" Zakariya ordered. He grabbed both Yusifina and Jirjis by the arms, dragging them toward the city gate as a volley of arrows rained down. Yusifina glanced back in horror as she watched Mariam's body struck again and again.

"Don't look back," Jirjis urged. "We must keep moving."

They stumbled past the fallen bodies Zakariya had taken down earlier, reaching two horses tied just outside the city gate. Jirjis hoisted Yusifina onto one of the horses before mounting behind her. Zakariya mounted the other, cutting their reins free.

As they galloped out of the city, shouts erupted behind them. "Stop them!"

Zakariya twisted in his saddle, shooting arrows as he rode. Each struck its target, but more pursuers emerged from the shadows.

With the great Iteru River to their left, the horses raced along the dirt path leading to the next town. Jirjis pulled on the reins, swerving their horse from side to side as arrows rained down. But with no horses of their own, their pursuers were unable to follow for long. After a few tense minutes, the arrows ceased.

"Are you alright?" Jirjis muttered. His hand fell to Yusifina's abdomen, giving it a gentle rub.

"I'm fine," Yusifina said. She clasped his hand in hers. Was it just the chilly air of the desert night, or was his skin cold? Not just cold–it was freezing. She felt the urge to let go, but he held tightly to her.

"I'm glad," his gentle breath tickled her ear.

Zakariya had pulled ahead, glancing back periodically to ensure Jirjis and Yusifina were still following.

With only the moon and the stars in the cloudless sky to light their path, they followed the river northward to the next town.

Dawn was just beginning to break on the horizon when Jirjis' grip on the reins faltered. Without warning, he slumped sideways and fell from the horse, landing with a dull thud in the sand.

"Jirjis!" Yusifina cried. She yanked on the reins, bringing them to a halt as she circled back around.

"What happened?!" Zakariya called out from ahead. He galloped back to join them.

Yusifina climbed down from her horse, racing to where Jirjis lay motionless on the ground. Her heart dropped when she saw the arrow protruding from his back.

"Jirjis no!" The princess shrieked. "He's been hit!"

Zakariya leaped to their side. "When did this happen?"

"Just when we…passed through the city gate…" Jirjis's voice was faint.

Yisei Ishkhan

Zakariya sucked in a breath. "That was hours ago."

"Why didn't you say anything?!" Yusifina cried.

"You must...keep moving. They'll be...after us. Go...leave me here..."

"Help him!" Yusifina's voice cracked as she turned frantically to Zakariya.

Zakariya hesitated as he assessed the prince's wounds. "He's lost too much blood. Even the most skilled physician wouldn't be able to save him."

Jirjis reached out, gripping Zakariya's wrist with his remaining strength. "Zakariya...promise me...you'll protect Yusifina...with your life. Get her to...Ethiopia. I have friends there. You'll be safe..."

Zakariya swallowed hard. "I will do everything in my power to keep her safe. You have my word."

"No!" Yusifina wept. "No! You're coming with me! I'm not going anywhere without you!"

"I don't have much time left..."

"You can't leave me! You're all I have left!"

"That's not true. You have our child...and you have God."

"You can't!"

"I'm sorry, Yusifina," the prince's eyes glistened. "I'm sorry."

With the remaining strength he had, he pulled her close, pressing his forehead against hers. His skin was cold, the warmth of life fading from him. When he pulled back, his head resting in the sand, he gazed distantly at the sky. The stars were beginning to vanish as the sun appeared over the horizon.

"It's so...beautiful..." he whispered.

The Tales of Abel and Mitra

Then he was still.

Yusifina's sobs broke the dawn's silence. She laid her head against his chest. Zakariya gave her space, heading off to tend to the horses. By the time he returned, Jirjis' body had gone cold.

"Your Highness," Zakariya said in a gentle tone, averting his gaze from both the princess and her deceased husband. "It's time to go."

For a moment, Yusifina didn't respond. When she did, her voice was barely more than a whisper. "We can't just leave him here."

"There's a place up ahead where we can bury him."

Yusifina followed Zakariya as he took Jirjis' body into his arms, carrying him over the dunes and into the flat expanse of desert that lay beyond. Several mounds rose in the distance, protruding from the ground like massive bee hives half buried in the sand—long-forgotten tombs of kings from some previous era. Zakariya dug a pit next to one of them, burying Jirjis' body inside.

"We don't even have anything to mark his grave," Yusifina said softly.

"It's better this way," said Zakariya. "No one can desecrate his remains if they don't know he's here."

"It doesn't feel right to leave him…"

"Your Highness, he's gone. What lies here is not him. It is merely a vessel. His soul has gone on to be with God."

The princess said nothing.

"Come," Zakariya gestured to the road. "We've nearly reached the next town."

She followed him back to the horses. They rode in silence, reaching the town of Pedeme within the hour. The mudbrick

Yisei Ishkhan

houses were clustered around a central market, bustling with life. As they entered, they earned stares from the locals—horses were a rare sight in Nubia, ill-suited for the desert, and typically only found in the possession of nobles or the military. Camels were the ideal beast for trekking through such terrain, and that was just what Zakariya was hoping to get his hands on.

Zakariya dismounted, approaching a caravan of camels. The merchant, a well-dressed Arab, eyed them with a shrewd glance.

"I'd like to trade," Zakariya said in fluent Arabic. "Two fine horses for one of your camels."

The man scoffed, waving dismissively. "What good are horses out there? They carry half as much as a camel and won't last a day out in the desert."

"These are the finest horses in Nubia," Zakariya said calmly. "Are you headed north? They'll fetch a heavy price on the Egyptian market."

"And what's someone like *you* doing with horses like *these*?"

"I'm a noble," Zakariya lied. "From Tungul."

"A noble, hm?" The merchant glanced past Zakariya, glimpsing Yusifina up and down. "I might be willing to trade if you threw in something *extra*."

"My wife is not for sale," Zakariya said firmly. "We need to get to the sea so we can make Hajj to Mecca. A camel is the only way to cross the desert."

"Your wife, huh?" The merchant huffed in disappointment. "Fine. I'll give you a camel for the sake of your pilgrimage."

Zakariya bowed his head. "Thank you, sir."

The Tales of Abel and Mitra

Once they'd secured the camel, Zakariya spent the little money he had to buy food, water, and supplies. As he haggled for waterskins with an elderly vendor, a bright yellow flag with a white crescent caught his attention as it flew above the town's garrison. His heart skipped a beat.

"Pardon me," he asked the vendor in a low voice. "How long has that flag been there?"

The old woman shrugged without looking up from her table. "The Mamluks rode in yesterday morning."

"What happened to the local garrison?"

"They surrendered without a fight–all eleven of them."

"Traitors," Zakariya grumbled.

The old woman chuckled. "Can you blame them? Why put up a fight for a battle they can't win? Pedeme has passed between Dotawo and the Mamluks for generations. What difference does it make if the border shifts a few leagues to the north or south?"

"Dotawo is the last remnant of Christian civilization in Nubia," Zakariya said. "Our ancestors fought off the Arabs for a thousand years. What would they think, knowing their descendants willingly let in the invaders? We'll become like the Egyptians, ruled by Arabs, Turks, and Circassians who know nothing of our culture and religion, until one day, we forget our roots."

"Why should I care?" The woman grumbled. "I have no descendants. My eldest son died from famine when he was a child. My younger son and daughter were captured by raiding nomads and sold to the slave markets in al-Qahira. I'm an old woman. I'll be dead in a few years, so why should I care about a future I won't live to see? Now, are you going to buy these waterskins or not?"

Yisei Ishkhan

Zakariya sighed, making his purchase before rejoining Yusifina at the edge of town.

"I've got what we need," he said, untying the reins of the camel. "Shall we get going?"

Yusifina glanced at the blazing sun overhead. "It's midday. We should wait until evening. It will be cooler."

"We can't stay," Zakariya said. "The Mamluks have taken Pedeme. If they realize who you are, you'll be in danger."

Yusifina frantically glanced around. "When did this happen?"

"Yesterday. It can't be a coincidence. Yudas must have coordinated his coup with the Mamluk invasion. We need to leave before they find out we're here."

"Do you think he's looking for us?"

"You're the last of the royal family," said Zakariya. "The only one who could pose a threat to his rule."

Yusifina's hand fell to her belly as she felt a kick from her unborn child within. She wasn't the last. Not yet.

Reluctantly, she mounted the camel. Zakariya guided them on foot as they left the town for the vast expanse of desert beyond.

"I apologize for what happened back there," Zakariya said.

"What for?" Yusifina asked, her voice distant.

"For telling that man you were my wife."

"Oh," Yusifina shook her head. "I didn't even notice. I don't understand much Arabic, so wasn't following most of that exchange." She glanced at the ground, watching their shadows dance across the dirt path, stretching longer and longer as the day went on. "Are we heading east?"

The Tales of Abel and Mitra

"First east, then we'll turn back to the south," said Zakariya. "I want to avoid the main road, so we don't have to pass through Daw."

"Are we really going to Ethiopia?"

Zakariya glanced up at her. "Is there somewhere else you'd like to go?"

Yusifina said nothing.

"Prince Jirjis said Ethiopia would be safe," Zakariya continued. "Now that Dotawo has fallen, it's the last Christian land south of Egypt."

"It will take us weeks to get there."

"Which is why we need the camel. Traveling along the river would be faster, but it's too dangerous. We risk running into Yudas' men if we take that route. This path is safer."

"Do you even know how to get there?"

"Roughly. We continue south, following the river until we reach the grasslands. That is the land of my birth–the southernmost region of the old Kingdom of Alwa, before the Funj conquest. Those grasslands are within view of the Ethiopian Highlands."

"I didn't know you were from Alwa," Yusifina said. "How did you end up in Dotawo?"

Zakariya's expression hardened. "Raiders attacked my village when I was a child. I was captured and sold to the slave markets in al-Qahira. I was bought by an elderly Circassian–a former soldier who took part in the conquest of Constantinople. He had once been a slave himself and was castrated as a boy, so he had no children of his own. He left me with his inheritance and freed me before his death. I used the money to travel to Dotawa and entered the service of Prince Jirjis."

Yisei Ishkhan

"Do you have any family left in Alwa?" Yusifina asked in a quiet tone.

"They're dead. My brothers were captured with me. They didn't survive the procedure."

"Procedure?"

"Castration. There were a dozen other boys captured along with me. I was the only one who survived."

Yusifina sucked in a breath. "That's terrible. Why do they do such a thing?"

"Castrated boys fetch a higher price on the market. It's worth it–even if only one out of every ten survive. But that's all in the past. I'd rather not dwell on it."

As evening approached, the winds began to shift. A storm brewed on the horizon, stirring up a wall of sand that swallowed the sun and obscured the path ahead of them. Luckily, they happened upon a small cave within a rocky outcropping. They ducked inside to take shelter for the night.

Zakariya unclipped their waterskin, taking a sip before passing it to Yusifina. "We're nearly out of water. We should stop by the river in the morning."

"Perhaps we should wait until later in the day before we travel again," the princess suggested. "We're far enough from Pedeme now, and the storm should cover our tracks. No one will find us here."

"Perhaps," Zakariya said. He removed the mats they'd purchased in town and laid them across the floor. "Get some rest. We'll wait until the storm passes and leave around this time tomorrow."

Yusifina lay on the mat, wrapping her shawl over her. She watched as Zakariya took a seat by the entrance of the cave, his silhouette outlined against the swirling sandstorm outside.

The Tales of Abel and Mitra

She drifted off to sleep.

***

A low murmur came from a hut at the end of the dirt path. Darkness enveloped everything else, leaving the hut as the only discernible feature of the landscape. Zakariya recognized the place immediately—it was his childhood home.

The building's thatched roof sagged under its weight, leaning awkwardly to one side, and was peppered with gaps where the sky peeked through. Had it always looked so run-down? He couldn't remember. It'd been years since he'd laid eyes on it.

As he approached, he realized the murmur had turned into the heavy sobs of a woman. Her anguished cries carried into the night, freezing him in his tracks.

"Mother?" Zakariya called out.

The sobbing ceased, replaced by a tense, suffocating silence.

"Mother!" Zakariya called out louder.

"Loku, run!" His mother shrieked.

Zakariya froze. *Loku*. He hadn't been called that in years. He'd almost forgotten that he'd gone by any name other than Zakariya. His mother's voice echoed in his mind, conjuring memories he'd long buried.

This is just a dream, he told himself. He knew he could do nothing to change the past. Still, his legs carried him forward into the hut.

On the ground lay his father's crumpled body—or what remained of it. The head was gone, severed cleanly at the neck. Splatters of blood drenched the walls. Zakariya's mother knelt at the center of the room, her body broken and bruised. Three men surrounded her, nothing but evil in their eyes as they held a gleaming blade to her throat.

"So, you *do* have children," one of the men said in the guttural accent of one of the neighbouring nomadic tribes. Zakariya remembered that voice–how could he forget the man who had slaughtered his parents?

"Loku go! GET OUT OF HERE!" His mother screamed, her eyes wide with terror.

Slit.

The blade moved across her throat with a swift motion.

"MOTHER!" Zakariya shrieked.

She crumpled to the ground.

"Take him and find the others," the man barked.

Before Zakariya could react, a bag was pulled over his head, muffling his screams. The world went dark.

***

A faint muttering echoed through the cave. No, not muttering–weeping. Zakariya stirred, unsure if he was still dreaming. His eyes fluttered open, and he found himself staring at the ceiling of the cave. He wiped the tears from his eyes. There was a rusty scent in the air.

That was when he noticed the drops of blood splattered across the ground. He leaped to his feet, instinctively reaching for the dagger sheathed at his belt. Panic set in as he glanced around. It was missing. So was Yusifina.

"Your Highness?!" He called out.

The weeping ceased, and a terrible sense of *déjà vu* overcame Zakariya. He followed the trail of blood to the far side of the cave. There was Yusifina, trembling on the ground

The Tales of Abel and Mitra

as she held his dagger clasped in her hands. Her forearm was streaked with blood.

"Your Highness, what happened?!" Zakariya fell to her side. He snatched the blade from her, cutting some cloth from his sleeve as he began bandaging her wound.

"I'm sorry…" the princess said through her tears. "I took your dagger…"

"Did you do this to yourself?!" Zakariya asked. He took her silence to be confirmation of his suspicions.

"I'm sorry…" she whispered. "I wanted to…but I couldn't bring myself to do it. All I managed was this. Now your blade is dirty because of me."

"Never mind the blade," Zakariya huffed. "Why would you do such a thing to yourself?!"

"I can't go on living. Not with my brother gone…and Mother…and Rehal…and Dawid…and Jirjis…" her voice caught in her throat. "I can't…"

Zakariya secured the bandage. "You must," he said in a gentle tone. "For Jirjis, and King Yuel, and everyone else. For your child."

"I can't. Daw has fallen; Dotawo is no more. This is the end of our kingdom—the end of my family. There's nothing left for me in this world…"

"Your child, Princess. Dotawa lives on through the child you carry. Jirjis lives on."

"I never asked for any of this!" Yusifina cried. Zakariya flinched at her sudden outburst. "I never asked to be born into the royal family. Why am I the last one standing? Why must I bear this burden alone? For a thousand years, our civilization has been in decline, chipped away piece by piece, until nothing is left. How can I bring a child into a world like that? There is no future for our people."

"I don't know what the future will bring," Zakariya admitted. "What I *do* know is if we give up hope, there won't be one. Every generation must make sacrifices for the next. We must press on in the hope that our descendants will be able to build a better future."

Yusifina shook her head. "I'll never make it to Ethiopia. Go on without me."

"I made a promise to Prince Jirjis," said Zakariya. "I'm not leaving you behind. Now, let's get you to the river. You've lost a lot of blood and need to drink."

He helped her to her feet, but as they made their way to the entrance of the cave, they saw it had been half buried in a pile of sand. Zakariya dug at the sand, only to find the storm was worse than the night before.

"We won't be able to travel in this weather," Zakariya said. "The storm should blow over in a day or two. In the meantime, we should search for another source of water."

"Water?" Yusifina muttered, suddenly realizing how parched her throat was. "In a cave?"

"You'd be surprised how many underground aquifers there are in the desert. Come, I'll light a torch."

Once the fire was lit, its flickering light revealed the cave was larger than they'd initially thought. Several chambers branched out from the main cavern where they'd spent the night.

"Perhaps we should split up," Yusifina suggested. "It would be faster."

The Tales of Abel and Mitra

Zakariya shook his head. "We don't know what else might be in here. There could be serpents, scorpions, jinn, or crocodiles."

"Crocodiles?" Yusifina said with a tone of skepticism. "This far from the river?"

Zakariya shrugged. "You never know. Stick close to me."

They made their way into the first tunnel, leaving the camel by the entrance of the cave as she chewed on her cud. The air grew stale as they descended, a deep chill setting in. Yusifina traced her hand along the wall to steady herself, the rough stone cracking under her touch and coating her fingertips with dust.

"The walls are straight here," she observed. "So is the ceiling and the floor."

Zakariya raised his torch, scanning their surroundings. She was right. The walls were perpendicular to one another and met the floor and ceiling at nearly perfect angles. He frowned. This didn't seem like a natural cave.

"Look!" Yusifina exclaimed. "There's something here!"

Zakariya instinctively pulled the princess away from the wall, worried she might've spotted a poisonous insect. But when he saw what had caught her attention, he breathed a sigh of relief. There was a carved symbol engraved on the wall–a loop resting atop a T-shaped cross.

"What is it?" Yusifina wondered.

"I've seen this symbol before," Zakariya said, "in some of the ruins of the temples in Egypt." He rubbed his hand across another portion of the wall, revealing other symbols weathered by time.

"Do you think that's what this place is?" Yusifina said in awe. "An ancient temple from the days of Kush?"

Yisei Ishkhan

"I think it's older than that," Zakariya said.

A piercing scream shattered the stillness. Zakariya spun around, scanning the darkness. He coughed as a cloud of dust blinded his vision. When it cleared, he found himself alone.

"Your Highness?!" He cried.

A pained groan came from the distance–from *below*. He fell to his knees and found a gaping hole had opened in the floor. Peering into the abyss, he spotted Yusifina sprawled atop a pile of rubble, clutching her side. Once the torchlight illuminated the chamber, Yusifina's eyes went wide in terror. She scrambled backwards, away from something just beyond Zakariya's line of sight.

"There's something down here!" She shrieked. "A monster!"

Zakariya cursed, leaping into action as he unstrapped his bow and dropped into the hole. He landed on his feet, his back to the princess as he notched an arrow and aimed it into the darkness. A massive beast loomed in the shadows, larger than any he'd seen before. Its body was sleek, with a slim snout and upturned pointy ears. The creature's golden, oval eyes stared forward, seemingly oblivious to their presence. After a moment, Zakariya let forth a deep sigh and lowered his bow.

"What are you doing?!" Yusifina cried.

"It's a statue," Zakariya scooped up the torch he'd dropped and took a step toward the looming beast. As he drew near, the flames revealed the beast to be the carved figure of a jackal, its forelimbs stretched out as it lay atop an elevated platform. Its golden eyes were polished gemstones, eerily lifelike. "See? Nothing to fear?"

Yusifina let out another cry.

The Tales of Abel and Mitra

"What is it?" Zakariya asked, frantically rushing over. "Are you injured?"

The princess remained on the ground, wincing in fear and pain as she clutched her abdomen. "I think…it's the baby…!"

"The baby?" Zakariya repeated in disbelief. "You're not due for a few weeks–are you certain?"

He paled as he glanced up at the hole in the ceiling, calculating the distance Yusifina had fallen. It wasn't far enough to cause serious injury to her–but *any* fall during pregnancy was dangerous.

"Take a deep breath," Zakariya said, kneeling at the princess's side. "Tell me where it hurts."

"I think it's coming out!"

Sweat dripped down Zakariya's brow. His calm demeanor faltered as panic set in. "Can't you…hold it in…?"

"NO!"

"Alright. Let me return to the camel and fetch supplies—"

He froze as Yusifina gripped him tightly by the wrist. "Don't leave me down here!"

"Fine…" he said with reluctance. "Just…take a deep breath."

She let out a scream. Her face was already dripping with sweat. "Do you think…my baby…?"

"It will be fine," Zakariya said, hoping to sound confident. "This is in God's hands, not yours. All you have to do is breathe. And push. Can you do that?"

She managed a nod, taking a deep breath. A cry followed that rattled Zakariya's eardrums as the contractions began. At first, Zakariya held the princess by the hand. But after a couple of minutes, her squeezes became so tight that he feared she would break his bones. He removed his outer cloak, cutting it into several pieces. He wiped her face, placed a bundle under her head as a pillow, and handed her a piece to clutch.

The sweat pouring off her alarmed him, especially given how little water they'd had in the past two days. They still had some left in the waterskins, but Yusifina refused to let the young guard leave her side.

"Something's wrong!" Yusifina gasped.

"Take a deep breath…" Zakariya urged.

But as he spoke, his voice was fading as if he were disappearing down a long tunnel. Yusifina's vision blurred, and the chamber seemed to spin around her.

A sudden voice whispered through the chaos. "You can do this…"

Yusifina's head jerked up. *Mother?* She glanced around, but there was nothing there. Even Zakariya had faded into the darkness.

"Everything is going to be fine…"

"Mother?!" She called out. "Mother, where are you?!"

"There's nothing to be afraid of…" the deep voice of a man said.

"Yuel?!" Yusifina exclaimed. "Yuel, is that you?!"

"Keep going, you're doing great!" A girl's voice said cheerfully.

"We're right here with you," said a boy.

Then she saw them. Her mother stood to her left, regal and serene, as she held Yusifina gently by the hand. Beside her was Rehal, Yusifina's younger sister, her dark eyes shining brighter than Yusifina had ever seen. Her brothers Dawid and Yuel, and her cousin Istifan hovered nearby.

The Tales of Abel and Mitra

"You're all here…!" Despite the pain, a light laugh escaped from Yusifina's lips. "I thought you had left me!"

"We'll never leave you, Yusifina," said another voice.

"Jirjis!" Yusifina exclaimed.

There he was, dressed in white robes, more regal and handsome than he'd ever been in life. He lowered his face, pressing his forehead against hers.

"No…" Yusifina said. "This can't be real. You died. I saw you die! All of you…are dead…"

"You're right," Jirjis chuckled. "In a sense, at least. But we're also more alive now than we've ever been."

"This must be some sort of dream…an illusion…"

But even as she spoke those words, Jirjis's gentle breath tickled her face. Her mother's skin was warm and soft as silk as she clutched her hand. Amazingly, there was no pain in Yusifina's abdomen at that moment, nor anywhere else in her body.

A blinding light suddenly radiated from behind Jirjis as another figure appeared. He burned with such a intensity that Yusifina couldn't make out any details of his features.

"This *is* real," a voice boomed, coming from every direction at once. "More real than the world you come from. Do not fear. One day, you will join your family here. But not yet. I still have plans for you."

"We've come to say goodbye," said Yusifina's mother.

"More like 'see you soon,' than goodbye," Jirjis corrected.

"I don't want to go back!" Yusifina protested. "I want to stay!"

"Our son needs you."

"Our son…?"

Yisei Ishkhan

The figure of light seemed to bow his head forward in affirmation.

"There was so much pain..." Yusifina winced. "So many tears...so much blood. My son...I don't want to bring up a child in a world like that..."

"You're never alone," said the figure shrouded in light. "Do you trust me?"

Yusifina held her tongue. Behind the light, the others watched her expectantly.

"I...I trust you..." Yusifina said.

"Then go. Your son needs you."

With that, the light faded, and Yusifina found herself back in the shadowy ruins of the ancient temple.

***

Yusifina awoke to the high-pitched cry of an infant. Her eyes fluttered open.

"Your Highness!" Zakariya's voice broke through the groggy haze. He loomed over her, and for the first time, Yusifina saw a smile on his face. "You're awake."

Yusifina groaned. She was fatigued, yet strangely free of any pain.

Zakariya held something in his arms—a bundle of swaddling cloth. He knelt by Yusifina's side, presenting her with the infant.

"It's a boy," Zakariya beamed.

Yusifina stared at her son in disbelief. He was so tiny, yet his screams were sharp, piercing the stillness of the chamber and echoing off the stone walls.

"Is he healthy?" She asked in concern, taking the baby into her arms.

The Tales of Abel and Mitra

"He's fine," Zakariya assured. "He's a bit small, but he's strong. I think he's just hungry."

Yusifina positioned the infant at her breast.

Zakariya glanced away. "I think the storm has died down. I'm going to head to the river and refill our waterskins. Don't go anywhere."

As he hoisted himself out of the chamber, Yusifina called out to him.

"Thank you. Thank you for staying by my side."

"Of course, Your Highness," Zakariya said. "Have you decided what you'll name him?"

The princess shook her head. "Not yet."

***

The storm had indeed died down, but with a newborn on Yusifina's hands, Zakariya insisted they remain where they were for a few days longer to give her time to recover.

Their refuge, as it turned out, wasn't a cave–it was the ruins of an ancient structure, buried beneath the sands and forgotten by history. In his free time, Zakariya explored its depths further, concluding it must've been a temple built when Nubia was under Egyptian rule millennia ago. The architectural style, statues of deities, and hieroglyphs along the walls were nearly identical to those he'd seen during his time in al-Qahira.

The room that Yusifina had fallen into appeared to be the central chamber of the complex, dominated by the towering jackal statue. Its shadow loomed over her like an ominous specter. It unnerved Yusifina, but she was too weak to climb out of the chamber, so she had no choice but to remain in its presence.

Yisei Ishkhan

Zakariya decided to shift their camp down to the chamber, leaving the camel above to guard the entrance to the temple. One afternoon, he returned from his explorations, carrying two objects.

"Look what I found," in one hand he held up a bronze pole with a carved serpent coiled around it. In the other, he had an old sachet.

Yusifina furrowed her brow. "Where did you get those?" She tucked the baby's face into the blanket, reaching to take hold of the sachet.

"Down in one of the lower chambers. There were some remains. These must've belonged to whoever was here before us."

Yusifina's hand flinched away from the bag. "Did someone die down there?"

"Yes. But it was a long time ago. Only a handful of bones remain."

That didn't make Yusifina feel much better. She accepted the sachet, digging through its contents. Inside were papyrus scrolls, crumbling under her touch as she handled them.

"What do they say?" Zakariya asked, drawing near with his torch so he could see what was written on the pages.

"Careful," Yusifina said sharply. "One spark and these will turn to ash." She squinted as she brought one of the scrolls close to her face, examining the faint markings. She could only make out a couple of words etched along the pages. "There are two scripts here: Greek and Coptic. But it's ancient, similar to the ones used by the priests in liturgy. But I don't think this is a religious scroll…" she glanced up at Zakariya, who still held the bronze serpent pole. "Were these found together?"

The Tales of Abel and Mitra

"They were."

Yusifina took the pole from him, examining it as she traced her fingers along its rough edges. She brushed the sand out of cracks around the serpent's eyes. "It reminds me of Nehushtan."

"Of what?"

"The bronze serpent that God commanded Prophet Maasa to make during the Exodus," Yusifina said. Then in Greek, she began reciting the verse from scripture. "And the Lord said: 'Make a fiery serpent and set it upon a pole; and it shall come to pass, that everyone who is bitten by the serpents, when he sees it, shall live.'"

"I don't understand liturgical Greek very well," Zakariya admitted sheepishly.

"No? But you seem quite skilled in languages. You speak Dotawo's dialect without an accent and had no trouble conversing with that Arab merchant."

"I only ever heard Greek at the cathedral in Daw. My village in Alwa was too poor for a church, so we only had a priest visit us from the capital once a year. As for Arabic, I picked it up during my time in Egypt. But the churches in Egypt use Coptic, not Greek."

Yusifina provided a quick translation of the verse into Nubian, before adding another: "Just as Maasa lifted up the serpent in the wilderness, so must the Son of Man be lifted up…"

She glanced down at her child, all bundled up in cloth and sound asleep.

"What is it?" Zakariya asked.

"I think I've decided on a name for my son."

"Oh?"

Yisei Ishkhan

"Maasa," said Yusifina, stroking her son's cheek.

"Maasa…" Zakariya repeated.

"Maasa was sent into exile out of Egypt," Yusifina explained. "And my son was born in exile out of Dotawo. Maasa was sent up the Iteru, while we follow the river in the opposite direction."

"Yes," Zakariya mused. "I think it's a fitting name."

"Who do you think he was?" Yusifina wondered, her gaze shifted back to the pole. "The man who carried this here."

"A traveler," Zakariya suggested. "Or a wandering eremite. He must've been here for centuries."

"Looks like it," Yusifina said, handling the scrolls with care as she placed them back into the sachet. She cast a wary glance at the statue of the jackal looming overhead. "I don't intend to stay here long enough to share his fate."

***

As they continued their journey south over the following weeks, the landscape gradually grew greener. First came sparse shrubs. A few days later, they reached the grasslands. Soon, lush foliage sprouted from the ground. One morning, when the skies were clear, distant peaks appeared over the southern horizon.

"There it is," Zakariya said. "The border with Ethiopia."

"I can't believe we made it," Yusifina said. It had been nearly two months since they'd set out from Daw, and the journey hadn't been easy with a newborn on their hands. Yusifina shifted atop the camel, positioning Maasa's head so he was facing the same direction they were traveling in. "Look there, Maasa," she pointed into the distance. "Do you see the mountains?"

The Tales of Abel and Mitra

The baby's sleepy eyes followed her finger before losing interest.

"It's beautiful," the princess murmured.

"It is…" Zakariya said, but his voice was distant. Something in the thicket had caught his attention. Without another word, he had stepped away from them, moving into the underbrush.

"Zakariya?" Yusifina called out to him in confusion. "Is something the matter?"

Stooping low, Zakariya began hacking aside branches and shrubs as he tried to get at something on the ground. "It looks like the foundations of a house here."

"A house?" Yusifina asked.

"I think…this is where I used to live…"

Before either of them could say another word, a deafening crack split the air. Yusifina flinched. For an instant, she mistook the sound for thunder. Maasa began to wail.

"What was that?!" Yusifina cried, sheltering her infant.

"Get down!" Zakariya ordered. He dropped to the ground, scanning the thicket. Blackened dirt smoldered inches from where he stood. Then he saw it—the barrel of a rifle poking out from the foliage. "You! Stop!"

The weapon's wielder fumbled, trying to reload. But Zakariya moved quicker, leaping from the ground and tackling the figure to the dirt. The rifle clattered away as Zakariya pinned down the man. No, not a man—a boy. He was dressed in nothing but a thin loincloth.

"Who are you?" Zakariya demanded, switching to the Alwa dialect. "Why are you shooting at us?"

Yisei Ishkhan

The boy stilled, but when he spoke, it wasn't in Nubian. The words fell from his lips in another tongue—one Zakariya had nearly forgotten. "You're intruding on our land!"

"Intruding..." Zakariya repeated the word. It felt strange to speak in his childhood tongue for the first time in so many years. "On *whose* land?"

"Loku?" The voice of an old woman called out from a distance. "Loku, is everything alright?"

Zakariya froze, his heart pounding in his chest. *Loku? Why was she using his old name?*

"Get up," Zakariya ordered.

He pushed the whimpering boy to his feet. The child couldn't be more than ten years old; his gun was nearly as long as he was tall.

"Don't hurt Granny," he pleaded in a tiny voice.

"*You're* the one who attacked *me*," Zakariya reminded him. But upon seeing the terror in the boy's eyes, his voice softened. "I'm not here to hurt anyone. Now, walk forward."

The boy did as he was told, making his way through the thicket to a clearing on the other side of the trees. Zakariya trailed him from behind, glancing back at the camel and Yusifina just before they slipped out of view. The princess stared back with a look of concern on her face, but Zakariya offered a reassuring nod.

The trees gave way to a clearing. Down a worn path sat a small wooden hut topped with a dome-shaped roof. Zakariya faltered as an elderly woman emerged, squinting at the pair through the sunlight. Her face was worn with age; her hair was gray and frizzy. But it wasn't any of these details that caught Zakariya's attention—it was the jagged scar stretching across her throat.

The Tales of Abel and Mitra

"What's going on?" The woman demanded. "Who are you?"

Zakariya lifted his hands. "I mean you no harm. We were merely traveling through the area when this boy opened fire. Thankfully, no one was hurt." He dropped the gun on the ground. "What are you doing with a weapon like this?"

"I found it in the caravan of a traveling Ottoman merchant," the boy said.

"Do you know how dangerous these are?" Zakariya hissed.

"Of course," the old woman said. "Ever since Alwa's central government was overthrown by the Funj, we have no one to protect us. We must protect ourselves."

Zakariya's gaze softened. "Next time, make sure you know who you're shooting at *before* you open fire," he handed the gun back to the boy, adjusting it in his hands and helping him aim the barrel. "If you want to hit your target, keep your eye on him. Understood?"

The boy glanced up at Zakariya in surprise. "Are you a marksman, sir?"

"No. But my former master fought for the Ottomans in Constantinople. He trained me in how to use firearms."

"You're a slave?"

"I *was*," Zakariya corrected. "It's a long story."

"Come," the old woman took the boy by the hand. "Let's let the man continue on his travels. Go inside. I'll make you something to eat."

The boy nodded, rushing into the hut. The woman sighed as she turned to Zakariya. "I'm sorry about that. We've had many raiders in these parts over the years. The boy just wanted to protect me, that's all."

Yisei Ishkhan

"I understand," Zakariya studied her face, catching every detail. His gaze lingered on the scar along her neck. "You called him Loku, didn't you?"

"I did."

"I was once called by that name..."

The woman gave him a quizzical stare. Then a glimmer of recognition flashed through her eyes. "Loku...no...it can't be!" Her hands shook and her voice trembled as she reached for his face. Tears welled in her eyes. "It's you...it's really you...! After all these years, I thought I'd never see you again..."

"I thought you were dead..." Zakariya whispered. "I saw those men slash your throat..."

"This?" The woman pointed to the scar across her neck. "By some miracle, I survived. But with everyone else dead, what reason did I have to continue living? It was hard for the first few years–but then I found that boy. He was just an infant, abandoned in the woods after raiders had pillaged his village and enslaved his family. I took him in and raised him as my own."

"And named him after me..." Zakariya noted.

The woman nodded.

"Zakariya?" Yusifina's concerned voice rose from the thicket. She emerged from the undergrowth, protectively cradling Maasa in her arms. She glanced from Zakariya to the old woman. "What's going on here?"

"And who's this?" The old woman gasped with delight. "Loku, is this your *wife*?"

"No," Zakariya coughed. "This is Princess Yusifina of Dotawo, who I've sworn to protect." Then, switching back to Nubian, he continued. "Your Highness, this is my mother."

The Tales of Abel and Mitra

"Your mother...?" Yusifina inhaled her breath. "It's a pleasure to meet you..."

"Adiit," the old woman said in Nubian. "Call me Adiit."

"Adiit," Yusifina smiled. "Please call me Yusifina."

"Oh, I couldn't!" Adiit exclaimed. "Loku said you were a princess!"

"I *was*," Yusifina said. "But what is a princess without her kingdom? I'm just an ordinary woman now."

"And what are you doing with a *princess*?" Adiit wondered, turning to her son.

"Long story—"

"Well, you have time to tell it!" Adiit exclaimed. She took her son by the arm and began leading him into the hut. "Come, I'll make us all dinner tonight. You too, Princess Yusifina."

Zakariya glanced back at the princess expectantly.

"I would be honoured," Yusifina said.

"They're staying for dinner?" The younger Loku asked, a trace of disappointment in his tone as he poked his head out the door.

"They can stay as long as they like!" Adiit said. "These two are very special guests."

Maasa let forth a cry, and Adiit squealed in delight.

"Oh! I didn't see you there, little one!" The old woman leaned over the infant and gave him a tickle under the chin. "These *three* are very special guests."

Loku gave the newcomers a glance up and down. "They don't look very special to me."

"Loku!" Adiit scolded. "This is Princess Yusifina and her baby..."

"Maasa," Yusifina said with a chuckle.

Yisei Ishkhan

"Maasa," Adiit said. Then, she turned to Zakariya. "And this is my son, Loku. He's the man you were named after."

Young Loku furrowed his brow. "I thought you didn't have any sons, Granny."

"I thought so too," Adiit mused. "I thought he was dead. But here he is, alive again."

The Tales of Abel and Mitra
The Tale of Abel and Mitra

Abel wiped the tears from his eyes.

"What is the matter?" Mitra wondered. "The story had a happy ending."

"Bittersweet," Abel murmured.

"Still happier than the endings of the other stories, no?"

"I guess so. But as you said before, no story truly has an end."

"Indeed."

"So, is the rest of their story happy?"

Mitra thought for a moment. "That is not up for me to determine. As I am sure you noticed, the details surrounding this narrative are sparse. The specifics regarding the political situation in Dotawo, and even the precise year that these events took place, remain a mystery. The only records that exist detailing Yusifina and Zakariya's tale come from a single source passed down for centuries that eventually found its way into my archives. Do you remember Nuwa Yuen-Serwanga from the story of Ismail and Mihai? It was his ancestors, the Serwangas, who kept this story in their archives, together with the relics that Zakariya uncovered from the forgotten temple. After Ismail commissioned me as an archivist, Natsuki was the one who compiled their story."

"So, you don't know what happened to Yusifina and Zakariya after this point in the story?"

"We can never *truly* know what happened," Mitra said. "For all we know, this tale could be a fabricated narrative. Perhaps Princess Yusifina and Zakariya never even existed."

"Oh..." Abel seemed dejected at the thought.

Yisei Ishkhan

"But I believe they did exist," Mitra quickly added. "As for whether the details of their story were accurately recorded, who can say? That is beside the point. Sometimes, there is as much truth in a mythical retelling of events as there is in actual history. The fact that a story exists at all, together with the relics, proves that there is at least *some* truth to the tale. We can speculate that Yusifina and her son Maasa survived long enough to pass those relics to their descendants. The House of Serwanga trace their lineage to Maasa."

Abel's eyes lit up. "Then all your stories are connected! Domingo and Sandoval's beaded bracelets showed up in Ismail and Mihai's story—Mihai was descended from the Sandoval family, wasn't he? And Natsuki Kirishima…she must be connected to Kirishima Hikaru in some way. Just like Nuwa Yuen-Serwanga is connected to Princess Yusifina."

"Of course they are connected," Mitra mused. "After all, everything in the universe is connected."

Abel tilted his head. "What about the papyrus records Zakariya found in the temple? Do you know the story they contained?"

"Indeed, but perhaps we should save that tale for another day," Mitra nodded up ahead, where the mountains of the Purvanchal Range loomed above them. "We have almost reached the Valley. It will not be long before we return to the Village."

Abel's stomach churned at the thought of the Elders confronting them upon their return. It was inevitable. They'd question how Abel and the others had managed to rescue Noa from the makarasa.

"Do you think anyone will believe our story?" Abel asked sheepishly.

The Tales of Abel and Mitra

"You know your Elders better than I do," Mitra chuckled. "What do you think?"

"I doubt it. But we can't lie to them."

"Then we will tell them the truth," said Mitra. "The truth about how I had to come in and rescue the four of you from the depths of the makarasa den because of your reckless behaviour." He glanced back at Abel with a smile on his face.

"They won't believe that," Abel muttered. "But I think we should keep your true identity a secret, at least for now. If they find out you aren't human, at least not fully, I don't know what might happen."

"Humans are afraid of what they do not understand," Mitra mused. "However, you do not appear to fear me."

"Why would I?" Abel asked. "There's nothing scary about you."

Abel flinched as something light landed on his shoulder. He reached to brush it away but froze when he spotted a flicker of light. He gasped as the shimmering scales of a silver phoenix's wing rubbed off on his finger. Even his faint touch had torn off a piece of the creature's wing.

"Is something wrong?" Mitra tilted his head back.

"Nothing," Abel said. "Just a silver phoenix landed on my shoulder. It was already dead."

"I see," Mitra nodded knowingly. "You only just noticed? They are all around."

As Abel followed his gaze, his breath caught in his throat. The forest was littered with the bodies of dozens of silver phoenixes–if not hundreds. They lay scattered about, their once-glimmering wings dull and faded. A couple were being preyed upon by golden dragons, but most looked as if they'd simply fallen out of the sky.

Yisei Ishkhan

"What happened to them...?" Abel whispered.

"They must be semelparous," Mitra noted.

"What's that?"

"A species that breeds only once in its lifetime," Mitra said. "They typically die shortly after."

Akavi leaped onto his shoulder, flashing colours along his patterned-back. He pointed two of his tiny limbs upward. Abel followed his gaze to the clusters of glowing, silver orbs hanging from enormous umbrella-shaped caps of the trees. He had noticed them earlier, but assumed they were some sort of strange fruit. Now he understood–they were eggs.

A pit formed in Abel's stomach. "That's sad. They'll never get to meet their parents."

"It is their nature," said Mitra. "I doubt they find it tragic."

"But they live such short lives," Abel frowned. "If they die after they return to Darkside, the silver phoenixes we see each Night must be the offspring of those from the Night before. Avi was right."

"He was," Mitra nodded. "Life revolves around cycles. Whether you live for a thousand Cycles like a human or a single Cycle like the silver phoenixes, no being can go on living forever. Not in this world, at least. The only thing that will remain will be the stories that are passed down to future generations."

They reached the pass cutting through the Purvanchal Range. Soon, they emerged on the other side of the mountains, greeted by the lush greenery of the Valley of Shambhala. Abel squinted as the light of Dawn beamed down. After so many hours on Darkside, even its faint glow from the forest floor seemed blinding. But Abel wasn't

The Tales of Abel and Mitra

complaining. He tilted his head back, relishing the warmth of the sun's rays filtering through the canopy.

"There you are!" Nineveh called out from the hovercycle up ahead.

Avi grinned. "We were worried you were captured by the makarasa again."

"We were just taking the scenic route," Mitra smiled. "This may be the only time we get to visit Darkside."

"I hope so," Nineveh huffed. "I have no plans on going back there again."

Avi gave Noa a light knock on the head. "Try not to get captured again."

Noa let out a groan. He was stirring but seemed to be only half awake. He rubbed his eyes. "I just had...the most awful nightmare..."

"I wish it *had* been a nightmare," Nineveh grumbled. "Then we wouldn't have to explain ourselves to the Elders."

"Look on the bright side," Avi grinned. "If we get in trouble for breaking the rules, we'll be suspended from our *morungs*. That means we won't have to work until at *least* the next Dawn! Mitra can entertain us with plenty of his stories in the meantime!"

"I could," Mitra mused. "I have plenty more to share."

"Better than listening to *Avi's* stories," mumbled Noa.

"Hey!"

"Alright, we can discuss this later," said Abel.

"Abel's right," nodded Nineveh as she prepared to start up the hovercycle again. "First let's face the wrath of the Elders."

They took off, with Mitra and Abel following close behind. As they zipped through the undergrowth, a thought

Yisei Ishkhan

entered Abel's mind. He was living in his *own* story. Perhaps someday, Mitra would find himself on some distant world, telling them the story about Shambhala.

The Tale of Abel and Mitra.

But until then, Abel's story is still being written.

Printed in Great Britain
by Amazon